MISSTEPS PERFECTING the SHUTTERBUG STRUT

Missteps Perfecting the *Shutterbug Strut*

J.L. Michael

This novel is a work of historical fiction: a spirited jaunt through the late 1920s. Actual events, settings, timelines, and business establishments have been included to formulate an accurate and informative representation of the era for the reader's enjoyment and experience. Any fictional characters are a product of the author's overindulgent imagination and are not based on, or associated with, any real or unaffiliated individuals.

That being said, all real-life personages—whether unsung or renowned—were selected due to their timely proximity or direct participation in the events portrayed. Great care has been taken to represent them in an appropriate and consistent light to their previously recorded qualities and contributions to society. It is the author's hope such instances will inspire the reader to seek further literature on their respective legacies.

For my daughter, Alexandra, who
indeed learned to swim in the
Amazon jungle.

Prologue

Omens, like shadows, often arise in the form of man or beast; in her case, both. Such hauntings occurred during the summer before everything changed—before her parents' permanent estrangement or any iniquitous hearsay she would one day reign supreme among the fallen.

The three siblings routinely mounted up to find a promising camping site along the Missouri River to cast their fly rods. She would often wander off to sketch birds and entwine daisies into the more unruly strands of her blonde hair. Each sunset, she'd pen a letter to post to some far-flung address across the world and desperately await a response. It was what eleven-year-old girls did, at least if raised in Montana and unwilling to admit that their British father spent his days not away on business, just away. The siblings would reconvene after dusk to set up their bedding and cook the day's catch over a fire pit. Thomas would play the harmonica, William would tell ghost stories, and they would all sing stupid songs until sleep came.

This camping outing would be their last for some time, perhaps longer. Her brothers would soon take sea passage to Europe to fight the Great War. Why they volunteered confused her. America had yet to declare, and it remained her simple belief that life was not some frivolous affair to recklessly wager. They were several years older and better acquainted with their Anglo-French heritage, whereas she had been raised pure Montana bobcat.

She'd miss them terribly, as she did their deceased sister, Emma.

As they sat one last occasion gazing at the stars together, she did not feel like singing, talking, or reminiscing about more innocuous days. All that stirred her mind was the unpleasant reality she would soon be sentenced to the sole care of her mother.

She'd hate them if she could for that unfairness.

And then it sounded. The bloodthirsty howl stung her ears and starched her back. While the region provided home to wolves, grizzlies, and mountain lions, none made so menacing a call. Thomas sprang up and headed for the horses as they neighed, unsettled in their tethers. He freed all three rifles from their saddle scabbards. Another wail rippled across the valley, muzzling the lesser chirps of the bordering woodlands.

They each chambered a round and searched the darkness, waiting.

A fleeting glimpse of the beast spurred her to gasp. The creature's eyes flashed a hellish red in the bold sturgeon moonlight and possessed malevolent intelligence. It did not appear to be of this world.

She struggled to hold steady her father's Mauser 98. "It sounds rather hungry."

"Looking for a meal, Alee. Not an appetizer like you," Thomas teased to calm her.

The high grass rustled to their left, now much closer. As quickly as they aimed, it vamoosed.

William cussed, which he held a habit of doing. "It's a Canadian gray. I'll take it down."

These wolves seldom raided from the north and acted more fearless than the local variety. The trio retreated from their camp to form a triangulated defensive position around the horses.

Alee's stance lent her to face the fire pit. Her heart thundered as she readied herself to pull the trigger, but when the beast raced near the flames, all she could do was gawk. It appeared to be some unfathomable hybrid between a wolf and a hyena. Brawnier than either, it flaunted an elongated jaw, gnarly fur, and a powerful rump slung low to the ground.

Her brothers opened fire as it scurried off.

Thomas retrieved an Eveready flashlight from his saddlebag to better inspect the grasslands. Alee kept vigil over the fire pit. The night had its way of teasing shadows. She locked her gaze on the silhouette of a tall man standing amidst the distant trees. He wore a cape and top hat. She retreated several steps. The menacing figure flashed red eyes and walked off in a stiff stride; the infernal beast following as if a pet.

Alee took aim and fired.

The entity bequeathed a subdued, taunting laugh, unfettered by her defiance. It vanished.

Thomas ran to her side. "What did you see?"

"I don't know," Alee spluttered, "but it's something I care never to see again." Short of a photograph, no one would believe her. Others took her to have a fanciful imagination, so no one ever did.

William lowered his rifle and pointed down. "You're bleeding."

Alee lifted her skirt, thinking she'd pissed herself, but her stream dripped discolored with blood. A disquieting notion set in over what it heralded. Henceforth, the rules would change.

Any hope to live a simple life was nevermore to be.

Chapter 1

Territory of Papua: August 1926

O ccasionally, the only unpalatable difference between adventure and misadventure is eating exotic foods as opposed to being exotic food. The sweltering rainforest teemed with blaring pitfalls shrouded in silence. It loomed an unforgiving wilderness, but to Alexandra Illyria Bathenbrook it served as a refuge from everyday life.

From a crouched position, she studied the indigenous tribesmen through her field glasses as they tramped over a dried riverbed half a football pitch away. They had emerged from the greenery parroting the stealth of bashful apparitions: stocky men wearing feathered headgear and nothing more. Colorful dyes graffitied their dark skin, which rendered them evermore ferocious to her fascinated gaze. Sharpened bones pierced their nostrils and jutted from the tips of crude weapons, touting a most unappetizing demise.

"They look like bloody cannibals! Why did I ever agree to this?"

"Not cannibals, Bannister," she said to reassure him. "According to the map, they're the next valley over."

Owing to erstwhile forays as an aspiring photographer, novice ornithologist, and fledgling explorer, Alexandra was well-rehearsed in stirring misadventure. At age seven, she had learned to swim in the Amazon jungle, and ever since, she'd fancied dipping her toes into unfamiliar waters. It failed to serve as a joyous footpath for everyone.

Patrol Officer Bannister, her hoodwinked guide, felt differently.

Alexandra sighed fretfully. "They'll shrink our silly heads, though, if we dare introduce ourselves."

He gulped. "How do you know they're headhunters?"

Her field glasses locked onto the shriveled skulls dangling from their spears. "Just a hunch."

Bannister wilted in posture, becoming one with the rainforest. He presented a strapping figure in his khaki uniform and Akubra hat. His starched mustache accentuated a resolute jaw and daring blue eyes, but perilous fieldwork did not fill his resumé. The valley dimmed under the cloak of storm clouds. He feared the headhunters might spot a reflection off of the tripod-mounted camera once the sun broke free. The fingers of the young lady in his charge massaged the flashlamp bulb, and she seemed the sort who'd risk snapping the photo.

He'd piss himself if he held anything in the tank.

"Quite a peck of pickled peppers I've picked," Alexandra jested.

The five tribesmen headed for the Ficus trees at which her Victorian Hasselblad field camera stood aimed. She retrieved her preferred pistol whenever traveling: a Colt 1908 vest pocket. It took up little space in her luggage, and while a meager sidearm, it served more dissuading than either teeth or fingernails. Her fevered mind calculated all the motion before her: the pace of the headhunters' steps, the churn of the turbulent clouds, the half-light cast upon the riverbed.

She made a final gambit that the synchronicity of all these elements would sway her way and reclaimed the bulb, intoxicated by the moment.

A wave of re-emerging sunlight rolled forward.

The tribesmen kept a steady gait.

It was going to be razor close.

She whispered, "Fortune favors the brave," and squeezed.

Despite beads of sweat tickling her nose and something slithering over a boot, Alexandra's focus remained squarely on the headhunters. Everything having fallen into place, she felt confident she'd pulled off a pitch-perfect shot undetected. The lead tribesman turned away just as sunlight exposed her camera. The second followed, and then the third.

You fourth bugger, don't you dare look back, she silently pleaded.

The last of them evaporated into the dense foliage.

She lowered the field glasses. "You can set down the camera."

Bannister did not hesitate. "Long way to come for a silly bird."

Her cattish grin failed to waver. "Not for me."

Two months ago, Alexandra had taken sea passage to Singapore to rendezvous with her father as he toured Southeast Asia. He would foot the bill. Her junior year at college concluded, it struck as healthy for her to get away from her mother over the idle summer months.

It was an era of irreverent behavior and momentous social change. Young women were lighting up cigarettes just to be rebellious, allowed to perspire while dancing, and no longer too timid to talk a bit saucy. Alexandra would vote for the first time this coming November, and as a dual citizen of England, she'd likely exercise the franchise there too, as women's suffrage stood on the brink of dropping to age twenty-one.

She found the times invigorating, as long as one didn't lose their head over it.

While Archibald Bathenbrook spent much of his adult life scouring the globe as a geologist for the British Colonial Office, Alexandra knew her father's genuine passion lay beyond discovering riches to be plundered by the empire.

The man found his greatest joy in birdwatching.

Upon arrival in Papua, he'd arranged with officials a trip up the Fly River to meet with prospectors and assess what natural resources might fill the vaguely charted interior of the island. These briefings were conducted over liberal amounts of gin and tonics, consumed for what they impishly deemed "medicinal reasons." The quinine in tonic water provided a remedy for malaria, which had afflicted him since Ceylon.

His eagerness to subject himself to such a taxing quest, however, held its appeal in spotting a *Paradisaea raggiana*—among the most colorful of the bird-of-paradise genus.

Prior to departure, he'd been informed that further upriver were nesting grounds for a grander prize: the *Paradisaea apoda.* Rumor held these birds lived in only two remote regions of the world: the islands of Aru and the higher reaches of the Fly River.

There, too, roamed the most feared of tribes—the cannibalistic Marind-Anim.

The hotel proprietor had shared tidbits of their little-known culture, for of the handful of whites who'd encountered them only a thumbnail returned. This perilous tease had taken the last wind from Archibald's sails. He'd retired to bed, asking Alexandra to offer apologies to their guide come morning. To idle in Port Moresby for another week posed an intolerable sentence. She had not sailed eight thousand miles to forgo such an escapade and prepped to conduct it in her father's absence.

When Bannister arrived at the Moresby Hotel to collect them, she'd stood in the lobby kitted out in a chic dotted net shirt, khaki waistcoat, skirt, and shoestring leather boots. Her rebellious hair clopped temporarily subdued under a floppy straw hat that boasted a robust brim ribbon. She had splashed on lipstick hoping a youngish man might show and knew upon their greeting she'd have her way.

... And here she stood.

Rain began pattering, eliciting riotous calls from the wildlife filling the leafy canopy. Alexandra lifted a pad from her canvas satchel and ruffled through the drawings of birds she had likewise photographed with her handheld Eastman-Kodak Brownie 2 along the journey upriver.

"Such risks and nary a hint of the bloody bird," Bannister winged, growing impressed as a duplication of the lead headhunter materialized onto a fresh page of her sketchpad.

Alexandra offered an unapologetic confession without breaking the rhythm of her hand. "I photographed the 'bloody bird' from the raft while you dozed."

"Then why are we risking shrunk noggins?"

"I deemed further exploration to be in order." She looked up and issued a contrite smile. *"Anyhoo,* whenever will I have another opportunity to see naked headhunters? It's unlikely back in Montana. I cannot fathom the discomfort of having their *schlanges* tied up to their waistlines so."

"'Schlanges?' Why would you refer to them like that?"

She held up her palms and shrugged. "Is that not what you call them around these parts?"

Bannister fumbled for a respectable response but could find none. His mouth fell agape, having never witnessed a young woman sketch a man's schlange tied up to his waistline.

Alexandra completed her drawing, bagged her utensils, and darted to her feet. "In the harbor, several sailors pointed down, howling, *'Nimm a meinen schlange!'"*

"We might have driven the Germans off this wretched island, but some of their coarse nature remains." He slung his rifle and tossed the camera across a shoulder but then paused. "Which way the river?"

Having always been directionless, Alexandra never felt lost. She pointed east. A fetid mist rose from the soundless jungle floor. She peeled an orange. "Have you seen much of the world, Bannister?"

"I served on the *Sydney*. We transported blokes to Gallipoli and returned with whatever remained of them."

Her mood soured on hearing the Great War had wrapped its ugly tentacles even as far as Down Under. It had irreparably sullied her life.

"Bully for you in making it home."

He hastened his pace to walk beside her. "You beguile me, Miss Alexandra. I need to learn more about you. What of your family? Your other talents? I beseech you!"

"My family background is too absurd to be believed," she conceded, forever uncomfortable when being beseeched. "As for other talents, I fare well at getting men to carry my belongings, unsolicited."

The massive Fly River stretched for a thousand kilometers, evolving in attraction and mystery the closer one delved toward its headwaters near the Dutch West Indies. Days prior, Alexandra and Bannister had journeyed up its lower course on the riverboat *Vanapa,* which conducted routine trips from Kiwai Island to a remote outpost called Everill Junction. Once docked at the wharf, supplies for those daring to live on the cusp of the known world were off-loaded, and the booty of prospectors secured for delivery to the coast. Presbyterian missionaries resided a settlement, and Alexandra had milled about its stilted thatch huts meeting the amicable villagers.

While capturing a shot of a *Paradisaea raggiana*, she'd spotted a sturdy raft, and a foolish impulse to go for the grand prize usurped better judgment. She had failed to notice the wooden handle on the back of the raft along their trek beyond the junction, having enticed the captain of the *Vanapa* to tow them, rendering the trip swift and the handle's purpose unforeseen.

Yet now, in the return riding a slight current, sixty kilometers spread a significant distance. Nature called. It often meddled as the biggest killjoy in her unorthodox travels. She tried to lose herself in a copy of *Picturesque Travel.* Not even the magazine's fetching tourist ads or stylish vignettes touting the beauty of the South China Sea could distract from her bladder's rebellion.

Seni and Inisi—the two young men manning their quant poles—knew the river and might have an answer to the fundamental question on her mind. They were good-natured lads and Papuan members of the Presbyterian congregation, caught somewhere in that difficult no-man's-land between the way things always were, and the way things forever would soon be. Though dressed in torn khaki shorts, sandals, and loose-fitting pith helmets, they did not speak English.

Alexandra often studied up on language when venturing abroad, but no literature existed on the finer pronunciation of Motu or the other hundred trans-Papuan dialects she'd have cause to use.

She maneuvered around supplies piled under an angled canopy. Female etiquette could, to some extent, be set aside in the jungle, yet some gender inequities would last eternal. Nothing she considered would be so convenient as her companions' ability to unbutton, unfurl, and unleash in a proud stance. She inspected the raft for any cracks to squat over, but the bamboo shoots were tied securely. It would be easy enough, as she'd already cut off her undergarments to use as toilet paper.

She moseyed over to Bannister. "Pardon me, but how does a lady tinkle aboard this vessel?"

He lifted his hat off his eyes and called out in Gogodala. Seni spoke, pointing near and far. Bannister forwarded, "They can stop on Snake Island. This handle is safer unless crocs break from shore."

"Snakes or crocodiles... *hmm!* I've tolerated worse company in powder rooms." Alexandra tossed off her hat, which freed her sun-kissed blonde hair to cascade down to the middle of her back; the cloying humidity having yet vanquished the everyday wave to its length.

The full force of the equatorial sun tolled. The many mucks of the wilderness stained her linen outfit. She stood drenched in perspiration, and, worst of all, smelled bad. Such muss could not stand, and there existed but one remedy.

She unstrapped her belt, wiggled out of her waist vest, and feistily battled the laces of her boots until they shared a pile.

"Tally-ho!"

The men cheered as Alexandra cannon-balled with a splash and vanished beneath the surface. It took several determined strokes before she gripped the handle. She floated on her back. Her eyes soaked in the colorations spawned by the sun as it sculpted faint rainbows in the river's rising mist. Hanging fruit bats set off to skim their bellies upon the water to cool off. She marveled at where she dallied and blithely debated whether innate courage or mental instability lay at the root of why she felt carefree. What made interior Papua so foreboding proved not what was known, but rather all that remained unrevealed. Native folklore spoke of monstrous antediluvian reptiles roving its rainforests and spiders that feasted on human prey.

Something high in the trees caught her eye. It resembled a hazy outline of a flying fox. Beyond its ungodly size, what rendered it compelling was that it did not hang from a branch but sat perched, encased in its wings. In Port Moresby, she'd heard of a winged creature the locals called a Seklo-bali, foretold to be a demon guardian of the river. It filled her mind with more wonder than worry.

"Something just nipped my foot."

A turtle poked its head above the surface. Bannister reached out a hand. "Come along. I'll pull you aboard."

"Not quite yet." Alexandra's saturated shirt failed to shield her bosom. Noting his interest, she flashed a coy smile and maneuvered to drift on her belly.

Bannister exhaled in exasperation, unsure if her provocations were intentional or just her insouciant manner of being. He pleaded, "I'll be up a creek if I bring back only half of you."

Alexandra grasped her lifeline, and he pulled her aboard. She tussle-dried her hair with a towel and attempted to squeeze moisture from her dripping clothes, but her soggy condition proved unsalvageable in such interminable mugginess. She took a squishy seat on a crate to take in the final offerings of sunshine before the full moon emerged to be their guidelight downriver. Bannister sat across from her, tight-lipped.

She knew why. "Chin up, good fellow. We'll soon be back at Everill Junction, no worse for the wear."

"I'll reside a penal colony once Government House learns of this."

His anxiety grated on her, being on holiday from her own. "Why did you ever agree?"

"You were a young American woman toying with my emotions," he protested. "When I kissed your hand... the look in your eyes and smell of your perfume captivated me."

"Mostly sweat with a touch of jasmine. You wouldn't have been so enchanted if you met me in Java last month, legless with dysentery."

It struck her as unfair. Losing herself in foreign lands always unearthed the best in her. In such a fleeting acquaintance, he could not know what an everyday wreck she truly was.

"I should have placed you in handcuffs and taken you back."

She abandoned efforts to comfort him. The raft drifted toward the reputed kingdom of poisonous snakes. The long islet cut the river into a narrow course to the left and a wider channel to its right. Bannister adjusted the mounted rudder to ride the faster waters of the narrows.

Alexandra's foot tapped out of cadence with the pulsing choral contributions of frogs, birds, and katydids.

Bannister scurried up and gripped his rifle. "Do you hear it?"

She focused on the ruckus. It held a rhythmic quality. Seni and Inisi stopped guiding the raft. They all stood in frozen silence: sensing, listening, waiting.

It rang unmistakable; someone was beating a drum.

Inisi shouted, *"Marind-Anim ti sasasa!"*

A dozen tribesmen emerged along the riverbank. They took a stance in the shallows, chanting in unison; their bodies rocking from side to side in a traditional war dance or show of force.

Alexandra could live with the thought of being killed, but to be eaten thereafter rested beyond her palate. She turned to Bannister, completely vexed. "Do you think they prefer to barbecue or boil?"

"You can suggest to them your preference," he grumbled.

For a moment, she set aside her astonishment to marvel at the tribesmen. The Marind-Anim were arresting in their grass skirts, feathered headdresses, and boned necklaces. War paint marked their bodies, and the spears they brandished were of great length.

She coveted a photograph, but sanity prevailed. "Do something! I'm too young to be served as a plat du jour."

Bannister adjusted the rudder as they approached the narrows.

Alexandra stood and reached for her smaller camera. A volley of spears stirred the air. She dove for cover behind the water barrels, as did the others. The frantic rush to starboard sent the craft into a spin and tilting near capsize. Seni grabbed a dock rope and jumped overboard.

The raft balanced out, and he held on for dear life, half-submerged.

Bannister struggled to work the bolt of his rifle.

Alexandra dared a peek. The warriors were moving downriver. "Do you plan to use that or just fiddle with it?"

He huffed, "The governor frowns on us shooting the natives unless it's a last resort."

A spear pierced the water barrel a few inches from their heads.

"I think we're about there." Alexandra ripped the Lee-Enfield 303 from his grip and chambered the round. She had graded well in her college rifle club and excelled in marksmanship on horseback. After adjusting the sights, she nodded to Inisi, who looked eager to get to the rudder. The river grew choppy, fueling the raft's unbridled drift.

Her aim fixed above the tribesmen, she fired.

The shot's percussion sent thousands of bats scattering, glutting the sky with rabid motion and an unremitting, deafening screech. Inisi used the distraction to alter their course and pull Seni aboard.

The current would dictate their fortune. They would either safely loop the upper tip of the islet or face doom in the narrows.

Alexandra admired the courage of the Marind-Anim, but not their tactics. "It recalls the blunder of LeGallais at Bothaville in letting De Wet slip away. If they waited, we'd be well-seasoned by now."

"Do you study military strategy at university?" asked Bannister.

"Forestry management, actually. My father speaks about birds, the Boer War, and little else."

"What will you do as a forest manager?"

She snickered, not knowing. "I can become a park ranger. Honestly, it seemed the best way to get out of a classroom, shoot a rifle, and take a few *walkabouts*."

He managed a smile. "You've finally picked up some Australian."

The gap between hunter and prey widened.

Alexandra retrieved her handheld Brownie camera. "Do you know who the first person to photograph the Marind-Anim was...? No one does. They were probably delicious. That leaves it up to me."

Bannister said, "You're bonkers!"

"Don't be silly. Jim Thorpe couldn't strike us from this distance."

A young warrior ran into the river.

Alexandra scored her photo.

The raft took a fateful turn toward the hostile riverbank, and a sense of doom set in. The last things she recalled were a winged shadow crossing over the water and a hurled object speedily heading her way.

Chapter 2

News had arrived of Rudolph Valentino's death, and the heartbroken women of Port Moresby cried. Alexandra paused outside a field currently serving as an open-air theater for the capital's white population, who were but six hundred in number. By happenstance, the evening's featured film proved Valentino's 1925 release, *Cobra*, and a sizable crowd stood gathered to pay the "Latin Lover" a last farewell. Bannister placed her camera and travel bag down. His ragged uniform and unshaven face bespoke of a sunbaked prospector limping into town empty-handed.

"Let's say we finish the show, Bannister. Would you scrounge me a cigarette?"

Alexandra took a seat under a palm tree, more so out of feeling faint than any desire to read inter-titles. She rested a hand over her bandaged temple. A black eyepatch applied at the local hospital covered the worst of the bruised discoloration. It rang difficult to fathom one's head could swell so without bursting. While her blood-stained hair proved a feral mess, at least her torn clothing had been laundered on the ship from Kiwai Island.

Bannister returned with her bounty. He planted it between her lips and lit it. Since regaining consciousness, Alexandra spoke little about their improbable escape. Bannister's fantastical account had left her flabbergasted. While her busted skull had been bandaged, she'd yet to wrap her head around its implications. Despite a cable having been dispatched from Kiwai, her father failed to greet her at Port Moresby Harbor. He held every right to be upset, but the penitence of an absentee parent lay in the forfeiture of unimpeachable say-so. Alexandra knew his anger would flash bright, fizzle quickly, and lapse into unspoken regret.

Everything had gone fine until it hadn't. Despite it all her doing, it would finish Bannister. She needed to come up with something to pry his cheek off the hook.

After all, he'd returned her to civilization... such that it was.

New Guinea had once been split between vying German and British interests. Administrative duties over the southern English realm were granted to Australia in 1905, and Port Moresby named the capital of the new Territory of Papua. German New Guinea to the north would be annexed during the Great War, and the Aussies accorded a mandate to oversee the entirety.

The port itself constituted an odd blend of Australasian customs, still rickety in its steps. Civil servants, merchants, and plantation owners accounted for most of its permanent inhabitants, with prospectors, traders, naval personnel, and anomalous tourists more transient in nature. Development into a modern tropical metropolis proceeded slowly. Electricity proved the latest jolt onward, with running water a mirage, but enough novelties existed to give the place some semblance of livability. Native workers were active during daylight, with most returning each evening to their shabby stilted houses jutting into the Gulf of Papua.

Alexandra broke a silly grin in recalling her first day touring the area. She'd been equally astounded to be served lunch by a tattooed Koitabu woman wearing only a ramis-grass skirt as in seeing a Motuan man—sporting a suit and spinning an umbrella—humming "God Save the King." In her everyday world, nudity and body art remained taboo.

"And truly... who wears tweed in such crushing humidity?" she blurted out to no one in particular.

Such sprang the oddities of the place. Peculiar, contradictory, but in its way, beautiful. Papua posed the most fascinating destination she'd ever traveled to, and it left her yearning more audacious gallivants. She rose to allow the passage of an enormous coconut crab carrying in its claws a chunk of its namesake. It was time to atone for her imprudence and find a soft mattress to sleep.

Atop the hill, the Moresby Hotel stood aglow in flickering lamps. A pleasant evening swirled, and the tepid breeze kicking off the Coral Sea played a gentle game with the leaves overhead. Alexandra and Bannister left the dark road to trample the stone pathway; the calls of the katydids fading secondary to the chatter of men on the outdoor terrace. Two wore the uniforms of the constabulary; shooting billiards under the shelter of a bamboo canopy. The proprietor lounged, reading the *Papuan Courier* and shooing mosquitoes.

Archibald Bathenbrook sat speaking over something jocular in his opinion; less so to the distinguished-looking recipient. He dressed in his standard tropical attire of a pale linen suit, loose tie, and beige Panama hat. Alexandra knew she held a gift for keeping him young, all the while graying his hair. He still offered a competitive reflection of what she could recall of earlier rendezvous. A dimmer fire in his brown eyes, a thinning hairline, and a slight shuffle from an arthritic hip seemed the only irrecoverable casualties of his interminable years championing new horizons for king and country.

The gathered men stood upon noting their arrival. Bannister said, "Crikey! Murray's down from Government House." He sought refuge with his peers, who were finding amusement in his predicament.

"You're late, Alee," Archibald said. "I feared you pulled a Percy Fawcett and become forever lost to the jungle."

"The harbormaster hesitated in allowing me ashore, fearing piracy. Good to see you, Father."

He kissed her non-bloated cheek. "May I introduce Sir Hubert Murray? We first met while serving in South Africa. Governor, my daughter, Alexandra."

Though wobbly, she managed a quick curtsy. "Your Excellency. Apologies for my appearance. I assure you, my father did not mate with a watermelon."

It spurred muted chortles from the billiard players, but none from Murray. "My dear girl, we feared for your safety. Bannister! Step forward and explain yourself."

Bannister did so, saluting and assuming a regimented posture. "No good explanation for any of it, sir!"

Silence ensued. The hotel owner asked, "Can I get you a drink?"

Prone to saying silly things when under duress, Alexandra replied, "I'd like some orange juice to avoid the scurvy."

A patrol officer, who introduced himself as Hornsby, carried over a chair for her to sit. The owner dispatched a Motuan houseboy to fix a bath. He informed, "Someone pinched my oranges a week ago."

"The cretin!" She vaguely recalled being the culprit. *"Anyhoo,* a Princess Kaiulani will suffice."

Archibald took a seat. "Come, Alee. Tell your tale."

"Wherever to start?" She settled into the teak and leather sling chair. Although not prone to fibbing, circumstances called for some degree of creative recollection. After a weighty pause, she spoke calmly for ten minutes, uninterrupted. *She had convinced Bannister that her father already awaited them at Everill Junction... He'd risked all to track her once she'd gone upriver without warning...*

As for the rest, she described it as lived. It transfixed her audience in competing waves of delight, alarm, and incredulity. A woman trailblazing the interior struck as inconceivable, yet they all concluded she'd pulled it off in spectacular fashion.

"Patrol Officer Bannister saved the entire expedition from the dinner table." Alexandra polished off her drink. "Thereafter, I did not wake until they loaded me aboard the *Mataram* in Kiwai."

"The cannibals scared off by a prodigious winged creature, you say?" the governor questioned. "Your story is unique, yet I suspect you're concussed or hallucinatory with fever."

"I am concussed, Your Excellency, as there were two of you when I arrived and three since I finished that cocktail. Perhaps you should hear it from my fearless guide."

Bannister came to attention. "She gave a spot-on account, sir!"

Murray grumbled. "What did your native guides have to say of this escapade?"

She shrugged. "Our guides spoke no English. Not even Australian."

Murray let slip a brief chuckle. "Though you can barely stand, my dear, you dance about magnificently!"

Alexandra reached into her satchel and produced a dagger. She'd likely be dead if it hadn't struck her camera, allowing her to get away with simply being knocked cold. It was a skillfully engraved piece of weaponry honed from the thigh bone of an ostrich-like creature known as a cassowary. She passed it to the governor tip first, unable to hold it still enough for him to safely grasp.

Archibald seized it, fearing a repeat of the "Coolidge Incident."

"I'd like to see a photo of those Marind-Anim," said Hornsby.

Alexandra shakily stood. "As would I, but my handheld camera is lost to the river."

Murray rose and placed on his pith helmet. "Chivalry would dictate we set out to find you. Such a venture could have jeopardized the lives of searcher and native alike. The punishment for misleading an officer is ten lashes with a rattan cane. I'm considering leniency."

Alexandra gasped and nearly tumbled over. Her mind locked up and retreated to some far-off place. She stood motionless, silent, her fixed expression mirroring Lot's wife outside the burning city.

Murray rushed forward and clutched her arm. "Does she require medical attention?"

"It will pass," Archibald assured. When it failed to, he tossed his drink into her face. It worked.

Alexandra licked a gin droplet running down her cheek. "That was rather unsporting, Father. You could have at least troubled yourself to get a glass of water."

Archibald said to the governor, "Alexandra is still young, foolish, and, while a finagler extraordinaire, has a good heart to her. I ask that you let her off, just this once."

"Gentlemen!" Murray kissed Alexandra's hand and winked. He headed down the dark path toward town, whistling a tune in a most upbeat manner.

Alexandra sought Bannister. "Thank you for lugging my camera. For everything, really."

"I hope to get to know you better," he confided.

"I'll soon be off to Sydney. Don't fret, Bannister. I'm a girl full of wanderlust. My priorities are not akin to romantic relationships. I can say 'goodbye' in forty languages, but 'hello' in only one."

She kissed his cheek and listlessly headed for her bath.

"Many thanks for seeing Alee back. No doubt she was a handful."

Bannister turned to Archibald. "Truth be told, she was more apt than I in the rainforest. I fear she holds an indifference toward death. At least she doesn't mind goading it a bit."

Archibald sighed. "I did a fair job raising my two sons but quite lost with my daughters."

"There are more like her out there?"

Archibald patted Bannister's shoulder in parting, and solemnly stated, "Not anymore."

It was the age of the majestic ocean liner, and Alexandra had booked passage on one of the true queens of the sea. In its trans-Pacific duties, the RMS *Empress of Australia* provided a luxurious ride. After boarding in Sydney, she'd postponed getting acquainted with its grandeur. It proved tricky enough walking a straight line on land, and the blurry image in her mirror still reflected that of a mutant.

She had finally broken quarantine.

The ship's decor displayed an Art Deco flair, which remained the rage, and she yearned to take a dip in its indoor pool. Two months of sweltering travel had weaned her slender frame to near-nothingness, but the multi-course dinners would dispel that quick enough. It went without saying they'd put her ashore in Vancouver halfway under the table. Prohibition loomed three weeks away, and she felt obligated to indulge before returning to the drought.

During her brief stay in Australia, she had sat for an interview with the *Sydney Mail*. News of her Papuan escapade had preceded her arrival, and the article made it to print the morning of departure. It pleased Alexandra that the journalist added a photograph of her in pristine outback gear prior to catastrophe alongside the shot of the headhunters. The right side of her face fostered a mutable palette of unpleasant colors partially concealed by an eyepatch, lending few aboard to make the connection in her mottled state of incognito.

Carrying a portfolio and a piece of cake, Alexandra navigated the ship's honeycomb of passageways until reaching the smoking parlor, which hosted the expected assembly of black-tied gents chatting over cigars. Two women invaded this masculine lair for a quick cigarette without protest.

She made it three.

The room's ambiance appealed to her untapped sophisticated tastes:

oak-paneled walls, mahogany chairs, crystal tumblers. A pianist and string bassist dished out jazzy selections.

Alexandra stopped at the bar. The tender lit a candle, and she set off for her father's table. It would be Archibald's last night aboard. He would disembark in New Zealand.

"Happy Birthday!"

"Whatever to wish?" He blew out the candle as she claimed a seat.

"I know what Mother would wish for." Alexandra snickered. "Did she forward her regards?"

"Remarkably, yes. Her heartfelt telegram inquired over the health of your uncle."

Archibald Bathenbrook was born the third son of an English baron, which meant he'd likely go through life a commoner and inherit nothing. Before marriage, he had attained a degree in geology, served with the King's Shropshire Light Infantry, and began his journeys throughout the world. England was an island, forever in need of importing food and raw materials to sustain itself, and a worldwide empire thereby established to see to it.

His duties in the Colonial Office were based on assessing distant lands for ore deposits, precious metals, and, of more recent priority— petroleum. During a visit to Alberta, Canada, in July 1895, Archibald's life took an American turn. To any geologist, Butte, Montana, presented the motherlode. The gold, silver, and copper within "The Richest Hill on Earth" elevated the region to global prominence. An American counterpart had offered a tour of its mining operations.

By chance, they traveled to the state capital to attend *Mark Twain's Tour Around the World* at the Ming Opera House. His colleague being a member of the prestigious Montana Club, Archibald found himself immersed in an invitation-only gala at the Hotel Helena to honor the man himself, Samuel Clemens.

Helena boasted it held more millionaires per capita than any city in the world, and the affair showcased an eclectic blend of upscale etiquette and wild west bravado. In attendance caroused ambitious courtiers biding their turn to dance with Larisa Monvoisin, the undisputed belle of the ball. The men of Montana waltzed stylishly with gun belts affixed, but only Archibald could blarney that he was the son of an English baron and his career entailed traveling the world. Her spirited personality once mixed well with his debonair manner.

Alexandra sensed her father's sudden melancholy. She asked, "Do you ever regret it all?"

Of his offspring, three were lost to Heaven, with a fourth broken in spirit. All his hopes for the future now rested with Alexandra. "I regret missing out on you growing into such a precocious young lady. But to lament one's marriage would be to regret one's children, so it does not come to mind."

She flashed a warm smile. "So, what did you wish for?"

"That someday you and I will return to Guiana and find that bloody bird and waterfall."

Liquor had loosened him up. She seized the opportunity. "When will you divorce?"

He sat not so oiled as to gush anything. "Your mother and I shared many fine years together, but my need to serve in South Africa put an end to that. We now have a suitable relationship. I partake in her fortune, and she longs to be a baroness."

He stood and fixed his bow tie. "Off for a tour of the loo."

Alexandra mumbled a curse over pushing too hard. To others, "Olde Archie" presented a gregarious fellow. If he bumped into a veteran of the Boer War, it would take an hour for his return.

It amazed her how the Brits spoke of that bloody conflict as if it were some grand fraternal sabbatical filled with wine, women, and sophomoric nicknames. She suspected it was how they coped with the utter horror of it all—the bodies of the fallen decomposing under the African sun, being picked apart by hyenas.

The lounge's instrumental duo played a dueling rendition of Louis Armstrong's "Heebie Jeebies." Jazz was to her liking. Alexandra leaned back in her chair, crossed her legs, and recalled with fondness her family trip in 1912 to British Guiana. It would be the last time they holidayed together, and it had been a somewhat happy gathering.

Her mother and sister remained in Georgetown while she and her brothers joined in seeking the famed Kaieteur Falls. It stood epic in a tamed corner of the Amazon and purported to be the largest single cascade of water in the world. Her father remained keener on spotting a Guianan cock-of-the-rock along the riverway, but such made sense, the English being odd birds in their own right.

Poor weather had turned them back.

Alexandra adjusted her eyepatch and sipped her whiskey, sensing a surge of testosterone filling the lounge. Even in her semi-grotesque state, there'd be a need to fend off buccaneers seeking to pass the voyage in her company. She spotted one amateur removing his wedding band to place in his pocket—the pros having done so just after boarding.

It struck as nothing new.

At seventeen, she had blossomed from a gawky, loose-limbed girl into a seductively angular young woman. During her first years in college, she'd engaged in three sordid trysts: one sober, twice otherwise. This rebellious stretch left her reputation not fleetingly tarnished but rusted into regrettable campus hearsay.

She felt on course in tempering such flippant behavior, *though if it were the right man...?*

"G'day. You're too lovely a lass to shivoo with the flies."

"I shivoo with all sorts," she cracked, not knowing what it meant. He was handsome, she'd give him that: six-foot-two, with a reddish tint to his brown hair. His face looked so smooth she suspected he had never used a razor and doubted he was older than twenty. "Alexandra."

"I've seen you somewhere," he said, squinting. "Aboard a ship in Port Moresby Harbor?"

She did not take him to be German. "Were you the one yelling for me to service his schlange?"

The man's eyebrows jumped off his forehead. "No. My name is Errol Flynn. I won a gold mine in a poker game and took sail there to get a lay of the land. I'm from Tasmania."

"Aren't you the lucky devil?"

"At least tonight." Flynn claimed the open seat. "Did a coconut fall on your head?"

"I had an accident evading cannibals on the Fly River." For an otherwise suave character, she felt Errol needed to polish up his pickup lines. "Fortunately, they find spoiled Americans hard to digest."

Flynn pushed back his slicked hair. "I'd like to see that jungle."

"Headhunters abound," she warned in all seriousness. While they'd likely fail to deflate Flynn's ego, they might just shrink his head. "They passed on mine. Too colorful a challenge."

"I disembark tomorrow. Why not greet the morning together?"

Alexandra spotted her father and strove to wrap things up. "I'm tempted, but the doctor informed me to refrain from intimate relations until the last of my leprosy clears up."

Flynn turned pale and skedaddled.

Alexandra uncrossed her legs and opened her portfolio. Her photographs stirred a sense of satisfaction. She had once longed to follow in the footsteps of Eliza Scidmore and become a contributing member of the National Geographic Society. Such ambition had faded off to wherever lost schoolgirl dreams resided. People yearned for pictorials with the stories they read and images of wildlife in their native habitats. This adventure rekindled consideration that travel photography might offer a vocation to pursue once escaping college.

Her father returned, accompanied by a man. It appeared debatable who held up whom. "This is my old chum, Crumpie Foster. We served outside Pretoria together."

"Of course, you did," Alexandra said. "I'm the wayward daughter."

"It is an indubitable pleasure." Crumpie swaggered. "Olde Archie and I go way back and served in Pretoria together. We were once snowbound in Lhasa, finishing the 'Great Game' with those Ruskies. Never so delighted to get that treaty signed so we could return to the blessed heat of India."

Alexandra recalled reading about the Great Game—the century-long competition between England and Russia to sway political influence throughout Central Asia. "Would you be so kind, Mister Crumpie, to pour my father back into his chair and join us for a nightcap?"

Crumpie tipped his top hat. "Past my bedtime. Cheerio!"

Alexandra produced her father's gift. "I took your advice: 'Find what they eat, when they eat, and then wait.'"

He marveled at the photograph of a male *Paradisaea apoda* in full plumage. "Brilliantly done!"

It raised her cheeks despite the pain.

Archibald had set in place contingencies for Alexandra to attain sole control of her trust fund. She had turned twenty-one in June. She had avoided eloping with some cad or birthing a child out of wedlock. All that remained now toiled getting a college degree.

It proved the only reason she'd gone to start.

"I can put off school and we can go after the cock-of-the-rock."

He exercised his gift for sobering up instantaneously. "We'll have none of that. Time to retire. I'll expect you at breakfast to see me off."

"Sweet dreams, Father." He made it out of the lounge in a straight-enough path. Alexandra hoped to emulate his exit, tipsy herself. To linger any longer would woo temptation not to reach her cabin door alone and allow some young buck in, like Flynn. A group of men browsing a shared newspaper at the bar rested their collective eyes on her. She worried about overstaying her welcome.

One stately man stepped forward, obstructing her exit. *"La femme photographe magnifique!"* The spirited Frenchman bowed and kissed her hand as his colleagues gathered around.

"Merci." Another man passed her champagne. The attention made Alexandra blush. The entire lounge rose from their seats, holding up their glasses. They appeared to be waiting for her to make an eloquent toast, but all that sprang from her lips was, "Huzzah!"

"Hear, hear!" several of them bellowed, while others applauded as she drained her glass.

"Thank you, gentlemen." Alexandra started on her way, flushed by the moment, but turned back. They appeared to be a group with much collective wisdom at their disposal. She asked, "Would any of you know, perchance, when the Treaty of Lhasa was signed?"

The tallest one, who espoused a military air, answered, "September 1904."

The stated date hit Alexandra like a sledgehammer. She could only manage a weak smile and nod. Her body teetered. She had been a postscript child, four years removed from the next youngest, Emma. It was her belief that her mother abhorred her for that inconvenience.

June 1905. It all served up bad math. Archibald Bathenbrook could not possibly be her father.

Desperately seeking her cabin, Alexandra lost her footing and bumped into a lofty man donning a top hat. She thought his fingers to be dreadfully cold and bony. He righted her fall before continuing down the passageway without a word. His loping strides lent his long white hair to bounce on his shoulders.

She moved along and noticed a bracelet missing from her wrist. The colorful braid of horsehair strands had been purchased from a Chippewa tribeswoman years ago. Though it held no monetary value, she cherished it as a talisman.

She felt too compromised to retrace her steps to find it.

Upon reaching her door, she could barely salvage the key from her purse. Tears streamed her cheeks as she collapsed on her bed. After crying for a few minutes, she retrieved a pen and paper. The impulse to confide her grief subsided. The world spun a blur, and she'd wait to post something sober when the ship made its later port of call in Hawaii.

"If you don't save me, William," she whispered, "who will?"

Chapter 3

Montana: June 1927

Alexandra Bathenbrook would start her life as a millionairess with one suitcase in hand and a rifle slung across her back. She left her room at Hamilton Hall a final time and cut through campus, which spread littered with streamers, confetti, and a few mortarboards left unclaimed from the graduation ceremony for the Class of 1927. She had treated Montana State College as a hideout more than an institute of higher learning, but her four years here were not a total waste. Fond memories of two-stepping with lads at the Bobcat Lair, cheering on Ott Romney's powerhouse basketball team, and hitching to the local hot springs for a steamy soak were portable mementos, easily summoned.

She learned that ardent boob-men only paid her passing heed, while staunch leg-men always locked their gaze. As for incorrigible ass devotees, they were but putty in her hands. She'd never fallen in love despite a long tally of suitors articulating their vows of eternal devotion, though willing to settle for feeling her up a bit.

Such flatteries aside, she'd made little progress eloquently managing herself in conventional settings. Alexandra needed to dig no further than being a newfound millionairess, alone on her graduation day, to realize she was an outcast of sorts. Why most people shunned her proved flummoxing, as she considered herself well-mannered, at times amusing, and she bathed routinely. She sometimes worried if her brief spell residing in New Orleans or her collegian reputation as a free spirit lay at the root, but neither was the case.

It had simply always been that way.

Before leaving campus, she stopped at a stone memorial for alumnae lost in the Great War and took a seat on the grass. It listed sixteen names, among them her eldest brother, Thomas. She had often spent time here to engage him in quiet conversation. He had been killed on November 29, 1917, at Cambrai—obliterated in a German Army artillery barrage so apocalyptic, the remains of the 2nd West Riding Division's fallen remained unrecovered a decade later. Alexandra had yet to move on from this loss. With no formal burial, he was nothing more than a ghost cast somewhere into the ether.

His parting words still haunted her: "I know you'll be the one to come visit me when you're older."

Most attributed Alexandra's disregard to take college seriously to her financial windfall upon graduation, but its origins were in graver reasoning. Thomas was gifted in most everything. He had devoted so much time preparing for a future never to be; all his admirable talents snuffed out in one ungodly finger snap. Life seemed too precarious to invest in. Yet now, facing an empty slate and a boundless horizon, Alexandra knew she needed a plan if she were to live hers to the hilt.

She bid farewell and picked up her sole suitcase, believing fresh starts were best initiated with limited baggage. She set off into the adult world, hoping not to stumble too much along the way.

Bozeman posed a contemporary town of seven thousand tucked within the Gallatin Valley and in the shadows of the Bridger Mountains. It did not entertain the uproars of the mining center of Butte, nor the tranquility of Yellowstone Park.

Like its geography, its flourish lived right in the middle.

Surrounding pea farms and prairie lands, having weathered extended periods of drought and wildfires, were readying to prosper. Alexandra circumvented a residential neighborhood and entered the heart of downtown along East Main Street. Trolley tracks and horse paths had faded away with the advent of the automobile. The long jaunt carrying a heavy Globe Trotter leather suitcase left her overheated due to her choice of a suede skirt and fringe jacket.

Dressing comfortably in springtime Montana proved impossible, as it could hit ninety degrees at noon and tease snow flurries by sundown. At least her Stetson hat hid the fact she'd once again lost her daily tussle with her flowing blonde hair. She veered into the Gallatin Bank & Trust. A manager informed her of a new policy forbidding firearms on the premises. He minded her Mauser 98 while she saw the teller.

The Wild West was yesteryear.

Cash-in-hand, Alexandra rushed to the Rialto Theater. The opening-day matinee of the movie *Metropolis* presented the best shot to say goodbye to Oliver Martin. She felt disappointed that he had not attended her graduation as promised. Soft-spoken and studious, he always dressed in the same wool sweater-vest and bow tie. A lot of books had been kicked out of his hands over his skittish school days, many of a fantastical pulp magazine variety.

Over the year, he had become her chief confidant.

Upon placement of an ad soliciting information on the lupine beast that had attacked her long ago, he had been the only one to return a serious reply. Her brothers had conjectured it to be a hellhound: beasts reputed to be messengers for the Devil and guardians of Hades.

It unsettled Alexandra for years.

Oliver had produced a faded news article discovered in the archives of the *Avant-Courier*, where he worked as a typesetter. A similar creature had been killed in 1886 after savaging livestock in the Madison Valley. The beast resided in Ioway Indian oral legend.

They called it a "Shunka Warakin."

Hearing it to be tertiary in origin had brought Alexandra great relief. As hoped, Oliver stood first in line.

"Hey, fella. Anything new crossing the wires?"

"Charles Lindbergh might visit. Keep that under your hat." After Alexandra concluded her hug, Oliver added, "I'm sorry. My mother's sick, and I've been working overtime so I can travel to Omaha."

She rubbed his arm. "I'm off to England soon to see my brother."

"Wow! I hope to visit someday. They don't take warmly to rifles."

"I'm still tinkering over a way to hide it in my suitcase."

They shook farewell. When Oliver disengaged, a fifty-dollar bill rested his palm. He said, "I can't accept this."

"Sure you can. I bet Nebraska is lovely in June. Safe travels."

A Model-T pickup came to a screeching halt. Kari Solvang stood on its bed, needing to plant a hand atop her black mortarboard to secure it from toppling. Her lively blue eyes and red-lipsticked mouth set off her ashen hair and complexion to the point they appeared electrified.

"Have you heard? He's heading this way!"

"Who, Charles Lindbergh?" Alexandra yelled back.

"No, the Dark Strangler!" Kari pulled her roommate aboard. "They spotted him near Great Falls."

Alexandra took a seat as the truck rumbled on. "He has only a few more days to get me."

Over recent months, the news services had ginned up hysteria over the strangulation killings by a new genre of thrill killer. The murders started in California and trended up the Pacific Coast. Tabloid reports speculated that the maniac copulated with his victims postmortem.

The entire nation trembled on high alert, awaiting portentous word of his whereabouts.

Alexandra's interest in serial murderers could be traced to her time in New Orleans. Her stay had come at the height of the notorious "Axeman Murders." With the great conflict extinguished but Spanish flu still ablaze, her mother had visited England. Alexandra had been abandoned to share a Creole townhouse with the ever-baleful Adelaide de Chantraine. Her aunt's cruel demeanor staged most demonstrable during tutelage on the corporeal nature of female sexual etiquette. It had been more vulture bites and wasp stings than any birds and the bees.

Kari lit a Lucky Strike and passed it over. "Have you decided yet?"

Alexandra lifted the cigarette from her puckish full lips. "I might freelance taking photographs of wildlife. Sell them to magazines. I'll settle somewhere along the Mediterranean first."

"Egypt? How romantic to kiss a man under the desert sky."

"Too many mummies." Alexandra blew out a ring of smoke. "I can barely tolerate having one."

"Sardinia?"

It elicited a raised eyebrow. "Too many Sardinians."

"Greece! The sun, the sea, the dark-haired fishermen..."

"I can't abide feta cheese!" Alexandra made a sour expression. Kari held the gusto for this to run all day, contingent on her knowledge of a globe. Her steadfast friendship kept Alexandra's waning spirits in check.

Upon becoming roommates, Kari took the bottom bed. It had suited Alexandra fine, being an upper-bunk type, not grounded whatsoever. She'd spent time with the Norwegian Solvang clan during school breaks, though she'd never quite taken to eating *lutefisk*.

They were now twenty-two years old, college graduates for whatever it was worth, and ready to howl.

Most of the passing cars were basic models, but a few ritzier offerings like a Mercedes-Benz or Alvis 12/40 spun Alexandra's head. She knew herself to be an abysmal driver yet skilled vagabond, and it pleased her she held no impulse to drop a thousand on something sporty. Some hailed having a vehicle as the pinnacle of freedom, but she considered them to be the epitome of captivity. With owning one came a need for a place to park it, which would metastasize into a house, marriage, and a sedentary existence.

Alexandra realized money would change her—it was inevitable—but at least for today, she would not buy a car. A year touring *wherever* awaited. Montana stood a long way from Tipperary—a long way from everywhere—and distant adventures beckoned. Once having her fill, she might return and purchase something fast, wild, and beautiful to build her life from the horse stables up.

The pickup slowed to cross a pole bridge, which offered a majestic view of the scenic canyon along the Gallatin River. Wildflowers and effervescent pines abounded, and occasionally a cotton-soft cloud settled upon a snow-capped mountain peak to form a perfect halo.

Alexandra lifted a camera from her bag. The Leica-1 35 millimeter, a graduation gift from her father, stood the best on the market. The compact unit with its chrome fittings and faux leather casing held innovative features, including a shutter speed dial, a collapsible lens, and an attachable range finder.

It was perfect.

While taking a photograph of Kari flaunting a coquettish pose, Alexandra spotted a hitchhiker. The disheveled man appeared middle-aged and gave nothing of a nefarious impression, yet he looked out of place. Months ago it would have been common courtesy to offer him a lift, but with a corpse-copulating madman on the lam, the unkempt straggler thumbed away, out of luck.

Alexandra retrieved from her suitcase a package left outside their dorm room. She studied the card. It read: *Alee, something to curl your hair when a man can't be found. –Love, the Girls.*

It stunned her since few of the coeds at Hamilton Hall exhibited any camaraderie, and she often served as a target of teasing. Other than Kari, the only classmate Alexandra felt a kinship with was Rebecca, who the others razzed by calling her "Becky Bucktooth." It struck her as unfair, as Becky's overbite appeared hardly conspicuous.

Alexandra opened the gift. The wooden box came inscribed with a logo: The *Electrex*. United Drug Company of St. Louis, USA. Within rested an odd, corded device. It looked more like something used in a malt shop than the pronged metal curling iron they'd heat upon the radiator coils on a Saturday night. It included unusual attachments.

Neither held a clue over what they gazed upon.

"It doesn't appear to have come with instructions, Kari. Perhaps we can ask your mother how it works."

The pickup slowed. Four cars idled along the roadside. A dozen young men dressed to impress were sharing a bottle and boisterous laughter. One car flaunted a University of Montana pendant in the back window. The damn grizzlies were invading.

Kari hollered, "Are you Missoula boys heading to the gala? I hear it will be the berries."

Two headed over. One said, "Sure thing. Promise me a dance?"

Alexandra stood and held out a hand. "It will cost you a hit of hooch in advance."

The lad flashed a grin and passed it up.

The pickup kicked up dirt and rumbled off, horn beeping in celebration. As the duped grizzlies gave good-natured chase, Alexandra waved them farewell. "Go Bobcats! *Too-da-loo*, boys!"

Six young women sharing a hotel room was not problematic. Five dolling themselves up in one modest bathroom—pandemonium. Alexandra slept while the other girls battled for the mirror amidst temporary truces involving swapped jewelry and makeup. For tonight, the newly christened Gallatin Gateway Inn served as the main stage for all of Montana. The hotel room came courtesy of Becky Bucktooth's father being a bigwig for the Milwaukee Road. The railroad magnates had financed the inn to cater to tourists visiting Yellowstone Park, and it would provide a fiscal boon to the state. A fleet of White Motor Company touring cars would transport those coming down on a new electric spur from Three Forks.

Among the inn's novelties; a phone in each guest room.

The ringing of one awoke Alexandra. Everyone was gone. She scrambled over to answer it.

Kari announced herself from the lobby. *"Get up. Let's blouse!"*

Alexandra laughed and hung up, in no hurry. Outside, a big band within a gazebo entertained a full dance floor, as two thousand attendees caroused beneath stringed lights and a clear evening sky. She wanted to be part of it, but not for too long, and went about filling the bathtub. She gathered neglected letters retrieved from her dormitory mailbox and browsed over them once taking the plunge.

One from the University of Chicago left her flabbergasted. They were offering her a stipend to travel to Mandatory Palestine and take part in an archaeological dig. She knew the article about her Papuan venture had hit the wires and gained print in newspapers. She was already booked to meet with James Ford, president of the Explorers Club, in New York. This proposal changed everything.

A starting point for a photography career now rested the table.

Alexandra passed on washing her hair, as it took forever and a day to towel dry. She rushed to answer the phone again. *"I'll be right—"* ... *"You're missing a bracelet. Find something to cover your wrist."*

The line clicked dead. The man's terse call was obviously meant for some other guest room.

She shifted into style overdrive: tossing on a silk envelope chemise, snapping herself into garters, wiggling into a beaded dress that came to a fringy halt at the knees, and securing a feathered headband. A few unclaimed necklaces and bracelets left strewn upon a bedcover were borrowed. With a touch of lipstick and eyeliner, she veered near full flapper disease, though she'd never make the ultimate commitments of bobbing her hair or donning a cloche hat.

She took the stairs down to the expansive main hall and lobby. The structure spread beautifully planned out in Spanish Colonial Revival Style, with its dark beams and doorframes accenting the yellow stucco walls to a tee. Once absorbed into the spirited crowd, she needed to bump and grind her way to a punch bowl. She downed the first cup in a gulp; the second, with sophistication.

Kari and Becky hunted her down in the company of two fellows.

"This is my brother!" Becky said. "He drove all the way from Iowa just for my graduation."

"Alexandra." With his thin mustache and dapper manner, she considered him harmless and did not protest his flask topping off her drink with either bathtub gin or smoky bourbon. She'd soon know.

"Robert Bucktooth, but my friends call me 'Smooth Willy.' I hear you're a veritable dervish of the 'Charleston.'"

"So veritable, I'm banned from South Carolina." She fanned herself with a napkin and panicked at having failed to put on any underarm protectorate or taken time to rid her armpits of stubble. "I assure you I'm not European. I simply forgot! Can we get some air?"

The five of them weeded through the crowd and emerged outdoors.

At the first notes of "Deed I Do," Kari sped off with her lad.

To Smooth Willy's request, Alexandra drained her cup and passed Becky her camera case. They took to the floor.

Alexandra removed her T-straps to avoid slipping on the grass. It proved a difficult dance to pull off holding shoes while keeping her elbows locked to her sides. She managed until the rhythm and beat sped from sweet to hot. It inspired her to stop obsessing and cut loose.

Midway through, the song came undone a few instruments at a time, and the crowd quieted.

Governor John Erickson hit the stage. "Come this September, our 'Treasure State' will host the man of the century... Charles Lindbergh, in his Spirit of St. Louis!"

The crowd erupted. Lindbergh had just completed his historic transatlantic flight, and his fame and status approached those of a deity. A fat man with thunderous handclaps guffawed, "Thirty-two hours of flight. Herculean feat. Truly Herculean!"

Alexandra nodded. How "Lucky Lindy" went so long without peeing filled her with envy.

The governor added, "And with great relief I inform that Canadian Mounties have captured the Dark Strangler at the border!"

Cheers again thundered, and the band fired up.

Smooth Willy grasped Alexandra's hand, but she declined his offer. He acted a real corn-shredder while dancing. "I twisted my ankle. Afraid I'm done for the evening."

He crowed, "I have ointment in my car that can soothe that in a jiffy. I'm a salesman for the United Drug Company and am a big cheese in the business."

"Your company should include directions with its hair-curlers."

"I know my onions. Which model is it?"

"The *Electrex*. I'd have you show me, but it's in my hotel room."

He flashed a predacious grin. "Let's blow this joint, and I'll provide firsthand oral instruction."

"Another time, perhaps." She looked away.

Smooth Willy remained undeterred. "In my car, I have powder that can rid your hair of lice."

Alexandra stopped twirling a curly strand in her fingers, taken aback. "My hair does not entertain lice!"

He plucked something off her head. "My mistake. It's confetti."

She grimaced. "I feel a terrible need for a water closet."

"Don't leave! Just gird your loins. A massage might relax you."

Alexandra grasped why girls joined convents. "I always have to pee in the thick of things."

"Have you considered a portable Gibbon-Walsh catheter? I have samples in my car. I can show you how it works. We can take a drive and look at the stars. Get to know each other better."

He certainly stored no shortage of things in his car. She debated whether he was seeking horizontal refreshment or a quick sale. "It all sounds perfectly romantic, but it can't wait." She burst out laughing, grabbed her camera, and headed indoors.

"Good evening, Alexandra. Such a surprise to find you here."

Alexandra cringed. "Good to see you, Mother."

Larisa Bathenbrook sat amidst a charmed circle of Helena's most prominent. Though in her early fifties, she had skirted many of the blemishes that come with age and caroused with the bravado of one knowing it. Her vitality was not mystical, but an intrinsic beauty fortified by a smart sense of style, enviable family genes, and tight laces to her whalebone corset. Emma had inherited her wavy black hair and destined to fill out into a similarly voluptuous woman if not felled so young.

Beguiling and pithy in public, Larisa was never far from snorting fire behind closed doors. She'd made decisions in her life that often riled her emotions. The eldest daughter of a Chicago banker who'd financed one of Montana's more lucrative mining holes, her preordained future had not suited her fancy by age eighteen. One dance with Archibald Bathenbrook had delivered her a means of escape. Their shocking elopement came at the cost of her losing her inheritance. She had been gifted the family's summer cottage in Helena under the condition that she never return to Chicago.

What she submitted to in order to rekindle her family's dark graces still haunted her intellect.

Alexandra could trace nothing to her mother unless she deemed perfect posture hereditary. Since starting college, they had not shared consecutive nights under the same roof. Larisa now used the Monvoisin mansion in Chicago as her primary residence, spending only the summer months in Helena. With each passing arose an opportunity to assess their ever-changing relationship.

The daughter now held the upper hand. Even the era swayed eyes her way, as a more flat-chested, athletic physique for females was in vogue. For once, Alexandra did not wilt under her mother's familiar, icy blue gaze, despite being caught dressed like a floozy.

"I missed you at my graduation," she poked, settling her camera case onto an open chair. "It would have been a kindness to have pretended."

"I was present in spirit, same as your father." Larisa turned to her flock. "The silly girl could have attended Smith or Barnard but elected to mingle with the local cowpokes and farm broods."

"I'm certified to mark trees for clearing, put out wildfires, treat poison ivy, and can shoot a rabid muskrat from two hundred yards," Alexandra made known. "Any such needs, I'm your gal Friday."

Larisa asked, "What are your plans to waste *my* family's fortune?"

"I plan to travel the world and take photographs of things never seen before," Alexandra said nonchalantly. "Build my resumé, so perhaps I can work one day for *National Geographic*. I'll soon be off to Palestine to assist with the excavation of Megiddo."

Larisa stood to confront her daughter eye-to-eye. "Need I remind you cannot step foot in the nation's capital? You're welcome to stay in Helena until you leave."

"I'll stop in to gather—"

Alexandra wavered upon observing a tall, morose man scowl at her getup in passing. Something about him vaguely rang familiar. She turned and frantically searched for the only top hat in town, but the man had inexplicably vanished in the crowd.

"Let's take a walk." Larisa grasped Alexandra's arm. Over their crisp steps, she berated, "You look ridiculous in that flimsy outfit. I warn you to be less insolent!"

"Yes, Mother."

They settled on the front lawn of the inn.

Alexandra freed her arm to reach under her dress for the crumpled pack of Egyptiennes Nerma cigarettes laced in her garters. Her father had sent them with the camera from Cairo, and as she seldom smoked, the carton might last her the rest of the year. "Have you heard from William lately? I plan to drop in over my travels."

"Nothing will ever change with William." Larisa retrieved a lighter from her purse and handed it over. "You must pay your respects to Mistress Adel... *to your aunt* when in Europe."

Alexandra lit up her cigarette. "Does she miss striking me with her whipping cane or allowing charlatans to kiss and fondle my..." She needed a gulp of air to finish. "I think not. I will never forgive you for abandoning me to that Satanic witch."

Larisa's smoky voice became stressed. "Everything we have, we owe to Adelaide. Someday, you might come to appreciate the many sacrifices I've made for this family."

"What family?" Alexandra rolled her eyes, not wanting to hear it. She thought to inquire about her parentage, but it a hazardous nest to kick. "Has Archibald Bathenbrook paid call lately?"

The smack left Alexandra's cheek red. "You respect your father."

It was not an answer either way. They returned to the lobby.

Alexandra felt embarrassed passing strangers had witnessed the reprimand. She reclaimed her camera case and retired to her room. Beyond the window, fireworks popped, eliciting a rapturous chorus of applause from those gazing skyward. Too dark to hope for a photograph, she smirked, wishing for inventors to concentrate their genius on a flash illumination method operable without blowing off a hand, or at the very least a tastier laxative than castor oil.

She opened her camera case to find a wrinkled cocktail napkin inside. Someone had jotted: *The date is written; the table has been set.* It read innocuous enough for such a festive setting, but what followed triggered a shiver: *3-7-77.*

The origin of this numerology remained debatable. Some believed it indicated a timestamp, while others contested it signified measurements for a coffin or a secretive Masonic denotation. The *meaning,* however, went undisputed throughout Montana.

Someone in her mother's circle had issued a threat or warning.

It meant, "Get out of town!"

Chapter 4

New York City: July 1927

Good Lord, please get me out of here! Alexandra's Montana-fledged sensibilities proved no match for the hullabaloos of Manhattan. It stirred like Chicago on Coca-Cola, and she felt the insufferable stimulation of a tasty insect dropped into the center of an ant colony. It was her last day amidst the madness, and she coveted a week on an ocean liner to recover before London, which, while hectic, served as a better-mannered metropolis and of more leisured stride. She posed in front of a fitting mirror, growing smitten with her reflection. Her current getup, though posher than the evening called for, would have to be the one. The boutique owner was spot-on in stating that the green tabard dress was a head-turner.

It fit Alexandra like a taut embrace.

Black, gold, and ivory embroidery gave it a sequined splash of class. The woman's talent with makeup brought out the winsome arc of Alexandra's eyebrows and favored the amber flecks in her playful hazel eyes. Black satin opera gloves and a peacock feather headband provided a final touch of swank. As an assistant struggled to corral Alexandra's hair into something sophisticated, a church bell outside tolled six times.

She would arrive late, but at least fashionably.

Alexandra marked her day dress and other purchases for delivery to her hotel and headed out the door. Dark clouds stirred above the towering skyline. She scurried down the sidewalk, holding high a leather messenger bag to fend off fleeting raindrops. If she had not spent the day signing documents with lawyers and bankers, she'd be in less of a rush, but windfall fortunes needed time-honored fiduciary management from time to time. She'd left the consultations with a scant clue whether they invested her money in a conventional portfolio or something more revolutionary, such as Chilean penguin hatcheries.

The rain picked up.

She skirted over to a crowded bus stand, screeched, and hustled to the bustling street corner. Rush hour during foul weather presented a perfect storm for not finding a cab. She briefly locked eyes with a man standing nearby. He was a handsome fella close to her age and one tall glass of water at a few inches over six feet. His dark hair rested neatly parted to one side, and he held an adorable cleft to his chin no bigger than a dimple. He popped on a fedora before turning away.

She inched her way over with inconspicuous canny until safely under his umbrella.

Without turning, he said, "If you wiggle any tighter, you'll end up in front of me."

When he faced her, Alexandra fell bedazzled. "I tried the bus stand, but somebody reeks of Limburger cheese. Your umbrella was my last port in the storm."

"Well, I'm tickled I passed the smell test." He offered a wry smile and more of the umbrella. "It seems unfair that I have a hat, brolly, and raincoat, and all you possess is the illumination of an Avalonian goddess. We'll share. By the bye, my name is Archibald Alec Leach."

"My father has the exact same name... except for the last part. I'm Alexandra Illyria Bathenbrook."

He shook her extended hand. "I hope you're not engaged in anything notorious, such as larceny. I would like to avoid arrest for sheltering a fugitive from police seeking to catch a thief."

"Not lately." Alexandra had already forgotten she was desperate for a cab. "Why do you ask?"

"Some find it fashionable to take these off." He used nail clippers to snip the price tag hanging from her headband. "Now you'll truly be the toast of New York."

"You've caught me in a pinch." She broke her captive gaze to loop her bag over a shoulder. "I need to flag a taxi to Midtown West."

"As do I. Not to be indiscreet, but what say you if one is waved down, we split the fare? No monkey business intended, I assure you."

"What's the fun in that?" She bit her lip, bemused it had escaped.

The rain was letting up. She stepped onto the street to try with more vigor. It worked. A Model–G Checker cab screeched to a stop. She waited for Archibald to open the back door, just resting her eyes on him.

Once settled in, she told the cabbie her destination, adding, "Please drive slow."

Archibald folded his brolly, and they were off. "If traffic ran any slower, we'd end up back in the Stone Age."

Alexandra found him amusing. His lighthearted style of speech struck charmingly disarming, with artful inflections to his subtle Cockney pronunciations. She could tell he expressed his honest thoughts in every word spoken yet did not take himself too seriously in speaking them.

"I meant to say 'carefully,'" she cheekily clarified. "We can't risk anything tragic marring your manicure."

He waved a playful finger. "My sacrifice for the theater."

An actor no less, her hormones happily pulsed. "Have you starred in anything familiar?"

"I just secured a minor role in a Broadway musical, *Golden Dawn.* The awful truth is, if it were any smaller, the crowd would need a microscope to spot me." He chuckled and straightened his tie. "It's a crazy business, but insanity runs in my family. It practically gallops!"

She nudged him. "I trust one day your name will hit the lights."

"And what amazing adventure are you seeking tonight? I have a suspicion I hate him."

Alexandra grinned, having already made him jealous. "A business dinner before going on holiday."

Traffic started flowing better. Their time together ran short. The inside of the cab grew steamy, fogging over the windows. Archibald made his play. "I am boxed up at the theater tonight, but might we *accidentally* bump into each other tomorrow?"

She hated to disappoint him... but did. "I'm afraid that can't be."

Archibald deflated in his seat. "I envisioned us traveling the world together: worshipping you night and day, champagne on yachts, seeing the Eiffel Tower and Egyptian pyramids hand-in-hand... The Taj Mahal!

We could have been a romance for the ages. You could have been my favorite wife, and yet here I'm left getting the icy mitt."

He ended his melodramatic homily with a humbled chuckle.

Alexandra fought off an irrepressible urge to grab his face and violently kiss him. "It all sounds lovely, but I sail for England tomorrow. And I should warn you I will not consider marriage until age twenty-five. I don't see the ladies waiting that long before one gobbles you up."

He perked up. "Every girl should be married. Tell me your birthdate and I'll divorce her."

"Once I settle somewhere, I'd like to write to you. Perhaps we'll cross paths and get a second chance at having an affair to remember."

He sulked, resigned to his fate. "If the play goes well, I can be reached at the Hammerstein Theater. If it bombs, you might find me in bum's alley or as an uncredited geisha in *Madama Butterfly*."

The cab pulled to the corner. Alexandra passed the entire fare up to the driver. "Drop my companion someplace to raise his spirits." She turned to Archibald. "I am truly crushed. Cash or check?"

He raised an eyebrow and leaned toward her. "People will talk, but by all means, *cash*."

She planted a soft, languid kiss on his lips. Once disengaged, she offered a parting smile and exited the cab. *"Sayonara*, Archibald." As the taxi headed off, she waved farewell upon spotting his forlorn face pressed against the steamy rear window. He looked like a man being shanghaied.

Something magical had eluded her grasp. At least if Archibald Alec Leach ever became a star, she could say that she had kissed him.

James Ford met Alexandra outside of Keens Chophouse. The rain subsided, easing any need to make an artless dash to greet him. His letter requested an informal meeting for her to share tales of Papua and hinted at potential inclusion in future projects.

For one interested in taking photographs of things never seen, there was no grander interview than this.

These were among the men—in spirited competition with their stodgier rivals of the Royal Geographical Society—at the forefront of supporting ventures into realms unknown. Ford came across a distinguished sort. He greeted her cordially and escorted her inside. The landmark restaurant boasted a no-nonsense decor with its brick-faced walls and white-draped tables. Other than its aged mutton chops, Keens held fame for its exclusive pipe club.

The main hall proved a boisterous mishmash of gaudy actors and city bigwigs jammed into one dark and crowded arena. Alexandra tried to stoke her failing embers of confidence, desperate not to fumble this opportunity. An attendant walked them to their private room.

Ford pointed out a glass-encased playbill said to have been held by Abraham Lincoln at the time of his assassination. He testified, "The theater is not named after *my* family, mind you."

Alexandra blurted, "I was once detained for an assassination attempt on Calvin Coolidge."

Ford halted his steps and looked at her, awaiting an explanation.

"Just a terrible misunderstanding," she clarified. *"Anyhoo,* how 'bout those Yankees?"

They settled in the Lillie Langtry room. Unaware if this setting had been reserved by intent or coincidence, the answer would resolve whether it were to be a case of the club courting her or the other way around. Two smartly attired gentlemen stood upon her arrival. They glanced at each other, stunned, possibly expecting someone of heartier physique and not dressed to the nines.

Ford introduced the older man, Frank Chapman, as a renowned ornithologist eager to discuss bird species of the Fly River estuary. The other man was George Dyott. The youngest of the trio at only twice her age, he served as the only one Alexandra held some familiarity with, having read somewhere about his daring exploits in aviation. Dyott was short, tight-lipped, and sallow in the face.

He returned little more than a grunt to her polite salutation.

"Gentlemen, this looks marvelous," she acknowledged as the waiter settled her into a heavy wooden chair.

Dyott whispered to Chapman, "It certainly abates that idea."

Things progressed nicely through the salad course. While the Explorers Club lay rife with pioneers who had traversed vast uncharted regions between the frozen poles, none had ever ventured into hidden Papua. Alexandra gave a calm and measured account of her quest.

The bone dagger of the Marind-Anim warrior engrossed Ford. His inquiries centered on anthropological aspects of study. Chapman listened with a fresh-faced glee, mesmerized by the photographs of exotic birds she gifted to him.

George Dyott exhibited no interest whatsoever.

They drifted into less formal discussions once their entrées arrived. The hot topic of the upcoming Guggenheim Tour that would see Charles Lindbergh visit every state ran its course. Ford found interest in Alexandra's plans to pursue some newfangled field, which she termed "Adventure Photography."

Dyott livened up with a few snickers and sighs of exasperation.

"I am under contract with the University of Chicago to rendezvous with Philip Langstaffe Ord-Guy to photograph his excavation of Megiddo," Alexandra confided, needing a sip of water. "Anyone with four names must surely be important. They expect me by October."

Ford asked, "Where will you set up your office for this endeavor?"

"I will tour from Lisbon to Greece and choose a location along the coast. I'll then entertain travel to any corner of the globe, except the north pole, as frozen lands aggravate a nipple condition and I've been on poor terms with Santa Claus since Christmas 1912."

She let out a deep breath and smiled, sensing by their palpable astonishment how impressed they were with her itinerary.

Dyott finally spoke. "It all sounds ridiculous to the fullest degree."

Alexandra glared at him but let it go.

Ford cleared his throat. "You must forgive George. He has just returned from Brazil, where he proved all the naysayers wrong about Teddy Roosevelt's discovery of the River of Doubt. He filmed the entire undertaking. Alas, for the Royal Geographical Society."

"Bully for you." Alexandra offered a fig leaf. "It is wise to dabble on both sides of the Atlantic."

"My father is English, and my mother is American," he snapped.

"As are mine." Alexandra gulped down her water. Dyott weighed on her. At least he possessed the foresight that film would soon surpass the photograph in popularity. Her neck muscles curdled into knots. She sought diversion. "Quite the baked potato, Mister Chapman."

He held up the colossus. "Bulbous enough to choke Beelzebub."

The odd mental image of a grand demon eating a baked potato unsettled Alexandra.

"How are your mutton chops?" inquired Ford.

"Far superior to those served at the Warm Springs Asylum, I assure you." Alexandra sat mortified it had slipped out. She shrugged it off. "I so regret I will not be home when Mister Limburger arrives."

Ford forecasted, "He'll be a club member soon. Might we speak of potential collaborations?"

She took another gulp of water. "By all means."

"We're promoting George's potential return to Amazonia to seek out the fate of Colonel Percy Fawcett."

The explorer had entered the Amazon in April 1925 searching for the fabled Lost City of Zed and now deemed vanished to the jungle. A rash of news stories had since fomented a frenzy of gossip and efforts to find him to the degree that it held a diagnosis: "Fawcett fever."

"I briefly visited the Amazon as a girl," said Alexandra.

George Dyott grunted in disbelief. "Amazonia is a veritable hell on earth. Hearty men in my company had daily cause to fend off death. Some failed. Surely you speak with a reckless imagination."

"I said briefly," countered Alexandra.

Ford continued, "The major newspaper syndicates are willing to fund George, however—"

"To cut to the chase," Dyott intruded, "they desire a photographer besides the two cameramen in my employ, as traditional photos are needed to post with their daily drivel."

"Two cameramen in case one gets eaten," Alexandra remarked, nodding. "That's good planning."

"The moneymen want George to pick you for the assignment," Ford finally finished.

It stunned her. She hoped only to have a few photographs published in their newsletter, *The Explorers Journal*. She dared to ask, "What is your opinion, Commander Dyott?"

He sighed. "The newspapers wish to pitch a damsel in constant peril to hook readers. A silly prop. It will line their pockets, and if you die some horrible death, they'll figure it all the better. Just look at the circulation stirred by that Wanderwell circus. It's also likely why the university in Chicago chose you."

He was making her feel quite small. About to pop off, she bit down on her lip. Hard.

Dyott pressed his napkin against her bleeding mouth. "Cannibalism may serve well in Papua, but not among the civilized."

She relieved him of his duties and held it in place, feeling stupid.

They all ate in silence for several minutes.

To get back on track, Alexandra spouted, "I'm fitter than you might think. I can do six push-ups... and not those of the girlie, knees on the floor, variety!"

"I highly doubt it."

She tossed his stained napkin onto her plate. "If I were a man, Mister Dyott, I'd challenge you to a duel, but as I am not and unarmed..."

She fumbled about trying to remove her long opera gloves, which clung to her slender forearms as if made of flypaper. Upon wrestling them free, she threw them to the floor.

"As I am not, and unarmed, I will..."

The men watched impassively once Alexandra's thighs became wedged against the table in her efforts to wiggle around an arm of the solid dining chair. She leaned forward, struggling to no avail, until the waiter stepped over to pull it back.

The Explorers Club discovered trifle evidence of cleavage.

Alexandra popped free and picked an open spot near the room's arched entryway. After straining to stretch herself down across the floor, she started pounding them out.

One... two... three...

The men observed, half-risen in their seats, baffled and speechless.

Midway through, a cavalcade of applause filled the main hall.

Alexandra struggled to make it to five push-ups before surrendering to her trembling arms. She fought the constriction of her silk body slip while attempting to rise, but ended her efforts, fearing she'd rip her dress—left to wiggle upon the floor like a hatching butterfly unable to free itself from its cocoon.

A pair of wingtip shoes settled beside her. She lifted her eyes to a fellow with blond hair gazing down. He stood under the archway, espousing a sense of gravitas, and backed by a posse eliciting hopeful expressions for an encore to her exhibition involving jumping jacks or squat thrusts.

The man greeted, "Hello, gentlemen. Quite the eventful evening."

"I say, the man of the hour! I cannot fathom how to explain it all," said Ford. "Our dexterous fourth upon the floor is Miss Alexandra Bathenbrook of Helena, Montana."

Alexandra took the man's hands, and he lifted her to her feet. He removed his fedora. "Lindbergh, Charles."

He appeared younger than in the newsreels. She'd noticed nothing Herculean about his feet, which seemed of average size. She muddled out, "September, you will land in Butte."

"I believe that is part of the schedule." He retrieved her gloves. "Shall you be there to greet me?"

Alexandra shook her head. "How did you avoid peeing on such a long journey?"

"One simple rule," he replied. "Bladder empty, petrol full."

The moment after Lindbergh bid farewell, Alexandra set off into a whirlwind of motion. She tossed the dagger into her bag, needing to pop a partially escaped boob into hiding while straightening her dress.

Dyott said, "One usually attends a cabaret for such jocularity."

"Let's end on a pleasant note over peach cobbler," said Ford.

She stomped a foot on the floor to halt her panic. "I'm more able with a compass and rifle in hand! I thank you all for dinner."

Once escaped into the balmy air and bright lights of the big city, Alexandra's anxiety subsided, leaving only humiliation and annoyance over which to fuddle. In the year of her birth, a socialite named Lillie Langtry had sued Keens Chophouse after being denied entrance into the exclusively male bastion. The court had ruled in her favor.

This victory for equal rights opened doors to public establishments for women near and far.

Alexandra did not want to raze the world but desired a stronger voice in it. Any chance of the Explorers Club viewing a female colleague as a compeer had been dented—taking *her* seriously, obliterated—and it was all her own doing. She asked a passing man for a smoke. He handed one over and fired it up. She felt a desperate need for a quick whiskey or slow brandy. Prohibition would soon be an ocean away, but alas, not until tomorrow.

"I have been dispatched to apologize for my boorish behavior."

"I came to dine at your invitation and should not have been a subject of mockery."

"Agreed," Dyott stated, walking closer. "My protest, though based in pragmatism, took on a tone of the personal. Men in dire jungle conditions must stay disciplined or they will revert to savagery. I could not safeguard the virtue or safety of a female under such circumstances.

Chapman suggested I disguise you as a man, but you are the essence of femininity. Now, Miss Bathenbrook, what would you have me do?"

Alexandra's anger diminished enough for her to foist some semblance of cunning to punch a hole in his rhetorical enquiry. "If you were to face this conundrum again, I'd advise that you agree to your financiers' conditions but arrange for the female candidate to arrive just before departure into the jungle, with no fanfare, to avoid the circus. I assume you'll be in the thick of it for many months, so send her back before the point of no return or if things get too grim. The newspaper syndicates will get their photographs, and you won't have to worry over her once the men tire of wanking the bishop or the food runs out."

Dyott seemed impressed. "I plan to depart this December and will consider your ideas."

He turned to leave, but she halted his steps in asking, "You flew in the war, sir. If you had crashed your plane and left terribly disfigured, how would you want others to treat you?"

"Like the whole man I once was." Dyott touched the brim of his hat and headed back inside.

Chapter 5

England

The open-air lorry in which Alexandra sat rumbled alongside the River Thames. She counted more cows grazing the pastures than people during her hitchhiking tour from West Wycombe to Cookham. The rural parish spread itself thirty miles west of London, and though somewhere near the bones of her supposed ancestors filled the ground, England remained a foreign land to her. She yawned, having spent the night at an inn beset by the ghost of a barmaid killed centuries ago by members of the diabolical Hellfire Club.

She hoped her pending reunion would be less haunting.

In 1922, she'd visited her brother and made a royal muck of it. She had been unprepared to witness his disfigurement. He did not require her hysterics as a reminder that the war left him irreparably scarred. A mirror sufficed. On this second opportunity, Alexandra committed to remaining composed and optimistic: keep a stiff upper lip, be full of good cheer, give it some stick, and whatever other British idioms came to mind. Will had grown up an aloof, rough and tumble lad, and they were never close. She'd attempted to establish a bond by writing letters, but for every dozen mailed, he'd respond with one posing little emotion to its ink.

He'd lived as a hermit since invalided out of the hospital and sent no pictures over the years, leaving her to wonder if an unwashed hobo dressed in rags would greet her: shoeless, with crinkly whiskers, uncut fingernails, and untenable long nostril hairs.

The lorry stopped. Alexandra hopped off and shouted thanks to the driver. Will's cottage stood up a narrow path amidst a patch of trees. As much as she felt sorrow and regret over the fate of her brothers, festering within endured a hidden rage at their abandonment over a decade ago.

They'd left eager to save the world, but neither returned to save her.

She took a seat along the riverbank. It stroked a pleasant temperature for an English afternoon, as spring decided to arrive before summer's end. Vibrant dandelions abounded, and animated squirrels chased down new leads on ripened berries. Rowdy lads passed by rowing skiffs, sending a gaggle of white swans to hasten their glide upon the tepid surface. There existed moments when the world appeared antiseptic, yet testimony otherwise prowled never far off.

Will had taken a terrible hit of shrapnel at Amiens in 1918. It tore a crater into the left hemisphere of his face, eviscerating his eye socket, cheekbone, and part of his temple. His left arm was lost at the elbow, and burns ran from his neck to his shoulders.

Alexandra picked up her bags and wearily marched up the pathway. She reminded herself, "Commander Dyott says to treat him like a 'whole man.' A whole man... *Olemén... Olemén...*" Someone watching her vanished from the window. She settled at the door and knocked. No one came, so she knocked harder. "William! It's your sister."

Nothing. "William! It's Alexandra! I'm being attacked by angry bees." To the continued silence, she again raised the ante. "Will! I am desperate for a loo. Let me in!"

The door finally opened. Before she could attain any sense of the stranger who answered, a large dog stormed forward and knocked her over. The cream-colored lab slobbered her face until called off. She sprang to her feet. "I'm sorry. I thought this to be my brother's cottage."

"You don't recognize the missing arm? Barnabas often tries to tug off the other."

On closer inspection, it was Will. She felt dumbfounded with delight. He stood dressed in a tweed jacket, well-groomed, and appeared the quintessential English gentleman. Alexandra soaked in with marvel the painted tin mask veiling his most egregious wounds. It blended in brilliantly with his skin tone and facial contours. They had even matched a fake eye near perfect to his other. Round spectacles held the prosthetic in place, leaving scars running into his brown hairline and burn marks the only blemishes left to direct view. It struck as a major improvement to the leather patch he'd worn five years ago.

She quashed her delight to casually state, "I departed Montana with one suitcase and now find myself overburdened with two. I was looking for a closet to hang some clothes and thought of you."

"Mother warned you might pop in. How long are you to stay?"

"For at least tonight," Alexandra suggested. "I slept with Suki last night at the George and Dragon Inn. She's rather naughty. Needless to say, little sleep was realized."

He lifted her heavier suitcase and escorted her inside.

The thatched-roof cottage spread quaint and clean. The sitting room held a phonograph, Crosley radio, two leather chairs, a sofa, and a square dining table. Stacked books rose to each side of a stone fireplace. Skimming the titles, she detected that Will, a once avid outdoorsman, had fallen casualty to intellectual pursuits.

The mantel hosted a shotgun, and a rug spread below: domain of Barnabas, half-chewed bone and all.

"It's all very nice, Brother."

"I have a girl who brings groceries and tidies up each morning."

Alexandra noted Will struggled when speaking, moving his jaw just the slightest to respond in a low but clear voice, void of much inflection. She said, "Do you venture out to shoot much? Pheasant and the like?"

He turned to her. "Only if the loader will also fire it for me."

"Good show! What's on the menu this evening?"

"Kidney pie. The guest room and loo are upstairs."

"You've truly gone native." She peeked into the den. A mahogany desk hosting a phone, lamp, and a wireless set dominated the space. Haphazardly resting on the floor, entwined in its leather straps and harness, sprawled a wooden arm.

Will gazed at his watch. "It's time Barnabas and I took a stroll."

"I'll cook up something more American. Ta!"

Alexandra flipped on the radio and inspected the small kitchen once they departed. She settled on omelets with roasted potatoes. While battling her ingredients, she wondered what course to take to dip Will's toes back into everyday society.

"I can't believe you have no *ham* to *cook* in Cookham," she jested upon his return.

Having won her battle not to set the kitchen ablaze, Alexandra plated and joined him. It surprised her to see him bow his head in prayer. They had rarely engaged in formal religion in their youth. Their mother was irreligious, and their father too often elsewhere to bring them to Saint Peter's Episcopal in Helena. She almost thought to join him.

Will seemed to enjoy his first taste of home. "How have you fared in London thus far?"

"Better since I became involved with this Japanese masseuse." She tightened and then relaxed her shoulders with a sigh. "She does such *wondrous* things to my body. I never knew."

He raised a perplexed eyebrow to her euphoria. "Anyway, will you be staying in England?"

"I'll be taking holiday across Europe. Care to join me?"

Will continued to slowly chew his food. "I think not."

Alexandra had swung for the fences and missed, in line with her nature. Laughingly, she recalled, "The last time I visited, Father took me to a dinner with the colonial secretary. General Allenby and some other la-di-dahs were present. My dining partner was a lowly ranked officer in the RAF named—"

"Yes, John Hume Ross," Will interrupted. "Both you and our father have shared the story."

At least it confirmed his long-term memory stood intact. She continued, not one to let redundancy interfere with the telling of a good tale. "*Anyhoo*, this Ross fellow came across so serene. Throughout the evening, all he wanted to discuss was his love of the desert."

Will wiped his mouth with a napkin. "Colonel T.E. Lawrence."

"The hero of Arabia? No, I don't believe he was there."

"John Hume Ross is T.E. Lawrence. He changed his name. They are the same man."

Alexandra could not fathom a person of such stature changing their name. "That would explain a lot, but I think not."

"You win!" Will refocused on his dinner, wishing for an ice pick to finish his eardrums.

Will had grown too familiar with dining alone, in peace. As she babbled when nervous, Alexandra considered herself the perfect remedy. "Any opinion on my going to Palestine? You might care to join me. There are places in the world a girl still needs a proper escort."

"That is impossible."

"Of course." She sipped her wine. "If Commander Dyott were to give me the call, I must be up for the physical challenge. I thought tomorrow we might rent a skiff and row the Thames."

Will shook his head. Alexandra operated unaware that others were not firsthand privy to the people she met or the follies she incurred. He tossed his fork onto his plate. "Have you traveled across the Atlantic just to torment me? I do not know a Commander Dyott, nor a Suki, nor do I have two arms for rowing!"

"I'd serve as the oarsman. I thought it would be an enjoyable outing for you. My apologies."

Will left the table, summoning Barnabas to join him. The door slammed upon their exiting.

Alexandra had achieved the near-impossible: making a man fearful to leave his home, flee his house. She washed the dishes and entered the den. On the desk rested a letter sent from Düsseldorf by a Gunnar Heise. Will having correspondence from a *Boche* troubled her. Next to it stood a framed photograph of Will in uniform with a young woman. She was a pretty thing, with a slight frame and dark curls cascading over her shoulders. It was easy to tell what the girl once meant to Will. He had rarely smiled, and in her arms, he glowed.

Alexandra penned her farewell note.

In departing, she noticed a newspaper clipping on the wall. It was the article the *Daily Sketch* had written about her Papua experience. At the bottom rested a pinned picture of the four of them: Thomas, Will, Emma, and herself. Tears filled her eyes, not in remembrance of lost days, but that Will displayed it so prominently. Perhaps it was his way of remaining connected or even proud of her.

She scurried upon hearing the door open.

Will removed his fedora and peered down at her bags. "I can still mount a temper. I acted poorly. You gave me quite a start today. I'm not accustomed to pleasant surprises."

"Rather stupid of me to drag you across the continent." Alexandra moved closer. "I always found the horse droppings to step in when we were kids. Little has changed."

He said, "Tomorrow, you will take me rowing. For tonight, all I ask is that once I retire, you not disturb me. I remove my tin when sleeping. Indeed, rarely wear it when alone. It is why it took me so long to answer the door."

"Take it off now so it will trouble you no further."

"I'm quite monstrous. It would be far too severe a shock for you."

"You're my brother. I'll entertain no more self-derision."

She lifted the glasses off his ears, taking care not to bend the prosthetic's thin casing or rip any skin off its adhesive. It surprised her how much foam padding filled its interior and how vacuous the area it covered truly was. Her stomach turned, her legs wobbled, but her hands remained surgeon-still.

"I am fortunate. Doctor Harold Gillies runs the best tin-nose shop in England," Will said with a wavering voice. "Recently, he referred me to an artist in Paris, Anna Coleman Ladd. An American, mind you. She has used her talents to paint new faces for thousands of veterans. It has allowed me to take Barnabas out for walks without scaring the children."

"I think such people remind us that the world is yet lost. We must send them a hefty donation."

"Agreed." Will half-smiled. "Let's get your bags upstairs."

William Bathenbrook sat helpless, having unwittingly fallen into her trap. Alexandra rowed them up the Thames, showing excellent form in her oar strokes while prattling on like an over-caffeinated race caller at Churchill Downs. Eleven years of pent-up older brother torment had hunted down its mark. He leaned back against the stern of the boat, accepting there existed no means of escape short of jumping overboard and drowning, which remained under consideration.

"After Mister Winston taught me how to light the cigar, he chortled a belly-hoot at my inability to breathe. John Hume Ross, who you oddly elect to call T.E. Lawrence, found the secretary's behavior uncouth, and then apologized for laughing, too."

Will had known all his life there was something peculiarly wrong with his sister. Alexandra was beyond brilliant yet failed in most everything. He recalled her mastering Mozart's "Rondo Alla Turca" but for one exception—every so often she would run a glissando. A tutor identified her as having a gift for languages. Several were taught simultaneously, yielding an anxious linguist fluent in seven tongues of gibberish, for Alexandra could not help but mingle her words in buffoonish foreign imbroglios. Her ingenious, slightly askew mind had not dulled with age. Just this morning—after stating having read *The Histories* without understanding a word—she'd orated a tactical account of the Delian League's flawed strategies to defeat Sparta that Herodotus might applaud from the grave.

Somewhere in Alexandra's head, one wire was faulty or missing.

As a girl, she had been a prolific bedwetter, rendering her self-esteem an equally leaky vessel. While that eventually dried up, the faded cut marks on her left wrist conveyed to Will more pressing concerns of emotional imbalance. And yet, she had matured into a stunningly attractive misfit; one seeking to travel the world and start a business. Will foresaw countless perils ahead, Alexandra being rich, socially isolated, and vulnerable to emotional manipulation and financial plucking, though he sensed she possessed a better grip on her impulses. He fiddled over where his duty in protecting her resided these days. Over breakfast, she'd voiced intent to marry some actor, but only after he divorced whoever he was married to at the time.

Alexandra had always been physically fit yet athletically clumsy. While faring well at rowing a boat, she'd drown many if piloting a Viennese gondola. She stopped sculling to catch her breath and inquired out of the blue, "What do you recall of my birth?"

Will sat up. He'd been only six and remembered little. "It was difficult for Mother. She left for Chicago to seek more suitable doctors and needed to convalesce for many months. Emma went with her, and Aunt Adelaide joined them. Thomas and I no doubt drove the nanny mad."

"I'm petering out." She submerged one oar to spin them around. "And where was our father?"

"I recall he planned to be home from… *wherever*, by August."

She regained her wind, and the skiff picked up speed. "Mother is evil, you must know."

He could not defend their mother's cold turn. "Alee, once attaining her inheritance, she lost all interest in being a parent. As the youngest, it was worse for you."

"Who were you trying to reach on the phone all morning?"

Her visit had come at an inopportune time. He knew she would not like his guests. "I planned to have friends spend the night and have found little luck reaching them to make other arrangements."

She smiled with joy. "And here I thought the hotel never booked."

It rarely was. "Gunnar and Hildegard are good people."

Her joy was felled a quick death. "They sound rather German."

"Yes, I figured that out. Thank you," he noted. "I had occasion to meet Gunnar moments before being struck down. I bayoneted him in the shoulder. Odd how some friendships can start."

Alexandra taunted, "Did he apologize for starting the war?"

"I do not believe he ever traveled to Sarajevo." Will did nothing more to stir her ire. She had been so close with Thomas—he was gone—and she would hold forevermore the Germanic people accountable.

They returned to Cookham Landing in silence.

Barnabas leaped off first to water the grass. Alexandra looped her arm within Will's. "I can spend another night sleeping with Suki while you entertain the happy Huns." She abruptly stopped walking. "Why did Father wish to get home by August?"

"You weren't expected until August," Will clarified. "Two months premature. Inexplicable you even survived."

Chapter 6

Gazing into the Mediterranean horizon, Alexandra sought her escape. She had spent a healthy part of the last six weeks frolicking the salty seas—from the beaches of the Portuguese Algarve to those of the Greek Islands—exercising a type of Polynesian ocean worship she had sampled in Hawaii. The waves had been middling, but time in the sun had left her skin nicely bronzed. Haifa provided ideal conditions for bodysurfing. The ankle waders found interest in her antics. Some offered applause, while others gawked as if she were a rumbustious sea creature that kept washing ashore.

There was one dogged frowner: a thickset woman with golden curls spilling out of her bathing cap, who, if raised in Japan, would have been trained in the art of the Sumo.

Now she stood waiting with two police officers, pointing.

Alexandra was unsure of her offense, awash in a strange land and knowing few of its rules. Her Jantzen swimsuit clung to her lithe frame modestly. Perhaps it struck blasphemously to display wet hair in the ancient Holy Land. She jumped bashful waves that broke close to shore and ducked under the churning lather of those so forceful they collapsed under their weight out to sea. Having the patience to corral the ideal wave proved key, and likely her only chance, short of swimming for Cyprus, to avoid arrest. She waited for her ride to conclude its stealth approach, rise, and fully show itself. *Here it comes!* she rejoiced. She swam to catch the wave when its crest was highest and face most powerful. Prone across the top, arms jutted forward, she propelled at breakneck speed. It all flowed with heart-pounding abandon until she glimpsed a gargantuan roadblock. It served as all the distraction needed for the wave to fold her into its white foam. She barreled into the barrier, lifting the woman off her formidable anchors.

The giantess crashed on top of her.

For a fleeting moment, Alexandra understood why many considered the hippopotamus the deadliest animal in Africa. She hurried out of the water to scoop up her beach bag and lose herself in the bazaar. She paused upon coming to a donkey cart displaying lemons and jugs of local concoctions. A glance back confirmed no one in pursuit, so she toweled off and tossed on clothes, doing her best to dry her hair without rendering it a cyclone-blown mess. She failed miserably, but her sunhat always saved the day.

Crumpled British pounds were liberated from her beach dress. *"Bir limonata, min fadlik."*

The merchant handed over two lemons.

Alexandra knew her Arabic came across poorly, but the ability to order lemonade anywhere in the world was of her highest priority. She looked at a man finding humor in her failings. He wore the light-colored linen clothes favored by the colonial English when in hotter climes. His brown tie matched his shoes, not to mention the shoulder holster visible under his beige jacket whenever he raised a cigarette to his lips. She called out, "You can salvage the situation at your leisure."

The man broke his lean against a palm tree and walked over. He placed a coin on the cart. *"Kub min easir allaymun, ya sadiqi."* As they waited on the results, he said, "You would have managed fine if this man were half-Turkish." The Arab presented a glass of lemonade.

After a parting lift of his fedora, the smart-ass returned to his tree.

Alexandra felt foolish. As she sipped her drink, she gave the man a few askance looks. While no Archibald Leach, he looked sweet in his own right. She rounded him out as an inch taller than her at an even six feet. His brown hair was short along the sides, with longer bangs pushed back under his hat. He appeared clean-cut and successful, but neither rich nor shy to crack a skull. She set aside his attention in spotting the zaftig charging across the sand.

The woman huffed and puffed upon arrival. She blurted in German, *"Sie müssen mir beibingen, wie es geht."*

Alexandra giggled. The woman wanted lessons. *"Ja, werde ich—"*

"She wants you to teach her to ride the waves!" the man yelled.

"You hush now!" Alexandra jeered back. *"Ja. Mittag morgen."*

"Ursula," the woman said. Her parting slap across Alexandra's back nearly broke a rib.

The loafer walked over. "You must be Archibald's daughter."

"And why would you think that?" Alexandra shot back, suspicious.

"The hotel said you were at the beach. You fit the description." He produced a CID police badge. "Detective Liam Kimball. The Colonial Office has dispatched me to escort you to Megiddo."

"Did my father send you or just some official?"

He shrugged, unsure. "My exact orders were 'Drive Alexandra to Megiddo and see to it she avoids stirring an international incident.' For a moment, I thought I was too late."

She smiled at his wry comment and started walking. "Those are my father's words. He knows me best."

The Appinger Hotel stood across town near the harbor, giving Alexandra time to flesh out this fresh man in her life. Kimball received the assignment being a fish in foreign waters, having been loaned to the Palestine office from Baghdad to assist with recovery efforts after the recent Jericho earthquake. He did not appear to mind the task, as it reunited him with the land where he had first steeled his metal as a volunteer in the Egyptian Expeditionary Force. As they strolled through the bazaar, he pointed out an alleyway where he had taken fire during the battle to seize the port in September 1918. He described the brave charge of the Indian 15th Cavalry Brigade up Mount Carmel, which had overwhelmed the Ottoman artillery and sealed the victory.

Haifa's population of forty-five thousand offered a foretaste of what a successful Palestine might come to be. It held a tolerant mix of Muslim and Christian Arabs, along with a growing influx of Jews. The dusty marketplace spread flushed with activity, fusing the city's diverse elements: Arabs dressed in tunics, Bedouin women peering from behind black burqas, with Western attire favored by most others.

Kimball cut a path through the pushcarts and tradesmen peddling their goods. Spotting a burgundy and gold silk headscarf that would match beautifully with her only packed dress, Alexandra stopped at a kiosk. "Are you charged with escorting me at all times, or would collecting me at my hotel at seven for dinner suffice?"

"Seven it is." Kimball tipped his fedora and headed off.

She bit her lip. Alexandra knew herself to be inept on dinner dates. She could flirt with fleeting wit, but in settings requiring etiquette and grace, her anxiety often spurred humiliating outcomes. She reflected on her previous disasters to recall what behaviors to avoid.

I fuss over what to wear and eat. My manner is overly mature and lends to high-minded yammering over my travels. Too much sauce and I'll saunter into sassier jabber.

She had not been intimate with a man in over two years and felt frisky. Liam Kimball struck her as a cut above the mundane. After a long debate, Alexandra left the market with the silk headscarf, confident that her evening with him would proceed swimmingly.

"And after I broke Mister Churchill's spectacles, Gertrude Bell quipped, 'You will die of thirst in the desert, Winston, if you can't *see that well.* Do you like my new headscarf? I strive to be fashionable.'"

Kimball nodded, having found no humor in the story, but some in her telling of it.

The restaurant within the Appinger was upscale. International tourists and the city's elite filled the tables. Though the hotel itself featured a western-oriented ambiance, the owners had ornamented the dining hall with the frills of timeless Arabia. Two musicians entertained the crowd with a windblown *ney* and a stringed *oud.* From her corner table, Alexandra paused to take in a breath. Rambling for thirty minutes about her travels proved exhausting, so she polished off her beverage to regain some equilibrium. She baited two lesser-known manmade wonders she'd visited were the Castelo dos Mouros above Sintra and Spain's towering stone bridges in Ronda.

Kimball nibbled on the hook. "Do you have any photographs?"

"In my room." She left the subtle invitation to just linger. Her milky cocktail was made from grapes and anise cut with water. *"Arak* tastes like peppermint. I'll have another."

Kimball called over the waiter. "Did you ride horses in Montana?"

"As often as palatable, the equestrian world was a penchant of my partaking." She crept to the edge of her chair, her posture pronounced and chest thrust forward. She wiggled her shoulders as if some tropical bird wooing a courtier during mating season. "I shan't imagine a policeman in Baghdad on horseback in these days of vapid technology."

"We use cars in the city and patrol the desert by aircraft." He commented on her odd posturing, "Did you strain your back when that enormous woman sat on you in the surf?"

"Yes." Her attempts to crack it back into place were proving futile. The waiter set down her drink. Alexandra slinked back from the table. She asked, "Were you engaged in any salient investigations before Palestine?"

"A streak of murders committed against young boys. Crimes too ghastly for dinner conversation."

The waiter placed down their entrées. Having been undecided over the baba ghanoush or shish taouk, Alexandra had settled on both. He had been more conventional and ordered one. She withdrew into her dishes to give Kimball a clearing to talk geopolitics. He shared his opinion that the Balfour Declaration of 1917, which favored establishing a Jewish homeland, had lit the fuse for clashes throughout Palestine, Transjordan, and Mesopotamia. The Arabs were growing disconcerted with British oversight due to increased Jewish immigration. The growing Zionist movement stood equally averse to the status quo. A bloodletting was in the offing. She listened with half-interest as geography held appeal—politics, none whatsoever.

Alexandra pushed her plates aside. The waiter rushed over. She informed, "I believe I'll order a nightcap."

The waiter bowed and cleared the table.

Kimball loosened his tie. "We leave for Megiddo in two days."

She lit a cigarette with the table's candle. After a satisfying exhale, she said, "We should travel on horseback. It would do us both some good."

He agreed but quashed the idea. "I'm afraid vapid technology will need to do the trick."

The waiter delivered another arak. Kimball said, "Your father seems an interesting man."

"He spies on me from afar and sends orders to his minions over the 'All Red Line.' How did you become acquainted?"

"I drove him around Baghdad. Supposedly, he has the king's ear."

Alexandra raised an inquisitive eyebrow at this news. She held a suspicion that her father's work went beyond geological assessments, but the ear of King George had never come into play. She said, "He'll be a baron one day. Soon, if my mother can determine means to poison my uncle without being rendered complicit. It results from my ancestor, Eckhart the Baleful, having killed many Normans some... some... *long time ago.* It is in family lore that after receiving this title, Eckhart cast off his unruly ways and became very pious. He would cleanse away his sins in the public watercourse. It is why I am a Bathenbrook, though I could have as easily been born a *Soakenstream*, or a *Scrubenpond*, or a *Cleanencreek*, or a *Washenlake*, or a *Swabenfirth*, or a—"

Kimball snapped a finger near her face several times. "You look a tad green."

"I feel greener than grass. Excuse me!"

Alexandra fled the restaurant and did not stop until finding a dark alleyway. Four araks and two dinners departed her company. She tore off her headscarf and wiped her mouth. Once recovered, she walked back into the lit square. The *Salat al-'isha* rippled the air from the nearby Istiqlal Mosque, but otherwise, the streets spread quiet. While those of Haifa intermingled during the day, they always retreated into their separate spiritual camps come evening.

She felt too embarrassed to face Kimball. The moon was not in a favorable phase anyway.

Alexandra spotted him standing an admirable distance away: sufficient to show concern, yet far enough to offer privacy. "You must think me a lush, but truly I am not! Don't tell Commander Dyott that I might cause a scene or two in foreign lands."

Not knowing the man, Kimball nodded. They started back to the hotel. He said, "Tomorrow, I'll borrow horses from the barracks, and we'll take them for a trot."

She liked the idea... almost. "Let's race them to the mountain's summit. A tribute to the Indian regiment's gallant charge. I am a girl who fares best with the wind in my hair."

He studied her soberly. "I believe that."

Alexandra smiled. When they reached the hotel, she extended her hand. "Tomorrow, then. The first to the top claims the steering wheel to Megiddo. Goodnight, Detective Kimball."

They shook. He held her hand for a few seconds to get a better feel for her. "I'm a splendid horseman, and please call me Liam."

"Well, I hope you win, Liam, for I am a terrible driver."

∽

Some would think it appropriate that Alexandra would begin her career as a professional adventure photographer at the designated site for the end of the world. The fortified city of Megiddo dated back to antiquity and had flourished for centuries along the trading routes connecting Africa and Mesopotamia. Egyptian Pharaoh Thutmose III had won the first battle in recorded history at its walls in 1479 B.C. It had been razed and rebuilt many times before its ultimate submission at the hands of the Persians a thousand years later. All that remained was an expansive mound of dirt, what archeologists called a "tel." Assumed buried within this hill were fabled artifacts of ancient history.

Yet, according to the Book of Revelation, a final apocalyptic battle on an undetermined date would be waged here, at Armageddon.

Professor Philip Langstaffe Ord-Guy presented this story to his guests. Their surroundings were nothing like Alexandra had imagined. When envisioning Palestine, what came to mind were ruined temples, arid deserts, and Bedouin camel caravans. The Jezreel Valley, however, spread lush with thriving croplands. The Carmel Range filled the skyline, and it all sensed little different from summertime Montana. Outfitted in lightweight desert garb of a linen jacket and skirt, with a black tie flapping over her white shirt, she felt terribly unsporty. Even her French pith helmet and leather boots proved wrong for the setting.

The excavation remained in its infancy. The camp comprised six canvas tents pitched around a shared fire pit. One permanent structure of flimsy construction stood near the road housing bunks for the workers, tool sheds, and artifact rooms. A latrine stood downwind, a parsimonious distance off.

The archeology team consisted of four graduate students who busied themselves kicking a soccer ball, a dozen Arabs away for a religious holiday, and a sour-faced assistant named Sigmund Coyle. Ord-Guy seemed qualified for his role. Oxford-educated, he'd headed up digs from Syria to Egypt. Alexandra thought he looked like an older reflection of Kimball with his short-cropped hair and disciplined eyes, but the professor held a thinner build, and his spectacles gave off the rightful impression of a scholar.

He continued his lecture as they ascended a serpentine path.

Alexandra assumed she would photograph sherds of ceramic pottery and uncovered burial chambers, yet Ord-Guy stated they could expect no such bounties for years. They reached the top strata of Tel Megiddo, which measured out at two hundred feet in height and covered thirty-five acres. The summit proved flattened soil filled with scrub.

"Knowing what I've seen and heard," Alexandra said, "I'm lost as to why the university hired me."

Ord-Guy lifted a pickax leaning against a dirt sifter. "It is for the wishes of our financier, John D. Rockefeller Junior. His wife Abigail read of your travels in Papua and convinced him having a female join the excavation would set an example for future archaeologists."

It impressed Alexandra that Ord-Guy could make the fact she was here as a token sound principled. She whispered to Kimball, "I fear Commander Dyott is right about everything."

"I am still unaware who this man is," he responded.

"Abigail is awaiting news of your arrival," Ord-Guy said. "Your camera, please."

"Never disappoint a millionairess!" Alexandra passed it over. In return, he handed her the pickax. She offered her most triumphant explorer's pose. "Limburger *cheeeese!*"

"Perfect!" Ord-Guy went to a corner of the mound. "We shall start tomorrow with photographs of the tel taken from superior height."

She asked, "Shall I get a ladder from the tool shed?"

Ord-Guy chuckled. He pointed down. Spread across a clearing rested a deflated hot-air balloon. "I believe it's in working condition."

The prospect thrilled her. "Can we give it a go today?"

"Our mechanic oversees it," said Coyle. "He's back tomorrow."

Ord-Guy said, "While unaware if I'm to be the first to use a balloon in this capacity, you will assuredly go down in history as the first female to conduct archaeological aerial photography."

Alexandra felt dazzled. "Professor, have you considered a grid for photographs taken two hundred feet up?"

"A smashing idea! Sigmund, do we have rope enough to dissect the entire tel? A layout of four-squared would suffice."

Coyle moaned and rolled his eyes. "Not likely, sir."

"Let's rile those lollygaggers off the pitch and get some sweat out of them. On the hop!"

They left the mound, with Ord-Guy and Coyle breaking off to gather the lads. Alexandra dipped into her tent. Other than her suitcases, it held a foldable cot, a lantern, and a washbasin. She lifted a set of car keys off the blanket and joined Kimball to say farewell, determined not to fuss over his departure.

He tried to start the engine, but it coughed and sputtered. Further attempts fared no better. He gave her a toying look. "Sand in the system. It happens when one struggles to stay on the road."

Alexandra was unapologetic. "I warned of my poor driving. You should have won the race."

That evening, she joined Ord-Guy, Coyle, and Kimball as they lounged on Roorkhee campaign chairs around the fire pit. It was the type of night Alexandra felt her favorite company: warm, still, and absent of artificial light. With the onset of electricity, people were forgetting the genuine allure of the galaxy left to silence. Coyle opened a bottle of ouzo. Alexandra vowed to restrict herself to one shot.

The group heard out Ord-Guy's theoretical debate if one could assume a ripple effect on history, stemming from Heinrich Schliemann's discovery of ancient Troy in 1878. Prior to the find, the legendary city was a forgotten land in a mythological war set in a Homeric tale. But in proof of its existence, Ord-Guy posited that the cunning ploy of the wooden horse, the beauty of Helen, and the gods of the Iliad were literal.

Coyle listened to the homily grudgingly, Kimball did so fascinated, while Alexandra reconsidered her poorly reasoned limit on ouzo consumption. Once the tale concluded, the graduate students could be heard lost to the darkness, grunting in their labors of lugging pikes and rope up the steep path. Archeology could be a tedious field, *unless...*

"I've received a cable," Ord-Guy said, "telling of an opportune development at a prior dig."

"The Byzantine ruins?" Coyle groaned. "What a waste of time."

"The earthquake has produced a sizeable fissure, revealing a hidden antechamber," Ord-Guy elaborated.

It intrigued Kimball. "What were you hoping to discover?"

Ord-Guy gleamed. "Proof of the *Nephilim*."

Alexandra and Kimball exchanged glances, both finding comfort they were not singular in camp unfamiliar with the term. She said, "If you could explain further, please."

Ord-Guy tried to oblige. "All cultures have verbal or written stories that are sacred cornerstones of their respective civilizations, but proof is often lacking. Mankind is now jilting tales of yore. If Noah built a great ark, it needs discovery upon Mount Ararat, or it will render scripture as mere poppycock!"

Alexandra and Kimball exchanged glances, both finding comfort they were not singular in camp suspecting Ord-Guy held no tolerance for ouzo. She asked, "And the Nephilim part?"

"I had this same conversation with a gifted protégé in 1913 while on a dig in Carchemish." Ord-Guy chortled. "I do not deem to boast, but that lad was T.E. Lawrence."

A witness! Alexandra placed aside any care about these mysterious Nephilim things. "I've been told that Mister Lawrence now holds a low military rank under the pseudonym 'John Hume Ross.'"

Ord-Guy's face flashed anger. "That is a preposterous canard!"

Alexandra tore the ouzo bottle from Kimball's grip. She poured herself and her newfound ally a nightcap. *"Mazel tov*, professor, with a *Mashallah* to boot."

"Can we get back to the Nephilim before anyone passes out?" asked Kimball.

Ord-Guy took down the shot. "As a man of science and faith, I believe in something more than a vacuous origin to the universe, but demand proof, damn it! I'm engaged in biblical archaeology to find proof of the Old Testament. Megiddo holds no such answers, but the site in the Valley of Sorek... *Mahatyam.*"

Ord-Guy slumped in his chair, having talked himself into unconsciousness. Alexandra motioned for Kimball to kick the professor so they could get their answers.

"Nephilim is the Hebrew word for 'The Fallen,'" Coyle dryly stated. "The giants in the Book of Genesis. They were the soiled offspring of

the daughters of man and fallen angels."

"Why would this other site hold proof?" asked Kimball.

Coyle shrugged. "It is in ancient Philistia. The most fabled Nephilim were Goliath and—"

"Peter the Great of Russia!" Alexandra interjected.

"—Og, the Amorite king of Bashan," Coyle finished, annoyed by the interruption.

"You must admit that Peter the Great was quite tall," she defended.

"So, too, Abraham Lincoln. Also, not Nephilim," said Coyle. "The story goes the demonic seeding of his children so angered God, He flushed the earth clean with the Great Flood. The professor believes that finding the remains of one Nephilim will change the world forever."

Alexandra noted Coyle's contempt for his boss, and she did not care for the cut of his jib. She said, "If such were found, the professor's ripple theory would impact Palestine. If Goliath were factually proven, David likewise is true. And if David existed, so too, the Kingdom of Israel with Jerusalem as its capital."

Kimball said, "Zionists could claim such evidence as proof this is truly the Jewish homeland. A spark for the tinderbox."

"For a policeman, you have a fair mind." Coyle left for his tent.

Kimball chuckled at the boorish comment. "Time to retire."

"Goodnight, Liam."

Once he departed, Alexandra spent an hour alone peering into the crackling fire. She discreetly rubbed her nether region and fantasized over nubile young women coupling with demons.

Chapter 7

Alexandra Illyria Bathenbrook—*first female to undertake archaeological aerial photography.* It would qualify as a flattering addendum to her obituary commemorative, though a tad wordy to fit across the tombstone. Many pioneers in hot-air ballooning had found innovative ways to leave more tragic footnotes ever since Joseph and Jacques Montgolfier constructed a prototype in 1782 capable of allowing mankind to touch the heavens. Introducing hydrogen had not helped, with the French particularly adept at blowing themselves up.

Pilâtre de Rozier—first man to fly in 1783 and first to die in flight, 1785. Sophie Blanchard—first solo female aeronaut in 1804 and the first female to blow herself up doing so, 1819. S.A. Andrées— first to lead a balloon expedition into the Arctic Circle in 1897 and the first to freeze to death upon crashing, 1897...

The list of gruesome and untimely deaths spread endless.

A robust breeze kicked up on an otherwise pristine Levantine daybreak. Alexandra hadn't yet digested her breakfast of plain yogurt and *maqluba* as she sorted through her gear. She kept reminding herself to pee before liftoff. She sulked in hearing the engine of Kimball's car turn over and lamented not sneaking out under cover of darkness to flatten its tires. He held the maturity needed in a man to keep her grounded and the humility to take it in stride when he would fail.

Barlow, the mechanic, arrived on a motorcycle, introduced himself, and left to fill the balloon and apply last-minute repairs to render it serviceable. It relieved Alexandra that he appeared sober and was an American. He had donated a leather aviator's cap and goggles for her to wear once aloft.

"*Pssst.* Alexandra! Are you decent?"

She flipped open her tent's flap and smiled at Kimball. "I try to be. I'm almost ready."

The flap dropped back down. After ten minutes, she joined him.

He asked, "You're really going to do it?"

"Of course! Adventure photography is my game."

"I've looked things over. The mechanic says Ord-Guy purchased the balloon for a song from the military, as it's old stock, missing its burners, and set for disposal."

She failed to see his point. "The balloon is tethered to the ground. I'll go up, take photos, and come back down. I've been in a balloon before. When I was a girl, my family visited Columbia Gardens in Butte. We all went up together in one, perhaps fifty feet."

"I believe you're set to go somewhat higher," Kimball reminded.

Ord-Guy joined them in high spirits, quoting Socrates. "'Man must rise above the Earth—only thus will he fully understand the world in which he lives.' We are off!"

They proceeded around the tel to witness the balloon rising into the air. A sputtering gas generator making a terrible racket continued powering a large fan. The khaki-colored envelope was nearly full, with the captured air being heated via its hastily installed burners. Ord-Guy reviewed the schematics for Alexandra to capture photographs of each of the sixteen squared-off grids at a height of two hundred feet, and then a more expansive focus from five hundred. The balloon's rectangular wicker basket could accommodate eight individuals. Sturdy line encased the envelope like a fishing net, with but a few noticeable omissions to the webbing. Two burners secured above the basket kicked up flames.

To Alexandra, it all appeared perfectly kosher.

Barlow wiped grit off his hands. He waved Alexandra closer and started pointing at things. "This altimeter will display your altitude. Two tanks of fuel and two sandbags to balance them out."

She struggled to tuck her rebellious hair into the cap. "Check!"

"These burners I made myself. Just pull this chain on the blast valve to rise." The flames kicked higher when he did so. "I used parts of an old flamethrower to put it all together."

"American ingenuity on display," Alexandra stated with approval. She took his hand and straddled the lip of the basket to board. "You are clearly gifted at making things work. Are you familiar with the United Drug Company and the operational mechanics of its *Electrex* hair curler? I can't grasp its use."

"I'll have it, and you, purring in no time." He winked. Eight braided uprights secured the basket to the envelope. Kimball pointed out that one rope appeared threadbare. Barlow shrugged. "She's ready to go!"

Alexandra affixed her goggles. "Will you wait for my return, Liam?"

Ord-Guy casually declared, "He needs to ride with you."

"Excuse me?" Kimball protested.

"I entrusted Coyle to break the news, and yet again, he has failed me. He was to be Alexandra's second, but he left this morning in haste for Jerusalem. We need two to ensure even weight distribution."

"What about the lollygagging collegians?" Kimball questioned. "One must surely be eager to join in?"

"Indubitably," Ord-Guy acknowledged. "Never underestimate the foolhardiness of youth. However, I signed waivers promising they would not be engaged in unduly hazardous duties."

"See that I don't fall out of this thing." Alexandra clapped as Kimball climbed aboard. "Good show!"

Ord-Guy took a photo and passed over her camera. "Godspeed!"

Barlow unlocked the winch, and the balloon started its rise.

It struck Alexandra that she had forgone Lindbergh's golden rule. She sang Irving Berlin's "Blue Skies" for the balloon's entire ascent, which eased Kimball's grip on the basket rim. They framed a plan for him to man the burners while she worked her camera.

The breeze pushed them directly over the tel.

The series of photographs taken at two hundred and five hundred feet went slowly. Because of the tel's immense size, the collegians needed to function as central locus markers in sixteen grids, so she could pinpoint separate shots within each. Once developed, Ord-Guy would assemble the images into one master map.

Alexandra reloaded her Leica-1, placing another completed roll of film into a cylinder. The balloon ascended and settled at one thousand feet. Those on the ground appeared as diminutive dots. She conducted photography at will to capture any anomalies in the landscape that would otherwise be untendered by the earthbound eye.

Faint crackles pinged the air. They came from a ruined stone house along a hillside. She leaned over the rim to better inspect. The frayed upright snapped, depressing her side of the basket. Alexandra jolted forward and teetered at the navel—feet kicking air and momentum favoring a toss overboard. Kimball grappled her waist and pulled her back in. Her backside crashed into his pelvis.

He was unmistakably aroused.

She flicked her rescuer's arms free from her hips and turned to face him. Flustered, she huffed, "Detective Kimball... sheath your weapon!"

He held up his hands. "Stop leaning over, waggling your bum."

"I believe Ursula cracked my lower spine. Any undulations are purely medicinal." Alexandra patted down her clothing and returned to her side of the basket. She lifted the binoculars.

Four Arabs idled at the ruins. One held a rifle. Another one waved up at her. A bullet zinged by.

She reported, "We are under small arms fire."

Kimball took the binoculars. "We're exposed up here."

After liftoff, the generator had been switched over to power the winch. With the racket it made, no one below seemed aware of the gunfire.

She said, "We should warn the camp. Do you have a pen?"

He searched but found only folded papers on which to write.

Alexandra claimed a lipstick case from her satchel and hastily sketched a diagram of the tel and the area from which the Arabs fired. She concluded with a narrative of what was transpiring.

"Are they still attempting to bring us down, Liam?"

"They are. We need to figure out a way to send down your note."

"Check!" Alexandra sat and wrestled off her boots. She stuffed the note deep inside one and handed it to Kimball. "Try to hit one of the lads. The redhead, preferably. He ogles me."

Kimball let it go and watched it descend. He jerked back after a bullet clipped the basket and refocused the binoculars to gauge his success.

"Missed the redhead, but they're running to it."

She wrote a second note for her remaining boot. "Try this one."

Kimball lifted the note free out of curiosity. Written in red lipstick: *Don't lose the first boot. Very expensive.* He shook his head and tossed it overboard. Alexandra rose and snatched the binoculars.

Another armed Arab joined in, and a bullet zinged by.

Thankfully, the messages had sprung everyone into motion, and pandemonium was finally afoot.

She related the play-by-play to Kimball. "One lad just came out of Barlow's tent with a rifle. Another is speeding away on a motorcycle... Ord-Guy has poured another shot of ouzo... Barlow is taking up position and firing back!"

The balloon rose. No one manned the winch.

Kimball seized the glasses. "Barlow's loosened the slack and is pointing up." He fired the burners, and they rocketed skyward. The tether tensed at full extension.

The altimeter read two thousand feet.

Alexandra said, "We're surely safe this high."

"If you say so."

A bullet pierced the basket. "I failed to share a newcomer has a scoped rifle."

A second bullet ripped through the envelope. Kimball cursed and lifted a folding knife from his pocket. He leaned over the rim to cut free the balloon, but it was impossible. The braided rope would require continuous hatchet blows to break apart.

They started losing altitude.

He retrieved his Colt M1911 pistol, fired, and missed. Rather than go for the rope horizontally, he went right down the throat with the next two shots. It frayed. Stretched to full capacity, he heatedly scraped the blade across the wound until the twines fell away.

It finally snapped.

With only one tether, the wind took command and tilted them sideways. Kimball spiked the burners to straighten them out, but at this rate, their fuel wouldn't last much longer. Air continued to seep out of the envelope. He crossed to the opposite rim but stepped back when the basket tilted. The second ring hung under the damaged upright and was too compromised to hold his weight. He maneuvered to the far corner, aimed, and spent his final four bullets. Three hit their mark.

He again fired the burners, lost over what to do next.

They were close to entering a free fall nothing could remedy.

"There is another way." Alexandra shared her plan. While Kimball loaded the far corner with the sandbags and tanks as a counterweight, she removed her linen jacket and freed her shirt from her skirt. He took a seat and pressed himself into the sunken side of the basket.

Now the tricky part...

Alexandra turned and straddled Kimble. She waited for him to lock in her ankles before taking a seat on the rim. Looking down, she let herself fall backward. With her kneepits clasping the rim as if a trapeze artist, she grabbed the tether and carved away. She gripped the knife so fiercely that her hand cramped after a few minutes.

Desperate with tears, it finally snapped free.

The balloon righted itself but continued to descend.

Now, the trickier part...

Alexandra rocked to gather momentum, tightened every muscle of her core, and stretched her arms up for the basket's lip. One hand caught the rim but slid off.

She fell back to once more hang upside down. Her back spiked with pain. With another burst, she grasped the rim tighter but had no leverage to pull herself up. She fell back again, nearing surrender, doubtful any strength remained for one final and desperate attempt at salvation.

Alexandra Illyria Bathenbrook, age 22—Died in a balloon crash due to an inability to stage a sit-up with a cracked spine incurred when a giant German woman crushed her while bodysurfing.

Such an epitaph read unacceptable. Alexandra screamed out to Kimball. He released his grasp on one of her ankles and reached a hand over the lip. Unless they fired the burners soon, they were done for.

This needed to be the one.

She reversed the knife in her grip. Rocking to gather momentum, she grunted and thrust herself upward. With fierce might, she slammed the knife into the basket. It stuck like a grappling piton and allowed her to remain upright long enough to lock a hand across Kimball's wrist. He rolled forward and yanked her aboard. She crashed on top of him in a rather unseemly position: her face flush against his crotch, *and dear God*, vice versa. At least the recent distractions rendered him deflated. She sat on his face upon rising to fire the burners. The balloon was now in free flight and captive to the wind. Tel Megiddo fell out of view.

They drifted across the valley and away from any gunplay.

Alexandra rested her hands on her knees, trying to recover. "Well done, Liam. At least Commander Dyott is not here to witness this."

Kimball frantically lit a cigarette. "Who precisely is this man?"

"He will soon take me into deepest Amazonia in a bid to rescue Percy Fawcett."

It left Kimball gobsmacked. "It will be less painful and quicker if you jump and die here."

"Yes." She collapsed to the floor. "But such is not my destiny."

"Now all we need to do is fly this thing. Any thoughts?"

She laughed. "I have faith you'll sort it out. Yet, despite your yeoman efforts, I fear we'll end up shattered to pieces. Our deaths, however horrific and painful, must not be in vain." She sprang up, retrieved her camera, and took a photograph of him.

To his annoyance, she explained, "So they can identify our disfigured remains. Now take one of me."

"Not too many balloon deaths are scheduled for today. They'll figure it out." They drifted inland, which ruled out crashing into the Mediterranean. "Look down. Nazareth, where Jesus lived."

"It is a lovely way to tour a country." Alexandra spent the last of her film on panoramas. A vast lake spread itself not far ahead. A mad idea filled her head. "I need your suspenders."

"Pardon?"

"My films must survive the crash."

Kimball did not argue. He slid off his jacket, snapped them off, and handed them over. While he tried to determine the best altitude at which to keep the balloon, he watched with curiosity as Alexandra cut open a burlap sandbag and emptied it over the rim. She removed her aviator cap and deposited into it her film cylinders. She padded the burlap bag with her jacket. Into this nest, she placed her cap and camera. Using the knife, she carved four slits into the bag, finagled two buttons into the gashes to one side, then tossed the suspenders over the burner rail to secure its final two buttons into the bag's opposite side. Her makeshift suspension device dangled in the air, bouncing with each shake of the basket.

It was brilliant, but not waterproof. He said, "I plan to crash us into the Sea of Galilee."

"Absolutely not! The balloon must land ashore."

He bargained that he'd need to find an opportune time over the water to toss her overboard.

The lake where Jesus had performed many of his miracles came into clearer view. They were on course to pass over its southern shoreline and now in the hands of greater forces, descending at a steady rate. On the far shore rose barren highlands that offered little room for landing. The last tank of fuel was down to vapors.

Kimball fired the burners a final time to give them a fighting chance of closing the gap. He threw overboard the remaining sandbag and an emptied fuel tank to lighten the load. He tossed his jacket and holster to the floor—wallet, badge, and cigarettes soon added.

Alexandra started disrobing. "If we don't crash soon, they may find us naked. What a scandal that would stir." They passed over the western bank. He had gauged it all to a tee. She said, "You go first."

He reminded, "Chivalry dictates ladies first."

She calculated they had ten seconds to decide. They were under a hundred feet in altitude. The balloon would not reach the opposite shore. She pulled the burner cord.

Enough fuel remained to pop them higher.

Kimball shouted, "What are you thinking?"

"We'll take our chances and jump closer to shore." The balloon drifted down again. She took his hand, and they waited. It was going to be dreadfully close. Two hundred feet was a death wish.

One hundred downright frightful.

Fifty would have to do. "Tally-ho!"

Alexandra crashed awkwardly into the water. She pushed to the surface and searched if the balloon would make it. It had risen in the loss of their weight, and she rejoiced in witnessing it crash along the scrub-filled shore. The placid lake bathed her in warmth, and the oddest thing—her back seemed to have popped into normal alignment.

Kimball surfaced a distance away. "I'll come to you!"

"If you wish to impress me, Liam, walk over." She pointed to a small fishing boat already making its way over to scoop them out. "I'll meet you aboard!"

Alexandra waded, lost in total harmony, knowing what relief Charles Lindbergh must have felt upon landing outside Paris.

Chapter 8

His chin troubled her. Alexandra did not fancy being alone in remote places with weak-chinned men. Photographs of serial murderer H.H. Holmes illustrated he had used such a placid chin to lure countless women into his Chicago murder castle, never to be seen again! It often proved tricky to weed through what type of chin a man held. So many camouflaged them under beards, goatees, chinstraps, and the ever-fiendish chin curtain. The only weak-chinned man Alexandra trusted was her dentist. He operated out of an office in downtown Helena, but if his chair had been deep in a forest, she would still have been at ease as he sported mutton chops, which all but promised, "I offer no deceit to conceal my weak chin. I celebrate it. You, therefore, can trust me." She did not prefer men with jutting lantern jaws or chin clefts so vivid one might confuse it for misplaced buttocks, but she found no hard reasoning to distrust those who featured them. Archibald Leach sported the perfect chin, and she would find comfort in his dimpled presence anywhere.

Sigmund Coyle, however, presented the ghastliest sort—a "heavy stubbler." Heavy stubblers all but mocked, "Yes, I have a weak chin. I place menial effort to conceal it, so you will ultimately be uncomfortable whilst alone with me in remote places."

"Why do you keep looking at me? It's quite distracting!"

"It's nothing." Alexandra offered Coyle a shallow smile and gazed back out her window.

The car rumbled over poorly groomed roads twenty miles west of Jerusalem. Despite Coyle's report that the dig site in the Sorek Valley remained undisturbed, Ord-Guy wanted photographs. As she was developing her film and sightseeing, Alexandra's marching orders were to pay it a visit. It seemed the least she could do after ruining his balloon. Her time in Jerusalem had exposed the devastation incurred in the Jericho earthquake. Crumpled houses littered the arid landscape, with even landmarks such as the Church of the Holy Sepulchre having sustained damage. She had hoped to entice Kimball into driving her, but he was wrapping up his last days with the Jerusalem bureau on a hashish smuggling investigation, so Coyle had collected her to conduct the day trip. She didn't understand why they backtracked the same roads he had traversed just days prior.

The valley spread desolate, hosting small Arab settlements, patchy olive trees, and an occasional shepherd overlooking his flock. What appeared on paper a quick trip was taking hours.

"Would you pass me the map in the glove box?" asked Coyle.

A flyer written in Hebrew fell out with the map. Alexandra could not read the words but knew what the red hammer and sickle symbol stood for. "Mister Coyle, are you perchance a communist?"

"They leave such leaflets everywhere. Ah, here we are."

He steered the car down a rocky pathway and stopped next to a hill strewn with rubble. They exited the vehicle and walked up the slope. The midday sun boiled what it failed to melt outright. Coyle removed his pith helmet to wipe his sun-scorched neck and forehead with a handkerchief. His curly brown hair clung matted in sweat, and his sunburnt arms shone lobster red.

Alexandra scouted the tel's perimeter. "Are you sure this is the correct place? It appears undisturbed."

"Yes. I recalled it but a short distance from Tel Batash."

Alexandra sensed she was getting the brush-off and lifted a map from her satchel. Compass in hand, she studied the landscape and pointed.

"There! On my map, the ruins should be a half-mile southwest along that ridgeline."

Coyle jetted up from his seat. "What map? Who gave you a map?"

"No one." She stepped forward to show him. "The professor listed the site's location over the phone using Tel Batash as the benchmark. I just didn't know we passed it."

"I'm to walk a half-mile on account of your slapdash scribblings?"

She took offense at his critique of her map. "You're rather slothful for a field man."

"I am of the intelligentsia," he proclaimed. "Hard labor is the toil of the *lumpenproletariat.*"

She chided, "Then wait here. I know exactly where I'm going."

Coyle's upper lip started twitching. "We shall go together."

As they made their way, he humored her request to discuss his previous work here. The valley had once been a borderland between the kingdoms of Philistia and Judea. Its proximity to Elah—the plain where David had slain Goliath—left it plausible the giant's remains rested somewhere nearby. Ord-Guy had run out of financing before getting much accomplished.

Alexandra adjusted the rope coiling her shoulder. She walked laden with her satchel, camera case, and a carbide lamp. Perspiration stained her shirt in unflattering abundance. Coyle lugged a shovel and mounted surveying transit. She resented his being able to drop buttons on his shirt and wear shorts.

"You speak in a rather dour tone about your vocation."

"Any search for biblical relics is fruitless," he asserted. "One cannot find what never existed. There is no God. It is bunkum for the masses."

She dampened a cloth to clean the dust off her face and passed over her canteen, as he had mentioned misplacing his. "You must have taken umbrage at the outcome of the Scopes monkey fiasco."

"Umbrage?" The 1925 trial—the first broadcast live on the radio—had ended with the controversial conviction of John Scopes for teaching theories of evolution over Divine creation. Coyle handed back the canteen. "It's a step in freeing humanity from the yoke of religion."

Coyle certainly spoke like a communist. She pushed on. "Why is Tel Batash noteworthy?"

"It may veil Timnah. The town of Samson's Philistine wife."

"The dreamy guy with the long hair? Does the professor believe he was one of these Nephilim?"

"No. They weren't all giants. For her beauty and cunning, he proposed Delilah was."

They climbed to the top of the mound. To one side stood an area of high pillars, broken walls, and the stone-arched facade of a crumpled structure. Byzantine ruins stood ubiquitous from the Black Sea to the Aegean. Archaeological interest focused on what might lie beneath them. Coyle set down his tools and took a seat.

Alexandra climbed over toppled debris as if a child relishing a playground. She landed at the entrance to the gutted structure. Passing under a cracked archway, she entered the ashlar-constructed edifice. Its interior lay exposed to the sunlight. Wisps of white hair entwined in vines and a fire pit lent evidence it served as a place of shelter for shepherds. A black snake sunned itself nearby.

A thick, jagged crack cut across the stone floor. Near its center existed a narrow cavity.

Alexandra peered down, but only darkness greeted her. She unloaded her rope and used a bowline knot to tie one end around the base of a fig tree. Once tying the carbide lamp to the opposite end, she struck its flint and lowered it into the gloom. An antechamber had indeed been exposed. The fissure opened into a wider arena.

"Sigmund! Come! Be aware there are mole vipers."

His reply he'd be over shortly sounded like carte blanche for her to proceed without him. Alexandra returned to her worksite. Wiping her hands free of moisture, she gripped the rope and descended. She landed on debris piled along the floor. The illuminated walls were constructed of rough stone and not leveled brick.

Another mole viper slithered nearby.

While having encountered more deadly snakes in Papua, this one shared a tight space. The serpent led her to a collapsed wall and vanished into a crack. Alexandra cast the lamp into a gap in the stones. An earthen pit spread before her. It spread the width of eight cars parked side by side. After wiggling through the gap, she hopped down into the dark chamber.

What she looked upon was of momentous historical consequence.

Encased in the clay rested skeletal remains in rows. Fragments of burial urns littered the area. She kneeled to pick up a sherd from a broken juglet. Upon cleaning off the encrusted residue, she could detect an engraving of a sea merman on the prow of a boat. Alexandra realized she lurked amidst an archaeological treasure trove. She wrapped the sherd in a cloth and secured it in her satchel. The skeletal remains were of people roughly five feet in height, which she surmised to be average in ancient times. It helped her to scale the final remains she came across.

What she gazed upon were the bones of a giant!

The man must have been twice-sized his burial mates. She took inventory of what she could detect: cracked ribs, pelvic bones, and an exposed femur. No skull appeared attached. She recalled David had taken Goliath's severed head back to Jerusalem.

Fortunately, Alexandra had packed well for the occasion.

She lifted a Webley & Scott one-shot flare pistol from her satchel. Once calculating a strategic firing angle, she shielded her eyes and pulled the trigger. The illumination shell ricocheted several times before settling into the clay. Exploding light nearly burned through her eyelids and uplifted hands. Between recovering her vision and allowing for the smoke to clear, only a few seconds remained to take photographs. Lanterns would be needed to attain better images.

Filled with excitement, she backtracked to the fissure. Her palms were raw from rope burns. She hoped to climb out, as Coyle could not pull her up. *Where was a jutting, lantern-jawed man when you needed one?* her mind chimed with indignation.

It failed to matter. The rope was gone.

Alexandra called out to Coyle and then spotted the canteen. It held an engraved monogram: *SIC.*

"Mister Coyle! What are you up to?"

His head blotted out the smidge of sunlight beaming down. "I'm afraid my comrades are insisting you die down there."

"Who are these comrades? I do not care for them whatsoever!" Alexandra shuddered at the prospect of being buried alive. She could hear him talking to others. "I demand you end this tomfoolery!"

A man swathed in black Arab garb peered down the hole and laughed. Coyle knelt alongside the fissure. "I tried to keep you free of this. It's nothing personal."

"It is to me." Alexandra sensed little sand remained left in her hourglass. For the first time in a long time, it troubled her.

A madness had gripped Coyle, perhaps from the heat. Perhaps he operated in league with an Arab cabal to hide the geopolitical ramifications of his findings, or maybe the many years of suffering a weak chin had finally made him snap. She shifted into panic mode and shouted, "I need an accurate spelling of your name, Sigmund."

He produced a pistol, aimed, and fired.

She jumped out of view a moment before the bullet pinged the debris where she had stood. From the darkness, she taunted, "There is a fatal flaw in your plan. I am an American girl with an influential British father. If I disappear, no stone will be left unturned. They will search with a fine-toothed comb, high and low, from hill to dale, beat every bush, check every nook and cranny, pull out all the—"

"I get your point," he yelled down. "I beg you to shut up!"

"I am writing notations on your treachery. You will be arrested, tried, and hopefully executed in a most grotesque fashion."

The rope fell.

Alexandra searched for something to use as a weapon. She hoped he would come down. Several minutes passed, but he'd failed to take the bait. She ventured as close to his firing range as she dared. "Others are aware I am in your care. It is your move, Mister Coyle."

He peered down. "You win. Grab the rope and we'll pull you up."

Alexandra doubted his sincerity, but it struck as suicide to stay. She grabbed hold, and they lifted her back into daylight. A beefy, lantern-jawed Arab of pale complexion grasped hold of her as his clone held the rope. The brute flung her to the ground and crushed a knee across her shoulders. He ripped her arms back and trussed her wrists.

She spat dust from her lips once settled against a stone.

Coyle walked over, waving his pistol. "You think yourself too clever, Miss Bathenbrook."

Alexandra looked away and said nothing.

He left to converse with his henchmen. The two goons spoke broken English with Slavic accents. It did not sound like they were debating a means to abort their plan, but a manner to kill her and cover their tracks. Alexandra knew upon registering Coyle's smarmy grin that he'd come up with something.

He failed to share it and descended the rope.

She watched and waited. One henchman opened a crate containing dynamite and lowered down sticks, while the other occupied himself shoveling beyond her view. The brute who had manhandled her ran wire and placed explosives along the pillars with the skill of a professional. They could implode the antechamber and seal it with the topside ruins, leaving it just another pile of stone defaced by the earthquake. It would re-entomb the historic remnants resting within, and with her death, the secrets it held would be forever silenced.

The brute pulled Coyle back to the surface.

The second thug appeared, carrying a shovel. "Grave is dug."

"No grave, you idiot!" Coyle fumed. "They must find her with all her belongings. I will put her in my car. There is a bend in the road, and we'll send her off the cliff."

Alexandra hissed, "I can only hope the wrath of Nebuchadnezzar falls upon you!"

The deceitful archaeologist claimed her camera case. "It's a shame that a woman smart enough to know the king responsible for the destruction of Philistia must die in such a manner... *but you must.*"

"I did not know that," she confessed. "I have simply always liked the way the name rolls off the tongue."

The bestial thug escorted her down the tel and situated her in the bed of a truck. He started shoveling another pit, all the while sweating profusely. He appeared to be a frustrated gravedigger.

"Pardon me, Igor," she interrupted. "I'm not to be buried, just burned up in the car."

"How you know name Igor?" The big oaf continued digging.

BOOM!!!!

Alexandra felt the explosion as much as heard it. She turned away as a vomit of small debris peppered the lorry and a plume of smoke enveloped the sky. Coyle and the other henchman rushed down the slope encased in dust. They tossed their tools into the back of the truck.

Coyle yelled, *"Popost'v gruzovik, glupo!"* and jumped into the bed.

The engine growled, and the vehicle jerked forward on its way, bouncing and rattling over the rough terrain. He popped out Alexandra's chambered film, placed it into an empty cylinder, and handed it to the oaf. *"Dlya Moskvy."*

It now rang obvious to Alexandra that Coyle worked in league with Moscow to extinguish any revelations of this biblical finding. "Are you willing to commit murder in the service of Uncle Joe Stalin?"

"I am a soldier of the Comintern. All power to the Soviets."

She looked up. The hum of a passing biplane dissipated. "Do you know much about aerial policing?"

Coyle folded back the rear flap and peered out. A biplane came into view far down the valley. It made a wide turn and started back. The lorry came to a halt at his car. He hopped down, needing to catch Alexandra once the Russian tossed her out. She fought and kicked as they dragged her to the car and threw her in. Coyle raced to the driver's side with her camera and satchel. Being under aerial observation had unnerved him.

He turned over the engine and followed the truck onto the road. They proceeded higher along the ridge.

To quell his captive's restlessness, he pressed his gun barrel into Alexandra's temple. "Not another movement."

She stopped trying to free her trussed wrists. "This will not end well for you."

The biplane swooped in low and buzzed the car. It continued onward before commencing another turn. Coyle slammed on the brakes. One of the Russians leaned out of the truck cabin to shoot at the passing plane. The driver took a sharp turn down a steep trail, and the lorry descended back into the valley. Coyle struggled to shift the car back into drive. He finally popped the clutch, and the car jutted forward, only to splutter to a halt. Just ahead, a truck and a car formed a roadblock.

Riflemen stood behind them.

The biplane made another run, this time unleashing its machine guns. Small plumes from the bullet strikes raked the dust and cut across the middle of the lorry. The riddled vehicle exploded. Alexandra closed her eyes on seeing the Russians step out, engulfed in flames, only to collapse and become part of the inferno.

Coyle flung open the door and yanked Alexandra out by the arm.

He pressed his gun to her head. The Palestinian policemen and British soldiers took aim and barked orders.

She sensed his grip weaken; he was yet ready to die for the cause.

Coyle dropped his weapon.

The soldiers swarmed in and grabbed them both. Coyle's wrists got cuffed, while hers were freed.

Alexandra took a moment to catch her breath and rubbed the rope burns on her wrists. "Quite the turn of events, Mister Coyle." Reeling back, she unleashed a punch to his nose. She was still swinging and kicking away when two soldiers pulled her aside.

They settled her at the rear of the vehicle.

"You actually were kidnapped," the familiar voice of Liam Kimball sounded.

She hid her pleasure in seeing him. "Who said I was kidnapped?"

"The bureau received a call. A man insisted your life was in peril near Tel Batash. Knowing you were scheduled to be out here, I took it seriously."

Alexandra licked her cracked lips to moisten them. "Who is this guardian angel of mine?"

Kimball handed her a canteen. "He didn't say. Harsh voice. Slight German accent. A patrolman will escort you back to Jerusalem. You must provide a statement. I'd take you myself, but..."

"Understood," she said, dejected. He would be off to Baghdad in two days, and she had left him an infernal mess to clean up. "I must treat you to dinner tomorrow. We can take in the city before heading our separate ways. Who knows, you may even prevent another international incident."

"It seems likely," he teased. "I'll bring along a parachute and a grappling hook. Better still, a flare gun and fire extinguisher. One never knows with you."

Alexandra stepped closer and straightened his tie. "I believe we already established on the balloon you are well-equipped for the expedition that awaits."

Alexandra smoked an after-sex cigarette at the Hotel Fast. Sunrise approached, and the dusty streets stood deserted under the dim glow of streetlamps. At least residing a room on the third floor offered a wisp of dry breeze filtering in from the open balcony doors. She studied the waning moon as it slid into hiding behind the ancient city walls and firmed up the tie on her silk robe, for like herself, it was coming undone.

She had forgotten how much a proper fucking inflamed her emotions. Vulgar and ruinous schemes fevered her mind, and hushed voices scolded she had just laid fatal waste to another defiler. Mawkish feelings for a man were an intoxicant of which Alexandra knew nothing. She had entertained bouts of infatuation, lust, and longing, yet never felt a trace of romantic love. She did not feel it now and would likely be unaware when she did, for it might feel much like now, which stroked pleasant, though nothing sweeping.

Two forces had offered her tutelage on how to mollify male passions. They had voiced contrary views, offering advice on how to conceive a child and on how best to avoid it.

A group of girls at Hamilton Hall had gabbed over little else, posing as amateur astrologers tracking the moon. They were willing to gamble their futures on the sketchy science of synchronizing their fertility cycles with lunar phases to avoid pregnancy. Comprehending terms such as waxing, waning, and gibbous, were of greater importance than studying the periodic table.

As the dormitory stood off-limits to males, it often meant a yay or nay to an awkward toss in a car or a more tender roll in the hay. If the timing of the carnal act were in doubt, they had concurred that smoking innumerable cigarettes afterward would foil any chances of conception. It was hard to know how seriously to take them. They had also snickered about coeds who pleasured themselves with electrical devices, which to Alexandra sounded weird and too futuristic to hold water.

Adelaide de Chantraine had provided more austere instruction on how Alexandra needed to comport herself to breed with *"Le Maître."* These lessons were conveyed to her at age thirteen, and being more impressionable than in her collegiate days, they had solidified firmer in her mind. Alexandra never took chances beyond the quarter moon, as her cycle ran unsynchronized, leading her to ovulate when the night sky lay flushed in darkness and bleed when the moon floated full. It appeared to be in a safe phase, yet as she gazed into the coming dawn, her worries mounted. The girls of Hamilton Hall had never stated their self-certified dogma applied to multiple sexual interludes in one evening.

She took another drag on her cigarette and smiled, sensing Kimball's discharge running down her thigh. Without thinking, she reached under her robe, wiped it with a finger, and rubbed it across her lips.

"What are you looking at?" Kimball asked from the bed.

She failed to turn. "The Jaffa Gate, picturing you marching through when General Allenby took Jerusalem. I wonder if I'll ever have cause to send a son off to war."

He sat up and lit a cigarette, noting she had pilfered several during his slumber. "Do you plan to share everything with Ord-Guy?"

With her film incinerated and the sherd confiscated by the Bureau of Antiquities, there existed no evidence to present. They had placed a gag order on her under threat of arrest and designated the tel off-limits to bury the matter.

Despite incarceration and death, Coyle's apparatchik had won.

"No," she answered. "At least civil conflict may be averted."

Kimball had arrived later than expected. They had wasted no time in small talk, undressed, and got right to it.

He asked, "What are your plans?"

"I received a telegram. The authorities in British East Africa want to hire me to photograph a lion kill."

"You don't sound too keen about going."

She snorted with disdain. "I thought it was the call from Commander Dyott. Regardless, it's unlikely I'd be able to scrape up sea passage to Brazil this late in the game."

Kimball pushed back his bangs and shook his head. "Why is it so important to you?"

"It was to be my forty days lost in the desert."

It irritated Alexandra to no end he failed to understand her nature after all their time together. They had agreed to visit each other down the line and stoke their fledgling relationship, but people voiced all kinds of nonsense when in the throes of passion.

He warned, "Don't go to Africa alone. A lot of ways to die there."

"I've cabled my brother." She scoffed. Her thoughts grew fast and iniquitous, her voice testy, and she felt out of sorts. "He was born in Rhodesia. A sort of homecoming, though I'm sure he'll decline. He was wounded in France. Thomas was killed. I know a thing or two about how you men think, despite having so little interest in the subject. You deem yourselves impregnable until taught otherwise. Runoff to play in the big game, unable to idle the bench. You got lucky, but my brothers just abandoned me! Terrible things happened to me! Sometimes acting recklessly rids such wretched fog from my mind."

Kimball watched as Alexandra untied her robe and tossed it to the floor. She remained with her back turned, naked, gazing out the balcony door: posture stiff, arms locked, fists tight. She began panting and shaking. Sweat beaded her skin, as if she were overheating.

He rushed over to embrace her.

Alexandra opened her eyes. Their first go had been awkward. She did not like a man on top of her making love, and perhaps she would know she was in love when she could tolerate it. A physical lover, she preferred to ride cowgirl, and thereafter, with her on top, their carnal unions rubbed more pleasing.

Flashing a lurid gaze, she took his manhood into her hands. "I need to be taken forcefully."

He became caught in her spell.

She gasped as he spun her about by the shoulders.

His arms enveloped her midriff and chest.

She let out a groan and exulted in being so flagrantly ravaged.

Kimball climaxed, relaxed his grip, and collapsed back onto the bed.

Her ravenous impulses subsided, she tossed on her robe, lit another cigarette, and returned to the balcony. The shady silhouette of a man standing under the Jaffa Gate caught her attention.

The voyeur's eyes flashed red and he departed.

Discovering the remains of a Nephilim had jolted Alexandra to the core. She wanted to greet the coming sunrise in peace, but it was not to be. One impudent string kept looping through her thoughts—*If Nephilim were real, demons once roamed the earth...*

...And if they still do, will one soon come for me?

Chapter 9

Alexandra stood in the observation carriage as the train chugged along the thirty-hour trip from Mombasa to Nairobi. Despite the open windows, the perturbed air remained stifling. Perspiration discolored her white blouse and khaki skirt no matter how fiercely she fanned herself with a dated issue of *Vogue* magazine.

Thus far, the journey proved disappointing.

An occasional hillside and the bare sands of the Taru desert offered uninspired breaks from the dry scrublands to either side of the rails. Catching a fresh breeze or sight of any wildlife were fleeting pleasures, but at least there resided unexpected company to chat up.

"Men of my village built this railway. Those who returned held much fear of the lions."

Alexandra shifted her gaze from the window to her escort. There breathed a calming and mystical manner in how he spoke, and she intuited he had come not for money, but a veiled sense of duty.

She debated her sanity in being here.

The endeavor had been labeled a case study on absurdity upon its inception in 1896, but completing a five-hundred-mile railway linking the Indian Ocean to Lake Victoria had transformed British East Africa immensely. The "Lunatic Line" opened interior Africa for expansion, and the exploited riches of the continent eased export to the world. Since the end of the Great War, ivory, cattle, coffee, and cocoa were being challenged by a new cash crop: safari tourism. Kenya's endless savannahs had bloomed into a newfangled playground for adventurers indulging in elaborate treks into the bush and sportsmen testing the steadiness of their aim in big-game hunting. The risk of getting mauled by feral beasts embodied part of the allure, though it remained unacceptable when such a fate befell a white traveler on holiday.

A sensationalized incident involving rogue lions attacking an eminent safari party had trumpeted its way into the headlines of European newspapers. This made for poor marketing.

A vivid demise was owed to these "Killer Lions of Ankole."

The Uganda Railway had commissioned a renowned "Big-Five" hunter to conduct the dirty work and Alexandra to verify the bloody business. They would publish her photographs to placate the local officials and reassure those yet to punch their tickets for the Rift Valley and beyond. Alexandra felt neither surprise nor disappointment that her brother had declined his invitation to join her.

It shocked her, however, to find a colleague of Will's named Simra awaiting her ship at Port Kilindini. She knew little about this composed, cordial Sikh other than he worked at a hospital in Maidenhead, where he lived with his wife and two children. With his trimmed beard, impeccably tied blue *pagri*, and wrinkle-free tunic, he obviously took care to fit in among the British without betraying his inbred ideals.

Alexandra found Simra's accented English pleasing to her ear. He struck her as a serene man, but not one to trifle with. A quote from the Roman poet Horace came to her mind in summing up her initial impressions: "New skies the exile finds, but the heart is still the same." She would treat him as an equal when social norms permitted... and even when they did not. As her booking dictated a first-class berth and he remained regulated to a second-class carriage, the observation car provided their only venue to share time.

Alexandra said, "Do tell my brother's instructions."

Simra spoke direct. "To see you to Nairobi and help you avoid any international incidents."

When she tried to ship him back to London, he had mentioned having family in Nairobi. That had quashed that. She teased, "I'm sure Will advised not to entertain the many questions I might spring on you?"

"He stated avoiding questions would only prolong my suffering. He then doubled my wages."

She nodded. "Will has a limber mind."

Simra said, "William is a good man. He has helped my family."

Before she could pry into that topic, the train slowed. It signaled to Alexandra it to be her turn to sit on the engine seat, but such had not worked out the first two times it to be true. First-class passengers signed a ledger to note their interest in taking in Africa alfresco. They had scheduled her for Voi. Upon reaching the station, a steward named Azrail ushered her forward, only to find two bellicose Belgians had plopped themselves down, upsetting the order of things. Their drunken discord held sway, and Azrail had escorted her back onto the train.

Alexandra despised line cutters. Respect for the queue served as a cornerstone of civilization, and being bumped left her upset. At the next stop at a village called Manyani, the untenable scenario played out again.

The Kenya Colony held forty separate tribes within its borders and many spoken dialects, with most of its native population practicing Christian or indigenous religious beliefs. Adherents of Islam lived along the coast and the borderlands with Somalia. Alexandra held few worries about her safety in the Anglophile regions of Nairobi, but the prospect of going unescorted in Mombasa troubled her. The city remained under the authority of the Sultan of Zanzibar and yet divorced from its history as an underpinning of the slave trade.

During the voyage through Suez and the Red Sea, she learned some Swahili to help navigate the city. Upon boarding, she'd observed Azrail kneeling on a small rug in the salat posture, praying in Arabic.

She had later warmly greeted, *"Jambo! Habari gani?"*

"Salamu, memsahib," he had politely responded.

Her greeting to him on this occasion—silence. The episodes of being back-benched filled her with unspent venom and a suspicion that her status as a "memsahib" lay at the root of Azrail's conduct.

He waved her to come. She asked Simra to join her. They stepped onto the tracks and proceeded forward.

The Belgians were walking back. A layer of dust coated their faces and clothing. One goaded, "The seat is ready for you and your wog."

Alexandra poked the man's chest. "Best mind your manners, sir!"

The dust-covered Belgian grumbled something in Flemish to his colleague and continued walking.

A spotter armed with a buffalo rifle lent down his hand to assist Alexandra's climb onto the engine seat. The simple slab of wood lay mounted above the metal pilot, which jutted out to knock obstacles off the tracks. In Africa, obstacles meant foraging animals with hearing problems or Cape buffalo, which as a species were too ornery and stubborn to move along. The spotter, an older Bantu man with gray hair and windburned skin, motioned to Simra to step up.

After hesitating, the Sikh did.

"I sit this seat with President Roosevelt!" the spotter asserted.

"Bully for you!" Alexandra settled in. Theodore Roosevelt's 1909 excursion to Africa had opened the minds of the American public to the grandeur of the continent. She sorted through her satchel to retrieve her binoculars, not knowing if the next stop to be ten minutes, three hours, or an incalculable hit of a waterbuck away. The engine hissed and kicked up steam. Those on the platform waved farewell.

The whistle blew, and they were off.

Azrail yelled up, "Behind us, all dust. Ahead, Africa most beautiful!"

Alexandra realized her assumptions were unfair. He had supplied a huge favor in delaying her turn. She yelled back, *"Asante, Azrail!"* and settled in to fill her heart with Africa.

With the engine thumping and vibrating behind her, she planted one hand over the brim of her straw sun hat; its extended black tassels flickering the wind like the tail of a kite. The train crossed the Tsavo River. The spotter informed her the bridge's construction had been suspended in 1898 when two lions of diabolical cunning started terrorizing the workers. By the time the man-eaters were killed, over a hundred laborers were lost, all devoured.

"And then crept the lions through the grasslands, night and day. Tore our men to pieces and then dragged them on their way," Simra recited. It came across as a recollection of a bedtime story heard as a boy or a pinch of Rudyard Kipling. "They moved as shrouded as a ghost and as silent as the darkness. A roar, a scream, circling vultures left to feast upon their carcass."

"You know this place, Simra?" asked Alexandra.

"My father died here." He nearly managed a smile. "I thank you for allowing me to visit him in this manner."

"This is evil land," said the spotter. "In Kikamba, Tsavo means 'place of slaughter.'"

Alexandra trembled. Sometimes beautiful places held ugly secrets if one dared to peek under the rosy veneer. If two lions could kill that many robust men, she held much to fear in the coming weeks.

Rolling hills soon replaced the arid plains; flushed in green with the arrival of the rainy season. All manner of God's creation fell into view of Alexandra's camera lens. Herds of duiker, reedbuck, and the deer-like dik-dik, reaped the grasslands. Bush elephants and a lone black rhinoceros drank at a waterhole. Colorful birds poked for bugs on sausage-looking baobab trees, while a pride of lions lazed under the shade of a flowering acacia. Through her binoculars, she observed a cheetah run down an ill-fated eland, and a blue-furred lesser-kudu outrun hyenas to live another day.

From the mist surrounding snow-capped Kilimanjaro to the untarnished flatlands of the Maasai, it was indeed Africa: most vicious, most wild, and most beautiful.

Upon entering the carriage, Alexandra's finagler reflexes activated. She held no interest in upsetting others or being the subject of scurrilous gossip yet wanted her way no less.

She regarded her audience with toying eyes and loudly cleared her throat. "My uncle, Baron Niles Bathenbrook, who some of you might affectionately know as 'Squibbly,' has dictated to this manservant the need to accompany me every waking step in most perilous Africa. Thus, he shall dine with me. I thank you all for your understanding."

Once her announcement circulated across all linguistic channels, the still atmosphere greeting her and Simra's arrival returned to its previous loquaciousness. A steward settled them at their table. The dining carriage featured impeccable service, and the menu's tidings of orange-glazed chicken and vegetable rice arrived steaming hot. Simra ate fastidiously, as if a man experienced to the pangs of famishment. Over dinner, Alexandra came to terms that the only practical location to set up her photography business would be London. It held favorable marks for language, shipping access, and would allow her to check in on Will.

City life would overwhelm, but she'd just need to tolerate it when not away. Knowing her tendency to allow things to drift amiss, Simra seemed a good bet for mature guidance. After her debauchery in Jerusalem, she felt spiritually cleaner in his company.

"Tea or coffee with dessert, Miss Bathenbrook?" asked the steward while clearing her plate.

"Tea, please." Alexandra gasped at her own words, and it all became crystal clear. No one except the key founders of America had made the connection—*the British ruled the world by doping tea*. A sinister plot for global domination likely started by the East India Company and, to this day, played an ongoing role in assimilating the masses. It was why America, the coffee-chugging behemoth of the twentieth century, stood primed to claim rule of the world. The only people immune were the Chinese, but she'd need more caffeine to sort that out.

She vowed this to be her last cup of the subjugating potion and took a sip. "I never partook of tea in America but have found it a pleasant diversion whilst traveling. How much tea do you drink?"

"Three cups daily." Simra gazed out the window at the setting sun enveloping the plains.

Alexandra assessed him as too far gone to salvage. "Tell me of your war experience."

He cleared his throat and stated matter-of-factly, "I served as a medic in the Sixth Poona Division. We landed in Mesopotamia in 1915 and failed to reach Baghdad. We endured siege and starvation at Kut along the Tigris. I weighed ninety-five pounds when the Turks took us prisoner and marched us through the desert. Before my death, they conscripted me into an Ottoman unit that had lost its medical staff."

"What you've endured sounds ghastly." She'd fail to believe such a tale coming from a lesser man. "How did you make way to France?"

"I treated the Turkish wounded before deserting. I walked across the Nefud to rejoin the Anglo-Indian units advancing up the Levant. Arabs captured me under the command of T.E.—"

"Lawrence!" *A second witness!* "Perchance, did you meet Colonel Lawrence?"

"Briefly, to administer a bandage to a minor arm wound."

"Are you aware he now serves in the Royal Air Force under the name John Hume Ross?"

Simra expressed surprise at this. "It may be so, but I have heard he is serving at Miramshah in Waziristan under the name T.E. Shaw. A brother-in-law served at the fort and wrote this."

Alexandra crunched her eyes. The cloak-and-dagger of this enigma required satisfaction. Either Lawrence rejoiced in being an international man of mystery or operated as a terribly clumsy spy.

"Pardon my interruption."

Simra continued. "They sent me to the Western Front. I was first to take William off the battlefield."

His story touched her heart. One day, she would need to serve as a correspondent to witness the horrors of war firsthand, but for now, it satisfied her to learn a smidgeon more about Simra.

"Do you enjoy hospital work? Seeing to the care of others?"

"I am a janitor," he stated. "I am grateful for my health to work it."

Alexandra sipped a cocktail on the front verandah of the Norfolk Hotel, ever-vigilant not to abuse her after-dinner alcohol privileges. Due to its altitude, Nairobi offered a temperate climate, yet it remained malaria country. Apart from her quinine, gin and tonic would be the poisons for the duration. Dining alone during her travels always rang awkward, but at least tonight she had learned that antelope, while gamy meat, held exceptional flavor if smothered in a mushroom demi-glace.

An oasis of urbane comforts, the Norfolk had been built five years after the founding of Nairobi in 1899. The city had rapidly evolved from nothing more than a desolate railroad depot into the administrative center of the Kenya Colony. A postwar influx of soldiers seeking cheap land, expatriates fleeing the blasé ethos of Europe, and other colonial types had spiked its population. Tourism revenue now filled the coffers.

Alexandra had taken in parts of the city during a rickshaw ride from the train station to the reception desk. Its municipal buildings and shops stood coated in a dusty red film roused by each passing vehicle. Well-ordered houses and meager thatch huts lay beyond, with larger plantation estates lost in the bushlands. She had checked in late afternoon, and from her terrace watched zebras grazing the plains. She had washed up and dressed down in record speed, eager to take it all in after two days idle on a train. The glowing cusp of the African sunset, however, put an end to that notion. The hotel staff warned that spotted hyenas and leopards still wandered into town under the cover of night. She was stuck—a single young woman among clannish gatherings of foreigners. The Norfolk served as the prime refuge for safari parties plotting their pending escapades or celebrating their successful return.

It felt odd enough to dine alone amidst such company. Standing at the bar like some vixen looking to bag a foreign sugar daddy struck her as intolerable.

She overheard a man's recollection of the Harry Thuku incident of 1922. An angry mob had been gunned down while protesting for the prison release of the nationalist. The man boasted about having shot from this very verandah his share of the hundred or so natives killed.

His boorish compatriots chuckled heartily.

Africa was forever a harsh continent in which to live: rife with famine, disease, tribal conflict, and fearsome beasts listing "human" high on the menu. The British espoused the overriding benevolence of colonial rule in bringing peace, infrastructure, medicine, and Occidental modernity to woeful lands. While having a train to ride or a stable banking system proved accommodating, Alexandra did not believe it to be worth the gift of freedom. The sorry state of the proud Shoshone, Blackfoot, and Crow tribes in Montana offered evidence enough.

She believed it preferable to experience a shorter life on one's own terms than a longer one under the thumb of others.

It was how *she* would proceed.

"Is she waiting on a rich chap or here to seduce one?"

"*Shhh*," the woman whispered back to her man. "They say she's American... and stop gazing at her bum!"

Alexandra rolled her eyes. She descended the steps to pass through the lobby. After firing off a telegram to Montana, she departed to share company with the papyrus trees filling the interior courtyard. She had arrangements to rendezvous tonight with a hunter who would guide her to Uganda. Simra was off among his people, as Nairobi held a small Sikh community living amidst the city's white residents and native Kikuyu.

And why are there so many German soldiers walking around? she continued to mull over.

An odd-looking fellow approached.

"Would you be Miss Bathenbrook? I am Jean-Luc De Pauw, your humble servant."

"Hello," she greeted as he kissed her hand. He was a short, square, robust chap with a fuzzy beard, which rendered any determination of his chin inconclusive. His bushy eyebrows likely hosted their own ecosystems. De Pauw spoke with a Frankish accent, which made it all the more curious why he wore a spiked German *pickelhaube* helmet.

Alexandra took a quick liking to him. "We won the war here, too? I have not heard differently."

"We have a peculiar way of celebrating the armistice. Would you care to join me at the club?"

She studied her dress, a simple gray cotton V-neck, thinking it would suffice. "Will they force me to drink *Weizenbier* and eat sauerkraut? They make me terribly gassy."

"I think not, but at Muthaiga, anything is possible." He removed his helmet to place it upon her head and offered a favorable review of the finished product. *"Parfaite!"*

Chapter 10

The Muthaiga Country Club stood a bumpy ten-minute drive north of the city center. Along the way, De Pauw spoke about the pompous atmosphere and boorish imbroglios standard for the institution, of which he was a proud member. It provided a venue for the elite to hold their soirées, gamble, keep a room, and engage in the favored elixir of socialite cliques—gossip. While many of the male members were reputable sorts of high political or social standing, Nairobi was evolving into a dissolute playground for the wayward offspring of aristocratic Europe, who, while born into privilege, were dealt a losing ticket in the primogeniture lottery.

They came to flaunt their disdain for the ways of yore and squander their second-rate inheritances. Among the most notorious firebrands were the "Happy Valley Set" who spent much of their energy outdoing their reputations for vain and hedonistic antics.

"Don't get me wrong," he reassured. "It's mostly harmless fun."

They're English. How outlandish could it be? Alexandra told herself. "Just don't leave me alone."

Armistice Day had been celebrated solemnly, but the cessation of hostilities in Africa were not agreed upon until three days after the eleventh hour, of the eleventh day, of the eleventh month. It had taken that long for the terms of surrender to reach German General Paul Emil von Lettow-Vorbeck and his ragtag army in Northern Rhodesia. Over four years of warfare, the respectfully coined "Lion of Africa" had outwitted, outmaneuvered, and outfought the larger Allied forces sent to rid German influence from the continent, making fools of them all.

Once De Pauw escorted Alexandra into the lavishly decorated dining hall, it grew clear the Muthaiga Club marked this second date in a more waggish fashion of self-mockery. Some men wore field-gray German uniforms, with a few of the women outfitted in the khaki garb of the British irregulars: topi-hats, spine pads, cartridge belts, and all.

Not everyone roamed so attired, with linen jackets for the men and airy dresses for the ladies showing off an uppity frontier adherence to customary style. Amidst the room's white pillars, they danced, milled about the champagne tower, or gathered to enjoy the music of a six-piece orchestra. Alexandra found it a bit suffocating but savored hearing the Jazz Age had made its way to Africa.

No sooner had she shared a toast with De Pauw that he set off for the private lounge where the stodgier members sat reading the *East African Standard*, shooting pool, and discussing politics under the glassy-eyed gazes of the wildlife mounts along the walls.

Alexandra's solo traveling circumstances had not improved. She now stood alone at another bar, offering an uncomfortable nod or a shy smile to those passing. A couple soon dropped by. They were in their late thirties and full of good cheer.

"How I love German women!" The man grinned and took hold of Alexandra's hand to kiss. "Baron Bror von Blixen-Finecke... and this, is my lovely Cockie."

Though wearing a dented steel Brodie helmet and inebriated, Cockie rubbed off as the more sophisticated. She said, "Jacqueline Harriet Alexander. Here all by your lonesome?"

"Alexandra Bathenbrook of Montana." She blushed. "I came with Jean-Luc De Pauw."

"Montana! I have yet to shoot a grizzly bear," Blixen pronounced with excitement. "I'm afraid Jean-Luc won't soon return. He is a fine shot but a tiresome gambler, so he takes longer to lose his money. We must dance. You can share the wonders of America before others whisper what a terrible rogue Bror Blixen is reputed to be."

He lent out his escort arm. *"Komm, Fräulein."*

Alexandra said, "As long as it won't stir an international incident."

"One dance is a courtesy." Cockie downed her champagne and shot an annoyed smirk at her man. "A second, all the better."

They settled into the pack, gliding arm-in-arm. Blixen had come from Sweden and earned a reputation as a daring white hunter. Despite his amicable banter, Alexandra sensed by his grip that he acted a fearless sort, accustomed to taking what he desired. His opaque eyes were those of a tracker—cool enough to persuade a charging elephant to consider otherwise—and his imparted expertise in the ways of the bush struck profound. Overall, she found him to be a decent guy. No less, she needed to lift his drifting hand back up to her waistline.

Once having an opening, she spoke of her dalliances with American beasts of the wild, refraining from mentioning upper-class fraternity boys at Montana State College.

"Did you know the lead male in a lion pride mates with two lionesses at the same time?" Blixen inquired.

"I did not." She tried to divert him from the persistent topic of animal sex customs. "Did you serve in the war, being from Sweden?"

"We all did our part, whatever little it accomplished."

Alexandra came to a sudden start; more so at hearing two shots of gunfire crackle just behind her than Blixen's squeeze of her bum. Those dancing loosened their embraces as the band lowered their instruments.

A man holding high a Webley revolver shouted, "After four years of folly, I bestow upon thee the *'Löwe von Afrika!'*"

The crowd burst into applause and catcalls.

Blixen led Alexandra through the thicket of revelers. Cockie greeted them with glasses of bubbly and a wobbly stance. "Perhaps I should take her prisoner. What a handsome threesome we would make."

The band struck up a military march. Four men in ragged uniforms carried a filanzana onto the dance floor. Upon this makeshift throne rested a stuffed lion's head with a gold-marked pickelhaube atop its thick mane. Everyone found great humor in pelting the effigy with whatever was in hand.

Cockie leaned into Alexandra. "Do my breasts appeal to you?"

"Pardon?"

"There you are, Beryl. It's good to—"

Alexandra stiffened upon a touch on her shoulder and turned to the arriving man, who cut short his jauntier greeting. Upon observing his error, the man espoused a pained grin, took a step back, and dipped his head. "You look similar, but she would never wear a German helmet."

Blixen frowned. "Don't play the white knight this evening, Denys."

As far as Alexandra felt, all lay forgiven. She could not lift her eyes off this pleasing stranger. He was not overly handsome, twice her age, yet something inherent struck her fancy. She did her level best not to overreach and be the first to introduce herself.

Blixen stepped in before anyone started melting. "May I present Denys George Finch Hatton, my ex-wife's lover and my best friend."

"Alexandra Illyria Bathenbrook." She sensed that Finch Hatton did not appreciate Blixen's blunt introduction. He shook her hand and held it longer than called for.

She asked, "Are you another renowned hunter?"

"Only in the bush. I'd be delighted if we might share a dance."

Finch Hatton presented more debonair on the dance floor than his redoubtable Swedish colleague. It came easy for Alexandra to lose herself in the study of the boyish glint yet faded from his eyes: how his thin face balanced out his bent nose; his charming grin; the light brown hair neatly parted, with little call for comb or effort.

Intrusive thoughts kept pulling her away from enjoying the moment, however, and entangling her in a web of algebraic distraction. It was dangerous when she started thinking in numbers. She held an astute mind for mathematics, which aided in converting currencies or deciphering train schedules, but otherwise posed a pitfall for torment.

She'd met so many people with lengthy names it felt like falling into a Tolstoy novel. Considering titles and nobiliary particles only accounted for half a name, it became ridiculously clear why the "Lion of Africa" had outwitted them. The sum of his garish moniker equaled an insurmountable *FIVE*, trumping their lesser numerical tallies, which, while impressive in Nairobi, failed to cut the mustard on the battlefield.

Having only three names sounded rather pedestrian. "Cockie" had needed to claim a beguiling sobriquet just to mix with this crowd. Alexandra pondered whether she'd need to add one to get on equal footing. It would have to be preposterous to match the times.

"Bumsy" came under immediate consideration.

"Who is this woman you mistook me for?" she asked.

Finch Hatton riposted, "Beryl... I'm not sure of her last name. She started the spring engaged to one man and ended up engaged to another by summer's end. I've been off in Tanganyika, so I couldn't say if it has changed once more. A rather spirited young lady."

Alexandra peered at a tall, long-limbed woman leering at them from the bar. "Would she be the light-haired Amazon conversing with Baron Blixen and Cockie?"

He glanced over. "That's her. They're all great chums."

Alexandra deemed some likeness in appearance and age, but this woman's face stretched narrower, the nose more aquiline, and the tight lips thinner than her own. Beryl's short, curled hair gave off a sleek, tomboyish appeal. By the venom shooting from her tautened blue eyes, Alexandra surmised this blonde tearaway fostered willful plans to one day add the surname Finch Hatton to her signature.

The band picked things up with "The Charleston."

"Do you ragtime, Finch Hatton?"

He consented and started slowly, but she soon got him up to speed. By the time it ended, Alexandra agreed: the first dance was a courtesy, and this second one all the better. They retired to the bar to share a drink. She laughed at his claim he'd once waltzed with a Kolb's monkey until champagne spattered her face.

"We have no need for American trollops," Beryl haughtily spewed, setting down the guilty glass.

A pervasive hush swept across the ballroom, and a crowd gathered. Idle chatter over who was sleeping with whom still took a backseat to a visceral catfight. Any semblance of proper English decorum was about to pop off.

"Trollop?" Alexandra fumed. "My uncle happens to be Baron Niles Bartholomew Bathenbrook!"

"Which means your father is likely a chimney sweep in Leicester!"

"So says the tart of the town!"

Someone observing yelled, "Slosh the Yank already!"

Finch Hatton deflected Beryl's swing. She spat, "Perhaps we should duel to settle this affair."

"I'm an excellent shot," warned Alexandra.

"I was thinking horses, you cretin," sniped Beryl, still under Finch Hatton's restraint.

"I am an even better shot when mounted!"

Their audience stirred in a blissful tizzy.

Bror Blixen appeared to be nearing orgasm.

Beryl freed herself. "Tomorrow at the racecourse. Noon! Eight furloughs. No guns."

"I'll need riding breeches," Alexandra said, twitching with agitation.

Beryl nodded. "After you've eaten my dust, your father can collect the horse droppings."

The slap landed flush, leaving a red mark across Beryl's cheek.

It took two men to remove her from the area, cursing and swinging as she was. Alexandra wiped any guilt from her hands and removed her pickelhaube helmet. "Please return this to Jean-Luc De Pauw," she asked Finch Hatton before fleeing the room.

The cars used in the Kenya Colony sported canvas tops and only a front shield for a window, which allowed for ventilation and reduced heating from the sun. Parking lessons appeared optional, as those in front of the club were left haphazard along the grass.

Alexandra walked among them, smoking a cigarette bummed off a chap entering the pink stucco building, which pulsed a rosy hue from the torchlights impaled around the grounds.

Odd noises filtered through the darkness: shrieks of hyraxes from the surrounding Ficus trees; the bark of a baboon, seated atop a safari wagon; and the sated moans of an English woman being fucked by a German soldier a few vehicles over.

Alexandra waited to ask anyone exiting to give her a lift into town and felt satisfied when Finch Hatton proved the man, though it had taken him long enough.

"Quite a kerfuffle you left in there." He placed on his slouch hat. "Haven't tasted so much excitement since Lord Delamere jumped his horse over three kneeling maidens in the lobby."

"If you colonials keep up these antics, you'll find yourselves less English than the Australians."

"Is that a bad thing?" he wondered aloud. "You have not caught us at our best, but we raised a lot of money at the door for the local health clinic. It's not all about sin and sauce."

"No offense intended. I can't place you fitting in with it, however."

"I don't. And you? Montana? Your manner takes me back to fond moonlight walks along the Thames."

Alexandra feared him correct; just like Will, she was turning English!

"I'm a bit of a chameleon. My mother tongue is American, but I adopt my father's ways whence among the British species."

"When," he corrected. It was his wagon on which the baboon sat. He waved his hat. "Shoo!"

It scampered off. "You've taught the animals English. Using the loo must be next."

He held the door as she climbed into the large open-air wagon, which could accommodate six tourists and held camping and survival gear strapped along its frame. He hopped aboard and they were off, circling several trees and one lazing giraffe.

Complete mystery awaited ten yards beyond the headlights.

"What sort of dilemma have you shown me into tomorrow?"

"I'm to blame?" he questioned. "We dance here without gunfire from time to time."

"This has nothing to do with me. It's about this Beryl woman's infatuation with you," Alexandra said. "What do men see in a cultured huntress like her?"

"I suppose they believe they'll be the one to tame her. She was born here and grew up wild. As a child, she used to go hunting with youth of the Maasai with only a spear. A friend's pet lion bit her once, and she bit it back. That has an appeal around these parts."

Alexandra shrunk in her seat. She had slapped a real tigress, and perhaps the most formidable foes in life were those known by only one name. "Does she ride well?"

Finch Hatton crunched his eyes. "She's the best trainer in Kenya. Lived at the stables after her first marriage bottomed out. The natives call her '*Memsahib wa farasi.*' In Swahili, it means 'Lady of the horses.' You're likely in for a bit of humiliation."

Alexandra shrugged. "Well, at least I didn't challenge the Red Baron to aerial combat."

They pulled into the rotary fronting the Norfolk. Finch Hatton opened the door, taking her hand as she stepped down. He escorted her to the lobby.

"Do you have a good thing going with Baron Blixen's former wife? I would very much like you as my second tomorrow at the track, but don't want to impose."

"I do," he said hesitantly. "No imposition. I'll pick you up at ten."

Alexandra liked that he could be playful with no hints of infidelity. "Goodnight, Finch Hatton."

❧

The following day, Alexandra settled into a small changing closet at the stables, finding trifling fun in being an underdog at thirty to one. She had woken hours earlier, opened the morning edition of the *East African Times*, and then everything slid sour. According to the paper, the foremost world events were wire scoops that Leon Trotsky had been purged from the Communist Party, and some German rabble-rouser named Hitler would publicly speak for the first time since the failed Beer Hall Putsch.

The top byline in the local section: *Fracas at Muthaiga leads to International Horseplay.*

All of Nairobi stood alerted that some two-name American hussy had slapped a local celebrity, and this threat to king and country would face a reckoning at noon today. The outlandish article could have at least included her middle name to make her sound more respectable! That second dance no longer felt "all the better."

As promised, Finch Hatton arrived to drive her to Nairobi Racecourse. They were met by officials of the Kenya Jockey Club, who informed her of the official betting line and pointed her to the stables.

The loaned riding breeches fit well. She tucked in her linen shirt, tightened her belt, and tied her hair back in a ponytail. Alexandra knew horses and could even lasso a wayward calf upon one, but nothing about the strategies to race them for a fast mile. She reemerged outdoors. The sun shone fiercely, and sunstroke never prowled far in places that hugged the equator. She placed on her topi-hat and cussed.

Half of Nairobi had shown up.

They sat on the bleachers and lined the fences: women shading themselves with parasols; farmers with kerchiefs around their necks; Kikuyu dressed in their colorful garb; and white-clad bureaucrats down from Government House, taking lunch to witness the spectacle. Alexandra headed for the safe harbor that was Finch Hatton, who stood sharing laughs with the resurfaced De Pauw. A native stableboy idled close, holding the halter leads of two saddled horses.

"Sorry about last eve," De Pauw tittered. "Got caught up in a winning streak before losing it all at the end! I hope to make it up with a small bet on you at forty to one."

"Bravo, Jean-Luc!" The odds were worsening, and now a proven loser was rallying to her side.

Beryl galloped by on her mount. She blew a kiss in their general direction; its target and sentiment undetermined. She broke her prize horse into a sprint and thrilled the crowd with two jumps over oxer barriers along her loop of the track.

Alexandra grudgingly admitted her foe looked splendid and in her element on a saddle.

"Miss Bathenbrook! I've brought you lemonade."

"You are sweet!"

Alexandra shuffled over to Simra. She felt guilty about keeping him away from his family and hoped his religious upbringing meant he did not wager on her. After a sip, she said, "I'm off tomorrow for Uganda and don't expect passage back until late December. You may leave at your leisure. Thank you for such fine traveling company."

Simra bowed his head. "As you wish."

"Pssst! That stallion of Beryl's is the favorite in next year's Kenya Derby," a man idling nearby touted. "She likes to go overland. Don't get pinched back."

Alexandra thanked him for the advice, half-clear on what it meant, having to juggle enough dialects without adding track-talk to the list. She glimpsed a towering figure in a top hat immersed in the crowd, but the man walked off before any solid identification. *Is that man stalking me?*

She shook it off and emptied her glass. "Someone pray for me."

"Let's see if I can help with this," Finch Hatton said to get her head back in the game. He settled next to the first horse: a homebred, well-groomed three-year-old with a roan coloring. "According to Beryl, this is the safer option. Good potential, even temperament. As for—"

Alexandra was already running a hand over the lean, light bay colt. It showed a silky black mane, lively eyes, and had been kicking up some when she had first come out. The British loved the sport of horseracing because it relied on bloodlines, but Alexandra believed the spirit of the beast a better gauge. Some animals clearly possessed souls: a loyal dog, a fine horse. She'd heard that elephants held great wisdom and mourned their dead, no lesser pained than humans. It was among the reasons she could never fully fall for a big-game hunter such as Finch Hatton.

Not even for the man himself.

He could see that she had made her choice. "An Abyssinian. Swift, but unruly. A known biter."

"Me too."

"You'll need to choose and show a knack for it," one official noted, "or you'll have no further takers. About plumb out of former husbands and scorned lovers... *Haw-haw.*"

Alexandra continued stroking the colt's neck and peacefully meeting its eyes. They were kindred spirits. "Does he have a name?"

"Wanderlust," Beryl informed. She raised her goggles, slowed her approach, and dismounted. Her white riding breeches matched her blouse. In her nasally, high-pitched voice, she scoffed, "It will be such a hoot when he tosses you. It's your turn. We can get a block if needed. Otherwise, as you Americans say, 'Monkey see, monkey do.'"

Beryl gracefully remounted.

Alexandra ignored the taunt. She took hold of the colt's reins and effortlessly sprang into the saddle. She quickly discerned the difference between the English snaffle bridle and the western, to which she was accustomed. The offer of a whip was waved off, as she would hand ride. In a measured trot, she directed Wanderlust onto the grass track to get a better feel for him before opening him up to cut the warm breeze. She liked his action and sensed him to be on the bit.

Those of Nairobi were getting a first take on her.

Alexandra noticed many Kikuyu looking on with broad smiles, perhaps tacit fans of the American memsahib. At the head of the final stretch, she finished in hand and eased Wanderlust back to their starting point. By the time she dismounted, the bookmakers were breaking a fresh sweat, and the odds leveled off at twenty-to-one.

She smiled at Finch Hatton and handed him her topi-hat to hold.

Beryl grinned, unpleasantly. "We should make a private wager to raise the spoils. Once I win, you will return to Muthaiga, place your silly German helmet on, and drink two mugs of beer and eat a large bowl of sauerkraut in front of any who may wish to observe."

De Pauw defended, "She broke me under interrogation."

Alexandra eased her glare and bent her lips. "And if I win?" She leaned forward and whispered in Beryl's ear.

"You slay me!" Beryl brayed. "Whatever does it matter?" She took her horse to the post and set up wide to leave a place for her rival to claim the rail position. Alexandra didn't bite and directed Wanderlust even wider.

Beryl said, "Any further, you'll be starting in Uganda."

"Soon enough."

"We both know you'll lose, and Denys will be mine."

The snappish banter ended. Alexandra could sense Wanderlust was tight and struggled to hold him still.

The starter's revolver pointed high in the air. It was race time.

Boom!

Alexandra found herself two lengths back before the ringing in her ears subsided, taking on turf kicked up by Beryl's stallion. She leaned forward and pressed Wanderlust to close the lead by half and ran him under control along the stallion's right flank. All she could hear was the thumping of the two beasts over the grass, though she detected in fleeting blurs onlookers waving their hats and other hooplas that entailed a boisterous soundtrack.

Wanderlust fell back, taking the first quarter pole wide.

Alexandra kept her hold snug and let him even out on Beryl's off-side as they approached the backstretch. Face to the sun, Alexandra's jockeyship fell pitch-perfect with the powerful strides of her horse. It felt like the rhythmic pumping of a vigorous heart. She knew he wanted to break loose and plotted her strategy to let him have his way.

Entering the far turn, Beryl acted brash enough to peer back. She scowled and brought the whip into play across the stallion's rump. It opened the distance, but also a pathway to finally run the rail. Alexandra noticed and guided her mount hard to the left. Wanderlust darted to the lead so fast that Beryl failed to check him to the rail.

Down the homestretch they thundered, cutting a tremendous speed, with Beryl's stallion under punishment.

Wanderlust opened a half-length lead. Alexandra drove him home, shouting encouragement.

Spectators filled the track, jumping and shouting.

Beryl made her victory run to close within a neck.

The stronger stretch runner would be the victor—it was Beryl's stallion—lending it ever more gratuitous when a final swing of her whip tore a crease along the thigh of Alexandra's breeches.

Wanderlust crossed the finish line a head back.

Alexandra continued along the track at a relaxed pace to cool off her horse. The colt had run a spirited race; it proved her poor start that had cost them. She looked back as Beryl turned her mount to trot along the grandstand and bask in the laurels of those gathered.

Alexandra gave her nemesis time to soak it all up.

In her solemn loop of the course, she found consolation in the joyous smiles of the Kikuyu youth as they ran alongside, singing a cheerful tribal song. Most of the fanfare had ended by the time she dismounted where it had all started. Alexandra patted Wanderlust's neck a final time and released him to the stable boy. She wiped dirt from her eyes and walked over to Finch Hatton to reclaim her topi-hat.

She curtsied to his applause. "I hope I didn't cost you money."

"A few shillings." He shrugged. "De Pauw mentioned you're heading to the Sanga district."

"Yes, we're meeting a hunter named Big Jim Gustin. Have you heard of him?"

Finch Hatton nodded. "If you have any doubts how great he is, just ask him. He'll be happy to tell you."

Beryl took a brief stand between them. "See you at the club!"

"I'm pinched for time," Finch Hatton stated as Beryl set off and the last of the crowd dispersed. They walked over to his vehicle. "De Pauw said he can drive you up to the club, but I'll be free to bring you back."

Alexandra blushed. "I think it best we say goodbye. I wish you well, Finch Hatton. May I write now and then to check in on you?"

"I'd like that." He took off his slouch hat and placed it on her head. Olive with a dark brown band, it fit a tad large yet suited her perfectly. Flashing a clever smile, he said, "For the bush. I've yet to be eaten while wearing it. Are you sure about the ride?"

"Quite sure. A solemn walk back into town in the fresh air will do me some good."

To this, he passed her a spare rifle. "Better take this for the walk, just in case it's needed."

Chapter 11

There existed no further doubt: the rhino was flashing her the stink eye. Alexandra stood on the safari wagon's hood—a Holland & Holland two-barrel rifle in hand—unsure what to do. The big bull thumped closer while Jean-Luc De Pauw busied himself filling the gas tank. He said, "It's scenting the grass. If he thinks we're female, he'll try to mount you from behind."

"Mount me?" screeched Alexandra. "I don't look remotely like a rhinoceros!"

"I meant the wagon. They have poor eyesight. If he thinks it's a rival male, he'll knock us to pieces."

"I have some perfume. Should I sprinkle it about to make the vehicle smell feminine?"

De Pauw sighed. "They have a courting process. Once he figures it out, he may just move along." The rhino settled next to the wagon and scraped its head against the bumper. "What's happening now?"

"Its giant apparatus is extending. It's a good three feet in length and as limber as an elephant's trunk. It keeps sniffing me." She tried to keep her balance during the amorous interlude between monster and machine. The rocking stopped, and the rhinoceros headed off.

She sighed with relief—it sprayed—and from twelve feet away it covered her with musk-scented urine.

De Pauw emerged from hiding. "He took a liking to you."

Secretion dripped off her clothing. "I am grotesque to the extreme!"

"Don't flirt with the animals. Mount up!"

They closed in on Lake Mburo in the Sanga district of Ankole. After a train ride through the Rift Valley, they had taken the SS *Usoga* from Kisumu to Port Bell. Alexandra had passed the ferry cruise attending to De Pauw's unruly eyebrows, finding revenge in his winces upon each timber plucked. At least he would not be mistaken for a forlorn gorilla down from the highlands.

After a night at the Speke Hotel, their 150-mile overland jaunt commenced, the wagon weighed down with supplies. It was near the lake that the safari party had been attacked. The Uganda Railway held plans to extend the line from Jinja to Kampala to increase tourism.

These ghosts of Tsavo could not stir further headlines.

"We're close," De Pauw stated as the wagon's suspension squeaked along the trail. He waved to three Buganda men walking enormously horned cattle. "They're friendly enough, but one wonders."

Alexandra knew by the Bugandas' sparse dress and hard inspections that she no longer foraged in biddable Kampala. On the horizon stood a village. The mud and straw dwellings held thatched roofs and stood circled by clay walls to fortify against raiders or carnivorous animals.

She inquired, "What should I expect?"

"Big Jim will ask you to a footrace," De Pauw said. "He likes having someone slower at his side. Prickly sort, but an excellent shot and one who very much enjoys killing things."

"Lovely."

The campsite stood under a cluster of trees. A safari wagon and a lorry were parked next to five weathered tents within view of the lake. Hundreds of bohor reedbuck roamed close. A bare-chested man performed pushups to an audience of uniformed askaris.

The fellow sprang to his feet and walked over. "Jim Gustin. No man or beast is my equal."

"Alexandra Bathenbrook." She hopped out of the wagon. Her hand disappeared in their shake. "Quite middling in most everything at this juncture in life, I'm afraid."

Big Jim earned his nickname at six and a half feet tall. Alexandra had never come across a hulkier man. The dark-haired Kiwi flaunted trapezoids up to his ears, biceps larger than coconuts, and pecs more pronounced than her breasts. Along with the long beard, it all gave him the appearance of a yet specified hominid. He placed an Akubra hat on and looked her over.

"You sweat a lot for a woman and stink like rhino piss."

"One scented me. We have a date to mate come Thursday."

Big Jim did not suffer smartasses well. "No man or beast is my equal! Do you run swiftly?"

"Like a gazelle," she said, shrinking from his presence.

Any consideration of racing ended there. Big Jim pointed out the old cook and mentioned he employed a tracker seeking the whereabouts of the man-eaters. He led her to meet the native askari colonial soldiers of the King's African Rifles, which policed the territories.

Alexandra thought they cut a striking image in their khaki uniforms and red fezzes. She said, "It all appears a formidable military machine. We should mount invasion of Congo and teach those no-good Belgians some proper manners!"

De Pauw placed down a box of supplies. "I'm Belgian."

Alexandra cringed. "Rightly so, Jean-Luc, with fullest apologies!"

Big Jim donned a khaki shirt. "I've heard of you. Have you menstruated since leaving Jerusalem?"

"Why do you ask?" she quizzed suspiciously. "Who have you been speaking to?"

"I am merely asking because—"

"Was it *you* lurking near the Jaffa Gate? Did you see me naked on the balcony?"

"Whatever are you talking about?" he defended. "I've never even been to Jerusalem!"

"Then who informed you I engaged in sexual relations at the Hotel Fast?" Alexandra was hearing nothing in her alarm. "Do you know Liam? Did he say he was satisfied?"

"Listen here, woman," Big Jim demanded, "I've heard none of these things. I ask because lions can smell blood miles off if you were in a female way. Mates wrote to me about you in Papua!"

"Woo!" Alexandra smiled. "Such a relief! To answer your inquiry, I am neither menstruating nor pregnant, and thankful for the latter after the working over I received at the Fast."

The four soldiers looked on with bewildered captivation.

She noticed. "Do any of the others speak English, Jean-Luc?"

"Everyone but the cook and his goat," he informed.

Big Jim gave orders to the askaris. Three departed to download supplies while the youngest one came to attention.

"This is Kizza. He will protect you."

"A pleasure." Alexandra extended a hand.

Kizza did not shake it. "I am good protector."

"You have a Holland," said Big Jim. "Can you shoot?"

She had yet to fire the powerful gun. "I'd like to get a feel for it."

He escorted her beyond the camp for a clearer view of the grazing reedbuck. Kizza followed with her suitcase. The sun hung low in the sky as the herd migrated away from the lake. Big Jim asked, "What madness gripped you to poke about the Fly River?"

"I held little else to do that week," she replied.

They stopped and took up position. Big Jim whispered, "I have a hearty appetite. Find a meaty one and fetch us dinner."

Alexandra slid her gun free. It was a short-range weapon, more akin to a shotgun than a long rifle. Walking into the grasslands, she sighted a reedbuck yet eyeing her intrusion. The gun would have a potent kick. She planted her feet in a skilled firing stance: weight forward, elbows tucked, the stock pressed hard into her shoulder. She steadied her aim, took a deep breath, and then lowered the rifle.

"A man should pick out his own cut at the butcher shop."

Big Jim laughed, raised his scoped rifle, and fired. The reedbuck toppled as the rest of the herd fled. He left to claim his bounty. "These lions won't hesitate. What is the count, Kizza?"

"Eighty-four," the young askari voiced.

Alexandra stopped walking. "Eighty-four what?"

"People," Big Jim clarified. "Three lions, eighty-two natives, and one order of Italian takeout. The average Banyankole is a bony meal, but lions have acquired a taste for them."

She knew he spoke of the slave trade. The trail from interior Africa to the coast equated to a death march, with only one in five taken in chains surviving it. "When will we face them?"

"Soon." He stopped at the kill and held out his rifle. "Take this. Sight something and shoot it."

Alexandra took hold of the weapon. She had never used a scoped rifle. Once lining up a marshbuck, it rubbed unfair that mankind had introduced such lethal technology into the hunting equation.

There was no longer any sport in it. She eased her stance. "Killing for pleasure is repugnant."

"Aren't you precious?" Big Jim lifted the reedbuck onto his shoulders and reclaimed his rifle. "Go wash up. If you don't get out of those clothes soon, you'll smell like elephant fart."

Alexandra scowled as he left for camp. She knew it often required rugged men to get dastardly tasks completed but cared little for gloating. She noticed Kizza walking with a limp as they headed for the lake. A poorly wrapped wound dripped just below his khaki field shorts. "Your bandage needs changing."

"Thornbush. Kizza is well." The sprawling lake held its own horizon and stood as the prime gathering spot for the entire region. He set down Alexandra's suitcase and pointed to a muddy pool of water apart from the shoreline. "I stand guard and look to camp."

Alexandra caught a twitchy reflection of the setting sun glinting off binoculars. While washing would reduce the chances she'd find a rhinoceros sharing her cot, stripping down would increase the odds of her waking to the Kiwi canoodling her. With only two sets of clothing, selecting her next wardrobe came easy, and she went about disrobing. It had felt liberating wearing pants, but it was back to a skirt.

Once buttoning a fresh linen shirt, she went about cleaning her soiled clothes in the murky puddle.

"Do you like the army, Kizza?"

"Army good for Kizza. It has taught me many things."

The sun continued to inflict a toll despite her slouch hat. Alexandra entered the shallows of the pristine lake and doused her neck before getting back to work on her clothing.

"Hey-hey-hey!" Kizza raced over, rifle pointed. "Finish, please."

Not thirty seconds passed before the head of a hippopotamus popped up twenty yards out, like the deck of a submarine breaching the ocean surface. Alexandra rose from her crouch and retreated to dry footing. They headed for camp.

"I've been told Big Jim likes to keep close slow runners."

"It used to be Odezza," Kizza said. "Big Jim bother herd of buffalo. Poor Odezza trampled."

"Your leg will heal faster re-wrapped. Until it does, I will not abandon you if you're in peril."

Kizza stopped in his tracks. "You would do so for me?"

"Of course. Soon enough, if Big Jim stirs trouble, we'll be able to outrun him together."

The landscape of Uganda proved beautiful, perilous, and telling. Situated between the yellow savannahs of Kenya and the lush green jungles of remote Congo, it shared features of both, as if their olive-shaded offspring. Over her three days of walking the grasslands and forested inclines, Alexandra could see how a more foliaged terrain hindered tracking anything down. However exhausting these treks were, constant perils filled her every step: the brutal sun beating down, wildlife mingling feet away, potential hazards hiding in nature's camouflage.

She paused under an olea tree and checked its branches for any leopards or green mambas. After a sip from her canteen, she doused a handkerchief to chill her skin. Her camera hung around her neck, and she had bagged excellent photographs of wildlife.

What pleased her most, however, was the birding. Along the lake's vibrant wetlands, she had scored an African finfoot, cormorant, and a papyrus yellow warbler. Only a shoebill stork remained on her must-see list. Such experiences would be all-satisfying if she were not here to photograph dead lions.

She pressed her hands to her knees and threw up.

Kizza circled, knowing threats most often came from the flanks.

"Miss okay?"

She wiped her mouth, feeling dizzy. "As fit as a sunburnt fiddle."

Each morning, they had broken camp, driven into the hinterlands, and tracked for footprints. These daylong walkabouts offered Alexandra time to share small talk with Big Jim, who, however uncouth, acted serious in his work. He joined her in the shade, frustrated. Somewhere drudging to their left rummaged Jean-Luc and two askaris, hoping to flush out the lions in a pincer movement.

They were all becoming worn down.

"Are these the most menacing killers you've tracked?" Alexandra asked, trying to catch her wind.

"Nah... I once bounced a dozen shots off a saltwater croc named Matilda," Big Jim related. "She still slipped away."

"How do you know if a crocodile is male or female? Do they have pronounced genitalia?"

He scratched his head, finding no answer. "It ate forty men in Queensland. Only a woman holds such wrath. These lions are young males, but have nothing on a sixteen-foot, thousand-pound croc."

"Your tracker..." She threw up again. "I've yet to meet him."

"He's ahead of us. Might spear all three if we don't pick up our pace." Big Jim gulped from his canteen. "He is of the Kavirondo tribe. You'll know him when you see him."

A shot echoed from afar, followed by multiple volleys.

Alexandra confirmed she was good to go.

They galloped across the grasslands, rifles loose and at the ready. They slowed their approach.

Big Jim shouted, "Jean-Luc! Which way?"

"We got one! The others have fled out of range."

They walked in close formation to the kill. The lion neared breathing its last—two well-placed holes gushing red across its broadside. The beast's fledgling mane pegged it at three years old. Despite its youth, it was a large specimen: stocky, muscular, and eight feet in length.

The panting stopped, and it lay still; its snout covered in dried blood. Flies gathered.

Big Jim gruffly said, "It's getting late. Get the wagon so we can bring it back to camp."

"Well done, Jean-Luc!" Alexandra cheered. The sprint left her wobbly. She motioned for him and Big Jim to kneel next to the dead lion. It was just what the Uganda Railway had ordered. *Click!*

"One down and two to go," Jean-Luc bellowed.

Big Jim lifted his rifle, took aim, and shot a monkey out of a distant tree. "Bugger you all!"

"Shhh!"

It was Kizza who called for silence. They all joined in, scouring the terrain with their ears and eyes. The disgruntled roar again sounded. "These are bad lions," he warned. "Lions do not act this way."

Alexandra photographed her askari; his dark silhouette well-defined in the waning African sun.

Everything became blurry. She placed her camera away and worried if the wrong mosquito had found her, and she was experiencing the onset of something dreadful such as "sleeping sickness" or Yellow fever.

Kizza turned and stepped toward her, alarm filling his eyes.

Alexandra's eyes rolled back, and she passed out into his awaiting arms.

≈

She panted to catch her breath while resting behind a tupelo tree. The full moon would aid in betraying her hiding spot if the torchbearers rode any closer. The others had already been captured, and once she surrendered, the sordid game would be over. The horsemen regrouped not thirty yards away; the creepy masks shielding their faces and their white cloaks sculpting them as ghosts in the darkness. Being from Montana, she didn't understand this was how her aunt's people celebrated Courir de Mardi Gras. A huntsman holding a fishing net called out for her to show herself. She ran off toward swampier grasslands, hoping they couldn't follow, but the horses charged ahead, unperturbed.

Alexandra woke, twitchy and breathless. The fever dream was not original; indeed a too-often night terror. Other than the tent's flickering lantern, everything remained dark. She reassured herself, "It's not Louisiana," and lifted her watch off the blanket. Daylight lasted twelve hours along the equator. It read ten past six, with the evening or morning part remaining in question. She removed the cloth dampening her forehead and dipped it into a foldable canvas washbasin beside her cot.

While freshening up, she hazily recalled the dead lion, taking photographs, and thereafter nothing more.

De Pauw breached the flap. "Good to have you up and about."

"Did I get drunk last night?"

"Just too much sun. I've got coffee and biscuits at the ready!"

The prospect of both delighted her. "You are a lifesaver, Jean-Luc."

He headed off, giving Alexandra time to change out of her sweat-drenched shirt. She sniffed her armpit and cringed. Men could tolerate not bathing for long stretches, but she could not stand it. She reflected on the canvas bathtub folded up in the lorry's bed and yearned to become one with it. It proved a struggle for her just to tie back her hair before tossing on her slouch hat.

Beyond the lake, the first glimmer of daybreak escaped the horizon. Bwanbale, the askari who'd spent the night route-stepping the camp's perimeter, looked ready for bed. Alexandra claimed a campaign chair to await the sunrise with Jean-Luc. Birds were singing, and a breeze kicked across the lake. A dragonfly zipped by in chase of a red and black butterfly. De Pauw passed over a mess tray holding a steaming biscuit, a mug of strong coffee, and a scoop of local cornmeal called ugali.

She thought it all so perfect. "Did you serve in the war, Jean-Luc?"

"Stationed at Fort de Pontisse on the Meuse," he replied. "The Schlieffen Plan called for the German Army to seize Liège and take Paris from the west. We held them up. When the shelling stopped, the fort was destroyed, and I became a prisoner. I can still hear 'Big Bertha' ringing my ears."

His perseverance humbled her. She had barely survived one hit from "Big Ursula." Alexandra suspected her inquiry had stirred terrible memories. "I hope you've found peace here in Africa."

"Best tonic for a man! Fresh air. Quiet, mostly. Good company from time to time."

She smiled. "Is Big Jim sleeping in?"

"He's out on the savannah. Set himself up with a wood blind amidst the trees. He'll not forgive me until he claims one himself."

The askaris emerged from their tents. She waved to them and finished her tray. "Any updates from your tracker?"

"He just left. Kept mumbling over a 'fourth' but my Dholuo is awful. We'll stay in today. Rain is on the way."

Alexandra could spot no clouds but trusted he knew better. She returned to her tent to claim her rifle, camera, and dwindling *Vogue* magazine. When she popped out, De Pauw informed her that Big Jim had returned. They walked toward the vehicles to check on his success. Yesterday's kill lay sprawled across the safari wagon. Its head dangled like a macabre hood ornament. It sickened her.

Big Jim arrived. His sour face broadcasted failure.

"It's a new day," De Pauw shouted out. "How fared the goat?"

"Hyenas took it." Big Jim called over De Pauw and the askaris who had aided him with the kill.

Alexandra said, "I appreciate the need to stop these lions but protest this fiendish display."

"Are you a photographer or philosopher? Take some goddamn pictures!" When angry, Big Jim could petrify. She climbed atop the hood of the second wagon as the four men lined up around the mounted carcass. Big Jim held up the lion's head by its shabby mane. *Click.*

He yelled, "Breakfast now!"

Alexandra hopped down, offering him a sneer as he passed. Twenty biscuits and a bucket of ugali were about to meet their maker. Her abdomen unexpectedly let out a tumultuous grumble.

It was the worst sound in the world and an instant eyeball dilator.

Kizza escorted her toward a shady Boscia tree she had claimed as her latrine. Her digestive tract stirred in rebellion. She tried to reclaim mastery, slowing her pace from long strides to a loose-stool shuffle of brisk choppy steps. Meant to portray everything remained fine, it never failed to trumpet someone neared shiting themselves.

Alexandra feigned a smile to her escort, who looked on with concern at the deep inhales and exhales of her panic breathing. She had learned while down with dysentery in Java that discipline was key. If she started loosening her clothing prematurely, the battle would be lost.

Kizza took a mindful stance a fair distance off.

She relaxed, knowing she would make it, and then the horror... Something had violated her private space. The massive pile of turd under *her* tree was the product of a once-constipated elephant... or Big Jim. She moaned. Her eyes darted to her backup tree, which stood further from camp. She made a desperate dash for it, tossing off her belt and freeing her shirt as she ran. Upon reaching the trunk, she tossed her rifle, attacked the buttons on her breeches, squatted... *Victory!*

Her world made sense again. Something hit her on the head. She gazed up at four colobus monkeys prancing in the branches. Their white faces stood out amidst their black bodies, giving them the appearance of tiny old men sporting chin curtains. They were eating the tree's globose fruit and spitting out the waste. Another seed hit her. It did not neatly reflect the themes of safari advertisements included in picturesque magazine ads sent to better castles and mansions.

She cleaned off and rejoined Kizza.

The sky clouded over, and rain was not far off.

"When you're on the watch tonight, how do you know if whatever is approaching is a threat or not?"

"The glow of eyes in moonlight," he said. "If eats plant, they are green. If seek meat, red."

Alexandra froze upon hearing a spine-chilling roar. Shouts and the discharge of firearms followed. She ripped her camera out of its case and ran in agile strides toward the fracas. As the camp came into view, she discovered two tents collapsed and an askari running in terror.

She focused her camera lens, and to her shock, a frothing cat shuffled into view. *Click.*

It chased down the askari, leaped, and toppled the man. He gave out one cry as blood splattered everywhere.

The beast dragged him into the high grass.

Reaching for her rifle, Alexandra heard a scream behind her. Her mind cursed, *I've abandoned Kizza!*

She had outrun him a long stretch. A second lion pulled him away by the leg. Terror filled Kizza's eyes as the yellow sea of high grass devoured him. She gave chase. The sound of his cries and a bloody trail kept her on track. She almost stepped on him once catching up.

He grasped desperate hold of her boot.

Rifle lifted, she screamed and pulled the trigger.

Chapter 12

Abacksplash of blood and powder fumes soiled Alexandra's face as her shot tore off one of the lion's ears. It released Kizza and postured to leap at her. She fired again, right down its red-stained snout. The potent kick of the Holland & Holland tumbled her back. She crashed onto the ground. Ears ringing, she sat up.

A horrid tranquility set in.

The lion lay dead. An oozing crater pitted much of its face. Kizza's eyes called out to her, blinking rapidly. His leg dangled, mauled below the knee. She ripped off her hair tie and used it as a tourniquet to slow the blood gushing from his wounds.

"Good lord!" De Pauw arrived with reinforcements. Two askaris lifted Kizza and carried him off. He asked, "Are you injured?"

"Irreparably, I fear. Just give me a moment." She lifted her eyes off the dead lion and rose to her feet. They headed for camp.

The men rushed about, prepping one wagon for departure. De Pauw tended to Kizza before loading him aboard. The dead askari lay wrapped in a soiled blanket; his head barely attached to his body. Big Jim appeared from the brush, his rifle resting over a shoulder. He had gone after the first lion, wounding it, but returned empty-handed. Alexandra suspected thus far he considered her as a shapely-arsed annoyance and knew his ire would swell once learning she had taken down the second lion.

"Bwanbale is dead, Big Jim." De Pauw peered up from his crouch.

"I'm a hunter, dammit, not a doctor! I'm taking Kizza to Kampala."

Big Jim nodded and walked away without a word.

They loaded Kizza and the dead soldier aboard. The old cook jumped into the front seat, horrified. An askari started the wagon on its race against the storm before the trail became an impassable quagmire.

Alexandra waved farewell. It was now just her, Big Jim, one askari, and the enigmatic tracker left to finish the bloody business. The clouds grew dark and turbulent. Distant thunder rumbled. She knew they'd head out to track the fresh scent of their wounded adversary and retreated to her tent to wash off the blood splattered upon her face.

The day remained young, and more killing remained for the taking.

The rain, once it came, fell hard. An entire afternoon tracking the lion came and passed, with traces of its paw prints washed away by the downpour. The beast had withdrawn to the highlands, ending the hunt aboard the safari wagon and rendering the need to pursue it on foot. The last askari was held back to guard the camp. Alexandra hunted alone with Big Jim. Their soaked clothes and drained legs weighed down their progress. A reprise of lightning bolts crackled across the sky, and the showers subsided.

"We'll return to the wagon and camp there. Once night falls, the odds favor the lion."

Alexandra nodded, and they backtracked down the foliaged hillside.

Big Jim had taken time to load the wagon with blankets, kindling, and foodstuffs. Once their campfire flickered ablaze, he set a coffee percolator on the grill and opened two cans of peaches. A dozen biscuits completed the meal. He seemed drained of all malice.

Alexandra asked, "How long have you been in Africa?"

"Eight years. I landed in Egypt while an Anzac. That was after we abandoned Gallipoli."

She knew that soldiers from Australia and New Zealand were scandalously sacrificed during the disastrous campaign to seize the Dardanelles from the Turks. It had been British leadership at its worst. She said, "I would think surviving the horrors of war would leave one with more reverence for life?"

He shook his head. "By day, we would fortify our bunkers and set wire, hoping not to get plugged by a sniper. At night, cower in our holes, praying not to be buried alive by the artillery. It was a relief when orders came to fix bayonets and rush the Turk trenches." He sipped his coffee and chuckled. "And me, the biggest lug of them all, never hit by a bullet! Africa is a good place to hide from high-minded dictators, so casually ordering me to shuck my mortal coil. It has left me dead inside."

She could see Big Jim struggled to stay awake, and that he was not so much a born lout, but more a victim of the war. She held less interest in lecturing him than in offering him solace. "You might read the works of Doctor Albert Schweitzer. It doesn't need to be all dark."

"I congratulate you on saving Kizza and killing the lion. Now stop talking, please."

All kinds of howls, cries, and calls filled the darkness, but among them, not a single roar. It would be a long night. Not even the wagon would provide safety. Alexandra had heard a tale of a watchman who'd fallen asleep in an idle carriage along the Lunatic Line. A lion had wandered in during the height of the day and dragged him off.

Big Jim leered at her through the flames. "Would you like to finally meet 'Little Jim?'"

"Is that his name, your tracker? We could use reinforcements."

He gave her a queer look. "His name is Kavidi. I'm speaking of us warming up together."

She frowned. "Who'll shoot the lion if you're on top of me?"

"It would be a pleasant way to go," he said, half-asleep.

"Don't address me in such a forward manner," she spat with vigor. "The gentleman in Jerusalem needed to save my life... twice! You're well behind the curve, Mister Gustin, and lest I remind you, I'm handy with a knife. You have been awake for two days and should retire. I'll see to the fire and wake you in six hours."

Big Jim had fallen asleep before she finished.

Alexandra got up to cover him with her blanket. She fed the fire and took up position atop the wagon's hood. She did not take kindly to his presumption of her being a loose woman. Such innuendos had plagued her college years for one drunken misstep. She had left a speakeasy with two men. They had gloated loud and often over their dual conquest, rendering an insufferable blow to her reputation. As occasionally afflicts reprobates, both were found murdered in grisly fashion.

Alexandra remained grateful the police inquiry had never made its way to her doorstep.

No one knew her, or any of it, in Africa.

Yet hiding from a disquieting past and running from an inconceivable destiny were two different beasts entirely.

The night passed. They were the longest and most fearful of hours. Roaming green eyes, occasional red eyes, and recollections of Thomas took turns keeping her alert. She recalled his letters from the trenches. He had written how he loathed the watch. Terrifying noises filled No-man's-land after dark—occasionally from German sappers crawling forward to cut the wire, raid the trench, and slit some throats.

Despite its strain, she let Big Jim sleep the entire night. Memories of her brother had provided fine company, and she whispered them farewell once sunlight colored the hills a luminous shade of orange.

Big Jim woke, rubbed his face, and nodded good morning.

As Alexandra got out of her crouch on the hood, she spotted it. The lion loitered not far off; just resting in the grass, panting heavily. Perhaps its wounds had drained it of all fight, or as king of the beasts, it wished to die facing down its executioners.

"Mister Gustin... there!"

He stood tall enough to see it from ground level. He raised his rifle and waited. "Take him!"

Alexandra lowered her weapon. "I have killed my last lion in this life. He is yours."

She had filled the foldable canvas bathtub at daybreak and left it to bake in the sun. Two days had passed since the killing of the last lion and finally deemed safe for Alexandra to submerge into this overdue oasis. Outside of the monkeys making a racket amidst the acacia trees, not a creature stirred. She stepped out of her pants and peeled off her crusted undergarments to settle into her haven. For the first time since being startled by the hippo on that initial day, she permitted herself to relax.

If a gramophone were handy, she would play Beethoven's "Ode to Joy"—thereby uniting God's greatest natural backdrop to humanity's closest offering of perfection.

It did not take long for a troop of colobus monkeys to infringe on her solitude. The bravest among them came right up to the bush bath to steal a quick drink. She found them charming and did not *shoo* them away. More to herself, she sang, "Yes! We Have No Bananas."

One monkey picked up her silk French knickers in its tiny hands. It dipped them into the tub, smelled them, and then made a strange noise before repeating the process. Alexandra took it for granted that it had a penis. "You dirty little man," she quipped, splashing water with her hand.

The monkey squawked and splashed back.

She countered, and once hit with another well-aimed rebuttal, turned to a growing ruckus. Other monkeys were running off with her clothes. Lunging forward, she swiped her knickers from the primate's grip. It hissed, bared its teeth, and fled. Tranquility lost, she hopped out of the tub and into her knickers. The sniffer monkey frolicked closest, now dragging off her towel. She ran after him with desperate fury and stomped a foot on a corner of the towel. Once winning the vicious tug of war, she wrapped herself up and secured it across her chest.

The other monkeys had carried their ill-gotten booty into the heights of the acacia trees. Alexandra felt grateful they'd not absconded with her rifle to shoot her. *I don't have my rifle!*

It was this thought that thunderstruck upon spotting the leopard—the only Big-Five game that she'd yet to encounter and the one readying to finish her. The lean cat slinked through the grass in a taut belly-hug of the ground. Finch Hatton had cautioned her never to run in such circumstances: keep eye contact; back off slowly; and, foremost, not to panic. Her admiration for the man notwithstanding, Alexandra did not hesitate to turn, freak out, and run for the trees for all she was worth.

The leopard made its break, and the race was on.

She made it first into the shade and scurried up one of the taller trees. The monkeys squawked over the big cat's presence. They dropped her clothing to climb unencumbered, instinctively knowing they just needed to stay one branch higher than the foolish white woman to avoid being appetizers or entrée.

Alexandra paused twenty feet up.

With a determined leap, the leopard cleared half the distance. She jostled one limb higher, but it seemed the end of her line. She ripped off her towel and tossed it across the beast's head. It stuck, despite the cat's efforts to shake it free. The blinded feline dropped back to the ground, growled, and then scurried off.

Her tense body relaxed until she spotted the fourth lion. She thought to scream but paused, needing to calculate which to be worse: being devoured or alerting Big Jim to see her topless.

The lion looked akin to those killed: young, long, and hungry. It drew closer, eyeing her intently.

The monkeys scaled higher once the larger cat started climbing.

Alexandra shrieked as it ascended—ten feet away... eight feet... Six! She readied herself to jump but stopped upon spotting a dark figure running across the grassland in fluid strides; a long spear uplifted. The lion's front paws clawed her branch when the sharp tip of the spear impaled it against the tree. The beast roared and tried to break itself free. She stood mesmerized, her eyes fixed on the hunter. He was the most indigenous man she'd seen outside of Papua: lean, muscular, and barefoot. He wore only a red loincloth. An elaborate headdress of ostrich feathers circled his ochre-stained hair, colored orange. With one hand clasped upon a branch, she covered her breasts with her other arm and looked away from the lion's desperate plight.

Big Jim arrived. He raised his rifle and shot the lion at close range. It was the most humane thing he could do.

The lion went limp and remained suspended.

Alexandra opened her eyes, still balancing her bare feet along the tree limb. If not humiliating enough having Big Jim and the magnificent African bushman gawking up at her, De Pauw and two askaris arrived to join in on the spectacle. She chuckled. "Jean-Luc, you're back!"

"Have I missed anything? I see you've finally met Kavidi."

"And he has surely seen me. Might you toss up the towel?"

"I retrieved your camera," he teased. "Care for a shot? It looks adventurous up there."

She gritted her teeth. "Don't make me scalp you on the ride home."

Big Jim picked it up. "Does this count as saving your life?"

Alexandra rolled her eyes. "I will credit you if you get that to me straight away." He tossed it up. She reached out, almost lost her balance, and snapped her arm back once more to cover herself. The towel fell to the ground. "A rather poor effort, Mister Gustin. I beg of you."

Big Jim tossed it again.

Though it struck her, she let it fall. Between holding the branch and concealing herself, it would be impossible to wrap up, anyway. Her only desire was to return to her well-earned bath, and there was only one way to quickly go about it. She dropped the arm covering her breasts and endured their wide-eyed appreciation.

"Yes! This is what an American girl looks like standing near-naked in an acacia tree."

Click.

After completing her bath, Alexandra loaded her suitcase into a safari wagon and headed for the lake to collect her driver. Four lions had been killed, photographed, and her work here lay complete. De Pauw would take her to Kampala, and then she would backtrack to Mombasa, hoping to hit London by the new year. A tour of Rippon Falls was a must. To leave without visiting the source of the Nile seemed foolish. In Nairobi, she would gather her stored luggage at the Norfolk Hotel. She knew she'd find Simra waiting for her, now knowing the measure of the man.

The only thing left unrealized was a photograph of a shoebill stork.

She found Jean-Luc by the lakeside telling a tale to Big Jim, who stood knee-deep, washing up a cut on his arm. The two askaris idled nearby. Her farewell could wait until they finished. Camera at the ready, she searched but could not detect any storks high-stepping the reeds.

Big Jim called her over. "If I give you an address in New Zealand, would you take a photograph and send it to my mother? Can't seem to find a mailbox around these parts."

"Sure." She stepped closer and lined him up in her lens. For some reason, she'd miss the big lug.

He stood up and flexed his biceps. "No man or beast is my equal!"

The moment her camera clicked, Alexandra jumped back. The enormous crocodile had broken the surface, clamped down, and taken him under at the thighs.

Blood filled the water where he had stood. The askaris fired their rifles, but he was gone; the quicker the mercy.

One of Big Jim's legs washed ashore. Equally shocked, De Pauw walked over to let Alexandra cry on his shoulder.

❧

"Miss Bathenbrook, I presume?" The receptionist passed over a room key. "And might I say, well done!"

"Thank you."

Alexandra drifted through the lobby of the Speke Hotel, ready to celebrate completing her duties in Kampala with a splash of lemonade. The local officials were pleased with her work. She had visited Kizza in the hospital and donated two thousand dollars for his care. If infection did not set in, he would keep his leg. Having received no formal training on how a millionairess should act, she remained unsure if such a gesture rang patronizingly colonial or the correct thing to do.

She claimed a seat to wait for the owners of the canvas-topped Ford Model-T motorcars parked outside, which sported a decal: *Wanderwell-Around the World endurance record.*

With a lift of her slouch hat, she shook out her hair. *It was over.*

The hotel was named after John Speke—the first westerner to sight Lake Victoria in 1858. His claim that it served as the source of the Nile had spawned controversy. In those days, the mysteries of Africa filled the newspaper headlines: foremost, the great manhunt of the nineteenth century to find explorer David Livingstone. Yet today, many deemed Africa a familiar commodity, with the most daring voyagers now casting eyes on inner Amazonia, the polar regions, or the depths of the ocean. Some even imagined mankind amidst the stars.

Unnavigable horizons were becoming less storybook fantasy.

The Great War had changed social norms, indeed everything. The age of colonial rule had reached its zenith upon its onset and now on the wane. Through civil unrest, peaceful retreat, or bloody rebellion, aspiring nations were on a path toward self-determination, however intermittent and slow each might prove to be. Good men like Kizza and Simra would be needed to father them along.

Evidence of progress filled Kampala, to which the British applied a lighter boot. If the diverse people of Uganda could set aside their tribal differences and derive a unified sense of being of one nation, their homeland and future would become a creation of their own. The English had done so centuries ago, and it was among the reasons that, for so long a period, they had ruled the world.

Alexandra immersed herself in a dated copy of the *London Times.* An article about George Dyott's preparations to conduct the most anticipated manhunt of the twentieth century caught her eye. It stated the Amazon expedition had been delayed until spring 1928, for reasons unspecified. She pondered what future, if any, remained for her in adventure photography. In her brief time, she had too often tempted a sunrise not meant to be her last, to be her last. She had kept that one awful photo of Big Jim posing just as the croc surfaced to take him under.

It had shaken her in witnessing his life snuffed out so violently.

They are here. Alexandra peered around a corner of her newspaper to watch the trailblazers settle at a table. All four appeared exhausted, dust-covered, and defeated. She knew from the newsreels one of the three men: Walter "Cap" Wanderwell. In 1922, he had started out leading his team on a race across the globe in his custom-made automobiles. Alexandra's eyes, however, locked onto the sole female in the party, who proved unmissable standing at six feet and dressed in khaki breeches.

The young woman took off her leather aviator cap.

Over recent years following her escapades, Aloha Wanderwell had been elevated into Alexandra's absentee idol. She hid behind her paper and quashed an impulse to introduce herself. What of interest could she possibly say to a woman who'd entered the Muslim holy city of Mecca disguised as a man and escaped capture from Chinese bandits by fleeing to Soviet Vladivostok?

She peeked again, and this time they took notice as the men filed out of the lobby. She felt silly at being caught gawking and retreated behind her newspaper.

"Alexandra Bathenbrook, I presume?"

"Yes." She folded down her paper. "I am thrilled to meet you!"

"And I am so very thrilled to meet you!" Aloha took the chair across. She displayed a tomboyish appeal that did not match her high-pitched voice. "I read about your travels in Papua. I said to myself, *'This is a gal I hope to meet one day.'* And here you are!"

Alexandra sat stunned, having never examined her reflection in the mirror for any semblance of celebrity. She summoned a waiter. "You must share a drink if you have the time."

Aloha ordered lemonade. "Cap and the boys are fixing the axle on my vehicle. We're all down with malaria, but plan to push on for Mombasa tomorrow. All of Kampala is abuzz over your success."

"I did little more than evade being eaten," Alexandra said. "What you've done is remarkable. Do tell."

Aloha told her tale. On a whim, she had answered a newspaper ad and joined up with Wanderwell's troupe to become the first woman to drive around the world. The group spent the entirety of 1927 touring Africa. Such barnstorming was financed by giving lectures and showing films of their travels, but they'd come across shockingly few opera houses between Cape Town and Khartoum. They were so spent of resources that their cars had chugged into Kampala using crushed bananas for grease and elephant fat for engine oil.

It sounded as if they were nearly bankrupt.

Aloha ended her story. "So, what exotic lands are next for you?"

"Montana. Home." Alexandra shared tidbits about her travels and fading ambitions. "Adventure photography has been fun, but I shan't do it any longer."

"You mustn't!" Aloha perked up. "What I'm doing is but a novelty act. Once done, it's done. What you're doing will allow young women the world over to dream beyond laboring in a factory or secretarial work. You mustn't, you truly mustn't give up!"

It offered a lot to think about. "My travel guide is delayed. I'm left with an extra room. You and your friends may have it."

Aloha appeared ill; her complexion ashen and eyes heavy. She tepidly resisted, half-asleep in her chair.

While John Speke had a hotel bearing his name and Doctor Livingstone had been presumed, it had proven the ambitious reporter, Henry Stanley, who'd ushered both men to fame.

A young American upstart with a speck of courageous vision.

Aloha's heartfelt encouragement relit Alexandra's pilot light. She stood and marched over to the reception desk. "I need a second room for the night."

"Only the Royal suite is vacant. It comes with full room service."

Alexandra smiled at the receptionist. "That sounds perfect."

Chapter 13

London: January 1928

A new year found Alexandra once more lost in the world and teetering on the cusp of a momentous decision. She studied the large map draping a wall of her new office space. The painted canvas presented a tantalizing depiction of her pending playground, circa 1900. She'd discovered this treasure in an antique store; a triumph of pastel-brushed cartography too dated to be practical but not yet priced as vintage. The Treaty of Versailles had changed the face of the globe monumentally and established the boundaries of a new world order, which continued in flux. She reasoned that the League of Nations—likely in cahoots with textbook, map, and atlas manufacturers—tinkered with a few borders each year to force people to purchase updated travel guides.

The map could suffice as decorative, as she had found another means to help figure out the latitude and longitude of foreign capitals.

She debated a single question over four o'clock coffee: *New York or New Orleans?* The phone rang, jarring her concentration. She slid over her French press, took a seat on the desk, and lifted the listening piece of the candlestick unit to her ear. *"Alexandra Illyria, foremost mistress to adventure! ... Yes, Father. I'm all settled in."*

The line from Edinburgh crackled with static.

Once he concluded voicing his upset, she assured him, *"William misheard. I am not a lesbian, though in this era of wonderful nonsense, anything is possible. ... Hello... hello?"*

Her father's voice choked off, and the line went dead. Alexandra hung up the earpiece.

The first month of 1928 had been spent establishing her business—a daunting task Alexandra conducted with unforeseen acumen and diligence. She'd rented a street-level unit on Bond Street in the West End, amidst the hectic foot traffic of Mayfair and a short walk from Piccadilly. No cost would be spared to transform the brick-walled, wood-floored hollow into her vision of business-chic Shangri-La. The window-filled main room spread outfitted with rattan blinds, a reception desk, three leather sling chairs beside a coffee table, and pygmy palms plugged into the corners. To the rear stood her office, a kitchenette, a bathroom, and a small closet destined to become a darkroom.

Once her mailing address and phone line were secured, her arrival needed to be shouted to the world. She'd settled on a name for her agency while a sign-writer readied to apply his calligraphic talents. The man stated the need to reduce his font size, since her full name would not fit across the streetside window and hung shingle. This rang unacceptable, as diminutive fonts do not shout "Adventure!" Thus, emblazoned on her letterhead, business cards, and office facade:

Alexandra Illyria–Photographer
No assignment too perilous!

It held the added advantage of keeping the Bathenbrook family name distant from the mishaps and scandals she would no doubt inspire along the way. She had mailed a press release to news agencies and the most vaunted exploratory societies. Newspaper ads were placed in the larger metropolises, and the wait for inquiries began.

She would soon be off to Switzerland.

Alexandra remained lost in thought. *New York or New Orleans?*

It was, and forever would be, all about logistics. Choosing to trek afar for any assignment meant a commitment of weeks and might rule out grander opportunities. Transportation timelines needed to be tight to avoid loitering at hotels between ocean passage and designated dates with adventure. Alexandra discerned it to be beyond a one-person operation. To make it work, she required someone to man the fort while she found herself lost in travel, rendered incommunicado in the wilderness, or intoxicated. She had imported the perfect complement to pull it off. Her

Montana confidante, Oliver Martin, possessed the ideal skill set to serve as a travel agent, film developer, researcher, and purveyor of secretarial duties.

Archibald or Archibald? Alexandra barely noticed Oliver joining her. It was "Decision Wednesday," which had naturally been preceded by "Mail review Monday" and "Correspondence Tuesday." A trickle of inquiries about fees and availability was arriving via mail. No job would be rejected; rather, a letter stating "all booked up" would be sent, as *too busy* sounded successful. Such tidings were already dispatched to proposers as far off as China. She took a seat in a sling chair to warm up near the heating stove. The one hard date and epicenter of her coming months would be April 10th in British Guiana. Her father had sent word he would be touring the Americas and hoped to rendezvous with her in its capital of Georgetown. Her current dilemma centered on what jobs could be worked around it.

"It seems easier to find passage to Paraguay," Alexandra said. "No one goes to Paraguay! Is it truly via New York or New Orleans?"

Oliver had charted them out to be the only options for expedient ocean transport from either Livorno, Italy, or Hamburg, Germany. He said, "New Orleans is the choice if you're taking the Pensacola job."

"Pensacola!" she scoffed, thinking it ludicrous. A yachtsman named Charles Thompson wanted her to join in on a voyage to new harboring in Key West. It served as a viable route to Cuba, which was required to get to Guiana. "Any updates on his chin?"

"I found no pictures of this Thompson fella. This might sweeten the pot."

She skimmed over the new correspondence. A family in Baltimore wished for her to photograph their son's bris. "I don't see the adventure in that."

"If the rabbi has a shaky hand, it might be." Her puzzled look begged for an explanation. Oliver added, "It's the Jewish ceremony of circumcision. Removal of the foreskin from... the penis?"

"All these years, I thought they came in two varieties."

Oliver laughed, thankful for the levity, as her mood swirled churlish. At least she had warned that Decision Wednesdays overwhelmed her.

"Why New York? Do you intend to stop by the National Geographic Society in Washington?"

"I am not allowed to enter the District of Columbia until the end of the Coolidge presidency." Alexandra failed to expand on her other reasons. Her longing to reunite with Archibald Leach percolated, and the prospect of a return to New Orleans filled her with disgust.

"I see." Oliver let it go. "It is *'Decision* Wednesday.'"

"Louisiana it is!" She stomped her foot and exhaled steam. Her nasty mood resulted from many things: the cold and damp London weather stiffening her back, her lament that travel via the Big Apple appeared impractical, and, foremost, an article in this morning's *London Times.* George Dyott prepared to set sail with much fanfare from Hoboken, New Jersey, aboard the SS *Voltaire*, destined for Rio de Janeiro.

Alexandra finished her coffee. "I will skip the bris and report to Pensacola to sail off with a complete stranger, *then* ferry to Cuba, *then* sea passage to Georgetown. It's all quite maddening!"

She retreated to her office. The best thing about self-employment was Correspondence Tuesday could be blown off now and then. Now that she had a mailing address and a flat, Alexandra needed to catch up with her personal affairs and free up Will from receiving her mail.

Seated on the cold floorboards, bundled in an overcoat, she sorted photographs and letters to file. The chimney stood yet swept, nor any furniture ordered. She gnawed on a telegram sent by her wretched aunt in Toulouse, France: *Visit soon. The Master awaits your decision. Your pleasures ruling over the Fallen will be infinite.*

The bell overhanging the front door jingled. She tore the message into oblivion.

Oliver opened her door. "Walk-in customer. I know this man!"

Alexandra darted up. "Hide the coffee press and make some tea!" She took several deep breaths. Professional comportment was not her forte. She slid off the jacket and pushed back her hair before entering the sitting room. A middle-aged man studied the framed photographs displayed on a wall, which marketed her travels and experience.

"Good day, fine sir," she said maturely. "I am Alexandra Illyria Bathenbrook. How may I be of service?"

"Harry Price." He removed his top hat. His consternation over her youth rang palpable. "I am here on behalf of the Ghost Club, which sounds like a childish venture, but not too foolhardy for the likes of Yeats, Dickens, Sir Arthur Conan Doyle, nor myself! We investigate paranormal incidents. I wish to converse about Borley Rectory. It's haunted, they say. Have you heard of it?"

"No, but such phenomena fascinate me."

She hung up his overcoat and motioned for him to take a seat. A tall man with a thin hairline and a long, unyielding face, he came across as morose. His dark eyebrows shot up to the sling chair's crumpling of his rigid posture, which left his knees bent even with his head.

Alexandra cringed. Her father had shipped the chairs from Siam, and it had taken an entire "Shampoo hair Sunday" to assemble them. At least the mystery of those leftover pieces of teak lay resolved.

Price stopped fighting the quicksand. He asked, "Have you any experience in this field?"

"I haven't followed it much since Houdini died but I slept with the ghost of Suki in West Wycombe." She claimed the chair next to him and not the one across, as Price displayed a wide man-spread.

"Harry Houdini was my friend and a fellow champion in exposing charlatans soiling this legitimate scientific field." He passed her a photograph. "The manor is in Essex County. The Reverend Henry Bull built it."

The rundown Victorian dwelling posed a gloomy backdrop. "What plagues this rectory?"

Price cleared his throat. "The diocese is having difficulty finding new clergy for the many reports of paranormal activity. They have requested the club to investigate. I desire a preliminary study before committing my time and reputation to the undertaking. If these tales of spirits are communal hysteria or collective *bull*-crap, our interest might appear a comeuppance. To be publicly fooled is bad stew."

"What is the job, sir?"

Price shifted in his chair, grimacing in discomfort. He sank deeper and looked much like a bug being devoured by a Venus flytrap. "I arranged for a photography team to spend this Saturday night on-premise, but they backed out after visiting the grounds. I am seeking a replacement and shall pay you six pounds for your service."

Alexandra calculated it to be $7.56 using the 0.79% conversion rate applied. It a pittance, but the job was local. "Does the property have electricity?"

"Not in the slightest. If you accept, you will see it through?"

"I stand by my shingle," Alexandra guaranteed. "Excuse me while I review my calendar."

Oliver arrived with tea. She left for her office, leaving him private time to bask in the eerie glow of their guest. She hoped his obvious eagerness to ghost hunt didn't knock the fee down to gratis.

A war of spiritualism raged.

The ghastly toll of the Great War, and the ensuing loss of fifty million more to Spanish flu, had frayed the spiritual fiber of humankind, foremost in Europe. It had resuscitated a longing to speak to the dead. Self-proclaimed clairvoyants and mediums—some legitimate, most con artists—arose to fill this demand. Séances were all the rage. Moving tables, disembodied voices, and visitations by shady apparitions were regular fare once hands locked and the lights dimmed. Local playhouses filled beyond capacity to witness lesser shams. Price and Houdini alleged that science could lay proof of an afterlife and ridding the field of ghost hustlers paramount to the task.

Alexandra believed spirits existed. If she could uncover a trusted medium, she would pay any fee to have a brief reunion with Thomas and Emma. She returned to the reception area. "I'm pleased to report I can make my team available, but due to travel and equipment costs, the fee must be ten pounds. We will arrive at noon, map out each floor, and remain vigilant through the eve. Without electricity, photographs may be problematic."

Price grunted his agreement. "I must brief you before Saturday."

"Oliver is at your disposal."

Price struggled to rise. He let out a moan and placed a hand on his lower spine.

She asked, "How long have you suffered back pain?"

"Excuse me? I have no issues with my back," he exclaimed. "I take issue with your chair!"

Regardless, Alexandra said, "I, too, suffer spinal pain. I've engaged the services of a Japanese masseuse. She is a petite girl with fingers more gifted than Rachmaninoff's. This, after my first stab with Oriental practices ended in fiasco, as I had a Pavlovian response to strike my acupuncturist whenever jabbed."

Price looked at her, vexed. "Whatever is this to me?" He grabbed his overcoat and departed.

It amused Oliver. "Where are we to find a team on brief notice?"

"I'm already working on it."

Alexandra tapped her lips with a forefinger. She gave thought to disassembling the chair, but it was nothing that couldn't wait until "Office cleaning Thursday."

The Model-T sedan came to a halt. Alexandra exited and tossed an overnight bag over her shoulder. In recent weeks, she had taken the train out of Paddington Station each Saturday and disembarked in Maidenhead to mind Simra's six-year-old twins. He would then drive her to Cookham.

"See you tomorrow, Simra. Bye, kids!"

"Ta, Miss Alee!" the boy and girl beckoned as the car headed off.

Before barging in, Alexandra sat along the Thames. The wind gusts chilled, and not a duck, Dick, or debutante stirred its banks. Her visits necessitated tactical contemplation. With each overnight stay, she and Will had drawn closer. She believed he needed to regain comfort in female contact, confident no woman had touched him in a non-medicinal manner for ten years running.

As for his former gal in the photograph, Noel Boneje had been his fiancée. Alexandra settled on a strategy to remedy Will's isolation. Option one required him to visit London. If he resisted, option two entailed showing up at his door unannounced with a high-end prostitute. The cost of retrieving her Victorian Hasselblad camera would be enduring another insipid sales pitch for her to see a psychiatrist, but it a tit for tat world.

She spotted a man standing across the river. He sported a top hat and a dark cloak. His long, stringy white hair danced in the cool breeze.

It was him—Astor Lys. A Swiss solicitor and gifted pianist, they had been introduced in New Orleans during one of her aunt's unhallowed soirées. Even from a far off distance, Alexandra sensed a predatory malevolence in his gaze. She stood to confront him, but he vanished in the blink of her eye.

A shiver ran down her spine. She left to knock on Will's door.

He answered, brandishing a confused expression. "'Visit Cookham

Saturday' is not until tomorrow. What are you doing here?"

"Exercising my privileges on 'Anything goes Friday.'"

Will retreated to put water on to boil. He said, "Normal people telephone before pushing in."

"Normal people are not so assuredly home." She removed her coat and assumed a lotus position near the fireplace to sneak in ten minutes of tranquil reflection before the fireworks commenced. *"Anyhoo,* such from the genteel lad who coined the term 'Alec Babblebrook.'"

It still made him laugh. He left the kitchen carrying a tea tray with finger sandwiches. "What are you doing?"

"I've taken up *Dhyana* to soothe my conscience. Simra's children are teaching me."

Will hoped that they would not be irreparably scarred with limited exposure. "Simra is a private man. Don't intrude on his affairs."

"Such as you paying for his son's cleft lip surgery?" She had ferreted from Simra very little along their journey back from Nairobi but tapped his wife and children with better results.

Will placed down his teacup. "He told you this?"

"No, just about his war experience." She took a bite of her sandwich. The damn Germans had sold him on liverwurst. "He treated a wound of T.E. Lawrence."

Will needled one correction. "You mean John Hume Ross?"

"Don't be stupid," she brayed. "Everyone knows that John Hume Ross, who you foolishly insist on calling T.E. Lawrence, has henceforth changed his name to T.E. Shaw and is now stationed in Waziristan. He has no standing in Simra's war journey whatsoever."

Will dropped his sandwich, dumbfounded. "Did you bring a bottle of magnesia?"

"Only aspirin. Your tummy would settle if you got out more."

Will failed to see why it mattered to her. "Our conversations would be rational if you'd see the alienist I keep telling you about. You're a picnic basket short of a sandwich!"

"That's a tad under the belt," she protested, unaware why it mattered to him. *"Anyhoo,* I need you to join my investigation of a haunted house tomorrow. Simra has signed on and will drive."

"Join what? Come, Barnabas!"

With that, they were off, once more driven from their domicile.

Alexandra checked her watch. It usually took less time for him to flee. She stood, wanting to sort through the pantry before getting on with burning supper.

❧

William Bathenbrook knew that after their initial squabble, his evenings in Alexandra's company would smooth out. After dinner, they sprawled out on the floor to take in the hearth's heat and sip brandy. She read aloud the latest exploits of persnickety Belgian inspector, Hercule Poirot. At her insistence, her thigh served as Will's pillow. He had initially balked, thinking it unfit to relax so casually with a grown sister, but reconsidered since she was a lesbian. He nearly drifted into peaceful sleep as she stroked his face and hair. Alexandra might be bonkers, but she flaunted a nurse's touch and a soothing reading voice. He felt grateful for so many little things she had added to make his days easier: from perfectly pre-knotting his ties to teaching him a way to place on his prosthetic arm, as its straps and harness were not suitable for someone with only one arm to secure.

Tonight, he had received a bonus: spared his waltz lessons.

With the last chapter completed, she closed the book and pitched her offer. "This alienist to whom you subscribe. Will he find my lost sandwich? I'll attend one appointment if you join me at the rectory tomorrow, and upon our return, meet my masseuse. She's lovely, and I feel pained whence absent from her touch."

"When," Will corrected. *How did a Japanese lesbian masseuse get involved in this?* he dared to ask himself.

"It's a fine tradeoff. A night of ghost stories and a massage, while I risk chase all about London by men with a net and straitjacket."

He sniffed for cheese in the trap. "I'll only go on the ghost hunt."

"Not enough! You must also dine out with me on your thirtieth birthday."

She functioned like a strangler vine with an agenda, but as it was not until October and she'd likely be locked up receiving proper psychiatric care by then, he agreed.

Alexandra nudged him to get up. She grimaced upon standing and rubbed her thigh. "A woman in Nairobi beat me with her whip. Just innocent horseplay. She grew jealous I danced with a man. Very domineering in that way.”

“Please say no more.”

“I must retrieve the coat of arms.” She went into his study. The Bathenbrook shield featured a knight standing in a fountain. They each placed a hand on it and sealed the deal.

“The local pub serves a fair meatloaf,” he suggested as their future dining option.

“I’m thinking Kung Pao chicken in Hong Kong. *Anyhoo,* time for your waltz lessons.”

Will felt depleted. He knew better than to not read the fine print. He took a stance; his right arm extended, waiting for her to put a record on the gramophone. As he had no left hand to lead with, she had struggled to teach him the closed position steps, since everything needed to be reversed.

They danced to the notes of “Let the Rest of the World Go By.” It amazed Will that Alexandra could look at him unmasked—a smile on her lips and a caring glisten in her hazel eyes.

She asked, “Why did you tell Father that I’m a lesbian?”

“Because he spends too much time worrying over some heel trying for your money.”

“Well, we’ve spoken, so now he’s heard the truth from me.”

Relief flushed Will. The ringing of his telephone granted him leave. After taking the call, he rejoined Alexandra. “Gunnar and Hildegard will spend the night.”

She threw up her arms. “We won the war, you know!”

“Take my bed. I’ll sleep downstairs with Barnabas and still go tomorrow.”

“Yes, you will!” She kissed his cheek before heading for the stairs. “See if the Teutonic invaders care to come along. It will add numbers to the séance. Goodnight.”

As the end drew near, Alexandra chalked it up as the worst road trip ever. Simra’s sedan felt cramped for five adult passengers, and over the three-hour ordeal to Borley, she had served as the squashed *wurst* in a

Hun sandwich. She weighed the unsuited German pair with derision. Gunnar appeared clean-cut, placid, and rather eye-catching for a chemist. Hildegard came across as highly combustive, cultured, but irrational, as she dyed her hair black.

Really, who does such a thing? Alexandra failed to reason.

The Kraut couple had passed the trip squabbling about having joined this campaign: he a firm *"Ja"* and she a feisty *"Nein."* To help lighten the mood, Alexandra had tried to orchestrate a round of "99 Flaschen Bier."

It had flopped quickly. Thankfully, they were passing through Sudbury and closing in on their destination. Alexandra took out the pamphlet Oliver had compiled, which outlined the history of the rectory. Each time she had attempted to read it aloud, her audience had degenerated into juvenile banter.

She tried again. "The Gothic-style mansion had been constructed in 1862 on the grounds of a twelfth-century monastery, which held to it an unsettling history. Local lore tells of a monk and a nun from nearby Bures Convent falling in love and eloping with the help of a friendly coachman. Upon capture, the monk was hanged, the coachman beheaded, and the nun immured alive within the monastery's basement. It is to this tragic event that the historic hauntings are tied."

Will asked, "What's the most fun a monk can have...? *Nun!*"

Everyone snickered. Alexandra frowned.

Simra turned off Hall Road to enter the estate. The huge, unkempt property lay filled with bone-barren trees. Looming ahead stood the twenty-three-room monstrosity; a once opulent vision faded to ruin in its abandonment. The lofty gables and chimneys stood chipped. Some windows were sealed with bricks, lending resemblance to a place of imprisonment. It sobered up their horseplay.

They all disembarked, eager to warm up inside.

Oliver had arrived earlier with the keys and busied himself unloading boxes of food, flashlights, candles, and explosives from his loaner car. Alexandra walked over to greet her understudy. "Why are the windows and door open?"

"To help heat up the place." Oliver left to introduce himself.

Alexandra carried a box into the gloomy structure. It felt ten degrees colder inside than outdoors: so chilly she could see her breath. A flicker of light guided her down a dark hallway. She passed through the main foyer to settle into the drawing room, which would serve as their base for the next twenty-four hours. Its large fireplace stood already ablaze. The outlines of absent portraits pockmarked the faded wallpaper. Even with the shutters open, only a pittance of illumination cut through the dirty windowpanes. Upholstered chairs, a wood table, and a dusty piano filled out the room. No coat closet was required.

Picking up an empty Corona pop bottle left by laborers who'd abandoned their repairs, she feared desertion of another kind. To her, this was a job; to Will's friends, a silly midwinter diversion. The problem was Will. He did not respect her prowess as a businesswoman, and the others owed allegiance to him, not her. They arrived already peevish about their working conditions. Once setting down their packages, they crowded around the fireplace.

Alexandra clapped to gain their attention. "Welcome to the rectory. Our first goal is to make a detailed map of the house and grounds. Two teams of three or three teams of two would best suffice. What say you?"

"I say four teams of one and a half," Will snarked.

Alexandra took pause not to strangle him. Once everyone stopped chuckling, she said, "Three teams of two, it is. As Oliver and I have cameras, we need volunteers to join us. We must start a fire upstairs. Who will join Oliver to do so...? *Anybody...?*"

Everyone looked up. Rats were scurrying about.

She placed the bottle on the wooden table. "Who will join me in touring the exterior...? *Anybody...?*"

Everyone looked out the window. Snow flurries kicked about. Volunteerism appeared to be in short supply.

She asked, "Who will prepare a hearty stew for dinner?"

Hildegard held up a hand, followed by Simra. It was a start.

Alexandra said, "Those remaining must face the fate of the spinning bottle. The winner joins Oliver upstairs. Gentlemen, take a side."

Will and Gunnar shuffled over to the table.

She spun the bottle, and it came to a rest pointing at Will.

Alexandra concluded, "We shall all reconvene in this room in two hours. Godspeed and *chop-chop!*"

Everyone rolled their eyes and drifted out of the drawing room to conduct their duties.

Chapter 14

The lifespan of a snowflake in England proved briefer and less mischievous than a poorly timed wink. As they walked the muddy grounds, Gunnar comprehended Alexandra's account of how high the snow piled Montana. He had fought in Galicia, battling Russians and Rumanians as a soldier in the *Alpenkorps,* and knew what a Carpathian winter looked and bit like. Alexandra could attain little sense of the fair-haired, enigmatic German. She had experienced the Great War still a child, reading about the Huns' "Rape of Belgium." Maturity eventually opened her eyes that the world functioned less black and white as newspaper ink would have one believe, and that yellow journalism would stoop to no bounds to pry a daily nickel from a pocket.

With each step shared with Gunnar, she became aware it might serve her interest to be allies rather than foes.

The property spread over four acres. She jumped over a small creek, needing to grasp his hand to avoid sliding off the far bank. She briefly hugged him during the conclusion of his rescue. After holding her stare into his reassuring blue eyes, she blushed and pulled away.

"Your wife seems a spirited sort," she noted. "Whyever did you agree to join in this?"

"It sounded like a more interesting setting to play Parcheesi."

Alexandra was finding wry humor in him. The board game, religion in India, was catching on in England. "Your friendship with Will is most unexpected, seeing that he pierced you with a bayonet. How does one reconcile that?"

"He could not pull it out, despite many kicks to my chest," Gunnar recalled, amused. "When it finally popped free, with I left helpless, he looked me in the eye and let me live. A shell hit, and his arm landed next to me. Will helped me quit morphine. Simra patched me up. One does not easily forget."

"I suspect all of you are helping my brother with something very secretive."

"He's looking for a woman in France that..." Gunnar paused. "It's not my affair to tell."

They came to a shuttered summer house at the end of the property and headed back for the rectory along a stone wall. Alexandra jumped over the creek and stopped dead in her tracks. A dark emptiness blurred the snowfall. A nothingness shaped in the silhouette of a woman. Alexandra managed a snapshot before the figure gradually faded away. Price's report dubbed this path the "nun's walk."

"We should return to the rectory," she said, unnerved. "It's none too holy out here."

After warming up by the drawing room fireplace, Alexandra set up her mounted Victorian Hasselblad camera. Once night fell, taking any photographs within the house would be infeasible. She'd devised a strategy to lure any roaming spirits to her. Having little experience in using flash powder, she reasoned equal chance it would work out splendidly or spark an uncontrollable fire.

So dithered the incalculable risks that come with *adventure!*

She reclaimed her handheld Leica-1 to inspect the main floor. The barren library shelved cobwebs, and the windows in the dining room were bricked up, as Reverend Bull had grown tired of the ghostly nun watching his family dine from outdoors. Upon visiting the exterior courtyard, she waved to Simra, who busied himself chopping wood and filling buckets with well water. Near the kitchen, a row of servant bells hung on the wall, with each designated for an upstairs bedroom. She could hear Hildegard prepping dinner. Alexandra knew that if they were each to play a role in amending Will's shattered life, amity was in order.

One German down; one to go. She exhaled and entered the kitchen. "I have fared poorly in prior relationships with women. I truly long for a heartfelt bond with you."

From the hallway, Will cleared his throat and skedaddled.

The cook tautened her glare and grip on her cleaver. "Why do you laugh with *mein Mann* outside?"

It was not the sort of question one prefers to hear from a moody wife wielding a weapon. Alexandra's mind went blank. "He told me a nun joke popular in the *Vaterland?*"

"You lie!" Hildegard obliterated a potato.

"He said you make a bland stew! *Anyhoo*, can I help spice it up?"

"I add spice." Hildegard violently chopped off the stem of a carrot. "You suck on this!"

Alexandra bit down on the long root thrust into her mouth. Once exercising a hasty retreat, she clapped her hands and shouted, "Time's up! All to the drawing room. *Chop-chop!*"

She received a sluggish response. While waiting for stragglers, she admired Hildegard's playing of Johann Bach's "Air on the G String." Will arrived last. She said, "If I'm found dead, the pianist is to blame."

He chuckled. "Never play spin the bottle with a married man."

"Get inside, you turd." Alexandra informed her audience, "We shall have tea at four, a delicious stew by the redoubtable Hildegard at six, and Parcheesi galore thereafter. I have photographed a first paranormal entity. Otherwise, the house is secure. Questions?"

No one appeared eager to say much.

A bell chimed near the kitchen. Several hands went up.

"I'll start with Simra." The continued chiming was becoming annoying. "What is your inquiry?"

"If we are all gathered, who is upstairs pulling the bell cord?"

The others lowered their hands, awaiting her answer.

"I dare not guess, but as Oliver and Will are charged with that area, they can find out. You two, *chop-chop!*"

The investigative duo left and took the stairs. The second floor of the rectory held eleven bedrooms and a small chapel. They had earlier mapped, photographed, and secured all the rooms, leaving their doors open. A fire had been started in the bedroom of the late Reverend Bull, which stood closest to the stairwell. The Ghost Club termed it the "Blue room" and of particular interest. Bull had died seven months ago in bed—as had his vicar father from syphilis in 1892—and visitors routinely noted odd noises emanating from within.

They passed the chapel and approached the rear bedroom aligned with the chimed bell. The door stood closed. Will opened it and looked in. The cord hung near a barren bedframe, but nothing stirred. He shrugged, left the door open, and they returned to the Blue room.

Will took a seat. He thought Oliver to be a decent chap. Will had plagued such types in his unruly youth; pawns to lock in a school closet or bully in other ways. He wished to know the lad better, as they both held a role to play in Alexandra's new life in London town.

"Any plan for when my sister pulls down her shingle? I can't see this business lasting long."

"She's far too savvy to allow that." Oliver used a poker to rouse the miserly fireplace logs. "Don't you want her to succeed?"

Years ago, Will would have slapped him for mouthing off, but now it fostered an appreciation for his loyalty. "Do you have any sisters?"

"Two older and one younger," Oliver nervously confided.

"What if your youngest came home upset no one asked her to a harvest moon dance?"

Oliver shrugged. "I'd cheer her as best I could."

"Alexandra keeps voicing dismay over not being invited to Amazonia so she might die a horrible death. Should I cheer her on as best I can? I want her to live a long and happy life. Such cannot be said for any of her siblings. Do you host any romantic designs?"

"No! A guy like me can't carry a torch for a lady like Alexandra."

Will felt bad his inquiry had spurred Oliver's self-derision. He carelessly leaked, "If she shows no interest in you, trust me, it's not you. Her eyes drift toward the fairer sex."

Oliver squinted, unsure of the implication, which had been delivered with a wink. "Pardon me?"

Will leaned forward. "She favors the company of women."

Oliver was yet sold, despite another wink. "What of her plans to marry Archibald Leach?"

"Some phantom actor a continent away?" Will scoffed. "A ruse to veil a carnal relationship with her Japanese masseuse. So don't take any rejection personally."

Oliver smiled. A door slammed down the hall. He rushed out to investigate. The bedroom they had just visited now stood locked. "Will we be executed if we abandon our position?"

Objects crashed against the walls inside.

Will spouted, "I can live with that."

The muffled wail of a woman beyond the closed door sent them scurrying to face the fire.

❧

Four o'clock tea was never meant to be so tense. The six amateur ghost sleuths sat in the drawing room, fidgety, trying to ignore the disembodied screams reverberating from above. The god-awful racket finally stopped, allowing everyone a needed breath.

"How does a vicar get syphilis?" Simra unexpectedly asked, puzzled by the quandary.

"The usual *habits*," Will speculated facetiously. *"Nun* too holy."

Alexandra even laughed, desperate for levity. It sparked courage. "Who shall join me upstairs and open the locked bedroom door...? *Anybody...?* Don't tempt me to spin the bottle!"

Upon seeing her rise, Gunnar consented, which upset the cook. Hildegard joined them as far as the kitchen since the stew needed stirring and a further warning with the cleaver overdue. Alexandra lifted a set of keys from a hook and proceeded up the stairs, needing to click on her flashlight once outside the dim firelight from the Blue room.

They settled at the guilty door.

"You open it and I'll dart in," she told Gunnar.

He found the correct key and inserted it.

Alexandra jumped in. A blurry figure hovered at the window, which she took to be the apparition of the monk gazing out to the grounds for his lost love. It was cloaked in a hooded robe and softly moaning as it struggled to yank a long stick out of its belly. She aimed her flashlight, and it became clear that the spirit was pleasuring itself. Upon discovery, it whisked by, right through the closet door. Alexandra turned to flee and barreled into Gunnar. He toppled back onto the hallway floor, and she landed pressed against him.

His schlange felt a tad rowdy.

They both screamed upon detecting Hildegard's heel clicks coming up the stairwell in rhythm with the oscillating glow of her flashlight. It so petrified Alexandra, she could not extricate herself to hide in the room's closet, as sharing time with whatever had flown by spanking its monkey seemed the lesser evil.

The menacing light and heel clicks drew closer—*ever closer*—on a collision course. The gaseous outline of the monk suddenly floated out of another bedroom and headed down the dark hall.

"Es ist ein guten-schlange!" screamed Hildegard.

Alexandra panicked. She freed herself, ran into the closet, and slammed the door. She waited until all the commotion settled before risking a peek. Her eyes burst wide upon opening the door.

Murkily looking out the window again stood the specter.

Guten-schlange, indeed, her libido sang. She screamed and flew over the bedframe, traversing the hall and stairs in a mercurial fashion. Everyone gathered near the kitchen. Gunnar tried to calm Hildegard's twitchy fit. The others stared down the steps leading to the basement.

The piercing wail of a distraught woman echoed from below.

"Did you see it, too?" Oliver asked Alexandra.

"Yes, it was the monk," she said. "He was... how should I say...?"

Hildegard cried out, *"Schlagen die wienerschnitzel!"*

"What you English label 'jollying the Roger,'" Gunnar clarified.

"You mean 'fighting the one-eyed trouser snake'?" Will tossed in. "How do they say it in India?"

Simra replied, *"Kobara sohani,* as in 'charming the cobra.'"

Alexandra sighed. If Simra was joining in, things had truly degenerated. The screams continued.

"We've yet to inspect down there. *Anybody...?"*

Upon seeing Alexandra turn to get the bottle, Will rushed ahead.

She waited; arms folded, tapping a foot. Waiting... waiting...

Smaaaash.

Will returned, triumphant. "Sorry. It slipped from my hand."

Oliver sensed Alexandra was about to pop off. "I'll go!"

"Good lad," Will praised. He looked at Alexandra. "Godspeed and *chop-chop."*

"Wait." Alexandra took Hildegard into her arms and shuffled her back to the drawing room. She lifted two cigarettes from her wool overcoat. After lighting them and passing one along, they both took a long drag, though it had taken effort for Hildegard's shaking hand to find her mouth. Alexandra liberated a bottle of wine and claimed a seat on the rug. "You saw *it*, too?"

Hildegard stopped hyperventilating. "I thought he held a lance. *Guter Gott!*"

Alexandra laughed wildly. She snarked, "No man should become a monk armed like that."

"*Ja, wirklich!* How could the nun resist?"

They laughed, drank, and smoked for a while longer.

Two Germans down; two poltergeists to go. Alexandra headed off to take the plunge. Oliver followed. All sorts of rusted and moldy debris crammed the basement's pitch-black passageway. She tried to brush a cobweb from her hair, but it clung like cotton candy. The air smelt putrid, and they aimed their twitchy flashlights at each squeal from scurrying rodents. The wailing of the woman subsided, but the scraping of an animal sharpening its claws against the damp bricks grew louder the deeper they inspected.

"What do you think of my brother?" She asked Oliver, needing a distraction to calm down.

"He worries about your judgement. Work and women."

"I fare poorly with other women."

"So did I," he admitted. "It's a relief to know we both sail into forbidden winds."

Alexandra turned. "What does sailing have to do with anything?"

"You know." Oliver winked. "Dance to the tune of a gayer band?"

"Why are you speaking in riddles and then winking?"

He squinted to shield the light on his face. "Engage in the love that dare not speak its name?"

"Oliver, are you trying to tell me you're a *dandy?*"

"Your expression is telling me you're not a lesbian."

Alexandra could see Oliver's panic that his secret was out. "I am not a lesbian. Who doesn't fantasize about sucking a boob now and then? As for the rest of it, I think not."

"But Will said you're involved in an affair with your Japanese masseuse, Suki. He kept winking!"

"He only has one eye, Oliver. His blink is a wink. As for my masseuse, her name is Miyu. She is only seventeen years old and blind, as they train only the sightless in the art of *shiatsu.*"

Oliver teared up. "I offer my resignation."

"Don't be stupid," she chided sympathetically. "They are your personal affairs. If you get caught, I'll bail you out, but we must agree it is sound business practice not to muddle our work responsibilities with talk of our love lives."

"Agreed!" He sighed with relief. "Bravely onward, boss?"

"Good show!" They ventured forward, but after several steps, Alexandra spun about. "So, have you met anyone dreamy since moving to London?"

A terrible cry and the thuds of a pounding fist sounded from within the wall. Something was trying to break out of its encasement. Alexandra looked back. Oliver had gotten the jump and already halfway home. She joined him in flight and locked the basement door upon finding sanctuary. "Sequester!" she howled beyond panic. "We must sequester! Bring the stew and bowls!"

Everyone scrambled to transport dishware to the drawing room.

"Not you!" Alexandra grabbed Will by the ear.

"What happened to sequester?" he asked as she steered him up the stairs, not resisting his comeuppance.

"After I tinkle. Stand guard!" She released him and slammed the bathroom door. Once seated, she barked, "What is wrong with you? I am a lover of men! Stop telling people differently."

"I thought you clarified with Father you preferred women?"

"No! I'm sure that I'm not the only gal who longs to rub nipples with another woman, but as for the rest of it, no thank you." She flushed the toilet. "If it makes you feel any better, I just engaged in ravenous sex with a *man* in Jerusalem."

It didn't. "Why do you keep talking about your masseuse, Suki?"

"Because I want *you* to meet her! Her name is Miyu." Alexandra opened the door. "You've been absent from people far too long, Will. If you don't work it out, you'll be more socially inept than me."

He looked at her skeptically. "I think not."

She threw up her arms. "You're insufferable! Sequester!"

❧

Sequester sucked. The only thing worse was Hildegard's stew, which only Simra took down without complaint. The slamming doors, demonic howls, and other rasps beyond the drawing room's door were no longer cause for investigation and served as considerable distractions to each round of Parcheesi.

Things improved once they broke out the liquor.

As midnight drew near, Alexandra completed her tutorial with Simra on how to hold afar the flash powder tray when he fired it off. The tripod camera stood aimed and set, with only the spirit of a tormented nun, ridiculously well-hung monk, or headless coachman remaining to be summoned for one immaculate money shot.

She clapped to get everyone's attention. "We should conduct a practice séance. Can I please have two volunteers...? *Anybody...?*" She grumbled and headed for an empty wine bottle.

Gunnar and Hildegard, half-asleep by the fire, raised their hands. For some unknown, but likely highly germane reason, they feared the spinning bottle. Will and Oliver blew out candles to dim the setting. Simra took position behind the Victorian Hasselblad camera.

Alexandra placed five candles and a half-peeled mushy potato on a tray in the center of the rug fronting the fireplace. "We must make an overture to the spirits."

"A potato?" Gunnar questioned. "The ghosts would need to be starving Irish to go for that."

"Humor mich," she implored. "We'll sit cross-legged around the offering and join hands."

They did so. Hildegard had experience with séances. She said, "Do not break the chain or speak."

"Let's summon the headless coachman," Alexandra suggested.

"Why the coachman?" Will wondered from the sidelines. "He can't even eat the potato!"

"Ja!" Alexandra closed her eyes and focused on her breathing. Here she sat, holding hands with the Germans, free of homicidal urges. Something good had resulted from this plight. She tightened her grip and gave each a friendly shake. "It's wonderful we're comrades and finally at peace."

"Do you fear silence?" Hildegard scoffed. *"Halt die klappe!"*

They spent several minutes establishing a united mental rhythm to beckon the coachman.

"Good God!" Will rushed to the window. "He's coming for us!"

Those in the séance immediately broke the chain and rushed over to the window. They issued a collective gasp.

The lanterns hanging from the coach jiggled in unison with the clops of a horse. It proved too dark outside to discern whether the seated driver had a noggin. The carriage rolled by and came to a stop near the front door. Panic ensued.

Gunnar and Simra picked up chairs to barricade the door.

Alexandra checked her watch; he was right on time. "At ease. It's only Geldorf."

"Who is this Geldorf?" asked Simra.

"The medium I hired to conduct the séance. When introduced, we shall only provide our middle names to foil any attempts at deception."

Alexandra grabbed a flashlight and violated sequester protocols to go out and greet him. Outside the front door stood a short and portly woman buried in a thick coat, net hat, and many scarves. At her side slouched a lad no older than sixteen, dressed in a baggy black suit, top hat, and cape. He faced significant issues with acne on his pasty cheeks and used his shirt cuff to wipe chocolate drippings off his lips and chin. He looked like a magician's apprentice.

The coachman was not their headless man.

Alexandra gasped. "You're Geldorf?"

"'The Magnificent!'" the woman assured. She slapped Geldorf's hand as it drifted to pick his nose and finished cleaning his mug with a handkerchief. "Geldorf is always paid upfront."

"I can see why." Alexandra lifted the fee from her pocket. "You must be Misses Magnificent?"

"The mother, yes. I must say, Illyria, you have a bestial house. A slim thing like you should buzz about cleaning with the speediness of a hummingbird. Youth, today. So lazy!"

Alexandra calculated that a pending disaster held better odds than a pending tip. She cringed upon showing them into the drawing room. It had been difficult to find a medium in the British countryside on such short notice. "One and all, I give you, Geldorf the Magnificent!"

Looks of unadulterated disbelief greeted the announcement. Will cracked, "Isn't it past his bedtime?"

The mother claimed the empty chair nearest Simra. He advised her to move, as remaining there would put her in the danger zone of being blown up. She complied and took another.

In a high-pitched, nasal voice, Geldorf squawked, "I bid you mortals greeting and a visceral warning. My power in conjuring spirits lost to the otherworld is unparalleled. Those of weak heart, mind, or bladder should not partake."

Will and Gunnar chuckled, having difficulty holding it together. Alexandra surmised all her team-building efforts were going to ruin. She motioned for everyone to take their positions and form a circle on the rug. Geldorf's finger once more flirted with his nose, and her crew were wise enough to leave vacant the spot beside his favored booger hand.

"Mother! They don't have a table!" Geldorf whined. He tossed back his cape in a huff and took a seat in front of the fireplace. He greedily eyed the potato. "Who shall I summon?"

"In a minor upset in our blind vote, 'Well-endowed monk' has defeated 'Frisky nun' three to two." Alexandra winked at Oliver.

Will and Gunnar pouted, having lobbied hard for the nun.

Alexandra sat and everyone joined hands, with Oliver needing to grasp Will's shoulder to close the circle.

Geldorf's hand felt gooey.

He said, "Proceed around the circle and state your names."

Illyria, Vana, Wadsworth, Harry, and Schwanzus were barked out in quick order.

Alexandra had not seen that coming. She grew troubled that they were contributing to the delinquency of a minor. She winked at Simra, entrusting him to identify when circumstances proved ripe to capture the spirit on film. Everyone closed their eyes and fell silent.

After a minute of tempered breathing, Geldorf called out, "Oh, Well-endowed monk, we bring you gifts from life to death. Commune with us, Well-endowed monk, and move among us."

The entire circle repeated the chant multiple times.

An icy breeze infiltrated the room. Alexandra peeked. While the candles flickered, there were no bites on the potato. Geldorf's slouched posture, flabby cheeks, and limp hold on her hand suddenly became rigid. His eyes dilated, and he stared blankly ahead, mouth ajar, yet offering no words to its drool. She hoped that if he discharged ectoplasm it would not stain her overcoat.

"What heretical wretches herein gathered."

The disembodied voice disseminating from Geldorf sounded nothing like that of a well-hung monk: more so, an old, bitter crone. Its menacing tone starched the backs of all those seated.

"You befoul this house, yee buggering sodomite amongst thee."

Alexandra opened her eyes again. Everyone else already had, and for some unjust reason, they were all looking at her. She shook her head and silently mouthed, *"It's not me!"*

"Oh, yee, once at the right hand of God. Now more suited to wield the right hand of self-pleasure!"

Three options for that one. Alexandra smiled, finally off the hook.

"An aspirant lust of infidelities fouls this fetid air I breathe."

The accusation was fifty-fifty between Hildegard and Gunnar. He twitched first. Judging by how tight Hildegard squeezed her hand, Alexandra judged if this went much deeper, the cleaver would leave Gunnar *schwanzless!*

Geldorf remained entranced, and his mother looked concerned.

Five minutes passed in silence.

Geldorf the Magnificent remained in a deep stupor. He shook violently and emoted in a highly guttural voice of a man—hissing singular words in a strange, ancient tongue. The séance continued devolving into a far more disturbing and serious matter.

"Hither and dither, Wilhelmina, but hid not from mine eyes. Thou hast fled, but we shall soon take you back."

Most turned their heads toward Will, suspecting it a bastardization of his first name, but the soft whimpers Hildegard expelled informed Alexandra differently. Those within the circle became fretful in their seats and close to abandoning the ritual.

Alexandra conjectured Vana had changed her name, Harry was not an anal virgin, Schwanzus held lust for her, and Wadsworth often choked the chicken. It left only her secrets on the chopping block.

Lo-and-behold, what terrible mischief an omnipotent entity could have with that! She closed her eyes and braced for the worst.

"Alas, Alexandra... affianced to the Master. Your five male broods will luxuriate in more blood than Anna, the last pleasured mistress of the Nyírbátor. You shall then reign supreme among the Fallen."

Geldorf's mother stood and shrieked.

A blinding explosion of light violated the proceedings. The ghastly image of a horned demon materialized out of the smoky ether fogging the room. It hovered behind Alexandra, embracing her in its wings.

A curtain on one window smoldered.

Everyone screamed.

Geldorf broke out of his trance and shited himself.

The demon vanished.

The smoke and smell from the ignited flash powder lingered in the air. Alexandra opened her eyes, alarmed, as she had sexually climaxed. She shook free of her funk to witness Simra throwing buckets of water on a burning window, Hildegard passed out, and the shit-stained Geldorf fleeing with his mother.

By the licentious noises emanating from upstairs, it sounded like the monk and nun had belatedly found each other.

Alexandra cried out, "Did we get the photograph, Simra?"

"Yes! I hope Miss Hildegard is still alive."

She was.

Everyone watched as the horse-drawn coach sped off into the night beyond the frosted windowpane.

Alexandra looked at Will. "What's wrong with you?"

Yet ready to share what they all had witnessed, he asked, "Between supplies, building damages, and paying Simra, how much is this job costing you?"

"Quite a lot, I'm afraid." She shrugged. "But you see, we got the photograph. That's what matters."

Will shook his head. "Don't continue with this business of yours. I beseech you!"

"Oh, go smack your salami!" Alexandra stood in a huff. The fire was finally out. She harkened to all, "Let's report to the kitchen to wash dishes before getting disturbingly drunk. On the hop!"

Chapter 15

Switzerland: February 1928

*I*f the Swiss weren't so busy counting their money and formed a navy, they might just rule the world.* Such a supposition stroked Alexandra's thoughts along her arresting train ride over the snow-laden valleys and scenic chasms of the Alps. The surrounding hamlets held magical charm; the railway tunnels and bridges veritable monuments of architectural brilliance. Everything in Switzerland presented as first-rate and aesthetically pleasing, from its multilingual people to its high-altitude living. The Alpine resort town of St. Moritz stood among this wonderland's shrines, and for the coming week, the setting for the first-ever stand-alone Winter Olympic Games.

The American Olympic Association fostered plans of marketing Lake Placid, New York, to host the event in 1932, hence eager for a pictorial account of the international splendor these newfangled games offered.

Alexandra arrived for this assignment ahead of a blizzard, with just enough time to check into the ritzy Kulm Hotel, conduct some overpriced shopping, and get hit by a snowball along a horse-drawn sleigh ride. The storm regulated her first night indoors. As fortune had it, the hotel served as a hub for the games: housing athletes and hosting venues for the opening ceremonies, skating competitions, and a tobogganing *piste* known as the Cresta Run. Alexandra had met a smorgasbord of interesting people over dinner, including the twenty-four-member American team. Her evening flew by in cozy, warm fun.

The following morning, not so much.

The long black wool coat with a gray mink collar and matching sable-brimmed Cossack hat looked warmer in the posh storefront window. She stood in zero-degree weather with a snow-driven wind pummeling away. Her mindset drifted away from the aim of her camera and to the discomfort pulsing her chest. Though raised in Montana, Alexandra tolerated tropical climates far better than frigid, and it was mostly because of her breasts.

As members of the Muthaiga Club and the Kavirondo tribe had no doubt heard by now, they existed.

Since departing Africa, a dream about Jean-Luc De Pauw pestered her. In it, he sat tied to a chair. Beryl paced nearby, cracking a riding crop until he blurted, *"They're small, upturned, and perky!"*

Yet, it was not truly her breasts at the root of Alexandra's grief, but more precisely, her nipples. They grew too pert when stimulated. This cruelty of nature had caused her vast humiliation, particularly in college, as the girls of Hamilton Hall had often teased her in the washroom. They'd also quipped that when cold, men reacted opposite: their testicles rising inward to insulated pockets just behind the kidneys. For this reason, sex lasted longer in winter, since it took time for their return trip to the scrotum, which then allowed the man to jizz.

Alexandra held no plans to test this theory over the coming week, though the heated friction of some heavy petting would rub ideal right about now.

The 464 athletes representing twenty-six countries prepared to enter the *Eispavillion* for the opening parade of nations. Alexandra secured a prime location to photograph the procession in the unceremonious conditions. The storm had swept away the hung flags, banners, and other decorative grandeur. Most of the arena's seats stood empty. She was determined to capture photos that would nullify the event's problematic commencement.

"Are your nipples as frozenly erect as mine, Skendra?"

"Yes, but for reasons other than being attired like a Muscovite runway model."

Alexandra followed her French colleague's gaze at the line of athletes entering the arena. Many were handsome Nordic types. None of them appeared the least bit discomforted by their vacated testicles.

Skendra Lilleth dressed warmer, yet as fashionable, as her American counterpart. Alexandra had met the *Le Matin* newspaper reporter over cocktails, and a bond sprung up. The raven-haired beauty lived in Marseilles, spoke fluent English with a sultry accent, and was proving fun and flashy company.

The pulsating grew intolerable, with the procession mere minutes away. Alexandra hugged herself and jumped up and down, using her gloves to cross-pat her shoulders as if a flagellating arctic ballerina. It surely looked ridiculous, and yet she didn't care.

Skendra shook her head. "Come here, Alexandra, and hug me."

She stopped jumping, stared into Skendra's imperious blue eyes, and complied.

From the grounds of the Kulm Hotel, the lights of the bleached town below sparkled against the frozen shoreline of Lake St. Moritz. Silver-glazed massifs served as sentries around the Engadine Valley, barring for ages the sordid entanglements of the outside world. With the mountain passes again open and fewer flurries to the wind, the games proceeded in fine fashion. Alexandra settled into a routine of taking in a fireside breakfast, covering the events, and dining and dancing in the Kulm's Grand Restaurant to close out each day.

In this mecca for the winter holiday set, the rich unapologetically acted rich, and the beautiful engaged in the indulgences of the beautiful. The Olympics added an eclectic twist to the standard social pudding, and a spurring sentiment of experiencing life to its fullest filled the air.

Alexandra examined the glistening ice of the Cresta Run. She commented to her date, "Before I leave, I want to make a pitch for it. I want to feel the same thrill you feel."

"If I win the gold," he said, "I'll let you wear the medal on the way down."

Only twenty-six Olympians were women. Because of this hormonal imbalance, Alexandra being whisked onto the dance floor stood at most a quick sip of a cocktail away. Many male athletes seemed less consumed with chaste focus on earning a medal than in unleashing their inner horndog. A call for reinforcements was in order. Her hotel suite had an adjoining room. After the opening ceremonies, she'd recruited Skendra and a Swedish skier turned journalist, Inga Nilsson, to abandon their lodgings and settle in.

There was no shortage of athletic or social dramas for the three to cover professionally each day or gossip over at dinnertime. Winter games had been held four years prior in Chamonix, France, as a mere addendum to the perennial Summer Olympics. Unfinished storylines from that competition abounded. The Norwegians had medaled highest, understandably, as skating, skiing, and sledding were practiced in their daily commutes. The imposing Canadian hockey team had humiliated all competitors, outscoring them 132–3 to hoist gold. It caused such a stink, officials eliminated their need to qualify this go-around and placed them in the medal rounds to avoid stirring animosities. Sonja Henie, the Norwegian wunderkind, was now age fifteen, and favored to dominate in figure skating. For the first time since the Great War, German athletes would compete internationally.

Alexandra focused on the American team and capturing the overall spirit of the games. Skendra's journalistic efforts were tuned to the personal narratives of the athletes. Inga fixated on the Scandinavian teams and on claiming unofficial gold in the "sleeping with the most foreign men" categories.

Yet, as events unfolded, scuttlebutt shifted toward an ever-growing mystery—*who were the snowball assailants and how were they getting away with it?*

The attacks came after nightfall—pedestrians pummeled by a well-aimed clump of packed powder. Those using the electric *Strassenbahn* trams were often picked. Despite a strong police presence, the snowballs continued to rain down with inexplicable accuracy. No sighting of the miscreants, or even a trace of their footprints in the snow, could be found. Some believed it the handiwork of local youth, while others professed mountain spirits at play. Suspicion soon swung toward any English-speaking people, as many witnesses reported that after each ambush, they heard the culprits yell, "Bullseye!" Alpine troops were called in to capture the perpetrators.

Despite being a victim, Alexandra found the entire affair hilarious and advantageous. It served as a perfect diversion from *her* unlawful transgressions. The nippy weather had forced her to become an unsolicited hugger. She'd taken to introducing herself to any arbitrary passerby and embracing them for a socially inappropriate duration to siphon their body heat. She went about unfettered in these antics despite concerns of molesting someone who might file a police complaint, which would set off sketched portraits of her being posted throughout town, holding in many languages the caption: *Wanted for frotteurism.*

Since being hit by a snowball her first eve, Alexandra had taken strolls without being targeted. Tonight, she found a man draping her arm for added insulation. She'd met Jennison Heaton during trial runs for the skeleton competition; a suicidal sport of headfirst sleigh riding. The speed of the competitors racing brakeless down the vaunted Cresta Run thrilled her: how they shifted their prone bodies to manage the turns and curves of the half-pipes, the slightest miscalculation away from brutal disaster. Heaton served as the American flag-bearer and was in position to medal. He was among Alexandra's few dance partners who understood her waistline was not three inches lower than many foreign dabblers believed it to be.

They departed the bottom of the piste.

"The town voted to ban women from using it to toboggan," Heaton informed. "Too brittle a sex, they say."

Alexandra frowned, firm in her belief that females should have an equal opportunity to break their bones on the icy track. "Have you ever incurred serious injury?"

He placed a hand over his heart. "Only if you're not there to cheer me on."

"No need to get sappy."

They laughed over their contrived melodramatics and continued to the hotel. She had told him she would not tarnish her professionalism in any amorous affairs. It had not deterred him from seeking her out for innocent American banter.

She asked, "Have you met the Japanese delegation? They seem lost in the ways of the West."

"Just in passing. They're cross-country skiers. Their training methods are curious. They cut down a pine tree, shaved off the branches, and ever since have been lugging it with ropes up a hillside. It must weigh several tons."

"Weird." Alexandra had noticed how polite the eight men sat at their remote table each evening. They would offer gracious smiles and crisp head bows to anyone who passed, even the waiters. No one spoke with them, likely because nobody understood Japanese.

"Tell me more about your roommates," Heaton requested.

Alexandra chuckled. "I hardly know them."

She'd introduced Heaton and other Americans to Skendra and Inga, and good international relations were in the offing. She deemed the French journalist too mature, cold, and sophisticated for him; the type no man would dare cop a feel of on the dance floor. The redheaded Swede came across fairer in figure than face, hypersexual, and as one who'd become consumed in self-doubt if a man *didn't* cop a feel.

Alexandra judged neither right for such an All-American lad as Heaton. He would be a perfect match with a young woman who landed in-between the two, such as herself. The query made her jealous. As a foolhardy girl whose opinions changed quicker than the weather, she believed a guy like Heaton should have better sense than to take her vow of chastity so literally.

Gentlemen can be so infuriating at times. She sighed. "If you must, try for Inga. There might be a line."

"Tomorrow, after my races are over, why don't we go ice skating?"

Alexandra approved the idea. She faced him, reached under the flaps of his wool coat, and adjusted his tie. "Would you mind if we just stood and cuddled awhile?"

Before Heaton could answer, she latched onto him with the adhesiveness of a suckerfish. Five minutes passed. He asked, "Good?"

"A little longer." She placed a hand on his frigid cheek and planted a heated kiss.

Splat!

The precision snowball struck mid-necking right at the juncture of their merged lips. They shook off the shock, wiped clean their faces, and shared a determined look. Without sharing a word, they scooped up snow and sprinted toward their assailants, packing firm their weaponry along the way. Upon reaching the only hiding spot the culprits could have thrown from, they found no one, not even any tracks to betray their route of retreat.

This mystery perplexed Alexandra. The shellacking cooled off her friskiness.

As they ascended the steps to the hotel, a distant disturbance ruffled the crisp air. It sounded like a high-pitched holler of "Bullseye!"

❧

Another gentleman; perhaps civility is yet lost. It was the eve before the closing of the games, and Alexandra was concluding the best week of her life waltzing in the well-mannered arms of one Geoffrey Mason. The Philadelphia-born bloke had answered a newspaper ad seeking a fifth rider to join the United States bobsled team. He would leave St. Moritz with a gold medal. As she reflected on the week, Alexandra judged the Americans to be the politest dancers of the lot and the Argentines the crudest. All past squeezes were now forgiven.

She felt pleased with her photographs, which went beyond the standard mix of victors receiving medals or the actual competitions. Her favorite was an impromptu Ziegfeld Follies chorus line of all the female figure skaters conducting an on-ice version of the can-can. As for the great dramas, the Norwegians again dominated in medaling, with the upstart Americans rising to second. Sonja Henie won gold and was crowned the newest darling of the world. The Canadian juggernaut breezed through their two medal-round contests by a combined score of 25–0, with eyes set on crushing the Swiss come morning.

A Canuck named Frank tapped Mason's shoulder. "May I cut in?"

Having danced before, Alexandra knew his game. She smiled at Mason for his understanding. Contempt for the Canadians ran high, and tempers were on the brink of boiling over. She had made it this far without stirring up an international incident and wanted to finish strong. As they caught up with the dance flow, she warned, "It's a waltz, Frank, and not *aboot* riding the slope of my arse, eh!"

Despite the pending gold medal hockey match, his breath reeked of alcohol. "I want to plant my flag in you."

Alexandra simmered; past her tolerance for Arctic men pining to forage south of the equator. She glanced at the Japanese delegation sitting inert in a corner and stormed off the dance floor. Running to her table, she downed champagne and slammed the glass onto the floor.

Skendra and Inga put the wooing of the Austrian ski team on hold to check in with her. The hall rang so boisterous they could barely hear her screech, "We live in a world where the vulgar attain riches and they cast the genteel to the shadows. I won't abide it!"

Her two colleagues followed her across the crowded room. They settled at the table hosting the Japanese. Alexandra asked, "Do any of you gentlemen speak English...? *Française...? Svenska?*"

The delegation looked up at their visitors, stunned. They stood and bowed. After a brief discussion, one stepped forward. In all her travels, Alexandra had never come across a Japanese man with facial hair, but this one sported a goatee, which gave him a low-key hipster appeal.

He said, "Yes, English."

"My name is Alexandra, and these are my roommates, Skendra and Inga. We'd love to share a dance with you men of the rising sun."

The man took her hand and kissed it. "I am Subaru. *Konbanwa!*"

"Hai!" Yes proved the only Japanese word Alexandra knew other than *sayonara*.

Subaru lined up his team for introductions. There was a Minoru, a Sakuta, a Takeo, a Takeji, a Motohiko, and of all things... a second Subaru! As the women walked the tight reception line, each man crisply bowed and kissed their extended hands in the best vestiges of chivalry. It amused Skendra and made Inga giggly.

An eighth Japanese man arrived after introductions concluded.

Alexandra stepped forward to greet him. *"Konbanwa.* My name is Alexandra Bathenbrook. I'm very pleased to meet you. *Hai!"*

"Hai!" the man retorted. *"Isowaku Fugakyu."*

Alexandra's mouth fell ajar. She lost all sanity and slapped him across the face. He looked about, shocked, and it seemed the entire ballroom stopped in its collective tracks to glare at her.

Subaru rushed over. "What is this? He is trainer. His name is Isowaku Fugakyu!"

"I'm so sorry!" Alexandra wanted to melt into the carpet. "I'm from Montana... It's how we greet people... Would anyone care to dance?"

Subaru burst out laughing, which inspired his teammates to laugh along. He translated her offer, and two others stepped forward to lead the women onto the dance floor as the band kicked off a slow melody. He claimed Alexandra and displayed knowing a thing or two about smooth-stepping. *"Sugoi kirei.* In English language, this means, 'You look lovely.'"

She blushed. "Will Isowaku dance with me? I feel like a scoundrel."

"Isowaku no dance." Passing his men fielding their own European lovelies, Subaru shouted, *"Sutekina o shiri!"*

They both snickered and responded, *"Hai!"*

"Sutekina o shiri," he repeated softly to his dance partner.

"Hai!" Alexandra sighed. It felt so refreshing to be in the arms of a true gentleman. So mature. So friendly!

The song ended, and they applauded the orchestra.

Skendra departed, mentioning an Austrian rooster in need of a good plucking. Alexandra and Inga returned to the delegation's table to further coddle Eurasian goodwill. They summoned a waiter to fill the champagne bucket. Inga lit a cigarette and tittered, "I find you little men most captivating."

Soon everyone sat drinking bubbly and smoking cigarettes.

The frigid air had taken a toll on Alexandra's back. She rotated her torso from side to side and placed her hands on the small of her spine to thrust out her chest. Isowaku remarked on her discomfort.

Alexandra interpreted his feedback as best she could. *"Hai!"*

The orchestra ended its break and opened with "The Charleston."

To her surprise, Subaru took a stance and extended a hand. "You know this 'Charleston?'"

She took up his offer. "So well, I'm banned from South Carolina!"

It became apparent that jazz was even conquering Japan. Subaru performed moves never seen before. Other couples stepped aside to watch, with loafers rising from their seats to join in on clapping.

None would soon forget the display put on by a daughter of Helena and a son of Hiroshima at the Swiss Winter Olympics.

❧

"Keep rocking me, Isowaku. It feels *so* good. God, yes! Yes! Break me. Break me in two!"

"Hai!"

Alexandra drifted into ecstasy. Sharing time with those holding no comprehension of her language allowed her to speak uninhibitedly.

160

What he was doing to her felt rapturous. "Jostle me hard, you magnificent Asian Heracles! Rock me! Manhandle me!"

Isowaku stopped his gyrations upon noting the door open. He stood bent at the waist, looking down at the floor. The Japanese team, Inga, and a spattering of foreign guests peered in, inspecting the commotion.

Alexandra glanced over. She lay dangling the air atop him, her back against his back, their arms interlocked at the elbows in his attempts to apply an exercise to fix her spine. Thankfully, they wore clothing and faced in opposite directions. Everyone but the foreigners shuffled in.

Someone in Japan had forgotten to book a reservation for the delegation, so the hotel offered a tearoom as a residence. Mats were spread about, hanging laundry strewed by the fireplace, and a lingering aroma of boiled rice and sushi tickled the nostrils.

Isowaku placed his patient down and joined his countrymen. They raided the cupboard and started changing into snow clothing and Alpine boots. Subaru zipped up his bleached jumpsuit and affixed a bandana imprinted with the rising sun and kana symbols across his forehead.

They were Japanese men on a mission.

"Will you join?" Inga asked as she wiggled into an extra snow suit. "Some adventure with a log. I so love learning of other cultures."

Alexandra had dressed for dancing, not foraging a snowy hillside.

Subaru handed her some gear and a bandana. As her back felt better, the studded boots fit, and the snowsuit hugged cozily, she was all in. They all gloved up, tied firm their hoods, and marched out of the hotel using a secondary exit. She had no idea what she was getting herself into, but then again, rarely did.

They trooped out of town through the frigid air and up a wooded hill. Subaru explained to his female outsiders his men were preparing for the Onbashira festival, which was conducted every seven years and highlighted by the delivery of fir trees to replace the pillars of sacred Shinto shrines. The means of transport entailed riding the felled trunks down a mountainside. He failed to mention that many people were crushed, mangled, or killed while attempting such.

Under a bent crescent moon perched above the nearby peaks, they reached the summit and their trial pole, which was very thick, long, and wrapped with holding ropes. The men pushed it into final position at the edge of the slope. Being gentlemen, they allowed the ladies first seats.

One by one, the men mounted the log and took hold of a rope. The log teetered on the ledge.

The last of them jumped aboard in front.

It dipped, and they were off, rushing down the hill and cutting across the ice on a spinning death pole. With all the joyous howls and blinding snow kicking up, it was difficult to ascertain who was first and last to fall off... but fall off everyone did. Alexandra had not lasted long, but at least she was not crushed. She popped her head out of the snow and watched the pilotless log crash into a row of evergreens, doubting such a sport would ever make its way into the Olympics. She rushed down the slope to join the others.

Everybody reunited uninjured and passed ceramic flasks of saké.

"Our ride, bad," Subaru acknowledged, "but survival good, yes?"

"Hai!" She took the flask and sampled the saké.

"I so love learning about other cultures," Inga prattled. She was having a fabulous evening spending no time on her back. "Some wish for return to hotel to play drinking game. They call it *bukkake* and say it is very satisfying. Will you join?"

Alexandra wondered if the Swede were a prodigy who'd learned Japanese in an hour or merely drunk. Subaru had earlier asked her to take a last tour of the hamlet to find harmony in its splendor, reflect on their poor athletic showing, and renew their spirits of transient imperfection. Choosing between the groups presented a sticky situation. She elected to stay with Subaru and two others to take in the village.

Inga departed the forest with five of the delegation.

Alexandra asked, "Where are we going?"

Subaru said, "Last night to catch *wabi-sabi.* Seek it in sacred task."

Alexandra worried if she'd made the tidier choice. They picked up their pace once quitting the outskirts for civilian territory. As they were heading for the lake and lower village, she hoped *wabi-sabi* was not Japanese for "ice-fishing." They trespassed dark alleyways, with an occasional jump down an embankment needed to avoid well-plowed cobbled streets. Both Subarus handled themselves marvelously in the wintry conditions; Takeo, not so much.

The main thoroughfares stood filled with revelers leaving the many galas marking the end of the games. Subaru halted his posse behind a stretch of flat-roofed stone buildings two stories in height. They sipped saké and searched the snowbanks for something.

He turned to face Alexandra. "Triad is safe. Three on one, not safe. Moon very bad."

She squinted her eyes, unsure if *wabi-sabi* meant "outdoor sex with multiple partners" and wondered how he knew she was ovulating. "No *wabi-sabi.*"

Takeo unburied a grappling hook. Subaru pointed up. *"Wabi-sabi."*

So, it meant, "outdoor sex with multiple partners on a roof." While her nipples rose in favor, the rest of her stayed reluctant. "No *wabi-sabi.*"

With the grappling hook in place, the men climbed up without her. Subaru motioned for her to wait. Alexandra watched as the three jumped the slim gap to the next building, and then the next, as nimble and ghostly as snow ninjas. She remained alone, hugging herself for warmth. After ten minutes, she thought of returning to the hotel.

"Bullseye!"

Without the faintest warning, they were back, canon-balling off the roof into a snowbank not twenty feet away. They extricated themselves and huddled as police whistles sounded.

Subaru grabbed Alexandra's hand, and they set off running.

They traversed a loop and could now watch the police searching the area they had just reigned terror.

Without pause, Subaru-two unleashed the grappling hook.

Subaru pointed skyward. *"Wabi-sabi?"*

Alexandra wondered what grade of cheese fondue they served in Swiss prisons. *"Hai!"*

After the three ninjas climbed, they pulled her up the final few feet and took extra caution, as triads were invisible, but quartets were not. One rooftop... a second... then a third were crossed in a stealthy crouch through the moonlight. They settled on a ledge with a perfect vantage point to observe a plethora of potential marks milling among the shops and twinkling streetlamps below.

They all packed their projectiles.

Those standing at a tram stop appeared ripe for snowballing, but Subaru considered it better to wait for those enjoying a horse-drawn sleigh ride, as the man who could strike a moving target is viewed with the highest esteem. He also mentioned their love for American baseball as an explanation for their uncanny accuracy.

"You jerks hit me twice," she chided.

Subaru shared what she said. They all snickered. "You kiss man... *Splat...* Most glorious!"

Alexandra could only laugh. She had not come this far not to splatter someone herself. If the Japanese team had placed as much preparation in mastering cross-country skiing as in their *wabi-sabi* strategies, they might not have finished at the bottom of the boards, but every man has his priorities. They listened for the hum of the electrified *Strassenbahn* or the jingling bells of a horse carriage.

Everyone broke a grin once both sounded simultaneous!

Once given the signal, Alexandra unleashed her barrage. Her tosses hit the tram, but no passengers, which in her mind stroked good enough.

They backtracked to where they had climbed up; the thrill infusing them high on adrenaline. As each man jumped off, he yelled a single word. It was not "bullseye" at all, but something similar in Japanese.

The last to go, Alexandra picked out a snowdrift, made the sign of the cross, and followed suit. *"Banzai!"*

∾

A knock on the door jostled Alexandra from a deep sleep. She sat up with a sense of dread filling her hazy mind. *Are the police here to arrest me for my frotteuristic proclivities? What if Subaru got caught cold-handed, placed under interrogation, and spilled my name as an accomplice?* The knock sounded again. It did not rattle like the hard thump of a policeman.

She slid into her silk bathrobe and answered the door.

Jennison Heaton stood in the hallway. "We can sneak onto the Cresta. Get your things."

"I'll meet you in the lobby," she said, pushing back her unruly hair.

Alexandra headed for her closet and hastily tossed on this or that. The door to the adjoining room stood ajar. She went to close it and noticed a flicker of candlelight. She stuck her head in. At the frost-laced window, looking off into the world, stood Skendra smoking a cigarette. The candlelight danced upon her flawless nude body. Alexandra interpreted how the French temptress appeared—plush black hair spilled across her shoulders, her ample bosom—cast a favorable replica of her own mother when in her twenties. She reflected on what fun it would have been to have Emma along on such a trip, which brought a fleeting smile.

In being distracted, she barely took notice of the naked man tied spread-eagle across the bed. The French journalist dabbling in kinky behavior surprised her, but not the Austrian, as Germanic people were weird that way. Skendra shifted her eyes and stared into the nearby floor mirror. A playful grin lifted her lips, while her gaze mocked, *I can see you but will pretend not to.*

Flustered, Alexandra retreated and fled out the door. It relieved her to find Heaton waiting in the lobby, skeleton sled at the ready. They headed out into the coming morning.

Along their walk, she whispered a prayer, thankful fine young men such as Jennison still existed. He'd been spared the call to forfeit his life on the battlefield because of his age.

Like her, those of a more fortunate generation.

The international camaraderie and uplifting spirit she'd discovered at these Olympic Games etched into her a belief that the "war to end all wars" had truly come to pass. It was something to be grateful for.

As most Europeans believed Americans to be pompous pariahs, they sang "America the Beautiful" along their ascent so as not to disappoint. By the time they reached the top of the Cresta Run, Alexandra felt calmer. Being around other Americans and not having a single cup of tea had refreshed her sense of identity.

They rested before getting down to business.

Below, the serene beauty of the sleeping town spread before them— a panorama of purest ice and snow.

"I'll get it started, and then you jump on."

"Check!" Alexandra took a deep breath as Heaton positioned his sled. Tempting fate again in the Swiss Alps seemed ridiculous, but the world considered her chosen pilot the best at his trade, and fortune still favored the brave. "Aren't you forgetting something?"

He reached into his coat and placed his Olympic gold medal ribbon over her head. "Here we go!"

Alexandra readied her footing.

Heaton dashed forward and dove headfirst onto the board.

She set off, timed her jump perfectly, and wrapped her arms around his neck short of strangulation. They picked up velocity and zipped down the icy track at breakneck speed.

All she could think with her hair flying wild and her soul fully singing was what a grand time it was to be young, healthy, and to feel so free.

Chapter 16

Florida: March 1928

The streetcar ran south down Palafox Street, toward the bay, on a cloudless morning for sailing. Alexandra leaned against a window. A sack of groceries filled her hands, and her long hair kicked up in the warm breeze from under her beret. Holding additional bags beside her stood Charles Thompson. He seemed an ostensibly decent Floridian businessman of age thirty, and one eager to take his new yacht to sea. Alexandra had been wary of taking this job, but the fact that he sported a solid chin aided a good first impression. He'd likewise picked up her sole suitcase; her winterwear having been mailed back to London. They'd purchased staples to stock the yacht's galley, with Thompson stating plans to earn dinner by catching fish along the way.

He planned for a five-day voyage across the Gulf of Mexico to bring his ship home to Key West. He'd mentioned having recruited a friend to help work the helm, sails, and riggings.

"You don't strike me, Mister Thompson, as one of those laid-back 'conch' types."

"It's more a state of mind. And just call me Karl. Everyone on the island goes by a nickname, and for whatever reason that is mine."

They disembarked a few blocks from the Pensacola Yacht Club. She wanted to pry more information out of "Karl" before boarding. "Have you much sailing experience?"

"I've taken out lesser crafts. Never tried night sailing, but nothing like learning by doing. Hemmy's in it for the fishing." Noting her alarmed expression, he added, "We'll be fine."

Third-party involvement troubled Alexandra. She had yet to meet this "Hemmy" whom Thompson stated was new to Key West and an acquaintance of only a few weeks. She'd taken the assignment because it would provide a free berth and board to get a step closer to British Guiana. It filled her with apprehension as a young woman; isolated with two strange men, adrift in an unforgiving sea. Thompson admitted he had only sent her his letter as a lark since her newspaper advertisement held a waggish appeal.

As they stepped onto the pier, he pointed *her* out. "She's the Dickies of Tarbert, gaff-rigged ketch." He spoke with the pride of a new father, or at least a man who had worked hard to attain one simple dream.

Alexandra's face lit up. She was a beauty.

The ketch checked in at forty-eight feet long, 11.5 across the beam, and featured a Perkins Saber diesel engine for when the wind was down. Varnished wood planked its hull and deck. Its canvas sails were down; the mainmast to the fore and smaller mizzen astern.

Manning the deck making final preparations stood Hemmy.

From a distance, Alexandra gauged him to be of similar age to Thompson, but they were two different breeds of men. The refined skipper would set sail clean-shaven and wearing a tie. His bullish first mate sported a dark mustache, a stubble-covered jawline, and wore a stained Breton shirt over rolled-up trousers. Noting how vigorously he moved about testing the riggings, she suspected this Hemmy to be a hard-boiled, lean-forward type of guy.

He hopped onto the pier. "She's all set, Karl."

"I'm Alexandra." She extended a hand. "You must be Hemmy?"

He took hold of her suitcase, nodded, and boarded without a word.

Alexandra stepped aboard, flashing Hemmy a sour glance. She adjusted the red neckerchief dangling from her blue middy blouse. If her body were to wash ashore in the coming days, the authorities would start their investigation at the nearest French naval yard or inquire along Broadway if one of their Rockettes was missing.

Hemmy's firm gaze weighed on her as she took the companionway. He stood arms folded; cheerless eyes squinted at the sun.

"What is it, sir?"

"I'm contemplating if you can swim."

"As swift as a mermaid," she responded, before descending into the cabin. It held multiple sleeping berths, a gas cooker, sink, and head, all outfitted in upscale mahogany and brass fittings.

They would sail in comfort as long as they didn't capsize her.

On the dinette table rested a copy of *The Ingenious Nobleman Sir Quixote of La Mancha.*

The first three days aboard presented a whirlwind of desperate activity and breathless learning on the fly. As an experienced angler, Thompson possessed many photographs of himself holding an impressive catch on deck or dock. He wished to add images of a sailor's struggles captured in the moment rather than after the fact.

Through her camera lens, Alexandra found the grit and sweat of big-game fishing appeared akin to the strains of sailing. A stressed rod bent like the boat's tilt in a steep leeward heel. Blood-flushed forearms battling a sizeable Amberjack burst veins no less red than when gybing the mainsail. Teeth clenched in either endeavor.

She attained splendid shots of Thompson hand-feeding a pod of dolphins racing alongside the hull. Her favorite captured Hemmy's prolonged duel with a swordfish; the prize being his forlorn gaze after his line snapped to the indomitable force of the victor jumping the surface. Everyone played a role. Hemmy would reel in dinner, Thompson would cook up a well-seasoned tarpon, and Alexandra had taken command in serving meals and breakfast preparations. The only time reserved for leisurely chats over coffee spiked with Jamaican rum came at sunset. Alexandra came to trust Thompson implicitly, but attaining any sense of Hemmy remained elusive. With brief comments here and there, she gathered he had recently moved from Paris. He acted gentlemanly enough to leave the deck when a rain shower afforded her a quick wash in the buff. Otherwise, he placed more attention on ignoring her than casting any interest or a favorable eye.

Most of their time, however, focused on mastering the intricacies of sailing. Outsmarting the swift fickleness of wind and surf required full insight and constant adjustments. Thompson used the advantage of fair weather to teach his novices basic nautical skills such as the "points of sail" and how to trim the sails when heading up or ease the sheets when bearing away. Alexandra soon flashed more confidence in manning the helm than in driving a car, as there were no tedious street signs to ignore.

They took the precaution of keeping two on deck, which lent for little rest. Their course remained southeasterly, with favorable morning winds shifting west each afternoon. On the third day, they found anchorage near St. Petersburg, which would allow for a sound night's sleep.

Alexandra wrapped up washing the dishes as the men sat playing cards at the galley's table. At sea, on the move, the pitching of the boat went unnoticed, but now anchored, the wakes stirred by passing vessels made balance a persistent nuisance. It was close-quarters living, and she planned to go topside and read by lantern light once wrapping up her cleaning. Until then, Thompson continued in further sailing instruction.

He lifted his eyes off his poker hand. "Did you get that, Alexandra?"

She repeated verbatim, "'If another boat is approaching, port tack gives way to starboard tack.'"

"You've picked up the rules of sailing most astutely."

"It's clean and logical." Half-facetiously, she added, "It's everything else in life that remains so very confusing."

"We can deal you in next hand," offered Hemmy.

"Disturb a game amongst chums? I resent being the only one aboard without a nickname."

The men placed their cards down. Thompson said, "Name it."

"A nickname must derive from others," she countered. "If you can fashion one meeting my approval, I'll join the game. Mind you, 'Bumsy' and 'Cheeky' have previously been rejected."

Thompson rubbed his chin. Hemmy tapped a finger to his cheek. Both smiled but elicited nothing.

She rolled her eyes, figuring their silence veiled saucy options. "May I borrow this book by Miguel de Cervantes? Is it interesting?"

"You've never read *Don Quixote*?" asked Hemmy. "No wonder life makes no sense to you."

"I read voraciously. What is it about?"

"What is it about?" Thompson repeated. He continued rubbing his chin. Hemmy's finger was still tapping his cheek. They looked at each other. Thompson blinked. "It's about a *quest*. The noble mission to overcome life's trials without conceding one's courage or honor. To be better far than you are."

To Alexandra, *Don Quixote* sounded like the fanciful delusions of an impossible dreamer. "The world is too overbearing to meet such impeccable standards. What say you, Hemmy?"

"Thus, the challenge of the quest. It's a book a man can better understand."

The nonchalant manner in which he said it rang like a shot across her bow. "Are you saying that I, among those of the fairer sex, cannot grasp the importance of courage and honor?"

"I'm not saying that." He lifted his uncompromising dark eyes to her. "I'm saying it's *different*."

She sat, not wanting to pitch battle on wobbly legs. "I might have entertained such argue from my brothers. They've been to war and would have stated it without generic ridicule of half the planet."

"I've been to war," Hemmy snapped, "and only speak for me. Have *you* been to war?"

He had her there. "My father taught me that courage and honor must be daily affairs."

"Yet, it is a discussion unlikely held with a mother. Whatever your brothers have told you of war, they shared with you most protectively. I won't burden you with the reason."

"As they are not here," Alexandra challenged, "tell me of your war experience in fullest brutality. I've noticed the scars on your legs. Perhaps your candid words will leave me enlightened."

"My personal affairs are not your concern," Hemmy rumbled. "Seek illumination by asking your brothers to man up and teach you about life. Better yet, read the book!"

"Now take it easy, Hem," Thompson pleaded. "Points well taken."

Alexandra shot up from the table. Her impulse to fight shifted to flight, and her body quivered under the weight of Hemmy's jutted gaze. She fired her last salvo in a composed, but much-shaken voice. "My brother William lost an arm and half his face at Amiens. They obliterated my Thomas at Cambrai. How more vivid, *Hemmy*, do you expect them to be?"

With that, she fled the galley for the deck, entertaining thoughts of jumping overboard and swimming for shore.

Thirty pages into *Don Quixote,* she heard the footsteps. Alexandra sat cross-legged at the bow, her lantern flickering with the bobbing lights of the other moored vessels within the harbor. She did not grant her visitor a look and continued to focus on the novel between slow puffs on a cigarette. She knew it was Hemmy. If he were seeking direction, he could try his luck with the sexton.

She held no interest in fostering friendly social bearings.

"I tried to join up in 1918," he said, settling beside her and peering at the sea. "Unfit because of poor vision... Me! I left my newspaper job in Missouri to drive a Red Cross ambulance in Italy."

Alexandra lifted her eyes. The fighting along the Isonzo River had been brutal. Hemmy related that the Italians feared Austro-Hungarians, who stormed the trenches in sheepskin cloaks wielding primitive weapons such as war hammers and spiked maces. He'd arrived after the disaster of Caporetto, with the front collapsed to the gates of Venice and the Italian Army in disarray. Soldiers were being lined up and executed for cowardice. The battle line had stabilized along the Piave River.

"Just months in, I was bringing up provisions when a mortar hit," he continued, taking a seat. "It tore two soldiers next to me into pieces. I took shrapnel carrying another man to the rear."

Alexandra's sympathetic gaze offered peace. "I've asked many men about their experiences in the war, not to pry, but to better understand how they persevere. My brother has self-exiled for his injuries. He will know nothing of love or happiness unless I can drag him back into the world of the living. I reckon it is among my *quests.* How do you cope?"

Sailboats were built to get away from such thoughts. Hemmy tossed his indomitable manner overboard. "I'm a writer, so I write."

She smiled. "And what has been the hardest for you, if I may ask?"

"Coming to terms they labeled me 'unfit to serve.'" The corner of Hemmy's lip that had lifted collapsed back down. "The needs placed on a man to act bravely weigh daily. There is no shortage of rogues who have abandoned such callings, but to most men, a single lapse in honor proves forever haunting. We are born with less a fear of facing certain death than endure the lifelong shame of having tucked tail and run."

"My father served in South Africa. He told me of an artillery officer who found a white feather on his cot after abandoning his field gun to the Boers at Colenso. In seeing it, the gunner stepped outside his tent, lifted revolver to head, and fired."

"That is what I speak of." Hemmy exhaled hard. "We do not spare such things from the women in our lives out of vanity or disregard, but out of love. Will any of this help you with your brother?"

"It has helped me to understand that he deserves my forgiveness," she said, determining herself an awful and selfish person. "Thank you for this chat. I hope you write great works."

He stood to leave. "Long two days ahead. You should retire."

She felt too worn out to sleep. "I need to catch up on better judging men, and so much else. I finally have a book to guide me."

He smiled. "I introduced myself curtly. My name is Ernest."

"And I remain Alexandra," she teased.

"Karl and I settled that. For this voyage, you are 'Dulcinea.'"

She thought it held a certain flair. "Will I like this nickname?"

Hemmy headed down the companionway. "Quit malingering and read the book."

The following day, Alexandra read aloud to her boatmates as they harnessed a favorable breeze and sailed it for all it was worth.

On their last morning, a red sky greeted them.

The wind and surf picked up, and a squall along the western horizon started chasing them with a gnashing intent to its lightning and thunderclaps. They affixed life vests, donned slickers, and went about battening down the hatches and doubling the lines. Every decision to stay ahead of the beast held grave consequences. It worried Alexandra in seeing the men whisper and flash askance looks her way, but Hemmy had stated the manly code of keeping the darkest details private.

They raced within view of the island, with only traces of rain pinging the deck. Thompson ordered the sails dropped so he could bring them home on diesel. Soon, the shoreline ran but a hundred yards off.

They had made it.

Hemmy unexpectedly cut the engine. Thompson seemed fidgety. He said, "We need a word, Dulcinea."

Alexandra presented herself. "What is it, Skipper?"

He asked, "Can you take off your slicker and shoes?"

She complied. It left her in a thin camisole under her life vest and a high-waist wrap skirt.

"We've been talking. You see, I'm happily married, and Hemmy's recently remarried, and—"

"And you want fashion tips for beach attire to purchase for your wives!" she chanced.

"—and we're worried how it might appear coming into port with a young woman aboard," Thompson finished. "Island folk love to gossip. So, with you looking how you look, untoward rumors—"

Hemmy, having little patience for elongated sentences, barged in with, "He's taking forever to say we don't want the town to think we brought along a prostitute."

"An extremely high-end prostitute, mind you," Thompson specified, wiping his brow. "And—"

"And in the finest tradition of knight-errant extraordinaire, *Hidalgo Don Quijote de la Mancha,* you plot to disguise me as a man to safeguard my reputation from such scurrilous tomes of dishonor!"

"Well... that, too," Thompson said, "but mostly we wish to spare ourselves any marital strife. I'm afraid we must throw you overboard."

Before Alexandra could protest, Hemmy scooped her up and sent her airborne over the side. As she cursed their decision, he advised, "Swim to shore and walk up to Duval Street. We'll meet you outside the Strand Theater and take you out to dinner. *Hasta luego!*"

Alexandra could bob the surf in a huff or get swimming.

She got swimming.

❧

The island's power was out, and Alexandra found herself a storm refugee trapped in an otherwise empty restaurant. She held plans to check into the La Concha Hotel and then catch the ferry to Havana out of Trumbo Point. Thompson and Hemmy had placed calls to their wives to drive down to collect them, but love only ran so deep, so they remained stranded. After dinner, they tried poker by candlelight, but playing for peanuts became a bore.

Alexandra broke out her travel portfolio and ushered them from Papua to Switzerland to pass the time. While speaking of her follies in Africa, Hemmy showed great interest.

"And that's how I ended up near-naked in the acacia tree."

"Are there any pictures of that in here?" asked Hemmy.

She pointed to a photograph of her bare feet just above the impaled lion. "I have destroyed all other evidence."

They shared a friendly laugh. If Hemmy ever ventured to Kenya to hunt, she could see him matching up with Bror Blixen, though they'd waste a lot of time arm-wrestling.

Thompson remained perplexed about her business concept. He asked, "Will you realize a profit?"

"Not likely," she projected. "Regardless, I've walked in the footsteps of Jesus and photographed the snows of Kilimanjaro. Someday, I hope to be a contributing photographer for *National Geographic*."

The torrential rain flooded Duval Street with a torrent of water even a frisky salmon could not surmount. The two young men staffing the joint swept out the creeping lake formed at the front doorway.

Alexandra stood to stretch out her back. A brilliant flash filled the windows, and the ensuing boom followed close behind. "Let's give five-card draw another go."

Thompson shuffled the deck. "What's the ante?"

"How about an article of clothing?" Hemmy suggested.

Alexandra snorted, judging the idea madcap. "I think not."

"Strip poker. First one naked has to run two blocks and back."

"Do I need to remind we live here?" Thompson asked. They were all down to their driest essentials. "I have six articles on. You only changed into two. As for Dulcinea?"

Alexandra wore her sailor outfit, a lace camisole, and with undies, came in at four. She asked, "Where do you come up with these bohemian ideas, Hemmy?"

"Paris, where else?" He was sticking his neck out, only wearing a sweater and pants. "I played in mixed company at this quaint cafe along Montparnasse. Fortunately for all those participating, Gertrude Stein is an excellent card player. No one's outside anyway."

Oh, to be one of the boys, she tinkered. *Why not?* "I'm in!"

Thompson was cornered. He asked the workers, "Do you guys mind if we play strip poker?"

The two men rested their brooms and looked at him, puzzled, then to Alexandra. One said, "Sure... and good luck to you and Hemmy!"

"Let's hope the electricity stays out." Thompson dealt out the cards.

Alexandra moaned and tossed three back. "Goodbye, blouse."

Hemmy won the round with two pair. Thompson lost his tie and Alexandra her top. The restaurant staffers hailed a new hero.

Thompson shuffled and dealt again. Alexandra kicked back two, then sighed. The dealer took the round with three jacks.

She peered over at the workers, who would knight him if it within their power. Circumstances grew dire. She slid out of her panties and tossed them atop her blouse lying on the floor.

As she surmised from his forearms, Hemmy had a hairy chest.

"Anyone like to bow out?" Thompson asked. "No shame in it."

Alexandra matched Hemmy's stoic gaze with her own. She was down to only her skirt and camisole; he, to his pants. He smirked but refused to blink. She pleaded, "I need a winner, Karl. Deal away."

Hemmy picked up his first five cards, offering no hint as to his take on them. "What I like about you, Dulcinea, is you can act one of the boys without being any less of a lady."

She thought it a superb compliment. "What I like about you, Ernest, will be the sight of your pale buttocks as you sprint through the rain."

The moment of truth arrived. After the draw, Alexandra held three sevens. She showed her hand. Hemmy groaned and presented two pair.

Thompson folded and removed his sweater vest.

As for the hovering workers, paradise lay lost.

Hemmy walked to the door. Everyone followed.

The street remained pitch dark, and the odds of being struck by lightning appeared even-money. Alexandra said, "It's time, Ernest, to run where the buck-naked dare not go."

Once his pants dropped, Hemmy shot off like a rocket. He displayed remarkable speed running with the current, but at the turn, he slowed down. They all cheered him on.

Alexandra shielded her eyes, taking one peek. "You threw the last hand, didn't you, Karl?"

He only chuckled and patted her shoulder.

She shouted, "Naked man afoot!" to reignite Hemmy's pace.

Somewhere lost in the night, a ship's bell tolled.

The electric streetlamps flickered all at once, allowing observers to take full heed of Hemmy: a man among men.

Chapter 17

British Guiana: April 1928

Alexandra arrived in Georgetown from Cuba aboard a United Fruit Company Caribbean banana boat transporting rotted fruit and ten thousand flies. Such a fragrant passage left her unbathed and desperate for a good meal. This upper corner of South America stood dreadfully humid and a few decades behind the times. While she waited outside the customs building, melting under the midday sun, nothing of the port's ballyhoos came as a surprise. Moored freighters were being loaded with bales of rice and sugarcane. Sun-wrinkled farmers peddled plantains, and fishermen yelled out the going price for their fly-ridden catches.

Few automobiles rumbled over the dusty roads. An open-air bus ground to a halt. A sweaty crowd circled it, tossing up their belongings to a man standing on its roof.

Outside of the white colonials, the denizens held lineage to African slaves brought over by the Dutch or indentured servants from the Indian subcontinent who had arrived unchained. Only a few native Indians milled about. Regardless of ancestry, everyone went about their business dressed in light, loose clothing, wore some style of a hat, and sweated despite the waving of hand-held fans, improvised hat fans, or even flip-flopping empty hands. It surprised Alexandra that her father did not await her. She placed down her heavy Globe-Trotter leather suitcase and pushed back her sunhat to wipe her brow, quickly taken to cool fantasies entailing ice and lemonade.

Alexandra had yet to grasp being a millionaire. She splurged on hotels and bought trendy clothing, but such living seemed peculiar. Growing up, she lacked nothing other than access to her trust fund and attention. She had gotten by with financial support from her father and Will to go to college, travel, and have a few dollars left in her pockets for books, meals, and mischief. For this reason, after waiting an hour, her instincts favored walking to her lodging instead of hopping aboard a donkey-cart taxi. A government car pulled up, interrupting her exodus.

A uniformed patrol officer presented himself. "Miss Bathenbrook... fullest apologies for our delay."

She held no clue how he knew her. "What is this about, sir?"

"We are here via Government House to see to your transportation needs," the officer attested. "Your father's ship from Puerto Cabello is delayed. If you please..."

The driver loaded her suitcase and opened the back door for her. She slid in, and they were off. They passed a group of sailors enjoying shore leave from the Royal Navy cruiser docked at the harbor. The car came to a halt in the capital's mercantile district. Alexandra entered a boutique, closing in on the vapors. She kissed the young Guianese girl who handed her a glass of iced tea sweetened with molasses.

The elderly proprietor stepped forward. "Miss Bathenbrook, such a pleasure to be of service. Government House wishes us to attend to your formalwear needs."

A hive of seamstresses swarmed in from the sewing room and measured Alexandra out, jotting down numbers and running their tape as she did her best imitation of Da Vinci's *Vitruvian man*. She had planned out her wardrobe for going birding in the jungle, with no gumption for any need for a lavish evening dress.

The proprietor promised that the custom-fitted garments would be delivered within hours, and once more, the patrol officers whisked Alexandra away. They drove to Woodbine House. If one were to stay in Guiana, there stood no better place. The guesthouse had hosted Edward, Prince of Wales, during his royal visit five years earlier, and it remained the premier forum for high-society soirées.

The flower-filled grounds spread well-manicured and peaceful. A

Guianese bellhop and maître d'hôtel stood waiting for her arrival.

"Miss Bathenbrook, so honored by your stay," the maître d'hôtel said. "The governor has asked that we see to your every comfort."

With their mission completed, the patrolmen tipped their caps and departed. Alexandra's suitcase was already in tow as the hotel manager escorted her to a shaded table on the sun patio. Dwarf palms and crimson canna lilies ornamented the courtyard. A glass pitcher of iced tea, topped with lemon rinds, made the perfect centerpiece.

A smiling waiter poured out the first round.

As she lifted her drink, Alexandra paused, unsure if *iced* tea fell under her theorem on British indoctrination techniques. Being parched, she erred it did not. Two months free from the clutches of the empire's surreptitious nectar had allowed her to detoxify. She had said *nil* zero times, no longer pronounced schedule as *shed-ule*, and when the last time she'd uttered *whence* proved anyone's guess. An impulse to start a flower garden had subsided, Yorkshire pudding once again tasted repulsive, and even her teeth appeared healthier in the mirror.

Two cheerful local girls delivered trays of food. They passed to Alexandra a posy of pink and white sacred lotuses. "Miss Bathenbrook... so lovely you visit our country."

"They're beautiful. Who arranged for this?"

The bashful girl smiled. "Guiana be happy you're here."

The girls left to get a vase, leaving Alexandra to her feast. Served were fried plantains marinated in coconut milk, chicken curry with rice, and a fruit plate holding her favorite delicacy of passionfruit. She dug right in. Once stuffed, she requested to see her room, refraining from sharing her plan to nap to avoid someone being sent up from the lobby to sleep it for her. The interior of the hotel was ornately colonial, with brick pillars, crafted wood, and plush seating.

Her room held a sunny verandah, a listless ceiling fan, and its bed beckoned before she inspected much more.

Three hours later, a knock sounded the door. She tossed on her silk robe to answer. Six women carrying steaming buckets of water marched into the bathroom to fill the tub. One said, "Rest time is over, Miss Bathenbrook. The reception's only two hours off."

Alexandra remained foggy in the head. "What reception, miss?"

"Your big reception, sweetie... and won't you look divine!"

Three women stayed, and Alexandra took to the tub. They scented the bathwater with flower petals and eucalyptus oil. She lounged and pondered any chance the hotel would offer scones for breakfast, or if she'd have time to take in a cricket match. She must have been falling behind her mysterious overseer's *shed-ule*, for soon the women entered and began shampooing her hair. Once rinsed off and towel-dried, they seated her at the vanity. One woman combed out her hair, another worked on her nails, while the third laid out her undergarments, which had been washed and dried in swift fashion.

"You'll be the belle of the ball. Just you wait and see."

Alexandra wondered if she was being processed to wed a benevolent dictator or to serve as a semi-virginal sacrifice to a South American sun god. "They don't plan to marry me off, do they?"

"I've seen it before," the hairdresser conceded. "Rest assured, you'll look beautiful."

The full salon treatment raged on. They plucked things overdue for plucking and powdered regions Alexandra had never assumed needed powdering. Her hair they pinned high and fanciful. By the time they colored her eyes and lips, the room's clock struck seven.

Her dresses arrived. Alexandra inspected both options, choosing the simpler blue one as it was best to avoid black in the tropics unless attending a funeral or facing a firing squad. Elegant and sleek, it slid down her silk slip effortlessly. The hairdresser walked her to the full-length mirror. She had not kitted out in such luxurious style since her disastrous meeting with the Explorers Club.

She studied her reflection, chuffed to bits.

❧

"'Boomsie' it is?" Alexandra asked her dancing companion. "You must have been an artilleryman in the military."

"It became my nickname," Boomsie confided, "on account of my diverticulitis."

The ornate and expansive drawing room at Woodbine House stood filled with the colony's upper crust mingling in smart tropical attire. Alexandra had been introduced to most, sharing a quick shake or kiss on her hand as an honoree. A string quartet played the music of the ages, and it seemed to last forever.

Once free of the receiving line, she'd fallen captive to the dance floor, being handed from one luminary to the next. It started with a waltz in the arms of the governor, Sir Cecil Hunter-Rodwell, who knew her father from the South African War. She'd been passed down the ranks of Royal Navy officers wearing number 2 mess dress and now found herself with administrator Boomsie Hilton, who was doing a masterful job in mitigating the crueler dispositions of his gastrointestinal system.

If she consumed all the world's tea, Alexandra would still have difficulty comprehending the propensity of Brits to adopt chummy nicknames, or as with T.E. Shaw, invent a new one. While there were countless Alexandras throughout history, she felt confident there were likely to be few, if any, Alexandra Illyrias, and positively none with the surname Bathenbrook.

It was hers, exclusively, and the only thing other than her soul to which she held absolute ownership.

Women came into this world with the expectation they would surrender their family name for another. Alexandra might do so come the day, but she'd need to be disturbingly in love to make such a sacrifice. While there remained a chance she would have to entertain temporary subterfuge if becoming a spy or have cause to go on the lam, altering it for anything less baffled her.

She had yet to share more than a hasty greeting with the man responsible for her being her—Olde Archie. If he didn't cut in soon, she might have to wait to speak with him until morning.

While the reception and dancing registered as very nice and nerve-wracking, Alexandra sensed that not everyone circulating the room appeared so welcoming. Her contemporaries of marriageable age did not bother to disguise their trenchant snipes with glance or whisper. Prince Edward had caused a stir upon his royal visit by requesting his first dance to be with a Guianese beauty over the pick of the colonial litter. Alexandra suspected such snotty scuttlebutt to be reminiscent of that weathered by the lady dubbed the "Duchess of Georgetown."

A clique of bachelors, primed to chat her up, waited for their turn. Until then, they engaged in speculative conversations about George Dyott's mission. Colonel Fawcett's disappearance proved of local interest, as Georgetown often served as a base for explorers seeking the fabled riches of El Dorado.

None ever returned.

"May I, sir?"

"By all means," Boomsie boomed. He ceded Alexandra's hand.

"Jolly good to see you, Father. Pray tell, what the bloody hell is going on?"

"I'm unaware," he casually related as they danced. "Colonials will seize upon any occasion to host a reception. Their life under the harsh sun would otherwise seem empty."

"Rubbish! They're here to honor you." It was clear there swam no bigger fish amidst the Crown colony's waters than her father. "I've heard that you have the 'ear of King George.' What say you?"

"Bureaucrats, even governors, tend to render rosy reports to the Colonial Office on the state of their fiefdoms. Buckingham Palace has entrusted me to attain a more precise account of things. Word has leaked, and thus I am now gloated upon to the extreme."

"Bravo!" Before anyone could interrupt, she requested, "Escort me outside for some air."

He led her to the sun patio, stopping to gather her purse along the way. Several men stood about smoking, sipping cocktails, and chatting about the mission to find Colonel Fawcett.

Archibald assessed his daughter with prideful delight. "Much has changed since last we said farewell. I've fallen so much older, and you have gone about engaging the world with such panache."

"I showed up at the docks in sixes and sevens. It took an army to put me together." Alexandra sighed. He appeared worn down: his hair thinner, his mahogany walking stick no longer in hand merely for show. His voice sounded tired. She rummaged through her bag for a small cedar box and handed it over. "La Gloria Cubanas."

"My precious, Alee-girl." He kissed her cheek and did not hesitate to liberate a cigar.

"I suspect you've cued up some of my jobs. How else could the Foreign Office locate me whilst in Jerusalem? Have you?"

"They selected you on merit. I simply pointed."

"And the Explorers Club? Was my meeting on your accord?"

"The Explorers Club?" He scoffed. "It took them a year to find you in Montana."

"When shall we take to the river?"

"Two days. Residing in London has left an imprint on you."

Alexandra waved it off. "I'm wise to their wicked game, but they seized occasion to serve me iced tea. I shall sweat it free of my being over the coming fortnight."

The virgin rainforest along the Potaro River provided a birding paradise. Alexandra and her father left the capital at morning's first light aboard the R.H. *Carr*. The steamship piloted routine runs down the broad Essequibo River to the bauxite mining areas in Rockstone. There, they switched to a smaller launch and motored onward. Two water patrol officers, a cook, and three porters were at their disposal, all courtesy of Government House.

Archibald recalled Alexandra's baptism at age seven. To say she had learned to swim was a stretch but made for better conversation. That day, the boat had struck a branch jutting the surface, jettisoning her over the rail. Left to drown or thrash her arms and legs in a frantic survival dance, she had thrashed away, soliciting interest from a monstrous green anaconda too slow to fetch her as a meal.

Like any father, he had orchestrated a furious attempt at rescue, and like most English gentlemen, shared jovial laughter with the local guides once she was plucked out and deemed unharmed. *Sixteen years...*

Upon returning from the jungle interior to inspect nesting areas of the elusive cock-of-the-rock, they were greeted by enticing aromas and a lantern-lit table by the river. They took seats and served pepperpot smothered in cassareep sauce. Vivid starlight and the fitful shadows of howler monkeys running among the broccoli trees made for a perfect canopy. They tallied up their bird sightings, which they configured into a competition by allotting a point system to varied species. Alexandra scored first dibs of a red-capped cardinal, streaked antwren, and an antbird with a long Latin name she simply called a "fergus." Archibald landed takes in spotting a harpy eagle, tufted coquette, and a silver-beak tanager. It played out like a lavish safari without the gunplay.

These days, it was good to be a Bathenbrook.

"We must discuss your falling out with William," Alexandra insisted.

Archibald leaned back in his foldable campaign chair. "Your Uncle Niles is not long for this world. Perhaps neither am I. The Bathenbrook name cannot fall into the dustbin of history."

The problem with bloodlines in a longstanding military family was that so many were killed in battle along the way. Alexandra knew Niles had lost all his sons: one to illness, another to war, and the last heir to murder. Her other uncle had passed before marrying, and over generations, Bathenbrook sperm predominantly swam female.

She said, "You wish him to marry?"

"I want him to be happy and fruitful."

She questioned, "How does one tell a man that beyond his front door exist women willing to feign love, tolerate his wounds, and birth a child for the comforts of his money?"

Archibald sighed. "This matter must be remedied."

"Balderdash! Divorce Mother and remarry. Even father a bastard."

Her father took umbrage at the vulgar suggestion. "We will discuss this no further."

Alexandra finished her wine and laid down the gauntlet. "If you two cannot sort this out, you'll leave me no choice but to one day bear a son out-of-wedlock to carry on the Bathenbrook name."

Over the next two days, the jungle trek grew more arduous.

They hiked around the waterfalls of Amatuk and Waratuck and required mules and push-pole rafts loaned from an Arawak Indian settlement. The river originated in the Pakaraima Mountains and midway thundered Kaieteur Falls. Alexandra managed well along the steep trail; her feet singing in her father's gift of high-laced suede boots, custom-made in Venezuela. She felt at the peak of physical health and hungry for the challenge. Despite the sapping heat, Archibald kept pace.

Natural hazards abounded, but hostile natives were of no concern. Alexandra photographed snakes whose venom incapacitated so quickly they were nicknamed "two-steps" and colorful poison dart frogs. Tea breaks took a backseat to drinking water hidden within capadulla vines. At some point along the river, Alexandra returned to the Amazon. She had beaten George Dyott, who, according to radio reports, remained in Rio de Janeiro, caught up in red tape. If a telegraph office existed anywhere near, she'd send him a two-word message: *Stuff it!*

That night, they camped a mile from the falls—beyond its view, yet within earshot of its thunderous abuse of the earth. They woke early, hoping to reach their objective before daybreak. They made quick progress along the stony riverbed carrying light packs... and there it stood supreme.

Alexandra freed her Leica-1 camera and looked up in wonder.

The waterfall loomed four times the height of Niagara and twice that of Victoria, measuring out to 750 feet of heavy flow from its single-drop plunge to its first break. Its waters thereafter cascaded over foundation rocks, which lent to a permanent mist and an effervescent rainbow spanning over the jungle-laced backdrop. Dozens of Makonaima birds flew into the plunging water to get to their hidden nests.

"Its name comes from the Patamona Indian phrase 'old-man-fall,'" a guide said. "Legend holds a tribal chief named Kaie saved his people from the Cariban by sailing over its edge in a canoe to placate their foes' creator god, Makunaima."

"Kaie take own life not to please Makunaima," an Arawak porter stated in labored English. "Kaie take life to scare Kanaima from body."

The guide related Kanaima to be a Carib spirit that possessed people. They all basked in its presence, whatever its true backstory. Alexandra found the waterfall a stunning vision of destiny. They had vowed to one day return and made it so. The guides offered to take them to its summit, but the ten-hour round trip over difficult terrain led her to decline. She would not go alone, and it would be foolish to tax her father any further. They stood neck and neck in their scorecards, with the prize bird yet spotted.

She glimpsed colorful movement in the trees off her left shoulder. Perched on a limb, flaunting its disk-shaped crest that lent semblance to an orange penis, idled a cock-of-the-rock. There comes a time in every child's life when they are the ones throwing the games for their parents. To bring it to her father's attention, she removed her slouch hat and shook out her hair. "I've made a muck of all the hard work put into me. How bad does it look, Father?"

"You're as spry as the morning." His eyes burst wide, and he lifted his field glasses. "You've fallen a close second to your old man."

"Bravo!" She primed her camera. "A battle well-fought and won."

After pictures of the bird and members of the party posing amidst such a magnificent backdrop, the guides went downriver to catch fish for dinner. Walking closer to the pooled basin, Alexandra dropped her rucksack and removed her boots. She hopped across the final slick rocks to bathe in its cooling mist. The roar deafened. She returned to her father, a cleansed and saturated daughter, at peace with life.

Toweling off, she quipped, "Shall we try next for Everest? When I post these photographs in my office and people ask why, I shan't need to answer, 'Because it's there.'"

"I viewed Everest while in Tibet," Archibald recollected, removing his pith helmet to wipe clean his brow and neckline. "Those were days when I was still in fine fettle, before you were born."

"Yes, 1904..." Alexandra stopped drying her hair. She'd never quite found the opportunity to finagle confirmation if he had returned to Montana by December of that year. She had convinced herself it to be true, but... Archibald looked to be in a panic.

"Are you truly my father?"

He held no need to respond. The resignation on his face and forlorn silence were telling enough. "I should have told you long ago, but how does one find the courage?"

She wavered in her stance, devastated. "As I never found it to ask, and you never found it to tell, white feathers all around."

Hemmy had shared that upon being hit by shrapnel, he sensed his spirit leave him, only to return. Alexandra sensed her own flee, but her identity failed to survive the round trip. People abandoned their names, *yet what to do when the name deserted you?*

"No need to get into the thick of it just now. I have loved you as my own and cherish that you see in me someone worthy to emulate."

"If I were to bear a son, he wouldn't be a Bathenbrook." She lifted her restive eyes to him. "Just as we have, we can pretend. It has all been pretend."

❧

It had been a long, silent return to Woodbine House. Alexandra punished Archibald with indifference, nothing more, and even she pitied him for having to endure such a callous reproach. The sun patio in the evening belonged to her alone. Oliver had sent telegrams from London, and she opened them to plot out her travels. Guiana was not a busy steamer terminus, and though desirous to depart, she'd not fall to temptation and set sail in any which direction just to get away.

She was already aimlessly adrift.

The United Press wanted her to go to Nicaragua to cover the American military's skirmishes with Sandinista rebels; one of many Central America entanglements the newspapers termed "Banana Wars." The International Olympic Committee was so impressed with her work in St. Moritz, they wanted her to photograph the upcoming summer games in Amsterdam.

"May I join you?" To her non-reply, Archibald took a seat. "Your mother married me to be free of her family. We shared many fine years of traveling. You're not the reason our marriage came undone."

Alexandra lifted her eyes, not wanting it to linger any further. "Do you know who my father is?"

"Yes. Your late uncle, Gaspard de Chantraine. Your mother was engaged to him when we eloped. To return to her family, honor needed satisfaction. Your Aunt Adelaide is barren. She craved a child with pure Monvoisin bloodlines. Your mother served as a surrogate, but when the time came, Adelaide no longer wished to be a parent. So, all our wealth is because of you. I've long since forgiven Larisa, as she has pardoned my many dalliances."

Alexandra lit a cigarette. She had never met her uncle, but portraits revealed a tall, fair-haired man of noble lineage. "So, what port-of-call awaits you, Archibald?"

"You are not a cruel person. It is unbecoming on you."

"I no longer know what sort of person I am." She sighed. "Since leaving Mother, I've found my footing. My anxiety has lessened, and my bladder control has improved. I've built a purpose to travel the world beyond mere escape from everyday life. You have been my lone pillar ever since Thomas died, and the last person I expected to kick my legs out from under me."

"Then it is my duty, my highest privilege, to help Alexandra Illyria Bathenbrook back to her feet." He extended his hand. "With all the love and shared hopes of a father to his daughter."

She wiped her eyes and accepted the lifeline. "You never returned for me."

"I should have, but Larisa made it clear she would announce in the court proceedings you were not mine to take. She aspires to be a baroness, but I ask that you forgive her neglectful manner. She had a much harsher upbringing than you."

"I stand by my advice to divorce. Find a woman who can give you a son and true happiness, but don't you dare have another daughter."

The waitstaff returned, holding a tray with further telegrams on it.

Alexandra moved aside the table's lantern and took them in hand after thanking the man. She opened the first of the three to read...

Request you meet party in Cuiabá before 25, May. — G. Dyott

"They want me to go to Brazil!" Alexandra breathlessly shared. She ripped open the second and third.

Stipend forwarded to join Fawcett Expedition. — NANA

Steamer Georgetown to São Paulo. 23, April. — O. Martin

"The North American Newspaper Alliance is sponsoring me. A ship leaves in two days!" Alexandra looked at Archibald, her face aglow and spirit reignited. "Whatever should I do, Father?"

He did not share her enthusiasm but smiled for her. "We'll discuss what provisions you'll need over tea at the polo match tomorrow."

She rubbed his hand. "Sounds smashing!"

Chapter 18

Mato Grosso, Brazil: May 1928

The longest, most perilous train ride of Alexandra's life rumbled on, and she now knew why the Portuguese had never come to rule the world. Sure, at one point, they'd boasted a mighty flotilla, laid discovery to much of the unmapped earth, and could still whir a tearful *fado*. Their railway-building skills, however, were lacking. Details such as well-pillared bridges, smooth track beds, and firm ties seemed of minor priority.

"We approach the 'Descent into Hell.' Then, the 'Devil's Bridge' into the 'Tunnel of Fire.'"

"Adescida ao Inferno. Então a Ponte do Diabo no Túnel de Fogo," Alexandra confirmed.

"Your Portuguese has improved, Alexandra," Capitão Agostinho Falcoa said, as everyone in the carriage prepared.

She smiled at him, concluding the Brazil Railway Company needed to upgrade its marketing team.

The trek from the coastline to the Paraguay River stretched for nine hundred miles. The train was prone to derailments and wobblier than a tightrope walker in a second-rate circus performing during an earthquake... while inebriated. This would be her last day aboard, and Alexandra now understood why the conductor ended each stop by shouting, *"O Trem da Morte está partindo!"*

She had boarded six days ago in São Paulo. Ricardo, her contact at the North American Newspaper Association, had supplied the lowdown. *NANA* had bankrolled the Fawcett Relief Expedition to provide millions of riveted readers across the globe with a stirring resolution to the feted mystery of the lost explorer. The chief concern was that after seeing Dyott's party off—whom the local media deemed "The Suicide Club"—they would never be heard from again. Without her participation, there would be little news to keep public interest piqued. Ricardo would travel to the city of Corumbá in a month to await her reemergence from the jungle and get her photographs to the press.

He had handed her a train ticket, vials of snakebite serum, and attained information about her next of kin.

Alexandra's meeting with Capitão Falcoa provided a blessing. He had boarded in Boituva, juggling three oranges. In noting the 38 Winchester rifle strapped across her frock and the Colt revolver resting in her holster, he had teased, *"A invasão foi cancelada."*

She had rebutted, "Pity. My only plan was to conquer your heart," and a friendship sprouted.

They had taken meals together, played cribbage, and, to the nightly contributions of traveling musicians playing for tips, he taught her to samba. A more superficial woman might consider him unremarkable with his pockmarked face and gray fringes to his mustache, but Alexandra detected forlorn wisdom in his grin and gaze. She took girlish pleasure in his sanguine acts, his bravado, and it rendered consideration that she preferred older men.

He escorted four recruits toward a remote outpost for the harshest year of their lives. An overt sense of doom cloaked their faces, even in slumber.

The highland terrain the train rumbled through spread rugged and leafy. Alexandra removed her slouch hat and stuck her head out of a window, allowing a warm breeze to cool her skin. The wanton decision to cut her hair to shoulder length inspired self-ridicule, but it would require less fuss over the coming hard months.

If she survived to Corumbá, a week-long trip on a river barge would see her to a disrepute frontier town called Cuiabá. The great unknown of inner Amazonia lay beyond, where men as stout as oxen were felled by snakebite, disease, or whistling arrow.

It sounded like interesting country, and she was eager to arrive.

Falcoa joined her. "In two hours, we detrain in Porto Esperança."

She nodded, catching sight of a distant rainbow. "Will you stay in the army, Agostinho, or does some other life ever call out to you?"

"I am often lost in that other life." He lifted his peaked forage cap and pushed back his graying hair. "I see you still chase rainbows. Always do so!"

Alexandra had yet to pass through that gate separating one's envisioned life from its unavoidable path; indeed, so naïve, she did not even know it existed. She gripped the window frame. The engineer operated with a heavy foot, causing the carriage to rock. "Tell me about the life you lost."

"I married while at university. We had a daughter. She would have been your age." Falcoa's eyes creased at these recollections. "A horse coachman, drunk on *caninha*, ran them over in the thoroughfare. My daughter died quickly. My wife suffered far too long. The man knew a politico. He did not go to prison, so I shot him. The judge offered me life in the army... so dressed, I shall remain."

Those sharing the carriage abandoned their hammocks or seats to kneel in a prayer line. The only passenger who remained standing was an adherent of Candomblé, who traveled with a rooster.

Falcoa closed the window as they plummeted.

The train whistle sounded like a banshee. Everything started shaking. "Would you mind holding me?"

Falcoa took Alexandra into his arms.

He stroked her hair.

Eyes closed, head resting on his shoulder, she prayed as the train thudded across a rickety bridge that spanned a deep gorge. She could feel its wheel sets rise off the tracks before crackling back down. Darkness filled the windows, and smoke infiltrated the carriage.

The Catholics were in full panic. They called out, *"Matáro o galo!"* to the Candomblé worshiper, imploring him to cut the throat of his rooster in sacrifice. Before a knife came into play, sunlight filtered back into the carriage. Several passengers had passed out, and others used hand fans to revive them.

Falcoa released her and opened the window to allow in air. A tear ran down his cheek. Alexandra brushed it free and kissed him. He backed off, lending a tender smile to soften her look of confusion. While she was at the moment seeking the comfort of a father figure, he had forever lost a daughter, and such it would always be.

❧

"Good day, Commander. Apologies for my delay." Alexandra slung a rifle over her shoulder and shut the car door. "I've just come from northern Amazonia and fortunate to have found sea passage to spare me any need to hike straight through to you."

"*Hmmm.*" It rang as the inanest comment expedition leader George Dyott had ever heard.

"Hello, fellas!" Alexandra waved to the others, who'd been loading supplies onto a Chevy flatbed truck upon her arrival. "Do we still depart tomorrow, right on *shed-ule?*"

"*Hmmm.*" Dyott looked her over. He understood the boots, khaki safari shirt, and breeches. He even grasped her neckerchief, leather gloves, and slouch hat. The goggles befuddled him. "There is no aviation associated with the mission."

"Affirmative, Commander." She placed them in her satchel.

Dyott peered into her bag, which sagged full of lemons. "You may die of many things over the coming weeks, but we can assume it won't be from scurvy."

With that, he walked away.

Alexandra's driver left, pleased with his tip. She shed her gear, all on which her initials were written. Her rucksack, camera bag, satchel, mosquito netting, and tied hammock formed a hefty pile. She took in a better assessment of things. Dyott showed canny leadership by staging the expedition elsewhere than Cuiabá. While the town held many churches, it hosted bandits, as wherever prospectors convened to drink and gamble away their gold, scoundrels soon followed. It brought to her mind an image of Tombstone before Wyatt Earp and Doc Holliday cleaned it out. A missionary school in Buriti, thirty miles to the northeast, served as the point of kickoff.

Of the other men present, four were Anglo, and five of mixed Brazilian ancestry. She went about introducing herself. Gerard and Bill were wireless specialists who busied themselves with a Silver Marshall field transmitter for a final communique before departure. Samuel and Jack acted as filmmakers who would record the mission via motion picture camera. They all seemed like decent, everyday guys. Alexandra took a shine that she might grace the big screen, but Samuel whispered they were under orders to keep her out of the documentary. The five local *camaradas* were pleasant in their greeting. Kalin, Joao, Vincente, and Verisimo were jack-of-all-trade types, while José served as the cook.

Alexandra felt relief it was a small group, wanting to move swiftly through the wilds. It struck her funny that all of them admitted to being novices with firearms and unfamiliar with the jungle, though the camaradas were likely handy with their machetes.

She likewise noted no pack mules or horses grazed the dry grasslands of the abandoned *fazenda*. She did not want to overburden anyone with questions, except for Dyott.

"Hello again, Commander. Might we compare notes?"

He grimaced and set down a bag. "Our notes should be in perfect synchronicity and read, 'You are an employee of *NANA* and not an official representative of this team.' *Notas completas.*"

"Notas incompletas." It came across so very British for Dyott to sport a tie with khaki field dress, but if one were to pull it off, it could not dangle loosely. She reached out and fixed it, taking kindly to his look of shocked appreciation. She slyly whispered, "Don't worry. If anything happens to you, I'll see the men home."

"Have you traveled thousands of miles just to torment me?"

Though donning a pith helmet, Dyott remained several inches shorter than her, even in Brazil. "I would have preferred if you'd invited me. At least a letter of rejection would have sufficed."

He took pause to facepalm. "I explicitly advertised for men of short stature. They move through the jungle efficiently and do not consume as much food."

Having witnessed Big Jim Gustin devour half an antelope, Alexandra could understand such, but she was not *that* tall nor of hearty appetite. She said, "I'm prepared to accept your apology so we can move on."

Dyott's face turned red. "Thousands of applicants across the globe reached out to be part of this expedition. One pitched he worked in a Turkish bath, thus could tolerate heat, with most stating after years of marriage, they were seasoned to endure any hardship. As one recently married, I cannot attest to that sentiment, *but you're helping me to understand it better!"*

"Ah, that reminds me." Dyott had honeymooned on his ship to Rio. She dug through the lemons filling her satchel and produced a small box. "Many happy years to you both."

He opened the gift and examined the gold tie pin.

"A small biplane. I thought it a fitting tribute to your war service."

"Indeed, quite thoughtful." He sighed. "A letter would have been apropos. You should take time to wash up in the schoolhouse. We can reconvene for dinner."

So, we will be allies, she bargained. "Do you have interest in hearing about my adventures in Guiana?"

"Not in the slightest." With that, Dyott walked away.

It immediately became clear: male body odor was going to be an issue.

Grand expeditions into the unknown do not begin in the middle of nowhere, but at its edge. The arid, scrub-filled upper plateau of the Chapada dos Guimarães spread itself forever. Pockmarked with evasive valleys segregated by dramatic cliffs, it teased one to misstep toward unreachable horizons. The truck made excellent progress until a tire blew out. Morale sank low once evening hit and a driving rain left everyone wet, cold, and without dinner. They hastily erected a lean-to canopy, and everyone piled under seeking refuge: Alexandra, ten men, and ubiquitous male body odor. It did not help that the camaradas walked barefoot and beans were served for breakfast. The thunderstorm forced Alexandra to put aside reading Dyott's research journal, which held valuable insight into Fawcett's earlier forays.

At daybreak, they lifted the tarp, fixed the tire, and the truck again rolled across the plateau. Alexandra took a seat upon sacks of rice and returned to her studies. She sighed, as the rankness that had ravaged her all night still clung to her.

At least for now she had escaped the farting.

Percy Fawcett had first visited South America in 1906 at the behest of the Royal Geographical Society to chart out the contested border between Brazil and Bolivia. He had often returned before the war to build upon his theory that a great civilization once existed in the Amazon—the proof awaiting discovery. He found minor evidence, but nothing confirming the fantastic tales of a tribe of Atlanteans or fair-skinned Amazons ruling the jungle.

After recovering from wounds incurred at the Somme, Fawcett had returned in 1920, needing to abandon his outing prematurely at a camp he labeled "Dead Horse." In his writings, he attested coordinates of 11.43° south latitude and 54.35° west longitude to this location. It likewise served as the campsite from which he had dispatched his last letters in 1925 before his disappearance.

The question remained whether these coordinates were reliable.

George Dyott did not believe so. The dates associated with Fawcett's 1920 trip did not match up with the camp being so far north. Fawcett's wife had confided that he often placed false markers to keep his intended route a secret. Dyott would gamble that Dead Horse lay three degrees south of the stated latitude. If he were correct, they'd be on the trail, and if wrong, lost in the middle of hostile Indian country.

"Ship-ahoy!" Samuel called out in a rascally voice.

Alexandra shut the journal and stood next to him. They had arrived near the Rio São Manoel to find an armada gathered. She counted sixty bullocks, ten mules, and eleven men.

The pile of boxed goods boggled the mind.

"How does one take all of that into a jungle?" she asked Samuel.

"Slowly," he said, "but what do I know? *I'm just a cameraman!*"

She placed her forearm near his face. "Do I smell manly to you?"

He sniffed. "A bit. More so, like beans and lemon juice."

The truck departed, the supplies were repacked, and Alexandra inherited a mule of her own. The barrier posed by the shallow river proved of little consequence, and the troupe proceeded onward, hoping to find enough grass to feed their pack animals.

Over the coming days, guiding her mount at the slowest of paces, Alexandra felt as if she had signed up for a Texas cattle drive. Coffee and farinha biscuits served as breakfast, with rice and beans the sole listing on the dinner menu. The oxen often grunted with displeasure, flared their nostrils, and acted unruly under three tons of packed goods, despite the skillful handling of their Brazilian *vaqueros*. The beasts lugged a sizeable food larder, two wireless sets, motion picture cameras, camping gear, a generator, gasoline, and cooking utensils.

Four long containers shipped from New York were stamped: *D.M. Dyott—Fawcett Relief Expedition.*

Outside of keeping a sharp eye out for venomous snakes and avoiding scrub infested with *garrapatas* ticks, the trail grew tedious. The expedition party averaged only twelve miles daily under the pounding sun. Alexandra failed to find even a puddle to rinse off residual male body odor, which still clung with the fury of a trap-jaw ant. Each afternoon, she rode ahead, singing ragtime tunes with Samuel as they sought opportune terrain to pitch camp. Dyott didn't mind, as music served as an ingredient for good morale.

Fire pits were dug for cooking, light, and warmth.

As they descended the plateau, the foliage became taller, greener, and thicker. The armada soon hit its first significant obstacle: the Rio Paranatinga. It posed a broad stretch of water. The animals would need to be unloaded to swim across, and rafts built to ferry the supplies.

Alexandra secured her mule to a tree limb. The vaqueros were fearful of the electric eels inhabiting wide rivers, but she did not care. It was water. She washed her face and doused her hair to cool off.

"How does one take all this across such a river?"

"Slowly," Samuel said, "but what do I know? *I grew up in a city!*"

Dyott walked through the thick brush to join them. "This will be where we cross. First thing is to secure a rope to yonder bank."

Everyone dispersed to unload the pack animals and clear a path to the treacherous waterway. It would be long and arduous work.

Dyott informed Alexandra and Samuel to remain and dropped a large coil of rope on the ground. "This crossing will be an all-day affair. You'll go first to film it. By the bye, are you bleeding?"

Alexandra responded, "I will menstruate in one week, as I have not engaged in sexual intercourse since October."

Dyott and Samuel looked at each other, not having a clue what that was about. Dyott clarified, "Any open cuts? Piranha are timid fish unless they smell blood, and thereto, shred you to the bone."

"I'll certainly check." To lighten his burdens, Alexandra breezily jabbered, "I learned to swim in the Amazon at age seven. It is a rather uproarious story—" She stopped talking upon Dyott walking away and turned to Samuel. "Are we to take the rope across?"

"Probably," Samuel said, "but what do I know? *I can't even swim!*"

Alexandra took off her hat and boots. She disarmed before rolling up her pant legs. *Borrachudo* flies swarmed, and she smacked a few trying to bite. She looped one end of the rope into a two-half hitch knot along the trunk of a thick tree and tied its free end around her waist. It would be cathartic to get wet. She cautiously walked in, less concerned with the current than with avoiding cuts to her feet from sharp rocks. Wading out until the water reached her belly button, she scrubbed the man-stink from her skin. Once satisfied, she swam.

Upon reaching the far bank, she secured the rope to a Jatobá tree, refreshed and proud of her achievement. She wondered why those across the river engaged in raucous laughter, waving at her. Commander Dyott once more shook his head and massaged his temples.

"Wait there!" Jack, the other cameraman, shouted.

"They must think me an idiot," Alexandra mumbled. They had unveiled four foldable canoes out of nowhere—no doubt shipped from New York. Dyott, Samuel, and Jack soon arrived with the camera gear. She continued swiping at borrachudos. "Rope secured, Commander!"

"The swim was of no waste," he commiserated. "You were foetid."

Alexandra's jaw dropped. Between the nasty flies and his reference to the man-stink his gender had cast upon her, she would need to unleash her secret weapon come evening. Jack handed over her camera and accouterments before unloading the canoe.

Samuel tossed her a towel, which reeked of male body odor.

Dyott headed back alone to gather more supplies.

Alexandra tied off her wet hair and rolled up her sleeves. It was time to be a photographer.

The Gayapos posed the Indians of immediate concern. While they lived farther north along the Xingu basin, rivers were their highways, and they often paddled down the Paranatinga to raid the local Bakairi. They were distinguishable by their extended lip plates, the reddish-black body paint they applied to mimic insects, and the long clubs they used to break the bones of those they captured.

For this reason, after taking photographs of the canoes in use and horned bullocks swimming across the river, Alexandra put her camera aside to carry her rifle. She ventured with Samuel and Jack to scout the area for a place to set camp for the night.

Near a pool of muddy runoff, they wandered into a green anaconda hosting a tremendous bulge. Its size amazed them.

Alexandra said, "We must get pictures. Has it choked to death?"

"Maybe it ate a tapir," Samuel guessed, "but what do I know? *I'm a vegetarian!*"

Jack tossed a stone at the prodigious specimen to see if it stirred. It did not. Dyott dropped in. "It has eaten and will idle for weeks."

Alexandra said, "I once encountered a similar-sized serpent in—"

Dyott had already walked away.

"One of us needs to pose beside it for scale," Jack said, readying his tripod camera.

"You go!" Samuel protested. "How about you, Alexandra?"

She reminded him, "I am not associated with this expedition and cannot be filmed."

"We'll decide by rock-paper-scissors," said Jack. The Asiatic hand game had caught fire in the Western Hemisphere. He set out the rules. "Two rounds. Both losers kneel beside it for posterity."

They all agreed on the plan. Alexandra plotted her strategy. Jack yelled, *"Ro-sham-bo!"* and she put out a flat hand, beating his rock. Time for round two with Samuel. *"Ro-sham-bo!"*

Samuel cheered, having stoned her scissors. He then beat Jack.

Alexandra passed Samuel her Leica-1 camera, informing him she wanted a picture of Jack alone for the *NANA* folks and one of herself for her office wall. They settled next to the twenty-foot monstrosity. She volunteered to be the first to take the end with the head. She put her hand on it. It felt very reptilian. "Muenster *cheeeeese!*"

Dyott dropped in again. "Very nice. Just be cautious of the second one slithering behind you."

Chapter 19

The Fawcett Relief Expedition arrived at Bakairi outpost in one week. The government reservation dealt with all three classifications of Indians in the Mato Grosso. For the assimilated Bakairi, it gave them land to raise cattle and grow crops, a schoolhouse for their children to learn Portuguese, and medical care for the invasive diseases that had decimated their people dating back to the conquistadors. Those wary of foreigners visited to trade food for trinkets and cutlery. Alexandra scored vivid photographs of the Mehinaku interacting with members of the team. They were sturdy men with bowl-cut hair who had walked out of the jungle stark naked, carrying seven-foot bows.

Barbed wire surrounded the twenty scantily built structures to deter attack from more hostile elements, of which there were many. As explained to her, most of these little-known tribes lived where the team headed. The cannibalistic Morcegos were "bat-people" who sheltered in tree trunks and only emerged at night. Macahirys were likewise people-eaters only four days' march to the north. The Suyá and Xavantes acted the most warlike, but the greatest threat remained the Gayapos. A small garrison of soldiers dissuaded their attacks and safeguarded against non-Indians taken to banditry.

It was agreed that Alexandra would return with the cattlemen once the expedition took to the rivers. She had taken enough first-rate photographs it would not be tragic if her departure came now. At first sight of the Mehinakus, the vaqueros feared to venture any deeper into the wilderness, but Dyott insisted they continue. He had gained critical intelligence from a Bakairi named Bernadino, who'd been among Fawcett's local guides in 1920. Bernadino's front teeth ended in sharp points, and he wore scant clothing. He spoke some Portuguese and confirmed that Dead Horse stood near the headwaters of the Rio Batovi, located 14º south latitude.

After two days' rest, the cowboys agreed to stay on. Bernadino and four companions joined the party, and the expedition set off into thicker forest toward the tributaries of the Rio Xingu.

It was the land from which no white man returned.

Alexandra had learned early in life how to navigate the openness of Montana. Since Buriti, she had mapped their route so she might retrace her steps back to civilization. It had been a simple process along the open chapada, but now, descending into the muggy basin, trees a hundred feet high blotted out the sunlight. To circumvent this handicap, jungle explorers carved symbols into tree trunks. Alexandra chose an exclamation point as her mark. While carving this sign, she detected an etched *Y* in a tree off the footpath. She recruited Samuel to tag along.

Insects swarmed as they wielded machetes to cut through dense vegetation. A capybara scurried into the brush. They found a trail that held anthills and large trees felled by termites.

Human footprints marred the moist forest bed.

"Gayapos," Alexandra hissed, unslinging her rifle. They followed the prints, which led to a decomposed body. Samuel threw up. The dead were recycled quickly in the bush. Ants were having a feast, and little flesh remained. "Rush back and get the commander."

Samuel retreated down the trail. He soon returned with Dyott.

Alexandra lowered the kerchief covering her nose and mouth to better investigate. Two opportunistic creatures had staked their claim: a venomous pit viper coiled inside the ribcage, waiting for vermin to ambush; a pink-toed tarantula, plotting the same.

It was what death in the Amazon looked like.

She took photographs. "I'd guess three days ago, Commander."

Dyott stepped forward. "I concur."

Alexandra lifted her goggles. She spotted a club under the body and pulled it free. It was a four-foot-long *borduna*—the weapon of choice of the Gayapos. "Shall we alert the others?"

"The vaqueros will flee," Dyott warned. "What I like about you, Miss Bathenbrook, is—"

"I can be one of the guys without being any less of a lady?"

"—that you'll be departing soon. Not a single word!"

Alexandra and Samuel nodded. She led Dyott to another tree etched with a *Y*. They debated whether Fawcett had carved it during his 1925 expedition. If so, they could follow such signposts the entire way.

She wagered, "What was the colonel's aim? What comes after *Y?*"

It brought a rare smile to Dyott's pursed lips. *"Zed!"*

They rejoined the armada struggling through the dense green landscape and kept a lookout for the markings over the coming days with mixed success. A week removed from Bakairi outpost, Bernadino had guided them to the spot near the Batovi he claimed to be Dead Horse. Days later, they reached the Rio Arame; the end of the line for land travel. As they pitched camp along its bank, it grew apparent that unobservable shadows hiding within the jungle now watched their every movement.

Imperceptible, yet everywhere.

Dyott granted everyone time to attend to cleaning themselves up and resting before dinner.

One essential lesson Alexandra had learned during previous jungle explorations... sound orifice management was crucial. In her everyday life, careless gatekeeping that allowed a lemon squirt to sting her eye, a sophomoric finger to pick her nose, or the welcoming of the occasional penis was survivable. Most people who fell in the Amazon did so rife with fever, and outside of ingestion of dirty water, it was due to poor cavity oversight. Many in the expedition were worn down and sickly.

Ever since leaving Bakairi outpost, Alexandra sensed a cold turn toward her. The vaqueros did not want her company when they returned, fearing the temptation to capture a white woman would encourage Indian attacks. The camaradas resented her brandishing two guns, while they were armed only with machetes. She didn't know why the technical men were giving her the icy mitt. Time off the trail might allow for tensions to subside.

She slept most of the day, swinging in her shaded hammock without too much bother from garrapatas, piums, or tiny wasps; the latter having an affinity to infiltrate the eyes, nose, and ears. Arising before sunset, she visited José as he prepared dinner. He planned to serve beans and rice rather than rice and beans to celebrate her twenty-third birthday. As she did every night, she retrieved a bucket of boiling water, filled her canteen, and spiked it with lemon juice. To what remained, she added the rind, a sprinkle of cinnamon, and drops of eucalyptus oil.

Tossing her satchel over a shoulder, she carried her steaming bucket to the river. Many of the men were also washing up; their bodies riddled with blotches and eyes puffy from intruders. They had scratched some of their bites to the point of open wounds, which created yet another portal for parasites and disease.

Dusk provided the only time pests did not rove rampant, as if man and insect agreed to a brief ceasefire. Thereafter, all treaties were off, and voracious mosquitoes would report for the night shift.

Alexandra found a spot offering privacy and tended to her cleaning rituals. She stripped out of her dirty clothing and frowned upon noting a tear in her khaki breeches. Despite wrapping puttees to seal her boots, bugs always fell out, and they invariably infiltrated her camisole and panties. Squatting to pee invited the nasty critters to seize opportunity, thus she had voided in water at every chance to keep them away from her privates. Her goggles, gloves, and the cotton swabs filling her ears were last to go before wetting a cloth to wash up. The bugs melted right off to her citrusy mix, which stung when applied. It was a recipe she had heard of in Java and first tried along her swampy passage from Corumbá to Cuiabá aboard the ferry *Iguatemi.* Foot care came next. Dry socks were a must, so she rinsed and squeezed them out so they might hang on her hammock line for use tomorrow. She slopped liberal amounts of petroleum jelly to insulate any open cuts on her skin.

The crunching of twigs disrupted her brief peace. She removed her revolver from its holster. To calm down, she started talking to herself, waiting for cause to turn and fire. "Armpits hairy...? *Check.* Left bosom still swelled from fire ant bite...? *Check.* No botfly larvae wriggling under my skin...?"

"Check!" Dyott moseyed out of the foliage.

"You should take caution," Alexandra said, lowering the gun. She shimmied back into her shirt. "I might have taken you for something other than a 'peeping Tom' and shot you."

"Everyone appears on edge." Dyott passed her a crumpled pack of cigarettes she had dropped in camp. He settled on the riverbank, tossed baited fishing lines into the water, and tied them to an exposed root. Bugs did not seem to care for him much.

Two colorful macaws flew by, and the jungle started singing.

The more the others soured on her, the kinder he had become. Alexandra lit up a smoke. After taking a puff, she used the cigarette to burn off three ticks and two leeches latched onto her left thigh.

"Pedro is very ill. He must travel tomorrow if he is to survive. I want you to take him."

She assumed Dyott remained eager to get rid of her, his millstone. The government agent was a decent man who had not fared well in the wilderness. "Just the two of us?"

"I would also send two Indians," Dyott said. "I suggest you leave after breakfast and find your way back to the outpost. As Colonel Fawcett wrote in his journal, 'The exit from Hell is always difficult.'"

She sighed. Three weeks in, and it was already over. "It will please everyone to be rid of me."

"If we've been brusque, it's because you've humbled us with your goggles, cotton, and clever insect repellents," he confessed. "The men feel foolish over their jibes and are irritable for being chewed upon with no impunity. You have not affected this mission as I feared. Cursing, belching, and untoward flatulence have been well below the norm. I want it known I'm sending Pedro with you because you're his only hope. Your map to the outpost is spot-on, and your instincts and conduct have been as keen as mustard!"

She gave him a brief but appreciative smile. "You *will* say 'hello' to Colonel Fawcett for me?"

Dyott raised a skeptical eyebrow, betraying his unspoken doubts about Fawcett's survival. "I shall."

Alexandra gazed downriver and snickered. Some men were getting a head start on reverting into Neanderthals, waving their hoses side to side while urinating into the river. "You may have spoken prematurely, Commander, but boys will be boys."

"They are just guarding against the candiru." Dyott headed back to camp, whistling.

"What is the candiru?" she hollered, needing to know.

He informed, "It is a native fish, thinner than a pin, which can swim up a flow of urine to lodge itself in the urethra. There, it latches in and grows, unremovable. A most insufferable way to die."

"Can it swim up a woman's submerged, *you know*, when she pees?"

Dyott rubbed his chin, having had no prior experience with a female in the Amazon to have given it any consideration. "From an anatomical standpoint, I suppose it could just swim up, *you know*, any ole time."

Alexandra felt faint. "When did you plan to share this with me?"

He held up his palms. "One cannot think of everything... and I just did. So, check!"

❧

The nights stirred noisy and pitch-black, less the campfires. The roar of howler monkeys served as frequent lullabies. Bill and Gerry were night owls, attempting to touch base with the outside world via their wireless set, which functioned better in the evening hours. They occasionally pulled in static-marred news reports from New York or a music station. The camaradas always sang around a fire pit, and the cattlemen dealt with their beasts. Dyott wrote in his journal to close out each day. He had informed the vaqueros they would depart when the team headed downriver for the Kuluene—a large tributary to the Rio Xingu. The rapids would lead into the thickest of rainforest.

Once upon the water, there was no turning back.

It rained for much of Alexandra's final night. She awaited the sunrise, rocking in her hammock, calculating her retreat to civilization. She had seen Dyott leave camp. As he had yet to return, she worried.

"*Pssst.* Sam! Where did Commander Dyott go?"

"Probably to toilet," Samuel grumbled from his hammock, "but what do I know? *I'm still asleep!*"

She unsealed herself from her mosquito netting. "Get a flashlight, and your gun, and let's go!"

They strode into the darkness. The moist soil made tracking Dyott's steps easy. As she suspected, he had headed for the spot they had chatted the previous night to check on his fishhooks. It stood a quarter mile down the river, and the trail was now fraught with mudholes and swampy pools. The forest pulsed with the clamors of dawn. Among them sounded the guttural cry of a jaguar. Alexandra stepped around a stretch of muck, assuming Samuel would do the same, but he walked right into the bog, and she needed to extricate him.

"What if the commander is dead?" he asked. "Killed by Gayapos or in the belly of a snake?"

"Stop being such a nervous Nellie!" she snipped. Her adrenaline spiked, and her heart pounded furiously. They continued forward for another fifty paces. She clicked off her flashlight. "Wait!"

From her crouch, she noted something protruding from the ground. Five minutes of silent inspection followed, with the mass moving occasionally. Rustling spread through the trees ahead. The first glimmer of sunlight reflected off the river, and she waited for it to expand enough to allow for a clearer assessment of things.

Shadows emerged from the trees. Indians carrying weapons.

Alexandra tightened her grip on her rifle. "The commander is caught in quicksand."

Samuel begged for orders. "Do we rush forward, guns ablaze?"

"What do I know? *I skipped forest ranger class that week!*"

As they carried bows, they were not Gayapos. There emerged six, no seven—wait, nine—materializing from the haze; no different from images upon a blank piece of photographic paper once dipped in a stop bath. Everything in the Amazon was big, except its people. The men wore feathered headdresses colored yellow and red. Shaved sticks impaled their cheeks, noses, and earlobes. Their bows were up, but the six-foot arrows they used to hunt were yet drawn back. To Alexandra, they seemed more curious about Dyott being trapped thigh-deep in the muck than hostile toward his presence. As they would detect her once sunlight crept forward, the decision to fight or flee approached its zenith.

She chose option three. "Hold my rifle."

Samuel tried to grab her as she stood and trudged ahead.

In measured steps, she approached them, hand near her revolver.

The Indians' attention shifted from Dyott to her.

They whispered among themselves, offering curious glances. Alexandra had not believed the tales of a race of tall, fair-skinned women ruling in these lands, but by the natives' reaction, one would venture *they* did. The Indians studied her as inquisitively as she studied them. They lowered their bows and disappeared into the jungle.

She proceeded toward Dyott. "Good morning, Commander. Quite a peck of pickled peppers you have picked."

"Did you see them? They are of the Kuikuro tribe."

"Hearty men, indeed," Alexandra commented. He appeared too cemented to pry free by hand. She turned to Samuel and reclaimed her rifle. "Get back to camp and retrieve Jack and some rope. I am handy with a lasso and will take great satisfaction in corralling the commander for rescue."

Dyott tried to free himself. "I beseech you to find another way."

Alexandra continued with her instructions. "Say nothing of this to the others. It would reflect poorly on the commander. I'll remain here. If you hear gunfire, send everybody."

Samuel nodded and headed off. It would take him at least thirty minutes to return with help.

Alexandra squatted down and rested the rifle across her thighs. The fresh sunlight heating her damp clothing felt luscious. "Should I try to retrieve the Kuikuro so we can get a group photograph?"

"Have you ever considered psychiatric consult, Miss Bathenbrook?"

"I am *shed-uled* for August if I make it back," she freely related, casting a mischievous grin. "I recall during our dinner in New York, you snubbed my discussion of Papua. As we have time together, I'll start from the beginning... *So, there I was on a raft, drifting down the Fly River, whence—*"

"When," Dyott corrected. He struggled desperately to break free of the slop, but his efforts were futile.

"*—whence* spotted were ferocious cannibals of the Marind-Anim. They looked quite hungry!"

He sighed and dipped his head. "Have you no mercy?"

"It might seem odd," she continued, "but my first thought was 'would I taste better grilled or boiled?'"

As Commander George Dyott listened, he could only lament that it had not been Gayapos who had found him helpless and gone about crushing his skull with their bordunas.

One can but dream.

Chapter 20

Eureka! The radiance of a mirage has little to do with its actual splendor; rather, the direness of circumstances of those beholding it. Bakairi outpost had not struck Alexandra favorably upon her initial passing, and sight of it now brought only a half-smile, speaking to the smooth, though taxing, nature of the return. The Indian guides had scouted tirelessly, the sickly official had not fallen off his mule, and they encountered no hostiles. She had served as navigator, nurse, and hired gun. It left her exhausted. Once behind the wire, she slept for twenty hours, an arm serving as a pillow.

She awoke to a wooden tray hosting cornmeal and honey-coated bread. Her clothes were missing, so she wrapped herself in her blanket and feasted. Sunlight filtered into the stuffy room. Delighting in scrubbing down in a creek beyond the compound filled her sleepy head. Two topless girls entered the schoolhouse, carrying her laundered clothing. They flaunted dark hair and russet-tinted skin that held the faultless gleam of youth.

"Pekodo uagahuda tapadirei," one gasped, speaking in Bakairi.

"Olá!" Alexandra greeted.

Both girls ran their fingers through her hair before wetting towels to wash her. Alexandra assumed they had never seen a blonde-haired woman before. Upon noticing they ate ticks picked from her head, she tried a few herself. They tasted crunchy and bitter, but overall palatable if in a pinch. She closed her eyes and thought of Emma, who'd always bathed her when she was a girl. Her sister would quell her anxieties by singing French lullabies and see her off to sleep safe and sound.

A man entered, shielded his eyes, and spun about in retreat. Alexandra's lips burst wide. "Agostinho!"

"Perdão," he said. "Tell me when I can enter."

She felt no need to cover her breasts. "You may enter."

Capitão Falcoa walked back in, raised an eyebrow, and settled on claiming a chair facing away from her. "I am leaving with three men in one hour. I think it wise for you to ride with us."

It proved a godsend. "I'll join once my delousing is complete."

"Excelente!" Falcoa left to finish his preparations.

Alexandra stood to allow the girls to wrap up their duties and joined in the scrubbing. Once finished, she slid herself into clean jungle attire and rummaged through her rucksack to put together a valuable kitty, but the girls only claimed a set of earrings before scurrying out, giggling. Boots laced, slouch hat affixed, and weapons secured, Alexandra ventured outside. Her mules had been watered and fed. They remained tied to a tree, still burdened by the provisions Commander Dyott had supplied. Presented were three soldiers: hardened young men desperate to reunite with their families, dance with a woman, and once more smell the salt of the ocean.

"Olá! Meu nome é Alexandra." They stated their names and rank: Corporal Raul and two privates, Francisco and Danilo. *"Uma vez em Corumbá,"* she playfully informed, *"beba comigo!"*

"Viva Alexandra," they burst out, slapping each other on the back.

Falcoa chuckled at her offer to pick up the tab upon arrival in Corumbá. "Already you prod revolt."

As they mounted their mules, the men shouted, *"Viva o Brasil!"*

"Para o inferno!" cheered Alexandra.

They headed for Cuiabá.

A week later, the exit from hell continued forward. They began crossing the dry chapada with hopes of not running out of water, as no rain had fallen since Alexandra left Dyott's party. To fend off boredom, she taught the soldiers the words to the "Streets of Laredo." With Falcoa's help, they mastered one stanza each day in both English and Portuguese, which they cheerfully sang each night around their campfire. Each morning, they rode for the high country of the Serra Azul in better harmony.

Another sweltering day on the trail, Alexandra went to work on verse seven. "'Go bring me a cup, a cup of cold water. To cool my parched lips, the cowboy did—'"

BOOM, boom, boom... Boom!

Private Danilo slunk off the side of his mule and crashed onto the dried grasslands. Alexandra rode back for him, but he clearly lay dead. She drew her revolver and fired into the grove of trees from which the ambush originated. Falcoa called for retreat, and his men settled behind a fallen tree resting on the crest of a hill. Alexandra joined them. She dismounted and retrieved a box of rifle rounds from her saddle pack. Bullets continued zinging through the air and chipping off the bark of the surrounding trees.

"Privado! Pegue as mulas," Falcoa commanded, pointing down the slope. *"Corporal, esquerda.* You have the right flank, Alexandra, and I will take the center."

"Check!" They all positioned themselves, waiting for clean shots. They held the advantage of the sun at their backs, and all their mules were accounted for. Private Francisco rushed the beasts down the hill, out of range. Alexandra keened her aim on the heavier foliage on her side of the battlefield. Each time she saw movement, she parted a measured shot in rebuttal.

"Who are they, Agostinho?"

"Coluna Prestes," he speculated. "They hide in these parts."

The group included remnants from a failed military uprising in 1924, and over the years had lapsed into nothing more than desperados. They still numbered in the hundreds. After exchanging gunfire, Alexandra crawled to the ridgeline. Their path of retreat spread like a stadium, with a wide plain flanked by higher rock-filled scrub.

It offered ideal terrain for a round of "Sly fox, dead hounds."

She crept back behind the timbers. Falcoa heard out her plan. Corporal Raul nodded, stood, and bolted down the hill. Falcoa soon followed. Alexandra waited until they settled into position, reloading her rifle and firing her pistol to stall for time.

She discharged a few parting rounds and headed over the ridge.

Archibald Bathenbrook had spoken of a game the Boers often sprung on the regimented Brits before they wised up. Alexandra served as the fox, running down the middle of the descending valley, tossing in a zig or zag every few strides to avoid being shot in the back.

Gunfire erupted behind her.

She sprinted past the bunkered positions Falcoa and Raul had taken to each flank and dared a peek over her shoulder. Two dozen armed men cleared the ridge, sprinting downhill in pursuit.

Fifty yards ahead spread some cover if she could make it.

Alexandra sighed with relief once hearing the rifles of her comrades come into play. Taking position behind a thick tree, she lifted her 38 Winchester and joined in. The waylaid bandits fell in terrible numbers, with some now trying to scurry back up the slope. She patiently picked out her targets before firing. Each time, they cried out, fell, and rolled down the hill. Smoke filled the air, and the slaughter did not cease until the last of them clawed their way to safety beyond the ridge.

Everything fell quiet.

Twelve desperados laid the grasslands; some lifeless, most others soon to join them, as those wounded in such badlands were as good as dead. Falcoa motioned to Raul, and they both headed toward her position. Falcoa did so limping and crashed to the ground upon arrival.

He was snake-bitten.

Alexandra tore off his boot. "What kind was it, Agostinho?"

He shook his head, not knowing. She lifted snakebite serum from her satchel. Three vials rested in the case: one each for vipers, rattlers, and "other." They needed to choose the right one. She raced to his previous position and searched the brush but could not find the snake.

A wounded bandit stumbled toward her, cursing.

Alexandra drew her pistol and shot him through the head.

There was no time to fuss over it. She left to treat Falcoa. They reasoned it most likely to be a viper and chose that vile. She slammed the filled syringe into his shoulder. His swollen leg continued turning red and purple.

Alexandra wrapped it in a tourniquet. They would soon know.

Raul returned from reconnoitering the woodlands. He reported finding two mules tied to a tree; among them Alexandra's, carrying all of her equipment and film. The rest had vanished, along with Private Francisco.

Things were unraveling rapidly.

Alexandra closed her eyes and tried to push aside the dire moans of the dying bandits to concentrate. They remained sixty kilometers northeast of Cuiabá. To continue across the open chapada would be suicide. To the south stood rugged woodlands leading to the Rio das Mortes. Once recovering their mules, it would have to be the route, as it would pose difficult terrain for the outlaws to pursue them.

She shared her plan with Falcoa.

He said weakly, "I would like to die near water."

For three more days, it did not rain. They could find no trace of Private Francisco. Falcoa sat atop his mule, feverish and not long for this world. Corporal Raul guided the party through the thick foliage, swinging a machete. Alexandra served as the rearguard, but no bandits followed. With all supplies depleted, finding water loomed as gravest concern. The last time Alexandra had pissed it trickled copper in tone. Her kidneys ached, and her legs cramped afire. Her equilibrium was failing, and she imagined herself to be hallucinatory in most steps.

The sun continued its dip, and Raul stopped to start a fire.

Alexandra helped Falcoa to the ground and placed another blanket over him. When his shaking did not subside, she caressed him close to her body and tried to stay awake. She cried.

"Where are your wife and daughter buried, Agostinho?"

"Do not fuss with me." His complexion had faded to an ashen, deathly gray. "Find your way home. You have such a grand life to live."

She rocked him in her arms, knowing it would be a kindness to shoot him, and that she never could. So weak-kneed, she needed to use her rifle to rise to her feet. A few surviving drops of water were sucked from her canteen.

Far off in the sky arched the faintest of rainbows.

She wagered it was formed by a waterfall along the Rio das Mortes rather than conjured by a desperate imagination. A map she had studied placed telegraph lines running to Cuiabá fifteen miles south of the river.

Once cutting the wires, someone would hopefully show up for repairs. It seemed their only hope.

Alexandra looked up. To her bewilderment, Falcoa was walking. He lifted free his sword, and with one blow, decapitated Raul. He turned to her. His dark eyes menaced, vacant of life. She gasped, dropped her canteen, and drew her pistol as he staggered closer. Her hand shook violently. "I beg of you, Agostinho. Come back to me. Don't leave me here alone!"

"Join me, Alexandra. Come dance with me in Hell."

She collapsed onto her knees and burst into tears. A ghoulish mist fled from Falcoa's body, and he crashed next to her, dead.

Alexandra fought to catch her breath. A nearby shrub ignited in flames, and the malicious hellhound from her youth darted in and out of the inferno, gnashing its fangs and howling its horrific call.

The blaze grew wilder, and within it stood her demon.

She knew him as Olemén—an acolyte to an archdemon ruling Hades. They had met once before, though his voice forever stirred the wind. He relished playing an insidious game of allowing others to become close to her, only to then drive them away.

During her freshman year in college, Alexandra had found herself in dire circumstances. Olemén had appeared, filled her head with terrible grandeur, and a deal had been struck. All she had vowed was to one day reunite with him where hell fell upon the earth. She once more inhabited his realm, where the language of angels and demons was spoken, and no remembrance of visitation was permissible.

In the fiery haze, Olemén flaunted a rosewood tone—robust in his element. His humanesque physique was taut, alluring, and hairless; the diabolic wings, extensive. Horns sprouted from his skull and curled across the forehead. His barbed penis dangled at the knees, and in one spindly hand rested a chalice from which Alexandra knew instinctively not to drink.

"You must partake, my 'Golden-one,'" Olemén said. "You shall be lustrated in Phocaea and henceforth rule among the Fallen."

"It is only water, Sister. Drink!" Alexandra covered her ears. Thomas and Emma continued to call out to her. They scorned her ill-granted soul and unbridled spirit for her many denials of the Master. They derided her birth as a blasphemous error, and she an abomination.

"The date is written; the table has been set," Olemén hissed. "You know what you are. Submit!"

Alexandra screamed, "You are a deceiver!"

She lifted her Papuan dagger from her belt and hurled it, but Olemén was gone. She sat for a moment, unsure of where she was. A bush burned; her mauled mule rested flat, whimpering. Falcoa lay dead.

An unconquerable panic set in. She raised the revolver and pressed it against her temple. She cried out, "It wasn't supposed to end this way!"

Dark clouds swelled the sky.

Rain fell.

Chapter 21

London: August 1928

William Bathenbrook passed the photograph to Gunnar and Simra. It shook him in seeing Alexandra so enraptured by the demon's presence: head back, eyes shut, a satiated grin bending her lips. She roved far off since February and remained incommunicado with her office as of May. Will had elected not to discuss with her the event that had concluded their séance at Borley Rectory and now plumb out of patience to stifle his concerns any longer.

He'd drawn in Oliver, who said, "The 'Mistress of the Nyirbátor' may refer to Elizabeth Bathory, the Hungarian blood countess."

Will replied, "The photo is brilliantly horrific."

"Too brilliant," Oliver said. "Alexandra will be miffed to learn the Ghost Club has deemed it a forgery and plans to sue."

Hildegard fidgeted in her chair, upset over this infringement of their cabal. She yelled, "Tell everything. *Schnell!*"

Oliver quivered. "Alexandra suspects you're all conspiring over finding some woman in France. She is not a lesbian and often talks about anal sex! Can I please stop talking now?"

Hildegard lit a cigarette and laughed. "I knew it was her."

Will shook his head. "I plan to book sea passage to Brazil. Would you care to join in, Simra?"

Simra looked up. He blinked and said, "Yes."

Later that evening, with only Barnabas at his side, Will worked the knobs of his shortwave receiver. The atmosphere on most summer eves stirred unfavorable, and he picked up only blips from a Brazilian proxy of the Fawcett Relief Expedition. The last report forwarded by *I.A W* stated the undertaking to be struggling on the rapids of the Rio Xingu, had bartered with Anauqua Indians, and remained confident they were on the path to Colonel Fawcett. Rio de Janeiro operated three hours behind Greenwich Mean Time. Messages by *I.A W* came after midnight. Alexandra's name had never been mentioned. The prime reporting interval passed in silence.

Will continued to wait, deep in thought.

A year ago, he came across an article in the *Evening Standard* lauding the charitable work of his aunt, Adelaide de Chantraine. Beside her in the accompanying photograph stood a woman in her twenties: ravishing, bewitching, and hauntingly familiar. Will knew little about his aunt other than she had visited occasionally from France, and that she was childless. Yet, the young and elegant brunette held a clear resemblance; indeed, more so to his mother. With time on his hands, he'd opened an inquiry. His findings proved disturbing.

The Monvoisin aristocracy dated back eternal and mentioned in the fourteenth-century witch inquisitions conducted by the Dominican friar, Bernard Gui. It labeled them occultists in league with Satan. Will speculated that his mother had eloped to escape such dark practices, but when left destitute, found a way back into her family's malevolent graces.

He grew certain that the penalty his mother had paid involved surrendering one of her daughters.

Emma first came to mind. She had died in a Chicago fire alongside her Hungarian nanny while in their aunt's care. Will recalled with unease that during his mother's visit to England as he convalesced in 1919, Alexandra had likewise been placed under Adelaide's supervision.

It had not gone well. Six months later, their mother had been summoned home. Alexandra had fled to Montana and, thereafter, ingested pills. The suicide attempt cost his sister a four-month stint at the Montana State Hospital for the Insane in Warm Springs.

It failed to dissuade her from trying again.

Yet, the more Will delved, his focus turned toward shrouded stories about Abigail. She had been born a year after him and died of fever at age one. It remained such a hushed-up incident he could not recall where she was buried, though somewhere in Asia struck familiar. Will held guilt over preserving this longstanding family secret and stifling his newfound suspicions from Alexandra, but she had already lost so much.

Any false hopes might just finish her. He missed her terribly.

At three in the morning, pings came across the ether. Will jot down *1.AW*'s Morse code update and deciphered it—*Fawcett party perished hands of Indians. July 1925 east of Kuluene River.*

It ended there. He turned off his desk lamp and fell asleep.

Morning sunlight filled his den when the phone woke him up. Oliver passed along that Alexandra had disembarked in Liverpool and was taking the train down.

Will thanked him for the news and hung up the receiver.

He briefly fumed. It would have been a simple courtesy for her to have sent a telegram weeks ago from Brazil. She held such limited understanding of human relations; the interconnectedness, emotions, and duties of it all. It was why he believed—no matter how much of the globe she navigated and triumphed—Alexandra would forever remain among the loneliest and most lost people in the world.

"Yes, Father. I'm safely returned. ... No, I did not spot a plum-throated cotinga whilst in Amazonia... Hello... hello?"

The line went dead. Alexandra placed the phone down.

It struck her fancy to lounge in her well-outfitted office. A mark of success came with it, even if the ledgers were drowning in red ink. She took a seat at the warama wood desk she had shipped from Guiana, only to cover her face to cry. A fuzzy account of her quest for Cuiabá had been provided to the Brazilian authorities, with measures taken to safeguard Agostinho Falcoa's honor. She'd conducted her escape in survival mode, with all caution tossed to the wind.

Despite trying to piece it all together, something felt missing.

No comfort greeted her in London. She had called her half-brother to ask one question. His honest answer led her to hang up the phone abruptly. It was never his secret to tell, no less, she resented Will for not telling it. Time would be needed to forgive his role in the charade.

Oliver entered with her backlog of mail and placed it on the desk.

Alexandra lifted out a box wrapped in brown paper, which held a pungent odor. "When did this arrive?"

"July, postmarked from Nairobi. No return address."

She cut its strings and peeled the layers away. It became clear who'd sent it. Aside from the decomposed sparrow and dead jumping spider, rested a card. It read: *Stop writing him!* She tossed the box into her trashcan. Letters from Denys Finch Hatton, Kari Solvang, and her New York bankers were prioritized for later reading.

It was long overdue for Detective Liam Kimball to reply to her last correspondence. She felt ready to chalk him up as a one-night stand. Hypersexual thoughts had tormented her for weeks, and it was unfortunate timing to lose him as a safe harbor. Joining Oliver in the sitting room, she settled at her wall map to escape to other worlds. Despite having reached Kaieteur Falls, she had suffered a disheartening plunge from her fleeting pinnacle of self-confidence and achievement.

Outside, swarms of businessmen dressed in clothing better worn in the previous century scoured for lunch. Standing a head taller than most, glowering from across the lane, loomed Astor Lys. A grayish pallor shaded the sharp and gaunt features of his face. Oliver had scoured old newspapers for any information about the man. His only find entailed a *Chicago Tribune* article from 1894, which stated an Astor Lys had been sentenced to hang for molesting young girls he'd tutored in piano. The rope had snapped, and he had been granted back his freedom.

Alexandra felt conflicted whether he posed a genuine threat or existed as a figment of her guilty conscience. She tossed her dagger into her purse. The mailman entered. He handed over a letter postmarked from Morocco. Alexandra's eyes lit up, and a faint smile bloomed.

The reaction intrigued Oliver. "Good news, I hope?"

"I need a spot of air. I shan't be gone but a few hours."

"Have you been sneaking tea?"

"Whilst aboard the ship from Rio, they served little else. Ta!"

Lys remained outside. She twitched with unease. Needing answers, she rushed across the street, directly for him. He raced off in shockingly nimble strides and vanished into an alley.

Alexandra stopped, too fearful to enter.

His existence remained debatable; as too, her sanity.

A short walk found her idling pensively outside an office door. Etched on its lead glass: *Dr. A.S. Berger, Psychoanalyst.*

Here we go! The small reception area comprised four chairs and a young secretary filing her nails. A deep voice sprang from the intercom, disrupting the secretary's focus on her manicure. Alexandra reminded herself this was no time for Alee Babblebrook to roam unleashed. She entered the adjoining office. Dr. Berger stood at his desk. Just as Will informed, he was old, bearded, wore a bowtie, round spectacles, and smoked a pipe—criteria Alexandra believed all legitimate alienists should emulate. She said, "Good day, Doctor."

"And to you, Miss Bathenbrook." He extended a hand toward the fainting couch. "I understand you are here only for a single consult?"

"That should suffice." The pleasing office held a cluttered bookshelf, three potted ferns, and stood illuminated by lamplight wherever sunshine from the window lay absent.

Alexandra laid down and folded her hands across her stomach.

The doctor rifled through a notepad. "A brief mental health exam can determine how best I might aid you. What do you believe to be of greatest worry?"

She cleared her throat. "I'm prone to anxiety and say silly things."

"I see," Berger empathized in a soothing voice. "We can often trace adult anxiety to a difficult upbringing. Were you a happy child?"

"There was always a meal on the table and shoes on my feet, so no real complaints. In retrospect, I wish my mother had spent less time locking me in a closet whilst entertaining her lovers. Archibald Bathenbrook, who I just learned is not my true father, should have visited more. I'm beset with shame that my aunt exposed me to occult rituals. Then, of course, the tragedies befell my siblings."

Berger lit his pipe. "What do *you* believe is at its root?"

"It stems from *the voices.* Since coming of age, whispers have tormented me. They're demonic. Quite lewd, I assure you."

"One moment." Berger pushed the button on his desk intercom. *Click.* "Cancel my lunch with Doctor Zeldin, Miss Bevel. This patient needs more than one hour." He flashed a reassuring smile.

"Demonic whispers, you say? What do they utter?"

"Murmurs that I am to birth the destroyers of mankind and similar apocalyptic hodge-podge. I pay it no heed."

"Do these *murmurs* arouse you?"

"They do!" Alexandra freely admitted. "Thoughts of mating with a demon tend to pert my nipples. See?"

Berger looked over and gasped. His mouth fell ajar in listening to her unbridled confession over the iniquitous notions that filled her head—whispered by fallen angels who wished to couple with her, no less. And then flowed New Orleans. Odd tales of being drugged and posed on an altar—blindfolded and naked—so guests veiled in ornate masks and regalia could touch and kiss her belly.

After twenty minutes, it mercifully concluded. The doctor cleared his throat. "Dare I ask, have you engaged in many sexual relations?"

"I'm not a harlot, Doctor!" snapped Alexandra. "I lost my virginity during my first year in college. Thereafter, I've partaken in only three sexual affairs, with only the last in Jerusalem proving pleasurable."

"Is having so few lovers a problem?"

"No, but there is no shortage of men who think otherwise. I hope my engaging in coitus in the Holy Land does not offend your Hebrew faith."

"Not at all. Back to these voices. It must be rather taxing to fend off such thoughts."

"Indubitably. I'm petrified of being impregnated again."

Berger crunched his bushy eyebrows. "Have you considered the use of a prophylactic? A penile covering for the gentleman?"

"Do such coverings come in circumcised, non-circumcised, and barbed variations?"

Berger rubbed his beard, unsure. "I'll write you a prescription—"

"Doctor, truly! I was taught that a man's seed must never be spilt. I'm considering anal intercourse to beat the system. Semen is a bit too salty for my taste. *Anyhoo*, it's not as vulgar as drinking blood."

Click. "Miss Bevel... are you there? *Click.* Hello...? Hello...?"

To his sudden panic, Alexandra reassured, "I do not boast vampiric tendencies. I held cause to cut the skin of a mule and drink its life force to avoid death in Amazonia."

"One last query. Do you have thoughts of killing yourself, any fears others are out to harm you, or see things that are not truly there?"

"That rather sounds like three," she noted. "I've not contemplated suicide... *lately*. Other than visions of a Swiss solicitor competent in Bach and Beethoven stalking me and waiting for attendants in white coats to show up to restrain me, no issues whatsoever."

"I don't perceive a straitjacket to be in order," Berger assured. He stopped writing upon noting his patient's sudden expression of melancholy. "Has something I've said troubled you?"

She shrugged. "I found restraint in a straitjacket very calming, and it's among my unmentioned fetishes."

Click. "Miss Bevel, check if I can move my vacation up a week." Berger started to ask another question but stopped himself. "May we pause? I'll return momentarily... *I think.*"

Once the doctor stepped out, Alexandra rushed to his desk, curious about how well she did on the test. She skimmed over his notations. Filling the page were terms shrouded in Latin. He had set up a grid with three columns. A checkmark headed the first column. It relieved her to have scored well with such things as tangential mindset and psychothapy.

Partial credit—indicated by a question mark in column two—listed tinnitus and depression.

She grimaced upon seeing words in the last column marked *X:* lypemania and dementia among them. She was barely passing and would need to try harder on those.

On hearing footsteps, she scurried back to the couch. Dr. Berger entered, tried to smile, but settled on shaking his head and reclaiming his seat. They sat, sharing an uncomfortable silence.

The ticking of the wall clock grew thunderous.

Alexandra asked, "Have you determined a solution for my ailment?"

He stated, "I have diagnosed you with licentious female hysteria."

It confused her, as she received a checkmark for that one.

"Miss Bathenbrook, you pose a striking conundrum," the doctor attested. "You present as an intelligent, candid, and lucid young woman, yet the degree of psychosis and neurosis reflected in your daily life is mind-boggling. I cannot fathom how you've avoided a complete nervous breakdown and implore you to consider a course of hydrotherapy to ease your symptoms."

"I will not be chained naked to a wall and hosed down with ice water to numb my senses! Never again!"

"I am a doctor, not a barbarian. Hydrotherapy entails a very narrow and forceful stream of water into the pelvic region to inspire *hysterical paroxysm.* I can even strap you into the chair to hasten and intensify your orgasms."

While tempting, she passed. "The hospital staff in Corumbá, Brazil, conducted a similar procedure. I'm pleased to report they found not a single candiru parasite."

Click. "Miss Bevel, please inquire with the bank over the status of my retirement account." Berger shakily scribbled on a pad. "In place of structured treatment, I will provide you with a prescription. If you smoke or consume alcohol to reduce stress, I implore you to do so more often."

Alexandra left the couch to collect the prescription. She gazed at it with confusion: *One unit. Electrex Ultra.*

"You believe curling my hair will help?"

"It's a vibrator. It will ease these voices imploring sexual satiation."

"I already have one, but it does not work in Europe. Something about watts and voltage."

"This one will work. I suggest a vigorous stimulation of the clitoris, daily."

She hesitantly nodded. "Might you write a note confirming to my brother I attended this session and passed the examination?"

He started writing. "In parting, I advise, if you value your freedom, repeat nothing you've stated in this office to anyone, anywhere, ever!"

"Yes, sir." Alexandra shook his hand and left the office, pleased at having held her darkest cards close to her vest. She shuffled to the receptionist to pay her bill. As another patient was seated, she whispered to Miss Bevel, "I've been prescribed a vibrator to apply vigorously daily to my clitoris... What's a clitoris?"

The young woman pointed toward Alexandra's lap. "Down there. You'll figure it out."

Chapter 22

Casablanca appeared the perfect city to crowd-watch Europeans living in Morocco... if that was what one wished. Half of its population were émigrés, reinforced by tourists seeking time in the sun and a tang of the exotic. Palm-lined avenues and mercantile neighborhoods catered to Occidental tastes, while in its ancient medina the less familiar intoxicants of snake charmers, black marketeers, and kief dens whispered come-hither. It provided a titillating wonderland for the nice to play naughty.

Alexandra had voyaged here for heedless sex and to help hunt down a serial murderer.

From her room in the Transatlantique Hotel, she waited for the knock. During her first day, she had toured little of the city and neither ruled it in nor out as her next scene for business.

She felt determined to leave London.

Her reasons for choosing it—when she thought herself half-British—had evaporated quicker than an April snowfall, leaving her footing there muddied. The food and climate indeed sucked. She was fed up with her half-brother's resistance to changing his life, and now, the mirage of a ghoulish interloper intruded her world, stalking her upon streets to which he blended hand in glove. It all needed to be burnt down.

An ocean, fair weather, frequent ships to Europe and beyond—

Casablanca might just be the spot.

Lurid, carnal thoughts continued to consume her. When he arrived, she would make haste to mount his cock, despite her moon being primed for pregnancy. *Bugger the moon!*

The knock sounded. Alexandra ran to the door.

He stood holding his linen jacket over a shoulder; his fedora pushed back and his expression somewhat wary. Without a word, she pulled him in by his tie. As she ravaged his lips, her hands went about sliding off his suspenders and working the buttons of his shirt. They drifted deeper into the room. Seating him at the edge of the bed, she paused her assault to unbutton her dress. It fell to the floor, leaving her naked. No quarter was given. She coaxed him to suckle a breast while her hand freed up his manhood, which she stroked until it bared her proper adoration. He settled back, and she mounted him.

She rode him feverishly before surrendering herself to his physical dominance. He rolled her onto her back. His tight grip and heated thrusts felt much like her first breeding. Danny Dalton came to her mind: that wry upperclassman smile, to which her carefree freshman eyes could find no fault.

Poor Danny had been found weeks later, hacked to pieces.

She lost her nerve and forced her lover off.

He grumbled and withdrew.

Alexandra brought him relief orally, so as not to act a complete tease. She scooped up her dress and retreated to the bathroom, tossing him a towel before slamming the door. It took her several minutes to compose herself. She flicked on the light to slink into her clothing. While not wanting to venture into the evening smelling of sex, she used a fingertip to rub toothpaste on her teeth and left it at that. Liam awaited.

"You should know," she said, placing on earrings, "that despite recent diagnoses as a sexual deviant by an accredited alienist, I've not bedded another since Jerusalem."

"Where did you get the tattoo near your—"

"It's none of your concern," she snapped, cutting him off.

"Well, you look like you have the measles," Kimball teased.

Her body remained marked with faded bug bites. "I'm recovering from running out of lemons in Amazonia. Is this the same serial murderer you spoke of whence in Palestine?"

"Yes." He lifted his shoulder holster off the chair and stepped into his pants. "I'm meeting with a French policeman in an hour for an update. Afterward, I'll stop back, and we can get dinner."

"Afterward?" She stopped dressing. "I haven't come exclusively as a concubine, I came to help you with the case. We have four days before my ship sails for Marseilles."

Kimball frowned. "I'll fill you in along the way."

It proved a lovely evening to be out on the town. Since they had an hour to kill, Alexandra insisted on visiting Bousbir. The neighborhood offered a unique Moroccan experience, and no tourist checked their visit complete without at least taking a stroll.

Kimball shared details of the manhunt as they walked. They believed the killer's name was Ali. He preyed on young boys, having abducted and murdered a dozen in Baghdad. No known photographs of him existed. An eyewitness stated he had black hair and a mustache. The killings stopped months ago, and the trail had gone cold.

They were after a highly unsavory type. It sounded as generic as seeking an Englishman named George, who strolled with an umbrella and enjoyed spotted dick for dessert.

Alexandra asked, "So, why are you here?"

"Three similar abductions have occurred in Casablanca."

"Why do you believe it's the same monster?"

"Instinct! Same pattern. Boys raped, drowned, and mutilated."

They stopped at the central archway to the walled-off *quartier rouge*. The atmosphere vibrated with roguish energy. Alexandra spotted harlots of Berber, Nubian, or Caucasian background—*kaftans* rolled down and breasts exposed—greeting those who entered. Oriental music sounded from behind the tall walls.

Out here, it sprang unlawful to hold Liam's hand.

Beyond the gate, anything goes, like breaching the flap of the adults-only tent at a carnival.

The main drag hosted cafes and restaurants of Neo-Moorish design. Tourists crammed the arena, exercising voyeuristic pleasure in watching belly dancers and stripteases from their dining chairs. Shouting merchants peddled souvenirs from kiosks while prostitutes chiseled through the crowd, stalking those with feet of clay. Most visiting out of curiosity would venture home with a racy postcard, while the more investigatory would do well to avoid a lifelong memento of syphilis.

Alexandra wrapped her arm under Liam's, and they headed down a shaded arcade. She stopped at a kiosk stocked with odd jewelry and suggestive paintings. A necklace of eight polished stones interwoven with a copper chain caught her attention. Green onyx with traces of gold, both colors complemented her hazel eyes. Its clasp appeared incomplete, holding a big ring at one end, but no connector to the other.

She placed this purchase in her bag, and they strolled on.

After passing a cabaret, the alleyway thinned out. Tourists became few, with most entering or exiting various whitewashed structures wearing the uniforms of the French Navy, foreign Zouaves, or the infamous La Légion. The sounds of sex and the smell of hashish drifted out from open windows. They came to a draped door advertising a pornographic movie, and at Alexandra's nudge, Kimball paid the entry fee. They shuffled into the smoky theater mid-show and stood in the back. The scene was quiet and eerie. Gentlemen smoked cigars while puckish ladies watched the screen's black and white images flicker.

It played out self-explanatory; no flashcards were required.

The film featured a man dressed in a tuxedo spanking a nude woman prone across his lap. The woman was bound and gagged. Alexandra found it evocative. She held no interest in bagging a man who would worship at her feet but wouldn't mind one who sucked her toes now and then. This sensual display knocked that pipedream down a peg.

"Are we to be an item, Liam, or just passing ships in the night?" She took hold of his hand. "I've thought of you often over the year."

He whispered back, "What would you expect from me?"

"Will you do that to me? Discipline me when I misbehave?"

He briskly escorted her outdoors, saying nothing more of the matter. Police work awaited.

A short trek back in the real world landed them at Petit Poucet. They took an outdoor table. A waiter wearing a fez and a wool djellaba deposited a kettle of mint tea. A plate of olives, couscous, and a French police officer arrived soon after. Alexandra waited as Kimball walked him in from the street, chatting in English. The officer wore a beige uniform and blue kepi with distinguished ease. A facial scar ran across his left eye from forehead to cheek.

"Lieutenant Victor Paulin." He kissed her hand. *"Enchante!"*

"Alexandra Bathenbrook. I hope you don't mind my intruding on your working dinner."

"Men must work, and men must eat," Paulin playfully fiddled, "but it forever best in the company of a lovely lady. How have you found us in Morocco thus far?"

"Rather European," she confided.

"You understand what Detective Kimball and I are to be discussing is of the highest security?"

She cheekily assured, "I shall be as mute as that palm tree and as deaf as this table candle."

"Are you finished?" Kimball questioned. They settled in.

Paulin retrieved a pad from his leather valise. "He has moved on to Marrakech. A second boy is missing. The body of the first was found in a well. A witness has shown up. She saw a man passing out treats to young boys in the medina where our last local victim vanished."

In the ensuing silence, Alexandra felt obligated to ask, "Do you now have a sketch of the suspect?"

Kimball looked at her, disheartened. "Do you ask as the mute tree or the deaf candle?"

"I am asking as the curious concubine." She lashed out her leg under the table and cringed at seeing Paulin's face contort to the blow. "Pardon me, Lieutenant. I missed."

He laughed. "It's an ugly business. We'll speak in French."

"May I borrow a paper and your pen?" She did so to his nod.

After the waiter took their orders, Alexandra jotted down notes on what she heard. The witness stated the suspect wore Western clothing and had shouted words that were neither Arabic, Berber, nor their union of local *Darija*. Something foreign. Alexandra sipped her tea and flipped over the paper. The men exchanged jocular chatter at her expense. Liam crossed the line, requesting she be denied a travel permit to Marrakech.

Handiwork finished, Alexandra cleared her throat and once more inquired, *"Avez-vous maintenant un croquis du suspect?"*

Paulin smiled. "We have no artist, and to you, *touché!*"

The waiter delivered plates and a steaming tajine of food.

Alexandra held up her sketch of him. "You do now."

"I've rarely looked better," he said, tickled. "We shall dine and then reconvene the witness."

Kimball lit a cigarette, sighed, and retreated in defeat.

"Despite Detective Kimball, *my lover*, divulging my tendency to stir up a whirlwind whence in foreign lands, may I go to Marrakech?"

"I shared it with your security in mind," Kimball tried to defend.

"Oh, hush!"

Paulin finished his *harira* soup. He said, "We are dealing with a ruthless killer. I cannot risk your safety."

Alexandra sighed and stared out at the headlights of the passing traffic. They were going to make her work harder than necessary.

"Where did you serve, Lieutenant?"

"Verdun." He pushed aside his soup bowl. His face fell sallow, gaze distant. *"On ne passe pas."*

"They shall not pass." It was the rallying cry that had saved France. Verdun. No vaster slaughterhouse existed. Throughout 1916, the French and Germans had fed half a million men to the meat grinder. To this day, over 100,000 dead remained missing in *Zone Rouge.*

Alexandra said, "My brother William lost much of his face and an arm at Amiens. Thomas fell at Cambrai. I plan to visit Bourlon Wood, so my oldest brother may know I have not forgotten him."

"Then France is forever in your debt." Paulin flashed a sympathetic smile. He lifted his glass. "To the heroism of your brothers."

She raised hers. "And to you, Lieutenant. *They did not pass.*"

"Bourlon Wood is Zone Rouge. You cannot enter. It is impossible."

She'd heard such before. "So too seemed my going to Marrakech. Please, Lieutenant."

"As it shall be! Excuse me. I will phone to ready the witness."

Once Paulin left, Kimball critiqued, "'When' and 'whence' are not interchangeable."

"Your French is horrible," she spat with venom. The conversation upset her. She scooped chicken and vegetables from the tajine, shooting a frosty glare at her man. "As for tonight, *va te faire foutre!*"

The upscale district of Gueliz appeared the perfect setting to crowd-watch Moroccans pretending to live in Casablanca... if that was what one wished. Alexandra, however, wanted to experience, taste, and explore the real Marrakech. Lieutenant Paulin obliged, dropping her in the care of an acquaintance who had restored a rundown palatial riad into a guest house for visiting dignitaries. It stood in the neighborhood of Mouassine; well within the gates and blushing red clay walls of the imperial city.

She had purred at first sight.

It held lemon trees in the inner courtyard, and the view from the rooftop terrace proved hypnotic. The mosaic tiles and carved doorways filling the three-story structure struck as appealing as those adorning a sharifian palace. On her first day, after a five-hour car ride, it presented a paradise. Alexandra held no desire to leave its grounds.

Now, on day two, she worried that her opportunity to catch a serial murderer would tick away.

Dusk remained an hour off, and the dry air topped one hundred degrees. No matter how much Alexandra hydrated, she felt more prune than plum. Restless for an update on the case, she waggled her feet in the courtyard pool while sipping mint tea. She doubted it to be spiked with anything that might metabolize Francophile assimilation. While the French boasted a stout navy, they were too absorbed in speaking their beautiful language and eating shelled gastropods to ever rule the world. If she dabbed perfume to avoid bathing or let her armpit hair grow out, she'd reconsider, but for now, she drank *sans sousi.*

The riad held six lodging quarters. Alexandra exchanged pleasantries with the other guests as they came and went. They included a French military officer, an Italian couple, and an older man seated nearby who'd yet shared a word between his intermittent gazes. The codger wore a linen suit, a blue bowtie, and often murmured indiscernible mantras as he sketched in a pad. Upon arrival, he had wrapped his bald head in a turban and set up a chessboard on a round tiled table in the shade. Alexandra thought he looked like a pasty, pudgy spider awaiting an entwined meal. She asked the houseboy for more tea to quench her boredom. Kimball had yet to visit since settling her at the riad. She was eager to share her thoughts on the investigation, cruise the medina with him, and revel in her first adult spanking.

The witness had supplied a fair recollection of the suspect, lending a portrait of a six-foot tall, muscular man wearing a suit. The killer's facial features included thick eyebrows, lean eyes, and a broad nose undercut by a dipping mustache. A blotch of dark skin discolored his left ear.

Alexandra's new hypothesis rested on the fact that he had fled upon being spotted. If he'd retreated to Marrakech to blend into a larger, less cosmopolitan city, he would now likely be wearing a traditional djellaba. She believed the suspect's fatal blunder came in shouting at the old woman. It seemed impossible to decipher the language in which he had cursed. The woman's poor Arabic lent difficulty to merging the words with any of the world's known alphabets. They could as easily be Turkic, Serbian, or the cluck-like mating call of an ostrich.

It sounded something like, "Kala-kada-jemi-k-day-me."

Alexandra had played with it over the sweltering car trip from Casablanca and then given up. She'd asked Paulin to send a telegram to her London office to let Oliver tinker with it. He had a marvelous way of entering a library and leaving with answers.

Until her understudy's riposte, there was little for her to do.

She gazed at the codger and blushed once caught. *"Bonjour."*

He tilted his head and leered at her inquisitively. "I escape Paris to visit Tunis from time to time, but Morocco captured my interest. You speak English with a French accent."

"Vraiment?" She pushed her tea aside.

"I sense many contradictions and mysteries to you," the man said, resolute in his tone.

Alexandra chose only to smile. She lifted her feet out of the pool.

They believed the killer to be an early-evening stalker. After placing her sunhat on, she checked the pistol in her satchel. She headed out to sneak in some shopping at the nearest *souk* offering a clear view of an orphanage, madras, or underage vendors peddling goods.

Find what they eat, when they eat, and then wait.

Being under house arrest by armed security would not aid her surreptitious cause.

After years of unrest, France had claimed a protectorate over most of Morocco in 1912. Under the Treaty of Fez, Islamic law still prevailed, and the Sultan had kept his status, though his rule remained conciliatory with the French governing apparatus. For this political dance, slavery had not been abolished until 1922, although ownership of "abids" remained lawful practice. European women were a highly prized commodity and therefore did not wander the medina unaccompanied.

Paulin had assigned a young *tirailleur* named Idir to guard the riad's front gate. His tasseled *tarbouche*, blue jacket, red sash, and white pantaloons formed an inspiring uniform. With Idir's rifle and jambiya dagger at the ready, what serial murderer wouldn't stick around?

Once in the medina, Alexandra reconnoitered the stalls, buying fruit and spiced flatbreads stuffed with onions and peppers. Bumping into a loping camel or over-packed mule served as the greatest threat in her jaywalking ways. Though Idir spoke only a smattering of French, they communicated well. He waited outside a tent that sold female clothing, and she eventually reemerged with a stuffed sack. Entering a more breathable square, Alexandra's priorities drifted back to catching a killer. Ahead, playing in high spirits, ran a group of boys batting a cloth ball with crooked wooden sticks.

She watched them with melancholy and ran her eyes over the arena. Veiled women washed clothes at a fountain. Sun-wrinkled traders—their swathed robes sprinkled with the dust of the Atlas Mountains—squatted on rugs, displaying their merchandise. A dark-skinned *haratine*—kidnapped as a boy from Senegal—swept dung off the street.

After five minutes, she abandoned her surveillance and searched out a fresh path to the riad, as retracing one's footsteps was antithetical to exploration. Idir returned her before sundown.

Waiting in the courtyard sat Kimball. He looked exhausted.

Alexandra said, "Let's dine on the roof. The city glows a magnificent pink at sunset."

"Sounds perfect." He placed a dusty bottle of liquor on the table.

"Well done, sir." She asked the houseboy to fill her clawfoot tub and helped herself to one of Liam's cigarettes.

They headed up the stairs.

She kissed him. "I'm happy you're here. I didn't come to Morocco solely to hunt down a serial murderer, you know."

Chapter 23

Her lavish bedchamber showcased silk linens and Berber rugs that rivaled the comforts bestowed on a favored paramour in the Sultan's harem. Enough moonlight filtered through the open-shuttered windows to allow Alexandra to appreciate her lover's sweat-shined body. She broke her sticky embrace and walked into the bathroom, only to return with an uncorked bottle in her grip.

The lubricant filled her hand, and she greased his cock.

Seductive whispers trespassed Kimball's ears as she kissed his neck. She turned, leaned forward across the mattress, and offered herself: back arched, rump raised. His manhood pressed into forbidden realms.

Even oiled up, it proved a stubborn fit.

With a loud, licentious sigh, she bit her lip and implored him to ravage her at his leisure.

An hour later, Alexandra awoke and looked at her hand, which burned and pulsed. She darted up, worried that a scorpion had stung her, as she'd earlier killed one hiding in her shoe. More alert, she sensed a similar discomfort underneath her, as if she sat on burning coals.

She gasped upon sensing that the tingling blazed *within* and wondered if it resulted from spreading extra spicy *harissa* on her *khobz b'cehma* flatbreads.

She gulped down the glass of water on her nightstand. *Nothing!* It seemed unlikely stowaway Brazilian fire ants were marching up her rectum. The inferno grew maddening.

Kimball lay muttering in his sleep. She punched him. "Wake up!"

He opened his eyes and moaned in pain.

She lifted the sheets off and tried to mount him. He protested and shoved her off.

The fiery tickle became excruciating. She again attempted to straddle him, desperate to douse her inflamed back passage. "Chivalry dictates you allow me to mount you!"

He reached over and surged the flame of the nightstand's oil lamp.

They screeched in unison upon spotting how red, gorged, and angry his penis stood. It did not look healthy.

Alexandra could stand it no longer. She cried out and made a mad dash for the bathroom. She crashed into the tub, legs over the rim, praying the cool water would extinguish the burn. Her breathing turned rhythmic, as if in labor. Nothing was happening, and at this moment, she would give up half her fortune for a turkey baster.

Kimball plopped in beside her, panting. "What lubricant was it?"

Alexandra cringed, realizing her error. "I may have rubbed my back ointment on your... It's some secret Japanese concoction meant to spur blood flow to tight muscles. Very potent stuff."

"Water isn't helping." He groaned. "We'll go to the hospital."

"No! I'm too young to be hanged as a sodomite!"

"Have a better idea?"

"Don't blame me, Liam," she griped. "We both know Ursula's at fault for crushing my spine." The arsonist in her anus continued to run rampant. After finding no other remedy, Alexandra pushed herself out of the tub and sought her clothing to dress.

"Public hanging as sodomites it is!"

It had proven a difficult evening, but Alexandra found cause to rejoice in the oddest thing: her back pain felt *so* alleviated. She spurred Liam to dress less sluggishly. He secured his shoulder holster and slid on his blazer. They walked down the steps more rigidly than Mary Shelley's *Frankenstein.* They had sought treatment at the French hospital in Gueliz, claiming ignorance. Enduring the snickers of the medical staff had served as cruel and unusual punishment.

"Bonjour, Lieutenant," Alexandra yelled down from the inner rail.

Paulin waved from his seat in the courtyard as the houseboy poured out Turkish coffee.

Kimball asked Alexandra, "Will you require another enema?"

"Whatever they pumped in worked. I'm clean as a whistle and light as a feather," she said cheerily. "I can barely walk for reasons I shall place on you. Do you need to continue icing it down?"

He groaned, having no answer. It was not a treatment conducive to managing his workday. She assumed his penis would be out-of-order for the last evening of her stay. They hushed up before reaching the courtyard and joined Paulin. Alexandra noticed the codger watching her. Something about him both enticed and repelled her curiosity.

Paulin handed over a telegram.

She read her message and declared, "The killer is Persian! My man Friday believes Ali yelled, *'Go away, old crow'* in Farsi."

Kimball sat up. "Wears a suit. A tradesman based in Baghdad."

"It would explain why he is here," Paulin added. "He may have victims in many countries."

Alexandra said, "My work here is complete. After breakfast, I plan to sleep all day."

"You must dine with us in Gueliz tonight," Paulin insisted. "I know the perfect *brasserie.*"

"Oui!" She hoped the bistro was not popular with hospital staff.

The houseboy dished out olives and honey-coated pancakes.

Both detectives soon departed, eager to check in with informers and press forward with this latest information. Alexandra walked them to the gate and wished them good hunting. No guard stood posted. It would save her the trouble of slipping over the back wall.

She yawned and headed for her room.

"I heard you last evening. Your libidinous cries were of sacred delectability to my ears."

Alexandra covered her mouth, mortified. "Sir, who are you?"

"I've been called many things," the bald codger replied, motioning with a hand for her to be seated. "Some tout me as a grand philosopher, others a tormented artist, while there are those who simply refer to me as 'The wickedest man alive.' I do not judge. 'Do what thou wilt' is our only law."

Alexandra took a seat. "What is it you see in me?"

"I sense a young woman shackled. One yearning for the freedom to unleash a sensual, spiritual beast raging just under her facade of decency. I can help you break your chains."

She lit a cigarette and leaned back in her chair. Something in his proposal titillated her. "Swing your hammer."

He signed his drawing from the prior day and passed it over.

She examined his work. From an artistic standpoint, it sparkled with talent. He had cast her seated upon a thrown in Hades next to an archdemon. Cowering slaves—herded from the flames by robed skeletal minions—pleaded for mercy, bowed at her feet.

She caught his fallacious smirk at her lack of reaction, and assumed if anyone knew, he did. "What do you know of the Nephilim? Are they among us today?"

"I have heard things." He leaned forward, basking in a disquieting afterglow. "Rituals still practiced by the old aristocracy. They offer young brides. It is considered a great honor. Arcane sacraments are conducted from an early age to prepare them. Their submission must be voluntary by chthonic law. Each aspirant must perfect a song to lure the demon when ready to copulate. The quickened gestation is damaging to the reproductive organs, so Nephilim are most often the bride's youngest child. Such heretical spawn cannot reproduce, so she must first cede a daughter to continue the cycle."

Though portions rang familiar, Alexandra suspected he was toying with her. "Name one."

"I cannot. They wield great power over humanity, though do so from the shadows."

He spoke with a hushed sense of awe, as if someone observing the big game from the junior varsity bench. Never one to allow a conspiracy theory to pass without piling on, she said, "I suspect those known by only one name. Robespierre, Rasputin, Judas, Beryl, and the like."

He raised a puzzled eyebrow. "You have an interesting mind and delectable flesh. I am to preside over a minerval for postulants to our North African lodge of the Ordo Templi Orientis. Join us."

She finished her cigarette. "I think not, but thanks for the offer."

"Seek me out when you're ready," he insisted as she stood to leave. "For today, let us at least spar in chess."

"It's a losing proposition to play chess with a mind reader. Good day, Mister Crowley."

After napping, Alexandra revisited the hectic square from the previous day. Dressed in a loose gandora robe, her head and face veiled by a *tahruyt*, she blended into the crowd. Once more, the boys played their stick game. She slipped off her *balghas* and asked a henna artist to ornament her feet. Seated upon a plush pillow, she aligned her camera lens to the range of the youths and placed it away.

The henna artist sang as she ground her leaves to create a paste.

Alexandra scrutinized two men in tattered clothes loitering nearby. The desert nomads conversed between predatory gazes at her. She rubbed the handle of her Colt 1908 vest pocket tucked into her layered waist wrap. The artist decorated up to her calf along one leg. No one unseemly approached the boys. Alexandra continued to monitor the unkempt men sizing her up. They were of a type she had been warned about. It troubled her in how they rubbed their craggy beards—their mouths open, exposing a noticeable lack of dental hygiene.

Wistful thoughts about her miscarriage arose for reasons lost to her. Her son would be four if it had not occurred—she felt certain she would bear only boys. Why it filled her with guilt, she remained unsure. She had done nothing to cause it, only wished it, and it was so. Perhaps she was here, watching over these rambunctious lads, because she owed the world a life. She placed her ruminations aside in detecting a dark-haired man in a blue djellaba observing the game. The intermittent foot traffic made it difficult to identify him.

He took a seat next to a younger boy.

The man fit parts of her sketch. She extracted her camera and lined him up in her lens. A basket-laden camel lumbering to the fountain disrupted her first attempt to photograph. The man came back into view. He passed the lad a candy, and her spine ran cold.

It was Ali!

She snapped the photograph, paid the henna artist, and rushed to put on her slippers.

The suspect walked off with the boy, becoming lost in the crowd.

She ran through the square until spotting him, and yelled, *"Arrêter toi, crétin!"*

The man looked back.

Click.

He covered his face and fled.

Alexandra's blood was up. She dashed past the abandoned boy, unsure if the first pictures would neatly unveil the killer. Her tahruyt impeded her vision, so she tossed it off, barely keeping him in sight as he trampled over dusty alleyways. She got lost in the maze.

The dirty lane she found herself in held an unyielding odor from the human waste and garbage strewed in its gutters. Clucking chickens scattered before her, dogs barked ahead, and swathed heads peered out through windows.

Ali had vanished.

She stopped to catch her breath in an alley. In her wake stormed the two nomads. One lurched forward and slapped her across the face, knocking her over. She hit the ground hard and remained stunned.

Her assailant emitted a frenzied cackle, produced a rope, and closed in. Alexandra ripped free her pistol, aimed, and fired. The man hopped back, holding his thigh, his hand filling with blood. She shot him again, and this time he toppled to his knees. She shuffled to a wall before the other slaver could draw closer.

Pedestrians shouted, and high-pitched police whistles sounded.

The second slaver retreated into the crowd.

Alexandra tossed away her gun. People pressed closer. Some offered soothing words, while others cursed. There remained nothing else to do but curl up, cover her eyes, and wait to escape it all.

❧

A trace of sunlight breached the cell's barred window. It would scurry the rats, but not the cockroaches. With morning on the march, she grew eager for breakfast and to warm up, as the night had passed chilly. They had gone medieval on her, locking her in the prison dungeon, which in her assessment held pluses and minuses. The sparse cell was preferable to the crowded holding pen she'd briefly shared with apprehended prostitutes. She did not fare well among other women. The foiled slavers had learned what she knew to be true: harem life could never be for her. To ease her boredom, she tried to run in place. It would be easier if the rusted metal corset fit snugger across her midriff. The primitive device was chained to the wall and designed to torment its wearer by denying the ability to sit. It offered some slack, but her only fun came in testing how far she could lean forward without toppling.

She abandoned her efforts and placed a finger on her swollen lip. While her mother had often slapped her, a man had never hit her. In dabbling in a rough and tumble world, she accepted that codes of chivalry would not forever shield her. The slaver had struck her; she had shot him. It seemed an appropriate quid pro quo.

The cell door opened.

"Sacré bleu!" Paulin berated the guard, who held up his hands, confused, before receiving a swipe across the face from his superior's gloves. It registered as a disgraceful state of affairs.

Kimball rubbed his chin. "You put that on yourself, didn't you?"

Alexandra reached back and popped the latch. The archaic device clanged against the wall. She said with much excitement, "It was Ali. I got a clear view of him. Why is everyone frowning?"

"The man you shot is a notorious slave-dealer," Paulin said. He apologized to the guard and dispatched the underling to retrieve her possessions. "He will live the rest of his days a eunuch."

So far, so good, she thought. "What about Ali? Is he captured?"

No answer came. Paulin said, "A car waits outside to take you to Casablanca. The Sultan demands that you leave the country before midnight. Your ship sails at dusk."

It confused her. "I stopped a crime. Why am I being punished?"

Paulin better understood both sides of the equation. "The usual penalty for a Christian woman shooting a Muslim man is death by stoning. When they explained that you're an American and British subject, the Sultan thought it wise to avoid an international incident."

Alexandra snorted. She'd never been kicked out of a country before. "Can I at least remain in my cell until breakfast is ready? Last night they served me the most incredible *bastilla.*"

Kimball shook his head, exasperated. "We'll gather your belongings. I'll tag along for the ride and escort you to the ship. The Sultan ordered for you to be handcuffed until safely aboard."

She rolled her eyes as Paulin placed on the cuffs. She said, "You may want the film from my camera."

"You attained a photograph?"

"Of course. It's what I do," she brazenly informed. "My gift to you for your hospitality."

Paulin winked. "Something special will be sought from the kitchen."

Alexandra smiled at Kimball as he escorted her out of the dungeon. She said, "Will you at least spank me along the drive to Casablanca?"

"Seeing that you've misbehaved, certainly not." He could not help but chuckle.

Chapter 24

Alexandra arrived in Tiranë under contract with the *London Times* to record not only the ascension of a new European king, but a Muslim one to boot. Interest in the coronation stood high back in "Jolly olde." The English mulled over the Albanians with a blend of derision and awe—their hearts swept up in the poetry and travel logs of Lord Byron. He had framed a romanticized vision of this restless, enigmatic land. Romanticism notwithstanding, there remained but one unpoetic problem: the country held no hotels.

"Do you know where a foreign traveler might stay in the capital?"

"Anyone will take you in," the ministry bureau clerk assured. "We are hospitable people."

How can a country have no hotels...? In Europe...? It's 1928!

Alexandra left the building with her stamped press pass in a state of bewilderment. Her surroundings appeared little different from other unprogressive areas of Europe, with one key exception—it held no hotels! The weather stirred mild, lending to a pleasant day to be a nomad in a backward Balkan kingdom. She gazed across the cityscape, which comprised little more than a few minarets, a church steeple, and a clock tower. Along the wide boulevards stood villas, timeworn structures of Ottoman design, and partially constructed government buildings. Albania had only emerged as an autonomous nation during the First

Balkan War of 1912, though its people had inhabited these lands from time immemorial when they were known as the Illyrians. Tiranë had been designated as its capital in 1925. The master plan to erase the ethos of five centuries of Ottoman rule and embrace the promise of the twentieth century remained in its infancy.

Alexandra set down her suitcase on a bench shaded by a eucalyptus tree. She kicked off her shoes and rubbed her feet. Breaking in new heels could not have been more poorly timed. The pistons of her mind churned hot and over-caffeinated. She'd spent hours consuming *Türk kahvesi* before hitting up the ministry for its bathroom and to get credentialed. Many foreigners sat in the cafe speaking languages both alien and familiar to her ear: Romanian royals, Bulgarian diplomats, French sophisticates, and Italian businessmen among them.

None of them seemed troubled over where they would rest their heads for the evening. She learned via pidgin-English, or pidgin-everything, some were staying at their nation's consulates or with compatriots. They suggested she ask anyone on the street for shelter, as the Albanians' ancient moral code, the Law of Lek, embraced hospitality as a great honor. Most agreed that a Turkish roadside *han* provided the best opportunity to wake up with fleas.

"How can a country have no hotels...? In Europe...? It's 1928!" Alexandra huffed aloud. It was her second consecutive nation suffering a dearth of electrical outlets. At least in Morocco, she had exploited periodic access to Liam's penis to aid her diagnosed mental condition... not to mention a bed. Smoking and drinking to excess only went so far. She considered changing into something vampish to seduce a Hungarian count or Montenegrin diplomat to bed down with for the night. Being so preoccupied with her annoyances, she failed to notice a girl sitting on the bench. She was no older than eighteen, dressed in a simple black travel frock, and clutched a suitcase—a peaceful half-smile to her lips.

Alexandra stopped picking at a bunion. "Want a cigarette?"

The young woman continued to smile, unschooled in English.

Alexandra fired one up and took a calming drag. She belatedly introduced herself. *"Unë jam Alexandra."*

The girl placed a hand over her heart. *"Agnes. Zoti qoftë me ju."*

While she knew a few phrases of Albanian, Alexandra surmised that anything more coming from her lips in this mindset would not sound friendly. She looked away. No one would mistake them for sisters. The tiny thing stood five feet tall, tied her dark hair in a bun, and held thick eyebrows that vanished halfway across her tepid eyes.

The bench stood near the parade route. Workers went about hanging the national flag from the roofs of surrounding structures. Alexandra considered it an intriguing banner: a black double-headed eagle on a backdrop of red. The colors of this "Land of the Eagles."

"Do të donit pak mollë?"

Alexandra turned to Agnes, who held out a slice of apple. "Does it come with a hotel room?"

The girl's persistent, calm gaze grated on her. Since returning from Brazil, Alexandra felt as if something noxious festered inside of her. Here she sat, brooding at the selfless gesture of a girl reared in a land offering her young life little more than a setting for bloodletting. She knew a newfound millionairess, raised in the spoils of America, should act better, but she didn't care to. She put on her shoes and walked away.

A middle-aged woman, brimming with excitement, ran up to her.

"You must be the girl I'm looking for!" The woman thrust out her hand. "Helen Boylston of New Hampshire. In the cafe, I heard mention of a young American searching for a place to stay."

"Alexandra from Helena, Montana."

"I've lived in Tiranë for two years. My roommate has returned to the States, and I've been longing to share some apple-pie conversation with someone for months." Helen smiled grandly. "You must stay at my villa. We'll listen to jazz, talk horses, and fire a rifle off the balcony if such things tickle your fancy."

"They fancy me to perfection," gasped Alexandra.

She looked back. Agnes sat eating her apple, smiling contentedly. The tiny thing waved farewell, and it took the American millionairess far too long to push aside her good fortune and wave back.

Serving as a politician in Albania posed such a taxing and perilous vocation that its parliament, under no threat of firearms, had voted to abolish itself. In its place, they would form a constitutional monarchy, with the current president, Ahmet Bey Zog, elevated to royalty. He was an inscrutable fellow; born into a prominent family and both victor and vanquished in the bloody coups that had never allowed the fledgling democracy to shake off its training wheels.

Zog had attained the role of prime minister by age twenty-seven and had occasion to get shot by a fellow parliamentarian. The failed assassin ended up murdered in reprisal. It had cost Zog a brief exile, but he soon returned to rejoin the government.

Here, there were laws, and then there were *Laws of Lek.*

The powers of Europe had tried to quell the turbulent nature of the land by sending Prince Wilhelm Wied of Germany as de facto king in 1914. They built him a palace overlooking the sea, made him sovereign, and he had fled six months later. There remained international hope that a native-born monarch would fare better.

If Tiranë typically hosted twenty thousand, on this day, its population stood fivefold. The Albanian army had been mobilized to provide security and decor. Most in the crowd wore Western garb, with Muslim men donning a fez instead of the fedora favored by the Christians. Well-to-do families from other Balkan fiefdoms were present, hoping to introduce Zog to their daughters, as he stood an hour away from becoming Europe's most eligible bachelor. Schoolchildren in black and red uniforms trouped by singing patriotic songs, and bicyclists whizzed along the periphery.

A flair for the exotic to which Byron had written sprinkled the crowd. Many women wore festive native dresses, with some men sporting kilt-like *fustanellas.* What most piqued Alexandra's curiosity, however, proved the *malissori*—rugged mountain men, who with but a strategic glare could send the gangs of New York to flight. They dressed in bleached wool breeches and embroidered waistcoats; their heads swathed in headscarves, sashes loaded with daggers and brandished stocked bandoliers to feed their long rifles. Their high cheekbones came as a birthright; their many scars having been earned. Only those allied with Zog's formidable Matja clan had been allowed into the city.

Alexandra made her way through the crowd in search of a sweet spot to photograph the royal motorcade. Along the entire procession route stood soldiers serving as barriers. Each time she climbed onto a lamppost or the hood of a car, a gendarme rushed over to demand she step down. Anticipation of an assassination attempt filled the arena.

Albania was the cradle of the blood feud—Ahmet Zog was entangled in fifty such imbroglios—and it seemed likely someone would try to extinguish his rise to the throne.

Missing such a shot would be haunting.

Growing desperate, Alexandra pondered whether any nearby kiosks sold stilts. She threw up her arms in frustration and exclaimed, "My kingdom for a ladder!" In her theatrics, a hand-sketched map of the city fell out of her camera bag. As the streets held no signposts, she'd made it to mark off Helen's villa and other points of interest. She stopped chasing it from fluttering into the crowd upon spotting Agnes, who stood holding her suitcase and offering a half-smile. The sun hit the spot she stood, giving her an angelic glow.

Alexandra sneered and walked away. *And there he stood.*

The young malissori towered seven feet tall. She pushed her way through to him, hoping the colossus spoke English or at least was an enthusiast of charades. She settled in the middle of his rawboned posse.

"Hello, boys!"

They stared at her with curiosity as she held up her camera, pointed skyward, and patted her shoulders. The giant conferred with his peers. He looked down and said, "Okay!"

The man squatted, and Alexandra climbed onto his shoulders.

With her prime vantage point secured, she went to work. A military band marched by, followed by *baijraktars* of the loyalist clans, gymnasium students waving flags, and finally, the motorcade, flanked by gendarmes holding swords. Ahmet Zog sat in an Alfa Romeo; his pursed lips wrinkling his thin mustache as he waved to the cheering masses. A tall and lean fellow, he wore a military uniform festooned with medals and ribbons for great battles yet fought or won.

Gendarmes pushed through the crowd, shouting for Alexandra to get down. The malissori refused to let them near and yelled back. She could not interpret their exact words, but their body language suggested them to be the local equivalent of "fuck off!"

Zog's car passed, and Alexandra's camera scored perfection. She motioned for the giant to set her down, wanting to avoid an international incident. The gendarmes persisted. A plainclothes man with them reached out and grasped her forearm. "The new prime minister requests a word with you, Miss Bathenbrook."

"Mirupafshim, fellas!" Alexandra surrendered herself. She hoped Albanian prisons rewarded well-behaved captives with baklava. "Who is the new prime minister?"

"I am." He identified himself as Kostaq Kota. "We would like you to photograph the swearing-in ceremony. We will compensate you for your time."

Double-dipping. Ka-ching! Thankfully, she sported a nice dress and had purchased amber jewelry at the local bazaar to jangle her ears and wrists. "Why me?"

"You are an American woman. What can be safer than that?"

"You'd be surprised," she cheekily said. *"Anyhoo,* lead the way!"

A select crowd filled the parliament room.

They introduced Alexandra to Zog. It went so well, he required prodding to abandon their discussion and get on with the ceremony of being crowned king. They moved her to the back of the hall and briefed her on what photographs they desired. Kota—an Orthodox Christian and among those populating the more enlightened regions south of the capital—wished the focus to be on Zog's pledge to rule a non-secular kingdom, inspire a love of nation, and introduce judicial reform.

Zog entered and took a stance on the dais. His mother and sisters filed to his side. The siblings spanned in age from Alexandra's to that of the thirty-two-year-old Zog. All five fostered dark hair, wore fashionable attire, and appeared glum for women about to be elevated into royalty. Alexandra focused on Zog, who cooperated by often looking over and flashing her a dry smile. He swore allegiance to the nation on both the Koran and the Bible... King! Applause filled the hall.

Alexandra sat to replace her film. After winding in a fresh roll, she glanced up to one of King Zog's sisters. *"Mirëdita!"*

The tight-eyed woman barked, *"Ndaloni se flirtuari me Mbretin ose vini në shtyllë!"*

Alexandra looked about. It had not been a very friendly greeting.

A Bektashi dervish standing next to her said in English, "She said, 'Stop flirting with king or face impalement.'"

"That doesn't sound pleasant." She did not require further stink-eye from the sisters to exit outdoors. The day had turned into a bonanza. It called for a round of raki, which would be available at Helen Boylston's after-party. Alexandra took a seat on a bench and kicked off her shoes to rub her feet. Celebratory gunfire and music filled the air, while people line danced across the cobblestones.

One young girl appeared unhappy.

Alexandra walked over and knelt beside her. She brushed aside the girl's blonde hair to get to the tears. "What's your name?"

"Eva," the girl said in a thick accent. "I am lost to my family."

"I'll help you find them. Where are you from?"

"Budapest. I once went to America. It is beautiful."

"You're beautiful." Alexandra whispered, "Don't tell anyone, but the love of my life lives in New York."

Eva smiled. "Is he handsome and rich?"

"Very handsome. I'll be the money. Do you miss Budapest?"

"Budapest is home, but no, New York is where I'd rather play."

A pretty blonde girl a few years older ran over. *"Eva! Tesék!"*

"Nóvér!" They hugged, and the problem seemed solved. Eva shyly said, "My sister, Zsa Zsa."

Alexandra said, "I simply love the name. *Búcsú!*"

The girls vanished into the crowd. Alexandra lifted her camera to take a few parting shots of the festivities, and then her heart sank. She had left her camera bag somewhere. She ran back to the bench, but only her shoes remained. Looking about, she spotted a young man peddling away on a bicycle with it wrapped over his shoulder.

She noticed Agnes gazing at her, offering the same annoying half-smile. Alexandra grabbed her pumps and broke into a full sprint, needing to capture the rapscallion and retrieve her undeveloped film or disaster would loom. The farther from the center of town she ran, the dirtier the streets became and the narrower the alleyways. She struggled to keep the swindler in her sight. She skidded across a steamy puddle of livestock droppings and crashed into a dung heap.

Huffing to catch her breath, she burst into tears. *It is gone. It is over. I am lost.*

Helen Boylston once more proved a lifesaver; nothing new, her being a nurse. She had served with the British Expeditionary Force and witnessed the worst carnage the Great War offered. Treaties ending wars do not bring peace to those who survive them. To aid her emotional recovery, she'd toured Europe in a maroon-colored Model-T she nicknamed "Zenobia" with another free spirit: the author Rose Wilder Lane. They had fallen smitten with Albania and taken up residency, adopting the role of socialites.

Rose had since returned to her little house on the Missouri prairie. Having washed her guest's soiled clothes, Helen had gone about playing dress-up. Alexandra stood decked out in gorgeous ethnic attire. The gold stitchwork adorning her white blouse and red bolero bespoke the brilliance of some mountain seamstress worthy of Coco Chanel. Below a red waist sash, she wore a decorative black skirt, with leather sandals called shollas giving respite to her feet. A lavish silk headscarf tamed her hair and swayed to her mid-back.

She tried to remain still in the mirror. "Who do you expect?"

"It's an open house, so anyone and everyone." Helen affixed a chain along Alexandra's hairline, which held gold coins that dangled across her forehead. Helen added, "Perhaps the king himself."

Alexandra plugged in her earrings and clasped her bracelets. She looked at herself and smiled. She felt at home.

Guests arrived. Helen left to welcome them into her villa.

How does one inform a Balkan king that the only photographs of his coronation are gone? Alexandra applied lipstick and sighed, having no answer. She had not reported the theft, knowing the police would notify the royal family, and thereafter, she would be duly impaled. She planned to sneak to the port of Durrës come morning and flee to Italy.

The villa soon filled with colorful characters plating local delicacies and singing off-key to the jazz records spinning on the gramophone. Alexandra resigned herself to the balcony to sip champagne and greet those who came out for a spot of air. Most did not linger, but she needed to fend off an Italian diplomat named Ciano, who, while dreamy, was not her type. Stefan and Shpresa Veshi rejoined her. The young couple lived in Boston and were fun to gossip with.

A man arrived with two malissori. Stefan said, "The *Kapidan* of the Mirdita. Stay clear of him."

"Why? Does he have a communicable disease?" asked Alexandra.

Stefan could not say. He explained the Mirdita were among the most powerful of the fierce Catholic clans. They lived in the remote mountain regions to the north, and they had never bent a knee to the Turks. "The kapidan's father led a rebellion years ago. Soldiers under Zog put it down. It is odd he comes to Tiranë today."

Alexandra did not find the chieftain intimidating. Of average stature, in his forties, with a thick mustache and fading black hair, his suit and tie were modish. The man shared a pleasant conversation with Helen... and here they came. Stefan and Shpresa bugged out.

Helen escorted the kapidan over by the arm. "My dear friend, Gjon MarkaGjoni. May I introduce Miss Alexandra Bathenbrook, who visits from America."

Alexandra held out her hand to be kissed... Hand still out there... *Still out there...*

MarkaGjoni appeared lost in a state of mental paralysis, his blank expression shaded with melancholy.

She withdrew her hand, flushed with embarrassment.

Helen became spooked. "What is it, Gjon? Are you feeling ill?"

The kapidan kissed Alexandra on both cheeks. He related what had enraptured his mind.

Helen's lips twisted; her expression one of fascination.

"What is it? Have I offended the kapidan—"

In reaction to Alexandra's wide-eyed gasp, MarkaGjoni lifted a pistol from his waistline, pivoted, and fired. Everyone stopped talking as the man charging with a long knife crashed to the floor. The shot had blown off a sizeable chunk of the assassin's skull. MarkaGjoni tucked back his revolver and offered consolatory words to Helen about staining her throw rug. He dispatched a bodyguard to summon a gendarme. With that, he bowed and left the balcony to fix a plate from the buffet table.

Everything drifted back to normal. Alexandra remained shaken. "What just happened?"

"A blood feud," Helen said. "The dead man is of the Thaçi."

Alexandra needed some raki. "Why did the kapidan look at me in such a manner?"

"You remind him of a woman named Zana Rrëshani, whom he had loved from afar as a young man. He thought you were a ghost or reincarnated. He invited us to visit a village called Rubik tomorrow. It is where this Zana is buried. It would be quite the adventure!"

Helen left the balcony to report the circumstances to an arriving gendarme. A man named Karl Vengver filled the void. An architect from Prague, he had served with the Austro-Hungarian forces that had driven the defeated Serbian Army across the Adriatic Sea. He described his war experience here as a chilling affair. Some of his comrades had been devoured by wolves or felled by the malissori. He was looking for investment opportunities to build something beautiful in a land he once helped to raze.

Alexandra suggested a hotel.

Vengver left the chat, nodding with approval.

Stefan and Shpresa returned. A man had arrived with the gendarme. He walked to Alexandra and handed her a note. As no one knew she was even here, it struck her as ominous that someone had found her.

Shpresa translated. "King Zog sent it. You are invited to stay at the royal villa with his family."

It presented a unique opportunity. "How painful is it to be impaled?"

Stefan informed, "It depends on the skill of the impaler. We judge them on how long their victims suffer before death. The best of them can send up a greased stake to miss the vital organs and pop it out at the shoulder. Two days is the unofficial record."

Alexandra tapped a finger to her lips, considering the invite. She moved aside as the bodyguards rolled up the failed assassin in the soiled carpet for disposal. The morning ferry to Italy appeared all the brighter.

Gjon MarkaGjoni moved on to the dessert tray; his honor kept, but appetite yet satisfied.

Helen escorted the gendarme out and soon returned. "There is a girl downstairs asking for you. Her name is Agnes Bojaxhiu. She will leave tomorrow for Ireland to join the Sisters of Loreto."

"Why are her sisters in Loreto?" inquired Alexandra.

"Agnes says she is going to become a nun."

Alexandra sighed with relief. It wasn't the worst thing to be stalked by a future nun. They headed down the stairs. Waiting, holding her suitcase in one hand and Alexandra's camera bag in her other, awaited Agnes—beautiful half-smile and all.

Alexandra crushed the tiny thing in a hug, stunned by her good fortune. All of her film canisters were intact. "How did you find me?"

After Helen's translation, Agnes took out the map that had blown into the wind.

Alexandra jotted down her contact information on the map and held out a roll of Italian lira. "Tell Agnes that if she has any needs in Ireland, I am but a brief trip away."

Once translated, Agnes accepted the map but would not take the money. Alexandra hugged her again and finagled the lira into the pocket of her savior's frock. *"Mirupafshim."*

"Shkoni në veri. Përqafoni dritën." With that, Agnes walked off toward her new life in an unknown land. Alone, but fully with God.

Alexandra's cheek, where Agnes had rubbed it, tingled. "What did she say, Helen?"

"She said, 'Travel north. Embrace the light.'"

It had been a tough decision: risk impalement by crazy princesses or take a road trip with Helen Boylston. Alexandra set aside her musings over becoming queen of *Shqipëria* and chose the latter.

The sun had crossed the sky by the time Zenobia trampled the narrow valley track running alongside the Fani River. It was jagged and barren mountain country. Alexandra had grown up looking at the peaks of Montana—majestic ranges amidst panoramas of lush countryside spread to the horizon.

These badlands were different.

The intermittent breeze whispered caveats of ambush. Vines covered the rubble of stone towers and houses abandoned to flame and cannon fire. Untended, long-forgotten grave markers abounded. It gave Alexandra a chill of claustrophobia. Once the sun dipped, Helen struggled to keep from tumbling them into the river. She slammed on the brakes and turned off the engine upon coming to a fallen tree blocking the road.

They disembarked and started walking.

Alexandra spotted an old Ottoman bridge. Its humped arches spanned the river like a giant serpent. An eagle flew by, taking one final swoop over the water. She asked, "What can you tell me of Teuta, the fearless pirate queen? I once had a dream of her after reading a *Fantômas* comic book."

Helen said, "Teuta ruled the Ardiaei clan not too far from here. She waged war against Rome. Facing defeat, she jumped off a mountain into the sea rather than surrender."

It impressed Alexandra. Teuta had left more of a legacy than the mere obligatory offspring and headstone.

"Have you driven the war free from your memory, Helen?"

"It will always be with me. I'm ready to return home and try. I'm desperate for a cheeseburger."

The cries of wolves echoed through the valley. It was an unfortunate time to be lost and unarmed.

Leaves and sticks crunched ahead.

Alexandra waited, her heart pounding. A dozen people carrying torches crossed the bridge. The first distinguishable figure proved that of a woman. In her mid-thirties, flaunting golden hair, she issued a welcoming demeanor.

"I am Luljeta. Rubik is just over the bridge."

Working up from the riverbank along winding donkey paths stood the fortified stone *kullas* of Rubik. Two stories in height, they featured narrow slits that served as rifle ports more than windows. A half-moon emerged and reflected off the lazy river and the steeple of the village church. Luljeta escorted them toward a bonfire, and the several hundred villagers gathered to celebrate the visit of their kapidan.

Everyone had dressed in their finest. Alexandra rejoiced at having worn her native garb for one last fling. Most Albanians she'd encountered posed a Mediterranean appearance, but among the Mirdita, blonde hair and lighter eyes appeared more common. As the crowd parted, the older women reached out to touch her arm or spat before her path.

They whispered among themselves.

"Zana died during childbirth," Luljeta said. They settled within the circle. "They believe you are a *shtriga*, come to haunt the living. The kapidan is correct. You look much like her."

A line of men, laden down with their war accouterments, performed the "Eagle dance." They interlocked their arms and chanted battle cries, with the lead malissori swinging a saber. Gjon MarkaGjoni sat in a prime seat for the performance. Once it concluded, he introduced Helen and Alexandra. They took seats and were served plates of lamb. He stated his plans to head for his village of Orosh come morning, and Luljeta's family would host them overnight.

Some women remained beguiled. Alexandra asked, "What became of Zana's husband and child?"

Luljeta said, "The husband died a year before her death."

A well-wrinkled woman standing nearby pointed at Alexandra and cursed, *"Ajo ishte mbarsur nga Djalli!"*

The kapidan ordered his bodyguard to escort the woman away.

The musicians fired up an ancient melody. A few of the malissori cajoled their leader to dance for them. He stood to the cheers of his people and extended his hand.

Alexandra looked up in a panic but did not deny his request. She asked Helen, "What do I do?"

Helen suggested, "Sway as if your father is a cobra and your mother a belly dancer."

MarkaGjoni led Alexandra to the dancing area. The drummer laid down a methodical beat, and the screechy vibrato of a clarinet and violin soon joined it. She circled the kapidan to the hoots and howls of their clapping audience, a growing sleekness to her predatory gestures. He stood like an obelisk, tapping only a foot while brandishing a puckish grin. She smiled and raised the ante, articulating her hips with a sinuous seductiveness.

The *çiftatelli* concluded.

"Sonte, je bija e shqiponjës!" cried MarkaGjoni. He handed her raki.

The crowd roared. Some shouted, *"Ju jeni në shtëpi!"*

The plum liquor heated her throat and kicked her stomach. For at least tonight, Alexandra considered herself a "daughter of the eagle." Once things settled, she asked to visit Zana's grave. Luljeta claimed a torch, and they marched through the darkness toward the church.

"Do any photographs of Zana exist?"

"No one owned a camera in those days," said Luljeta.

The tomb stood in a hillside cemetery covered in vines. Nobody tended the grave of a fallen woman. They had marked it Zana Rrëshani, as those of Rubik would not allow her to further tarnish their village name. No stone for the child existed.

Luljeta said, "She was so lovely. I'm ashamed of what happened."

"What became of the child?" asked Alexandra.

"A victim of foul superstition. The elders swear the Devil ravaged

Zana. They left the orphaned child to the wolves, but they would not feast. The priest took it to France."

Alexandra squatted down and pushed away dead weeds. It revealed an inscription. Zana died on June 20, 1905, at age twenty-three—the precise date of Alexandra's birth.

Chapter 25

The exposé was shaping up to be one about planes, trains, automobiles... *and pleasure barges?* The Italian government, tired of hearing about "The greatness that *was* Rome" issued zestful collaboration in producing Skendra Lilleth's article on the "New Italy." As her photographer, Alexandra had traveled the country for a week and yet crossed paths with her colleague, as the French journalist remained upcountry interviewing such titans of auto innovation as Isotta Maserati and Enzo Ferrari.

"Is a photograph equating Mussolini to Caligula what they're truly going for?"

Galeazzo checked his itinerary. "Yes."

"Strike a dignified pose beside the car."

She hiked up the grassy hillside and waited for the morning sun to rise a little higher. For years, the government pursued an archaeological project to drain Lake Nemi and recover two sunken barges built by the notorious Roman emperor. The floating palaces were magnificent in size and once served as Caligula's playground for sex orgies.

The sun now appeared right, rendering the dark outline of the submerged barges visible in the turquoise pool of shallow water. The trick was introducing a hint of modern contrast. She had instructed Galeazzo to park his flashy Alfa Romeo 6C 1500 Spider at a specific spot along the shore. It would offer her photographs scale and juxtapose the sleek and hip innovations of present-day Italy with the ignoble monstrosities sunk centuries ago. It was a shame that Galeazzo—attired in a custom-tailored suit that perfectly complemented his playboy charisma—would appear so minuscule in the broad vista.

Through her camera lens it all looked perfect. *Click!*

Mission complete, she shuffled down to rejoin her tour guide.

"We'll stop for an early lunch," Galeazzo said.

"Magnifico!" Alexandra coiled herself up in the red sport car's leather seat. They sped off in a flash.

It proved hard not to fall in love with the rustic scenery of Italy when the shades of autumn colored the rolling hillsides south of Rome. Alexandra held a gift for making a splash in foreign waters. The ripples of her Albanian adventure had made it all the way to Rome. Count Galeazzo Ciano—who'd invested an hour chatting her up when they'd first met in Tiranë—awaited her. She couldn't help but admit he presented an impressive, if not subtle, suitor. His influential father stood as a founding member of the National Fascist Party and led the March on Rome in 1922. It had no doubt greased the wheels for Galeazzo's ascendancy in the diplomatic corps. Though still in his twenties, he'd already served as a consul in Rio di Janeiro, Buenos Aires, and as the Secretary of Legation in Peking. Pegging him as a ladies-man came easy.

Over their travels, Alexandra's resolve to end their days shaking hands goodnight in a hotel lobby neared capitulation, and the longer they spent time together, the better his odds grew.

Her windswept mane mirrored Galeazzo's breakneck driving. She gazed up in wonder at the passing scenery. "That's an impressive castle."

Galeazzo's greased black hair remained perfect. "It is the Palazzo Apostolico. The Pope's summer retreat. It must be good to be the Pontiff, except for all that celibacy."

He guided the car off the main road and drove into Castel Gandolfo. The quaint hillside town spread tranquil and pretty. They walked its flower-filled alleyways and piazzas, eventually settling in an outdoor cafe that offered a fine view of the forests surrounding Lake Albano.

They ordered warm bread, fruit, and a bottle of *grappa*.

"When I heard you were visiting, I postponed my return to China," Galeazzo shared, amplifying his pitch for her heart; or at least other parts of her. "Our time together grows short."

"And what fun it's been, but I recall making it clear that I am not currently looking for a husband or lover."

"Perendeshe e Bukurise," he said in Albanian. "It is what the men in Tiranë called you."

Alexandra blushed. "Goddess of beauty" sounded lovely in any language. Galeazzo spoke perfect English and fiery Italian. "If you want to impress me, say it in Chinese."

He met the challenge. *"Meinu shen."*

She broke her deep gaze and said, "Dinner tonight, then we'll see."

With the latest round of flirtations out of the way, they enjoyed a more cerebral lunch, chatting about the interesting corners of South America each had traveled. Alexandra wandered off to take photos. Chirping swallows crowded the trees, with a few rewarded with crumbs from those sitting in the piazza. She excused herself to find a bathroom and entered an alleyway. The cobbled lane ended at the entrance to a courtyard, which held a running fountain and stood filled with flowerpots and vines. She found the facilities and settled in.

While she sat, odd noises sounded from beyond a wall. The longer she listened, the more it signaled that people were bowling.

She vacated the lavatory and paused at a door. Another *thump* of a hard ball landing, *whoosh* of its fast roll, and a thunderous *kapow* of toppling pins echoed. She entered the dark end of a small arena. It indeed hosted two well-lit bowling lanes. Three elderly clerics were engaged in a rousing competition. Two wore black cassocks and scarlet zucchetto caps. The final cleric donned all white, and after rolling a spare, he skipped back to the scoring table, offering a waving hand to his competitors' high praises.

The truth was even stranger than Alexandra suspected—*they were no good "candle-pinners."* Half a dozen men observed. Their ridiculous outfits were akin to those of a Renaissance-era joker: gaudy blue, red, and yellow stripes coloring their baggy blouses and flaring skirts. They sported fluffy ruffs around their necks and black berets that clung with all the droopiness of a soggy pancake.

Thump... whoosh.... kapow!

The white-robed cleric sure acted a demon of the alleys. Alexandra just needed to take a photo. She crept closer, focused her lens, and took several of the clergyman knocking down pins in prime form for a man of his advanced years. Brandishing a stern face and round spectacles, he boyishly clucked each time... *Egad,* she realized, *it's Pope Pius!*

She lowered her camera and started back-stepping. Her bum jostled a table. She cringed while watching a dusty bottle roll off its edge to shatter on the floor.

The Pope fixed his gaze on her, his irascible face turning red with panic. He shouted, *"Afferrala!"*

It rattled Alexandra having an angry Pope yell and point at her. The moment the Swiss Guards realized she was trespassing, she fled. Once back in the courtyard, she slammed the door and jammed a rake through its handle to shutter the exit. Racing into the piazza in panicked strides, she shouted for Galeazzo to start the engine.

"What is the rush?" he called out. "I have yet to finish my grappa!"

"The Swiss Guard is after me! I've witnessed something so blasphemous, the Vatican might crumble if it became public."

Galeazzo speculated, "A naked girl in the Pope's company?"

"Even worse," she huffed, tossing *lire* on the table.

"A young boy?"

"I saw the Pope candlepin bowling!"

Galeazzo clutched his head in a dither. *"Madre di dio aiutami!"*

They rushed to the car and hopped in without using the doors. In the rear-view mirror, Alexandra spotted a swarm of Swiss Guards running across the piazza, waving their halberd axes. Galeazzo turned over the engine, slammed down the clutch, and left tire marks upon the cobbles as they sped out of town. Once circumventing tight turns, he eased up on the pedal along the main thoroughfare to Rome.

Alexandra elected not to share having taken photographs.

Galeazzo winged, "Can you fathom the implications if word got out?"

"Bocce lovers will surely convert to Protestantism," she speculated.

"If it is traced to me, my career will be in shambles. *Mamma Mio!*"

Alexandra agreed to keep what she saw a secret to placate his worries. Regardless, she did not want to risk Vatican torture or inquisition.

She said, "He might send out assassins to silence me, but I'll credit him this... the Pope is one helluva bowler."

❧

It stood out as a chin worthy of its own legend. Italo Balbo—Air Minister of the Regia Aeronautica, audacious Blackshirt leader, and international fascist superstar—exited his vehicle along a runway of Ciampino Airport. The world knew him for the impressive armadas he flew over the shores of the Mediterranean to parade Italian might. Mussolini needed to thrust out his jaw artificially to attain a poor semblance of Balbo's natural magnanimity, leading many to speculate that the well-liked aviator would one day become a palatable successor.

To Alexandra, his chin already inspired fanatical devotion. Balbo's white uniform, sturdy build, broad smile, and gregarious nature were all but lost to her in their introduction. All she could focus on was a deep desire to suck his chin. His bold and stylish chestnut-colored beard made it special and like no other she'd ever seen: restricted to the chin and darting out into a fine point with a floating mustache above.

Another fetish proved the last thing Alexandra needed. She hoped her nipples stayed in check.

Balbo said, "Skendra Lilleth sends her regards."

"Who...? Oh, yes! We plan to meet in Venice."

"And you, young Ciano," greeted Balbo. "How is your father?"

Galeazzo nearly flopped over at Balbo's slap to the shoulder. "He is well, Air Marshall."

"Come! Let me show you the future of Italian mastery of the sky!"

They entered his vehicle. The driver headed down the runway. Balbo discussed the upgrades in aviation technology his countrymen were testing. They passed Savoia Marchetti flying boats, outfitted with pontoons to allow for water takeoff and landing.

"Why don't you call them floating planes?" Alexandra questioned. "It would be a shame for the Royal Navy to be credited such machines, when it is your chin that deserves such praise."

"I like how you think!" Balbo declared. "You two must join us this evening at the opera."

"You and Skendra? In Venice? Isn't it a bit late to drive up?"

The car came to a stop beside a high-winged Caproni Ca. 101 three-propeller aircraft. "The Air Marshall does not drive." Balbo winked. "He flies." He laid out their itinerary. They could be in Venice in two hours, allowing her time to meet up with Skendra and shop for a dress.

They exited the vehicle.

Alexandra said, "I would like a photograph of you standing on the wings, Chin Marshall."

Balbo jumped onto the rear stabilizer and then onto the fuselage. He walked to the center of the plane and took a proud stance on a wing.

"Will this do?"

She aimed her camera. "I meant while in flight."

With Balbo's bold laugh, she attained her desired photograph. Another staff car drove up. Balbo jumped down and met the arriving air force officer. He read a note and barked irritably in Italian.

Galeazzo whispered, "Balbo just mentioned bombing all red cars south of Rome."

Alexandra bit her knuckles. "Should we cancel Venice?"

Balbo strolled over. "Some tourists have assaulted the Pope. We have dispatched the Carabinieri to monitor all trains and ports of entry. I pity these deviants!"

She assured Galeazzo, "I never touched him!"

He grabbed her arm and escorted her away for a private chat. "What are you not telling me?"

"Nothing!" She exhaled deeply. Flying would save her an all-day train ride and allay fears that Swiss Guardsmen would show up at her Rome hotel to drag her to the Vatican dungeons. "We must distance ourselves and go!"

"Balbo is an honorable man, but he will toss us out at ten thousand feet if Mussolini orders it."

"So... what have you two decided?" Balbo asked.

Alexandra looked up at Galeazzo, who nodded. "We'll get our bags and then, *Venezio, arriviamo!*"

∾

A stylish, highbrow crowd filled the foyer of the Teatro la Fenice. The ornate beauty of the opera house had so inspired Giuseppe Verdi that he'd composed *La Traviata* to honor it, and it served as a staple to open each season. Alexandra sipped champagne and chatted with Balbo, one ear keened on surrounding conversations.

Angry gossip about an attempted assassination of the Pope whirled.

Her rendezvous with Skendra at the Hotel Danieli rekindled their sisterly competition. They'd hit the boutiques and bantered on fun terms while sliding into their black evening dresses, elbow gloves, and applying makeup in tactical attempts to out-posh the other. Once their dates arrived, such comradeship ended. Galeazzo set his prancing eyes upon Skendra and was met with no resistance.

Their unfettered flirtations had monopolized the quartet's stop for cappuccinos at the Café Florian and continued in full annoyance.

It upset Alexandra on principle alone. She could not fault Galeazzo for his frustration with her after days of amorous rebuke, yet it bothered her how easily he dumped a partner in crime. She glanced at the frisky pair, thinking a child of unequivocal beauty might be conceived before sunrise if she failed to reassert some authority over her date. The lights in the foyer dimmed twice. Those gathered funneled into the opera house. Alexandra muscled in and kissed Galeazzo on the lips.

She slid her arm within his so he could escort her to their seats. Skendra fell in line around Balbo's extended arm. They walked up the red-carpeted staircase and entered the Royal Box.

The entire theater stunned with its golden frescoes and crimson tapestries, but nothing matched the indulgence of artistic detail given to the Imperial Loggia. In place of chairs, four thrones stood adorned with exquisite candelabras overhead, casting a radiant light on a mural-filled ceiling. Alexandra and Galeazzo settled behind Balbo and Skendra. The cacophony of the little people below evaporated once the lights dimmed.

A man took to the stage. He asked everyone to rise for a prayer dedicated to the Pope's health and recovery.

"Maybe he's so angry with *you* he had a stroke?" Galeazzo worried.

Alexandra rolled her eyes. The brief silence concluded, and they retook their seats. She whispered, "If I go down, you'll be lucky to end up a janitor at the embassy in Iceland. Can your father make inquiries to end this?"

"You don't tell a man nicknamed 'The Jaw' bad news," he warned.

Act one commenced. Balbo looked back, a finger pressed to his lips. Alexandra extracted a pen and paper from her purse and began jotting. She handed her message to Galeazzo. "Get on the phone to someone who has the Pope's ear and read this."

The note stated: *Dear Pontiff. I have photographs. Call off the dogs or I go public—candlepin gal.*

Galeazzo's face paled. He left the box to find a phone. Alexandra settled in to enjoy the show. Venice, with its historic architecture and romanticized canals, stirred epic in its beauty, but its air lofted foul and musty. From the moment of arrival, she was beset with nasal drip. She offered an apologetic smile whenever her sniffling disrupted Balbo's blissful devotion to the stage.

In the middle of act two, Galeazzo returned. He nodded and retook his seat. Relieved, Alexandra took hold of his hand.

Her stomach gave out a loud grumble. "My mouth is so dry. I need something to suck on. Do you have a mint?"

Galeazzo placed her hand on his crotch. "It is customary for a count to be served up *felatio* at the opera."

Alexandra's eyes burst wide. She slid her hand off his bulge and crept toward the other end of her throne. "You didn't pay for the tickets."

Act two concluded. The audience applauded and retired to the foyer for intermission. The men excused themselves to smoke cigars on the piazza. Alexandra pulled Skendra aside. "Galeazzo insists on felatio. You need to help me!"

Skendra's rosy lips curled with intrigue. "How explicit was he?"

"Around *this* explicit," Alexandra illustrated, book-ending her hands. *"Mamma Mio!"*

Skendra gulped. "We'll switch seats for the final act. Italo is married and has shown a virtue of steel. Do something about your sniffling."

"You're such a lifesaver!" Alexandra left for the restroom. She used some tissues to blow out the clog in her sinus canals, but it only inspired a fit of sneezing. Her head felt full of fluid.

"It's the mildew, darling," a woman touching up her lips said in a Germanic accent. She lifted from her neck an ornate silver pendant and unscrewed the top, revealing a tiny spoon and white granules.

Alexandra took it in hand, finding it a sweet piece of jewelry. "This will help my congestion?"

"It helps with everything, darling. One sniff for each nostril."

Alexandra snorted the first spoonful, dug in for another, and sniffed it to the max. It cleared out her sinuses. "Thank you!"

"Auf Wiedersehen."

The lights flickered, sending Alexandra to rejoin her party. They rushed up the steps. She sat next to Balbo, and Skendra settled beside

Galeazzo. The lights dimmed. For the first time in hours, Alexandra felt wonderful and worry-free. An opera posed a glorious forum for telling a story. Her moving up just one row made such a difference. The voices of the actors and the melody flowing from the orchestra pit took on an extra-dimensional quality. All her senses tingled, and she could smell the cigar residue on Balbo, hear droplets of rain pinging the roof, and read the sheet music of a cellist from an incredible distance. She studied Balbo, thinking the crème silk scarf dangling over his shoulders such an elegant addition to his tuxedo. She yearned to suck his chin.

Someone behind her moaned. The rear thrones of the Royal Box were slightly offset from those in the front, which allowed a narrow corridor for her to peek.

Skendra and Galeazzo sat serenely, eyes fixed on the stage.

Alexandra started flailing her arms to help direct the orchestra. She turned upon hearing a noisy slurping sound, but Skendra and Galeazzo idled peacefully. She returned to her duties as *maestro collaboratore;* the music flowing out of her fingers in an unsurpassed virtuoso. Galeazzo again moaned. Rather than turn, Alexandra removed her compact from her purse and opened it. She first checked her eyes, sensing that they were bulging out of their sockets, but they were only bloodshot and *primo* beautiful! She shifted the compact's mirror to spy behind her.

Skendra appeared missing! *Wait, there she is...* vanished!

Her head rose and dipped like a well-charged windshield wiper. The French vixen certainly knew how to service a count.

Alexandra peered at Balbo, who seemed oblivious to anything beyond the view of his opera glasses. She placed her hand on his crotch.

He glanced over to whisper, "Perhaps after dinner."

She slinked her hand back to her lap. The slurping proved distracting beyond belief. The titillating music of *felatio in teatro*, and the opera itself, came to their momentous climaxes. A thunderous ovation sounded as the audience burst from their seats.

"Bravissimo!" Alexandra shouted repeatedly. She lifted a handful of lire from her purse and tossed them over the balcony rail. She turned to Galeazzo and Skendra to applaud them as well. *"Bravissimo!"*

Skendra dabbed a handkerchief to her lips. Galeazzo appeared depleted.

"We'll meet the actors at the reception," said Balbo.

Alexandra kept clapping and yelling, *"Bravissimo!"*

"You can stop now," said Balbo. "The cast has left the stage."

The opera house emptied, but Alexandra continued to applaud. *"Bravissimo!"*

❧

The Teatro la Fenice showcased an impressive facade—particularly on a nasal decongestant—but Alexandra thought that the management should not have shortchanged hosting a snack bar. She paced the front courtyard smoking a cigarette, waiting for the actors to report to a cocktail hour in the Sala Grande. Her stomach demanded recompense for the upset stirred throughout the day.

It had rained, lending the reflections of the streetlamps off the cobblestones more enticing to her mind's eye than the twinkling of the solar system, the Hope Diamond, or even a stick of pink cotton candy. She had tried to cajole Balbo to join her so she could instigate an uninhibited suckling of his chin, but he was the second most popular figure in all of Italy and immediately mobbed by well-wishers. As for the whereabouts of the two ranking members of the Count Ciano Penis Admiration Society, Alexandra remained unaware: likely in a more discreet setting to fornicate, such as a dark alleyway or broom closet.

A few other VIP patrons out for some air started heading back inside. She joined them and eventually found Balbo holding forum with a rather brutish-looking penguin and two jutted-jawed goons. He broke off his conversation to tell her, "These men are with the *OVRA*. The ugly matter with the Pope is resolved."

"Magnifico!" She popped a kiss high into the air. *"Arrivederci!"*

Balbo shook his head as she marched off. Spread across a clothed table between mini champagne towers rested small bowls of iced caviar and plates of toasted ciabatta wafers. Alexandra muscled her way close. The tiny spoons perplexed her. Her trial scoop allowed for a mere pittance of fish eggs to place on the crackers. She savored her treat's salty pop and gooey texture and declared to no one in particular, "It rather tastes like jism."

Two older women turned to her, shocked.

Alexandra clarified, *"Sá di pene fluido!"*

The women gasped at her uncouth manner and scurried off.

After another dainty scoop, Alexandra picked up the bowl and emptied it into her mouth. She washed it down with two glasses of champagne. Everyone's attention shifted to the operatic artistes. She returned to clasp Balbo's arm. A petite man with a curled mustache introduced the cast as they entered the soirée to applause. A receiving line formed behind Balbo, as he stood highest in rank. Alexandra felt intoxicated standing arm-in-arm with a neo-emperor, as if one could get away with most anything.

First up came the actor who'd played Alfredo. Alexandra curtsied. She placed her thumb and fingertips together and stuck them under the tenor's nose. "You are no Enrico Caruso!"

Next up, the mezzo-soprano portraying Flora. Alexandra hand-scoffed, *"Mezza-mezza."*

The soprano who played Violetta was introduced next. Alexandra kissed her on both cheeks. "My Electrex-Ultra *vibratos* a prettier tune."

Balbo glared at her.

"Grande uomo!" she gasped. The baritone who acted as Giorgio proved much fatter up close. She did the fingers again. "A gifted contralto? *Au contraire!* As a comprimario, you were so compromisio!"

Her beyond the pale gestures alone annoyed. An undercurrent of disdain swelled among those gathered. She stepped to the maestro. "You are no Toscanini!" Someone tapped her shoulder. "The entire third act sounded far superior under my direction."

Alexandra paused and looked up at the two towering OVRA goons settled in front of her. At Balbo's nod, they lifted her up, tossed her over their collective shoulders, and marched across the room. As she floated the air in their firm grips, she wondered why the Italian people had turned on her. Their scowls and hisses appeared very striking to behold from so high an altitude. "Italo! Save me!"

Balbo did not acknowledge her; his face lost in a palm, head dipped and shaking.

"The promise of Fascist Italy has failed me!" Alexandra percolated. "My train arrived twenty-minutes late! My ravioli was so undercooked, it *al dente'd* a tooth! Your caviar lacks the appropriate *tessitura!* The Pontiff is a closet bowler! He's a filthy candle-pinner!"

People pelted her with whatever they could find to throw.

She made her final defiant barbs, laughing hysterically. "Il Duce's favorite ice cream is Dulce de leche! You will never rule the world again! Italo, I beseech you! I must suck your chin!"

Apparently, the orders given to the goons went beyond taking her outside. They carried her through the courtyard, across the street, and flung her into a canal. Its water stirred cold and smelled like sewage.

She surfaced cursing; waving a fist. One goon tossed her purse onto the ground. *"Parti domani, capisci!"*

"Capisci!" Alexandra yelled back.

Some jerk walked up to the waterline, and instead of aiding her, snapped a photo. She swam to a boat dock. Once dried off, she'd need to piece together at what juncture the magical evening had taken such a remarkable downturn.

Chapter 26

France: October 1928

Will was in Paris. Barnabas had chewed on his mask, and he needed to report to the local studio of Anna Coleman Ladd to get it replaced. It also happened to be his thirtieth birthday. He skimmed over Alexandra's latest photographs while she inspected the damage. The prosthetic showed few marks. Any pretext that "the dog ate my face" would not excuse him from dining out. She placed it down and rummaged through the suitcase Will had lugged from England. It contained her St. Moritz winter wardrobe and some letters. Regions of Turkey would be cold this time of year.

Will passed back a photograph, amused. "The sisters look like they want to stab you."

"Impalement is their preference. A hot, greased pole thrust up one's rectum is no laughing matter. You must trust me on this." Alexandra hopped onto the bed. *Cruuunch!*

Will sighed. He would not have his new mask until tomorrow. He rubbed his temples as she tried to pop out the sunken portions of the malleable tin. "Cancel dinner."

Alexandra was hearing none of it. "I set the reservations. I'll sort it out." She tossed on her cashmere coat and sable-brimmed Cossack hat, pushing the ends of her hair over her shoulders. "Be ready!"

Paris in springtime charmed incomparable; October, not so much.

A cool wind swirled, and thunderstorms loomed on the horizon. During her taxi ride through neighborhoods of Saint-Germaine-des-Prés, Alexandra read her correspondences. One came from Denys Finch Hatton, who'd recently guided British royalty on safari. He had included a photograph of himself with the Prince of Wales. Written on the back: *Dearest Alexandra—Brilliant time with our special guest.*

She filed it in her purse.

Her brief trip ended at Le Procope. Hemmy had recommended the belle époque brasserie; a favorite haunt for artists and literary types. She had reserved a private upstairs dining room but remained unsure how public the trail from the entrance to their table would be. It was *his* birthday, and stressing out Will did not suit her overriding intention. No one stood at the maître d' station. Things looked promising. A brass-poled staircase wound itself to the upper floor behind the waiting area. She peeked into both main dining chambers. The vibrant rooms featured red and gold decor, crystal chandeliers, and tightly quartered tables. Settling near the entryway, she waited for someone to show.

"Vous y!" A man in a tuxedo stormed past and took station at the welcoming stand. *"C'est pas encore ouvert!"*

"Excusez-moi?" Alexandra responded. "Do you speak English?"

"When I must." The boorish maître d' raised an eyebrow and grunted. "Do you have a reservation?"

"Under Bathenbrook." She drew nearer. "Is there a more discreet entry to the upstairs?"

He lifted his attention from the seating chart. "Your inquiry is superfluous. Your table is in the dining hall to your left."

"Au contraire. I spoke with Pascal, who assured—"

"Pascal is off tonight. I've bumped you for a more notable party."

Alexandra's eyes tightened. If she were certain the French penal system served fresh baguettes, she would bust the man's upturned beak. She regrouped her emotions, recalling she was a finagler extraordinaire.

"I see. The prince will be *very* disappointed."

Her statement lingered for several seconds. "What prince?"

"I don't want to give too much away," she told the snoot. "We'll just refer to him as the next 'King of England.'"

"Insense! I would know if the Prince of Wales were to dine here. I follow the gossip columns about his liaisons."

"And that is why *the prince* travels clandestinely and does not publicize his private affairs to French maître d's!" She dug through the photographs in her purse. "For example, you read nothing in the tabloids of his attendance at the crowning of King Zog of Albania."

"I only see you with King Zog. Those women look like they want to show you the guillotine."

"And do you know why...? Because *the prince* was taking a photo of *me!* Surely, you've heard about his trip to Africa." She shoved a second photograph up to his nose. "Is that not the Prince of Wales?"

Beads of sweat formed on the man's forehead as he read the back of the photo. He ran a finger to loosen his shirt collar, studied the seating chart, and then held out a hand, seeking it to be greased.

No bribe proved forthcoming. *"The prince* suffered a facial wound while on safari. He insists on being escorted to our table without untoward attention. Make it happen, or I'll bring this up with the Pope next time we bowl together."

"Ridiculous. The Pope does not... *Bon Dieu!*"

She placed the last picture back in her purse. "Please write your name."

"Why do you need my name?" the maître d' pensively inquired.

"So when *the prince* is negotiating new terms to divide German war reparations with President Gaston Doumergue, he can irately state, 'This maître d' upset me. It is why England demands five billion additional gold reichsmarks once destined for the French treasury!'"

Patrons filtered in. The maître d' gulped. "An innocent error. I have secured your table. *What else do you need?*"

She laid out her demands, concluding, *"The prince* will be incognito to veil his identity and facial scar. Our dinner must be kept secret from the press. His man will remain in our limousine. He tells the king everything... I mean *everything* that we do together."

"It shall all be as you wish," the maître d' promised.

"Eight o'clock it is. *Au revoir.*"

Alexandra took in a satisfied breath of chilly air once hitting the street. She pondered where best to shop for two British flags and a somewhat fashionable sack.

❧

William Bathenbrook, the unbeknownst next King of England, sat trying to see through the small holes cut into the black velvet handbag covering his head. It was of high quality and rested on his shoulders without being overly droopy. He did not know how it had come to this. He suffered mightily, but quietly. The yellow Rolls-Royce Phantom sported a black top, grille, and trim, with a late addition of small Union Jack diplomatic flags to each side of its headlights.

Will gazed through the raindrop-tainted window at the lights of Paris, which did twinkle peacefully in his mind. The gray wool trench coat Alexandra had gifted him fit well, and their only debate had been whether wearing a hat over his head bag would look peculiar.

He looked across at her. She sat humming a jazzy tune with the complete glam and confidence of a Muscovite fashion model. For the first time in his life, he placed partial trust that his sister knew what she was doing.

Alexandra patted down his white scarf. "By the bye, everyone will treat you as if you're the Prince of Wales."

"Why?" he asked, though his preference was not to know.

"Because I fibbed to get a private room." She finished touching up her lips and folded her monogrammed silver compact. "Walk in head held high and regal-like."

It was worse than he had feared. "I'm much taller than the Prince of Wales. Everyone will notice!"

"Don't be daft," she quibbled. "They'll be too distracted by the sack over your head to take notice of your height. Place your fake hand inside your coat pocket, and I'll guide you in, nice and slow."

Will exhaled. "For once, don't jerk about and rip my arm off."

Léon, the chauffeur, guided the car to a parking spot at the entrance. The rain kept pedestrian traffic low along the cobbled lane. Two burly men dressed in upscale livery rushed out with umbrellas. Will stepped out first, Alexandra looped her arm within his, and they were escorted inside. The restaurant was abuzz with raucous merriment.

An attendee helped to remove Alexandra's jacket. She elected to keep on her Cossack hat, as it meshed flawlessly with her silver-jeweled evening dress and provided a touch of bohemian chic. Will kept his coat. They were ushered up the stairs, with one bouncer remaining below and the other at the top of the steps. One private room stood filled with artsy, bright young thing wannabees having a gas, while the others held more curmudgeon groupings. Will finally relaxed upon stepping into their dining chamber. It looked like a library furnished with historic relics and a candle-lit table for two.

"See! Without a hitch," said Alexandra.

They took seats. The head waiter passed over menus. The wine steward awaited a decision.

Alexandra said, "The prince appreciates your discretion. We will start with a bottle of Château Margaux gran vin, 1921."

"You look lovely," said Will. Older brothers never truly surrendered their watch over the safety and fidelity of their younger sisters. It seemed to him that over her recent travels, Alexandra had matured from an unfailing calamity into a sophisticated woman, exotic in her allure and more sensible in scruples. The dress she wore was elegant, her makeup subtly captivating, and he felt it would be unfair to begrudge any man resting festive eyes upon her.

He asked, "How am I to eat with this on my head?"

"Garçon!" she called out. *"J'ai besoin de ciseaux."*

"Très bien, mademoiselle."

The scissors arrived before the wine. Alexandra cut out an oval. Will felt relieved not to have lost a nostril. He ordered an appetizer of garlic-buttered snails, a bowl of lobster bisque, and steak tartar for himself, along with onion soup and coq au vin for Alexandra.

The wine cork popped. Alexandra sniffed its bouquet. "This woman you're looking for. Noel, perchance?"

Will remained wary of sharing his suspicions about their deceased sister. "Yes. I hope she is well."

"If you do not get over her soon," Alexandra warned, "I shall help you along. A high-end escort might appear at your door someday, and utter, 'Hello, William. Alexandra sent me.'"

"I'd prefer you did not." He spotted an odd-looking fellow peering in from the doorway.

"I take your father's side on this issue. You must marry and carry on the Bathenbrook name."

"Our father." Will could tell by her tone the truth had cut deep.

The upstairs bouncer scurried the interloper away and took a stance in the doorway. A tray of snails arrived. Alexandra tasted one and shrieked, so Will polished off the rest.

"*Scusa mi intrusão.* I must speak with the lady."

Will again glanced over. The man, a lean chap with slicked-back hair, was dressed in a loose-fitting jacket and flashy tie. He jumped up and down, trying to see into the room. By his springiness, his shoes may have held rubber heels.

"I saw him dining the next room over." Alexandra waved him in.

"I am Dalí!" The man sauntered in, taking loping strides while pressing down the ends of his thin mustache. An intensely bug-eyed character, if one were to guess his profession, most would settle on "over-caffeinated hypnotist."

Dalí set out his hands and merged his thumbs as if lining Alexandra up for a photograph. He popped his lips with a palm. "Yes! I must paint you naked from behind."

"From behind what?" she asked, amused. "Do you always paint in the nude?"

"*Jag précis meine descrizione... Sei nudo!*" Dalí scurried to the window. He rested one hand high on the sill, the other on a hip, pushed out his buttocks, and glassily looked off into the night. "*Exactamente! 'Luna adorada av la nacht.'* It will be *minha meisterstück!*"

Will failed to calculate how many languages Dalí had mixed into so short a statement.

Alexandra gasped. "*Mon cuerpo desnudo skall vara dein musa?*"

Dalí tossed his hands in the air, overjoyed. "*Finalmente!* Someone who *spricht meine língua!*"

"*Por fin!*" She ran from her seat and kissed Dalí on both cheeks.

Will could not believe it. Alexandra had found the only other person in the world who spoke and understood her childhood international gibberish. As the soup was served, he sat back in his chair, trying to ignore their nonsensical tongue-twisting of Occidental languages.

It proved impossible.

Alexandra translated for Will, "Salvador wants to paint me standing at a window in the nude."

"That's the only part I understood." Will had read about a young Catalan setting the art world ablaze. He dropped his spoon into his soup and wiped his sack's oral hole. "You cannot pose. He's famous."

"What?" she asked, squinting. "It's difficult to hear you with that bag over your head."

Will broke a stick of bread, violently. "He's famous! Do not agree!"

She turned back to Dalí, shaking her head as they continued their mutant speech.

Dalí rushed to the table. "I *must* paint her. I feel it in my loins."

"No doubt, but I can't tolerate her naked image hung in a gallery stirring too many loins."

Dalí turned to Alexandra. "What tragedy has befallen your master that he veils himself?"

"He incurred a wound," she explained, a tad upset. *"Je me suis assis sur son visage."*

Dalí pounded his chest, needing to restart his heart.

"I must pass, Salvador," she said. He kissed her hand and bid his farewell. Alexandra retook her seat. "My bum was to serve as his muse. *Anyhoo,* my onion soup smells delicious."

They enjoyed the main course without interruption.

Alexandra relished seeing Will dine elsewhere than his cottage, in a foreign city, even with a bag over his head. She sensed great things in his future, and if he failed to seize them, she would be there to jam them down his throat. She poured the last of the wine. *"Garçon!* Macarons and coffee for dessert."

"Très bien, mademoiselle."

She asked, "What are your plans? I would like to visit Thomas."

Will was yet ready for such a trip. "Bourlon Wood is Zone Rouge. You won't get near it."

"I'll find a way. At least I must try."

They talked of lighter things. One letter he had delivered came from the National Geographic Society, requesting an interview. She confessed that seeking this opportunity had driven her every step since leaving Montana, and her fear that she would muff it up. *"Anyhoo,"* she concluded, "I'm forbidden to drop in before the presidential election."

"Oh, yes," he recalled. "The Coolidge Incident."

She left for the ladies' room. In passing his dining room, she waved to Dalí. He sprang from his chair and followed. She sauntered down the staircase. A sudden burst of flash powder halted her descent. By the partially blinded look of things, she could only conclude that word had leaked the Prince of Wales dined upstairs. A mob of reporters rushed to the stairs. The burly bouncer, Jacques, held the line, extending his arms from wall to rail. Léon, standing outside by the limousine, likewise fell besieged.

"*Bonsoir, messieurs!*" Half in the tank, Alexandra posed stylishly, and their cameras clicked away.

Three waiters rushed over to reinforce Jacques. Patrons left their seats and gathered to check in on the fanfare.

The supercilious maître d'appeared ill.

"*Qui êtes-vous...? Es-tu l'amant du prince?*" a reporter shouted.

It presented a free publicity opportunity. "I am Alexandra Illyria Bathenbrook. *Photographe d'aventure!*"

"How was the prince injured?" another yelled in English.

"A rather madcap mishap," she laughingly proclaimed, "suffered when I sat on his face."

It hit as if a bomb exploded.

The audience burst out in beguiled commotion. They gasped, laughed, and some applauded. Dalí bit his hand. It would be impossible to get to the car, and lingering might inspire a riot. Alexandra stepped down to Jacques, who struggled to keep the reporters at bay. She took a roll of francs from her purse and placed a fat tip in his pocket. "In the heroic words of your General Nivelle at Verdun, *'They shall not pass.'*"

"*On ne passe pas!*" Jacques yelled out to his colleagues holding the line. "Long live the prince!"

"*Vive le France!*" shouted Alexandra, blowing a kiss to the crowd. She ran up the stairs as further bedlam erupted. She tipped the upstairs bouncer. "*Merci! On ne passe pas!*"

"*On ne passe pas!*" the burly man shouted before heading down to reinforce the barricade.

Those dining upstairs peered out of their rooms at Alexandra. Dalí followed, sketching her arse. He gasped upon being caught. "The exquisite curve. A flawless inverted heart. I must paint you in the nude!"

She liked the thin, slope-shouldered Catalan. "Would you like to touch it?"

"If it were part of me, I'd do little else." Dalí closed his eyes and squeezed. "*Ay Dios mío!*"

Alexandra reentered her dining room. She tipped the wine steward and sent him off to battle. Dessert had arrived via the dumbwaiter, and she sampled a purple macaron.

"Garçon. Is there a way to exit from upstairs?"

The head waiter walked to the window and opened it. "Fire escape, Miss Bathenbrook."

"Please ask the artist who visited if he has a car I can borrow."

He left and soon returned with Dalí. The Spaniard rushed in and knelt, begging forgiveness for his previous impertinence.

Will motioned for him to rise. "You may confer with my mistress."

Alexandra shared her idea in gibberish. Dalí departed.

Will said, "I hope his painting doesn't hang in the Louvre."

"You've seen the works of these surrealists and cubist types. I'll not even look human." She dropped a small fortune to settle the bill while the waiter placed on her jacket. Handing him a fat roll of francs, she said, *"Merci, pour une soirée memorable."*

"Oui, mademoiselle. Good luck, and God save the King!"

She joined Will, who already had one foot out the window. They descended the slick metal steps and tracked the headlights of a Citroën automobile cruising down the narrow alleyway.

It came to a halt, and they rushed over.

Alexandra detected a lone jackal emerging from the shadows an instant before the flash powder ignited. She jumped in front to shield Will and hustled him into the car. The back door slammed, and they sped off. Dalí applauded. The older driver crashed into a trashcan before turning onto the bright and misty thoroughfare. He eventually turned his head. All he said was, "Picasso."

"The prince will remember you always!" Alexandra nudged Will's shoulder with her elbow, tickled he was laughing. "I told you we'd pull it off with no problems. I haven't had this much fun since Hemingway ran naked down Duval Street."

Dalí peered back, his mouth ajar and eyes somehow even buggier. *"Ernesto...?* Do tell!"

Chapter 27

She cringed and moved the phone from her ear. Over several days, Alexandra had attempted to navigate Paris incognito, twice changing her lodging. Despite her efforts, the pesky Parisian press corps kept finding her, *and now even her father!* Fortunately, the connection from Brussels was breaking up.

"I was misquoted. It was just a fling. I am not dating the Prince of Wales. ... Too much static, Father. ... Ta!" Alexandra thanked the hotel receptionist and informed Léon it was time to bug out.

The chauffeur asked, "Will the prince be joining you today?"

"Not today, Léon. He's likely up to some other royal mischief."

She placed a bouquet of sunflowers on the seat and removed her Cossack hat. Hours before sunrise, Léon smuggled her out of the city. Her dining escapade would haunt her for some time. She glanced over an edition of *Paris-soir*, thinking the photograph of her strutting down the staircase rather fetching. Dalí gazing at her arse had also come across well. The caption read: *Dame de l'intrigue Internationale.*

Having escaped with the aid of Pablo Picasso only added to the legend. Poor Oliver had cabled the British tabloids were swamping the office. Alexandra had no idea where to start in explaining that she was not on the shortlist to reign as the next Queen of England.

"I've been declared an 'International dame of intrigue.'"

"Superbe, mademoiselle!"

"I cannot fathom how they keep finding me."

"Perhaps you should set aside your hat," he suggested.

"Never!" Until all this royal mistress scuttlebutt died down, she could not return to London. Since Brazil, Alexandra sensed her life to be unraveling. It proved exhausting fending off the unassailable foes staining her mind with ugly graffiti. She was desperate to have lunch with Thomas in Bourlon Wood and talk it all out. It would be a long drive. She folded a blanket over her lap and tried to enjoy the scenery.

The panorama cooperated for several hours. They cleared the city of Amiens where Will had been wounded. An hour later, Léon, a veteran himself, mentioned they were approaching the outskirts of Zone Rouge, and to proceed further would be impossible.

It became clear what war looked like.

Alexandra asked him to pull over and left the car to walk along the road. It was an otherworldly landscape, as desolate and chilling as the surface of the moon. The rolling fields northeast of Paris were now a wasteland. Within this contested abattoir spread the residue of four years of pointless struggle upon such infamous battlefields as the Somme, Neuve Chappelle, and Vimy Ridge. She stood forty kilometers short of Cambrai and would get no closer to Bourlon Wood.

She walked into the field until coming to a sign strung across the barbed wire. The skull and crossbones forbade trespass. Spread before her stretched pockmarked fields, collapsed trench lines, rusted metal debris, and the sporadic carcass of a tree. The ruins of a once lovely countryside hamlet brought a tear to her eye, now identifiable only by a placard marked *Village Détruit*—a village that died for France.

Thousands of undetonated artillery shells and decomposed corpses remained within the shattered landscape, hidden in soil so toxic with chemicals that nothing would grow for one hundred years. It would only get worse ahead. She returned to the car.

Somewhere out there rested the remains of Lance Corporal Thomas Sawyer Bathenbrook—yet recovered, still unvisited, in Zone Rouge.

They had all been right. *It was impossible.*

Alexandra studied her French colleague. "I love your necklace. It's interesting."

"It's a *Croix-de-feu*," Skendra Lilleth noted. "I also like yours. Are you aware those are anal beads?"

Alexandra was not and stopped fiddling with her recent Casablanca purchase. Her face reddened, and she slunk back in her chair. Their table in a small cafe stood within the bustling terminus of the *Gare de l'Est* station. Having bumped into Skendra by happenstance, they'd sat for a quick drink. Her train to Istanbul would depart within the hour. The journalist presented a paradox, blowing hot and cold.

If she were to become a trusted friend or another liaison lost to the wind remained unclear.

"Anyhoo, whilst traveling in Albania, I learned their national hero, Gjergj Kastrioti, was honored with the title 'Skenderbeg' by the Sultan. It means 'Lord Alexander' referring to his comparable military prowess to Alexander the Great. Does this mean we share the same name? Are your parents Turkish?"

"Yes, I'm Alexandra." Skendra flashed a sly smile. "My mother was French. I know very little about my father. I was orphaned and raised by a prestigious family in Marseilles."

What else could be expected from an enigma? A call came over the intercom announcing Alexandra's train was set for boarding. She gathered her bags. "I guess this is farewell."

Skendra took hold of Alexandra's cheeks and seized a long and sensual kiss. Their lips finally parted. An impish glimmer colored Skendra's expression. *"Adieu, petite soeur."*

Alexandra remained stunned: eyes closed, mouth moist, and legs trembling. Pin drops tingled through her body, and her thoughts fell vacant. She stepped back, turned, and ran into the station. Once on the platform, she freed her ticket and shrugged off her reaction. She thought it likely ordinary for a woman to savor a passionate kiss from another, but as for succumbing to the rest of it... *maybe?*

That evening, Alexandra sat in her compartment, reading. The classy wood-paneled lounging space offered a sofa easily converted to sleeping berths, a drawing table, luggage racks, and a washbasin. The opulent blue carriages of the train she rode held the golden badge of the *Compagnie Internationale des Wagon-Lits* and the bold lettering "Venice Simplon-Orient Express." She would arrive in Istanbul in three days. She had accepted an assignment to help uncover the extent of ethnic cleansing the Ottoman Empire had inflicted on its Armenian minority during the Great War. The investigative team had not sought government permission, rendering this a risky proposition. They would rendezvous at the Pera Palas Hotel.

Her book of choice was *Mystery on the Blue Train*—the latest spellbinder featuring the overly fastidious and urbane Hercule Poirot. Needing a nightcap, she left to finish over a tumbler of something. At this late hour, few passengers would occupy the lounge carriage. She remained desperate to get her hands on an edition of the *London Times*, which an old fuddy-duddy had guarded with the fierceness of a British bulldog since boarding. As expected, the spiffily outfitted lounge stood quiet, with only a middle-aged woman seated alone and, of course... *the British bulldog monopolizing the newspaper.*

Alexandra bit her lower lip to avoid snarling and plopped herself into a plush armchair. She ordered a hot-toddy, her favorite cold-weather nightcap, and shook her head at the fogy's need to cling to the news of home. It defeated the purpose of getting away from it all. She'd given London little thought since departing two months ago.

The steward placed down her steaming drink, and she dove right in.

The middle-aged woman lifted her gaze from the window.

Alexandra flashed a smile, and the woman returned one ever briefer.

The news hog fingered a few keystrokes on the lounge piano on his way out, and by some miracle, left empty-handed. Alexandra sprang from her chair and pounced, rushing back to swish through the pages. The lead headline trumpeted that the health of King George had taken a sour turn, rendering England awash in worry. Runners-up included Herbert Hoover's campaign to be the next United States president and the latest scoop on the "London After Midnight" murder. She cheered in reading that Commander Dyott and the boys had emerged from the Amazon and were now sailing for New York.

Though they had lost all of their film, everyone survived.

It provided the perfect ending to her day.

"It smells tempting," the woman said, pointing to the lemon-spiked whiskey. "May I join you?"

"That would be lovely." Alexandra held up her tumbler and two fingers, to which the steward nodded. She placed down the paper and introduced herself as the tall woman took the seat across. Her guest held an everyday look to her: dressed nicely, but plainly, sporting a slight wave to her short, reddish hair.

"Have you enjoyed your trip thus far, Miss...?"

"Mary Westmacott." She played with the long strand of pearls double-looped along her neckline and stated with sadness, "It feels odd to be on such a flamboyant excursion on one's own. Bound for Baghdad is not what I planned for at this stage of my life."

Alexandra said, hush-hush, "If you find yourself afoul of the law there, ask for Detective Liam Kimball. Be warned, he might flee if you mention my name."

The steward brought their cocktails. Mary raised her glass. "To upcoming days beneath an unfamiliar sun." After the shared toast and a hard sip, she asked, "How are you enjoying the novel?"

Alexandra's expression went wishy-washy. "It is *not* one of Miss Christie's stronger efforts, though I'm glad to see Poirot solving a murder back in his native France."

"He's Belgian," Mary snipped, sitting up sharply. "What exactly do you find lacking?"

The inimical reproach surprised Alexandra. "The book's title, for starters. 'Le Bleu Train?' I think not! More like *'Le Blah* Train.' Why not one as ritzy as this?"

Mary frowned and let out an unappealing gurgle. Alexandra continued in her critique. "The first quarter of the book is *so* droll! It reads like a soap opera for bland and unlikeable hoity-toities bemoaning their wealthy la-di-das. I'm only at the midpoint but *already* know who the killers are."

Mary seemed to find this hard to believe. "I dare ask, Alexandra, who are the killers?"

"Major Knighton is *obviously* the marquise and conspired with the maid."

Mary discharged a snorty *harrumph.* "I didn't find it *so* obvious. What else?"

"Miss Christie has become *so* stale in this gathering of suspects thing at the end. If I were the killer, I would refuse to show up." Alexandra sensed she was on a roll. A hot-toddy always sharpened her intellect, and she was pleased it no longer rendered her melodramatic in speech. "It would be better stew if the culprit escaped and started threatening

Hercule whilst on the lam. Have Poirot *so* discombobulated he stops bathing, shaves his mustache, and even orders scrambled eggs. Then, instead of ending it in a *boring* casino or train, do so in Istanbul. Poirot tracks down the marquise and hands him over to the authorities, who publicly impale the killer to the detective's delight!"

Mary worked her pearls furiously. The sour, disturbed expression on her face indicated she thought differently. "You have a most vivid imagination, my dear."

"Hear, hear." Alexandra leaned forward and whispered, "We can't be *too* hard on poor Agatha. The papers *so* ravaged her about her disappearance and divorce. Let's just chalk up this disaster to her, you know, *'fragile mental state.'*"

Mary slammed down her glass and stormed out of the carriage.

Alexandra lifted an eyebrow, thinking it emotionally healthier to be a fan of Agatha Christie rather than a fanatic, like Mary Westmacott. She finally had the lounge to herself, except for whoever was playing "Clair de Lune" on the piano. The melody seemed to allude to it being acceptable to be alone in life, *though someday...*

She shut her eyes and smiled, lost in thoughts of Archibald Leach.

The lulling piano notes were interrupted by a sparkling glissando. "I first met Larisa Monvoisin on a piano bench. This was her song. She is the most ravishing woman I have ever ravaged."

It was him! Alexandra darted up from her chair. Her first impeccable view of Astor Lys confirmed her worst fears. He was something that appeared to have only one foot in this world. He stood thin, yet sinewy; old, yet virile. Though composed in speech, his voice thundered malice.

She frantically looked for the lounge steward, but the man roamed elsewhere. "Who are you, sir?"

"I am an empty vessel, allowed continued breath so greater beings can ensure you do not wander too far astray." Lys produced a decorative hand ax. "Your benevolent, albeit foreboding, shadow."

"You are nothing more than a demented man," she challenged. "An illusion! A deceiver!"

"Is that so, Dulcinea?"

He crept toward her; his eyes fiery red. "Didst thou not touch thy womb to safeguard thy inheritance? Was I not there when your raft entered the rapids? *Seul le Maître peut goûter votre chair.* Who guided you from the jungle as you dallied with death? Thine eyes betray a desire to fall. You were born an abomination, but upon your first bleeding, you became the most precious thing on earth."

Alexandra refused to believe him. She backed up against a window, closed her eyes, and trembled. Sensing him looming over her, she meekly asked, "What do you want from me?"

A low, taunting laugh preceded his answer. "Those you are meeting will spend years in a Turkish prison. You would not like the food served. Depart this train. If you do not, I will hack the heart from Liam Kimball, just as I have the other men you've so sluttishly allowed to soil you. The date is written; the table has been set. Nothing must interfere with that."

Alexandra did not move for several minutes—long after her eyes opened. She finally reached into her purse for a cigarette but instead freed her Papuan dagger.

Enough is enough, her mind thundered. She could no longer tolerate this enigmatic tormentor. If Lys were flesh, he would bleed. If but imagined, she would cut her wrists. She rushed out of the carriage, hot on his trail, but came to a halt in the passageway.

The steward stopped folding towels to tip his cap. *"Mademoiselle."*

"The tall man who just passed. Which cabin? Who is he?"

"No one has stirred, Miss Bathenbrook."

Alexandra feigned a smile, nodded wearily, and calmly headed for her compartment. A few tears moistened her cheeks. She could no longer tolerate insanity; not to this extreme. All she wanted to do was go home, but no such place existed. Death would need to rendezvous with her here: naked, alone, and welcoming.

She shed her clothing and placed the dagger on her left wrist.

Demons roared in her ears, imploring her to cease such madness.

She peered at her nightstand and postponed the final cut.

On top of it rested the braided bracelet she had lost over two years ago on the RMS *Empress of Australia.*

Chapter 28

New York City: November 1928

The Hotel Pennsylvania's Café Rouge offered a lively gathering spot for the late-night theater crowd. The immense room spread outfitted in a Tuscany-inspired terracotta and limestone finish. Spirited chatter and the jazzy tunes of an orchestra were in full swing. This was not just another dinner date.

"Do *you* find my name brings to mind that of an English butler?"

"That's so ridiculous," Alexandra said. Everything about Archibald Leach still made her heart go *boom-boom*. "It's terribly warm in here. Would you hang my jacket?"

In relinquishing her Cossack hat, the coat checker gushed, "Aren't you the one who sat on—"

"I was misquoted!" Alexandra snapped. She turned to Archibald. *"Anyhoo*, the joint looks jumping."

Their dinner progressed swimmingly.

Alexandra stared misty-eyed at her charming date as he offered a tongue-in-cheek overview of touring small towns throughout America in vaudevillian hits or misses upon his arrival from England in 1920. He chuckled over the ridiculous nature of such work: serving as a unicycle rider, stilt walker, and crooner of penny serenades. He was hesitant to follow his press agent's advice to change his name to something less domestic servant sounding. During their stroll through Herald Square, he'd mentioned hitting lean times, having lost his microscopic role in *Golden Dawn* once the show met its cheerless sunset. By his alarmed reaction upon entering the restaurant, it rang clear he was unaccustomed to such an upscale setting.

Alexandra finished the last bite of her chicken brochette. "That was the best application of cayenne and cumin I've tasted since Marrakech prison. How did you find your steak, Archie?"

"Deliciously unaffordable. It found me as usual, exceedingly rare."

The waiter offered the dessert menu. Alexandra ordered one and requested the check. She leaned back and rotated her shoulders, trying to crack her spine. In catching Archibald's eyes pop, she flashed one final shake of her bosom. "I injured myself bodysurfing. I miss my Japanese masseuse whilst traveling. She'll have me disrobe, lay down, rub healing oils into my back and bum, and apply a sensual massage."

"It sounds... Is there room for one more?" Archibald needed a sip of water to continue. "How do you manage without during your travels?"

"I've attempted many remedies but have found only two that ease my back pain. The first was crashing a hot-air balloon into the Sea of Galilee, but to do so again seems impractical."

"And the second, I dare ask?"

"I dare *not* say. I've been referred to a proctologist for treatment."

"Do Americans usually see a proctologist for back pain?"

She snickered. "Don't be silly. That would be asinine."

"I see... *I think.* Would you care to dance?"

"Soon." Alexandra wore the same sleek green tabard dress that had dazzled his eyes upon their first meeting seventeen months ago. Too splashy for her everyday travels, it chicly suited the New York nightlife like no other in her wardrobe. While stylish, it fit too snug to entertain anything rollicking flowing from the bandstand.

The check arrived. Archibald whimpered and loosened his tie. "'Tis a shame having no topper of alcohol."

He had suffered enough. "I smuggled in a bottle of *Veuve Clicquot.*" She plucked the billfold from his hands. "It's in my suite upstairs."

He shared a look of disbelief. "How can you afford all of this?"

"Don't let it trouble you. I'm worth millions," she casually stated. "I spent today sorting out my investments with my Wall Street moneymen. They kept insisting I invest big in dirigibles, but I convinced them to place a sizeable egg on a small flying operation I came across whence touring Key West. It's called Pan-American Airways."

"Aren't I, Mister Lucky?" To Alexandra's gesture, the Gershwin brothers' "S'Wonderful" would do, he escorted her to the dance floor. She melted in his arms and wondered if it was worth abandoning her self-fashioned business for a lifetime of carefree nights such as this. Archibald—so easy on the eyes, so humorous, so debonair—proved the only charming devil charismatic enough to tempt her to do it.

She felt a first inkling of falling in love.

"I've thought of you often over these many months."

He whispered, "Thoughts of you have inspired me to great lengths."

Archibald acted too much of a gentleman to even cop a feel. "Cold weather sets off my back. A firm hand to my spine helps with the pain."

He obliged, and her pelvis brushed against his.

Inspired to great lengths, indeed. She blushed and stepped back.

"So, you're sure I should not change my name for my career? Not become Harry Brandt?"

"Your name and your soul are the only things of which you have absolute ownership." Alexandra spoke deadly serious over this. "Once you surrender one, they'll surely come for the other."

He relaxed his shoulders. "You truly are an Andalusian goddess."

Alexandra suspected he'd soon have more pressing matters to worry over. From the surrounding conversations of those who'd attended the opening night performance of the musical comedy *Boom-Boom* at the Casino Theater, she predicted the newspaper reviews come morning would be brutal. Archibald held the minor role of Reggie Phipps in the production. He shared the lead in the song "Nina" with starlet Jeanette MacDonald and inspired the loudest laughter in his few acerbic speaking lines. As for the rest of the Broadway show, it lacked the harmonized music, wit, and comedic delivery of one destined for longevity.

Unless something changed, it would flop.

The ballad ended. Alexandra rested a hand on his smooth cheek, lifted herself on tiptoes, and passionately kissed him.

A delectable piece of baked alaska with two spoons awaited back at their table. Alexandra dug in, needing to cool herself off. She gave a passing glance to the check and tossed a nice tip into the billfold. The band played a brassy number, and it was difficult to hear much of anything. She lifted out her cigarette case, freed one, and waited for Archibald to light it, as he had already fired her up in every other way.

He lit one of his own and slumped in his chair. He called out to cut through the racket, "It seems the peanut gallery is not too high on the show. Backstage, we sensed *Boom-Boom* went *kaboom* halfway in."

Alexandra shouted back, "You were hilarious, but the actor playing Skippy Carr lacks pizzazz."

He cried out, "It must embarrass you to dine with a chump like me!"

"Don't be stupid, Archie!" Flaunting her wealth had wounded his pride. She loudly declared, "Archibald Alec Leach, I find you the most attractive man in the world. My suite has a wondrous view of the skyline. The moon is right. We must make love. Take me at your leisure!"

The cigarette fell out of Archibald's mouth. Those seated nearby gawked, stupefied. With her hands gripping the corners of the square table and head thrust back, Alexandra sensed how quiet things had fallen since the band had wrapped up its song. "Everyone heard, haven't they?"

"Just all of it," he confirmed, waiting for blood to return to his head. "Archie! There you are."

Two men rushed over. One said, "We've searched everywhere for you. You've got to come back to the theater. It's an emergency! Kendall broke his leg. We have no understudy for Skippy Carr! Lee and J.J. say you're the only one who can save the show! You'll need to rehearse all night to be ready by tomorrow. This is your big chance!"

Archibald's hands locked onto the table corners. "You don't realize what you're asking of me!"

The two men battled to pry free his grip, finally succeeding.

"No, no!" Archibald begged. "You can't do this! You mustn't!"

"Archie, you really must go," Alexandra intervened. "We'll finish the date whence I return from Washington."

He looked like a man being shanghaied. "Whence might that be?"

"Soon!"

ȣ

Monsieur Babe Ruth could not be hitting them out of the park any deeper. Alexandra operated in unrehearsed territory: poised, confident, and eloquent to the extreme, regardless of the stress derived from engaging in her job interview of a lifetime. She was not imagining it. Her reflection in the glasses of the man across the table confirmed this abnormality of social grace. Gilbert Hovey Grosvenor, president and chief editor of the National Geographic Society, was a pocket-sized fellow with a receding hairline, which lent his bushy mustache to stand out with vigor. Though his eyes remained crunched behind his round nose-pinched spectacles, his gleeful smile hinted that Alexandra's performance at Hubbard Hall far surpassed a *tour de force.*

It stirred downright *magnifique!*

"The magazine will feature 'Scenic Glories of the American West,'" one seated editor promoted.

"Montana bred," Alexandra replied, shooting him a wink.

Another pitched, "Next November's lead is 'Battlefields of France Eleven Years After.'"

She said, "I've visited Zone Rouge. It's nothing to blush over."

"Utterly remarkable you've ventured into primeval Papua," another gasped. "Your thoughts on returning up the Fly River by seaplane?"

Alexandra placed a whimsical hand on her chin. "To this time bring Gayetty's toilet paper."

The gathered editors all partook in jovial laughter.

The National Geographic Society had been founded in 1888 as a club for academics, travelers, and well-to-do patrons to discuss and promote knowledge and understanding of the world. Its monthly magazine had expanded to a circulation of over one million, with each issue offering compelling tales, maps, sketches, and photographs of diverse cultures, exotic lands, and natural wonders. "The Society" was pioneering new methods of night photography and colorization via the Autochrome Lumière process.

No realm short of the moon was its domain for study.

For Alexandra, sitting in the same room with such luminaries of a *"vive la différence"* approach to experiencing life served as the pinnacle of her young career. Her humorous and intrepid sagas mesmerized her audience and left them dancing to her strings. Each editor now pitched their projects against those of their peers.

"'Bethlehem and Along the Way of the Magi,' just in time for next year's Christmas," an editor spurted. "What say you?"

Alexandra tossed up her hands. "Sounds like a great opportunity to once more go ballooning!"

"'Java. Queen of the West Indies.' Will you return to that mystical land and photograph its splendor for us?"

"Just between the six of us," she leaned forward to tell on the sly, "I saw little of the island my first go-around because of dysentery. The Dutch nuns even named a muddy river after me. I'd love to return!"

The lucky editor expounded a victorious bellow to her agreement.

"'Across Madagascar by Boat, Auto, Rail, and Filanzana?'"

Alexandra clasped her hands together. "It has always been my dream to be carried through the most foreboding jungles of the world on a filanzana. Sign me up!"

Savoir-faire shined everywhere.

If she were any hotter, Alexandra would combust spontaneously. Contracts for her signature were being drawn up that would fill out her schedule for 1929 and beyond. She leaned back in her leather chair as the editors skimmed over her *pièce de résistance*, genuflecting in wonder and astonishment. The portfolio held photographs she had taken more so as a tourist. Many of these works were among her *crème de la crème,* and she was giddy over sharing them. A warm flush swelled her heart, soul, and mind. Her big gamble in 1927 had paid off. She felt proud, and perhaps her days of public gaffes and squishy self-esteem were misadventures *des jours passés.*

Now, if only she could suppress the incessant French superlatives exploding within her head. She hoped it was due to nothing more than her hotel having featured French toast as its breakfast *plat du jour.*

An elderly secretary entered the elegantly outfitted boardroom carrying a pile of contracts. She passed them over to Grosvenor for inspection. He slid them across the table. "Choose whatever you wish."

Alexandra looked them over, relishing her *carte blanche.*

The secretary handed her a gold fountain pen.

One editor fumbled while holding Alexandra's portfolio. It crashed to the floor. The others scrambled over to be part of the cleanup team. They halted their work and fell silent, examining two photographs. They were passed over to Grosvenor. He looked up, shocked. "Is there any sanitary explanation for these, Miss Bathenbrook?"

Ooh la la! Alexandra bit her knuckles, having wondered where they were hiding. "The first photo is me sprawled across the lap of artist

Salvador Dalí receiving a spanking. It was my parting gesture of gratitude for allowing me to pose nude for him."

"And this second one of him sucking your toes?"

"His parting gesture to me." She rolled her eyes and sighed.

The society leadership glanced at each other, unsure what to think.

"It was all Pablo's crazy idea," she jittered. "You know, gentlemen, when in Bohemia..."

One editor inquired, "Pablo, as in Picasso?"

"Is there another? He insisted we send copies to Hemingway in Key West to lighten him up."

"Hemingway, as in Ernest?" asked Grosvenor.

"But of course," Alexandra chortled, fingers crossed.

A bubbling of semi-contained laughter turned into a flood of delight.

"Honestly," Alexandra said, laughing herself. "Spending time with those two mad Spaniards was the most fun I've had since riding Subaru Takahashi's huge pole like a crazed woman in St. Moritz."

Silence again swept the room. Grosvenor asked, "Whose what?"

To their drop-jawed stares, she clarified, "Subaru Takahashi. He's only the twenty-sixth best cross-country skier in the world. Don't any of you read the sports page?"

From the continued hush, it was clear they did not.

"The Onbashira festival...? The Japanese Shinto practice of riding felled pine trees to the sacred temple...? Truly learned gentlemen, you must know of it?"

They all sighed and nodded energetically. Grosvenor wiped a tear of mirth from his eye. "Please pardon us."

Alexandra polished her knuckles on her shoulder—*still golden.*

As they settled down, she decided. It would be Java, Madagascar, and France, for starters. She took the fountain pen and attempted to sign the first contract, but it held no ink. The peevish secretary scurried out to retrieve another. Everyone sat idle, smiling.

The secretary returned with a new pen.

Alexandra winked. "To a long and fruitful relationship, fine sirs!"

Two brawny men abruptly stormed into the boardroom. They flaunted serious dispositions and flashed official government badges. One shouted, "Special Agent Grigsby, United States Secret Service. Alexandra Bathenbrook, I am placing you under arrest!"

Sacré bleu! She peered up at the two special agents looming behind her. "Whatever do you mean?"

"Come peacefully, or we'll cuff you," warned Grigsby.

She panicked once Grosvenor pulled the contracts away. The secretary confiscated the pen. "Is this about killing those banditos in Brazil? Turning that guy into a eunuch in Morocco? Blowing up the archaeology site in Palestine?"

"You know what this is about," Grigsby insisted. "You fired a gun at President Coolidge and have violated your parole."

"But Mister Hoover is our new president," she defended.

"The inauguration is next March." Grigsby gestured for her to stand.

"Mister Grosvenor, please allow me to explain," she pleaded.

Alexandra huffed when he shook his head. All the editors left their chairs to cower along the far wall. She bit her forefinger deep enough to draw blood and dove forward to sign her name on a contract. Within seconds, her hands were behind her back and the cuffs clicking on.

Sprawled across the table, she pleaded to Grosvenor, "I saved the president's life! You must let me explain. I beseech you!"

The second special agent searched Alexandra's crammed suitcase. He removed her *Electrex Ultra* and set it on the table.

The elderly secretary placed a hand on her forehead, sighed, and succumbed to the vapors.

Not knowing what sort of weapon it was, the agent began frisking Alexandra. He stopped along her buttocks and lifted her skirt. "She has something sticking out of her knickers. It looks like a grenade pin."

"We'll conduct a comprehensive cavity search once returned to the station," Grigsby said. "Whatever you do, don't pull it!"

It was too late. Alexandra's eyes burst wide. *Oh, l' humanité!*

In August 1921, Alexandra Illyria Bathenbrook had been riding her horse along the Missouri River. She observed a fly-fisher knee-deep in the water, and though his chin placed her life in no jeopardy, the large grizzly plodding toward the river imperiled his. She had galloped over, yelling a warning, but the elderly man remained unaware. Rifle in hand, she had fired a warning shot to scare off the bear. Several men had rushed out of a car parked atop the hillside, firing guns at her. She had skedaddled, only to be later arrested and charged with the attempted assassination of the Vice-President of the United States. It had taken a full day to sort out the facts, and the local sheriff had prepared the fluffiest flapjacks for breakfast.

Thankfully, more cerebral leadership now filled the ranks of the Secret Service, and no jail time was required.

With her fancifully luggage-labeled Globe Trotter leather suitcase in hand, Alexandra entered Union Station humming James P. Johnson's "If I Could Be with You (One Hour Tonight)." She studied the scheduling board, undecided about her next destination. Being the unwitting fiancé of Lucifer, her final terminus would be Hell, but for today, better options beckoned.

A few weeks remained in 1928 to wander aimlessly, completely adrift, yet for once not entirely lost. Perhaps she'd visit Emma's grave in Chicago or ride all the way to Montana just to see if the sky remained beautiful in her absence. Thereafter, a return to New York for some quality Archibald Leach time and then sea passage back to London.

Yet sometimes in life, people simply followed wherever their inner demons might lead them. Since nearly ending her life in France, her malevolent voices had subsided, having been forewarned about the consequence of pushing her too hard.

For an insouciant vagabond and finagler extraordinaire, no date was set, nor destiny written.

While there would no doubt be further missteps perfecting her shutterbug strut, Alexandra knew, no matter which path she chose, one thing would always remain paramount in her travels—*Adventure!*

She concluded her humming. It was time to sing.

~la fin

About the Author

J.L. Michael is a Maine author partial to old-school jazz, vintage travel posters, and historical literature that champions daring quests into realms unknown. The majority of the author's time is spent pursuing the honor code of an impossible dreamer, which includes acting as an able Healthcare Director, committed spouse, and steadfast (though imperfect) role-model to an eight-year-old best-thing-ever. When not thrashing away on a keyboard, J.L. can be found lounging beachside atop the hood of a Jeep Wrangler, contemplating a next escape to distant exotic lands or plotting further misadventures to include in the sequel to this novel.